Her Beast

S.M. LAVIOLETTE

CROOKED SIXPENCE BOOKS are published by
CROOKED SIXPENCE PRESS

2 State Road 230
El Prado, NM 87529

First printing July 2022

10 9 8 7 6 5 4 3 2 1

978-1-951662-61-5

<u>Praise for Minerva Spencer & S.M. LaViolette's</u>
<u>THE ACADEMY OF LOVE series:</u>

"[A] pitch perfect Regency…. Readers will be hooked."
(THE MUSIC OF LOVE)
★*Publishers Weekly STARRED REVIEW*

"An offbeat story that offers unexpected twists on a familiar
setup."
(A FIGURE OF LOVE)
Kirkus

"[A] consistently entertaining read."
(A FIGURE OF LOVE)
Kirkus

<u>Praise for THE MASQUERADERS series:</u>
"Lovers of historical romance will be hooked on this twisty
story of revenge, redemption, and reversal of fortunes."
Publishers Weekly, STARRED review of THE
FOOTMAN.

"Fans will be delighted."
Publishers Weekly on THE POSTILION

<u>Praise for Minerva Spencer's *REBELS OF THE TON*</u>
<u>series:</u>
<u>*NOTORIOUS*</u

★A *PopSugar* Best New Romance of November
★A *She Reads* Fall Historical Romance Pick
★A *Bookclubz* Recommended Read

"Brilliantly crafted…an irresistible cocktail of smart
characterization, sophisticated sensuality, and sharp wit."
★*Booklist STARRED REVIEW*

"Sparkling…impossible not to love."—Popsugar

"Both characters are strong, complex, and believable, and the cliffhanger offers a nice setup for the sequel. Readers who like thrills mixed in with their romance should check this out."
—Publishers Weekly

"Packed full of fiery exchanges and passionate embraces, this is for those who prefer their Regencies on the scandalous side."—*Library Journal*

INFAMOUS

"Realistically transforming the Regency equivalent of a mean girl into a relatable, all-too-human heroine is no easy feat, but Spencer (Outrageous, 2021) succeeds on every level. Lightly dusted with wintery holiday charm, graced with an absolutely endearing, beetle-obsessed hero and a fully rendered cast of supporting characters and spiked with smoldering sensuality and wry wit, the latest in Spencer's Rebels of the Ton series is sublimely satisfying."**—Booklist STARRED review**

"Perfect for fans of Bridgerton, Infamous is also a charming story for Christmas. In fact, I enjoyed Infamous so much that when I was halfway through it, I ordered the author's first novel, Dangerous. I look forward to reading much more of Minerva Spencer's work."**—THE HISTORICAL NOVEL SOCIETY**

<u>Praise for Minerva Spencer's *Outcasts* series:</u>

"Minerva Spencer's writing is sophisticated and wickedly witty. Dangerous is a delight from start to finish with swashbuckling action, scorching love scenes, and a coolly arrogant hero to die for. Spencer is my new auto-buy!"
-NYT Bestselling Author Elizabeth Hoyt

More books by S.M. LaViolette & Minerva Spencer
<u>**THE ACADEMY OF LOVE SERIES**</u>
The Music of Love
A Figure of Love
A Portrait of Love
The Language of Love
Dancing with Love*
The Story of Love*
<u>**THE OUTCASTS SERIES**</u>
Dangerous
Barbarous
Scandalous
<u>**THE REBELS OF THE *TON***</u>
Notorious
Outrageous
Infamous
<u>**THE MASQUERADERS**</u>
<u>The Footman</u>
<u>The Postilion</u>
<u>The Bastard</u>
<u>**THE SEDUCERS**</u>
<u>Melissa and The Vicar</u>
<u>Joss and The Countess</u>
<u>Hugo and The Maiden</u>
<u>**VICTORIAN DECADENCE**</u>
<u>His Harlot</u>
<u>His Valet</u>
<u>His Countess</u>
<u>Her Master</u>*
<u>Her Beast</u>*
<u>**THE BELLAMY SISTERS**</u>
PHOEBE*
HYACINTH*
<u>**THE WILD WOMEN OF WHITECHAPEL**</u>
THE BOXING BARONESS*

Prologue

London
1857

Sukey popped the cork on the fifth bottle of champagne that night and swayed drunkenly as she stood beside the chaise longue where Malcolm was sprawled. "Open up, Mal!"

He obligingly opened his mouth, but when she poured the contents of the £20 bottle from a height of at least a foot she missed Malcolm's head completely, hitting his chest, instead.

They both chortled like the drunken fools they were as the expensive alcohol ran down his naked chest and stomach, the bubbly liquid strangely pleasurable on his hot skin.

Malcolm blinked his bleary, champagne-misted gaze at the man kneeling between his thighs. "It's coming your way, Bri," he warned.

Brian merely grunted, too busy trying to throat Malcolm's prick, even though he never managed to swallow more than two-thirds before he started choking.

Still, God bless the man for trying.

Sukey staggered back several feet, until she bumped into Malcolm's desk, still clinging to the bottle with both hands. The slight swaying of her body and her owlish gaze told Malcolm that his wife was one step from passing out.

"I love you, Mal," she said, clumsily hoisting her arse up onto the desktop without letting loose of the bottle.

Malcolm grinned. "I know."

His answer sent Sukey into whoops.

"You're so—so *bad*," she gasped in between snorts and chuckles, the champagne bottle slipping through her fingers and falling to the rug with a dull *thunk*. She sighed and then flopped onto her back across the desk, her lush body laid out like a delicacy.

"Spread for me, Sukes," Mal said in a voice made harsh from too much drink, too many cigars, and too much silly laughter.

Sukey lifted her heels onto the edge of the desk and then let her legs fall open like a butterfly, giving Malcolm a prime view of her pretty pink cunt.

He groaned. "So fucking beautiful. Touch yourself."

She slid a finger into her slick folds and spread wider as she circled her swollen nub with one hand and fucked herself with the other.

"Good girl," he praised as he drank in the gorgeous sight of her "C'mere," he ordered after watching her for a few minutes, his balls so hard they felt like steel. "Need to taste you."

But Sukey was too far gone to hear him.

Malcolm tried to push himself up and go to her, but he'd forgotten about the man attached to his prick.

Brian grabbed his thighs and yanked him down, shooting him a hot, sultry glare. "Stay put."

Malcolm was too dizzy to struggle against Bri's strong hands or his hot, sucking mouth.

Sukey didn't need him, in any case, and she sped toward her climax like an out-of-control locomotive. "Mal… I'm—" The muscles in her spread thighs strained as her back arched off the desk, hips jerking and bucking as she screamed out her pleasure.

"Fuckin' gorgeous," Malcolm growled, reaching for the champagne bottle he'd set beside his chair earlier. He lifted it to his mouth and took a swig, purposely spilling the last of the bottle onto his chest. It rolled down his belly to his groin and Brian hastily licked up the expensive liquid.

"Tha's right," Mal slurred as Bri cleaned off the mingled champagne and spunk from their earlier round of fucking, allowing some of the liquid to run onto his sac.

"*So good,*" he muttered as Bri tongued his tight, aching bollocks.

Malcolm struggled to keep his heavy lids up; he wanted to watch Bri pleasure him—the man wasn't only talented with his mouth; he was also as beautiful as an angel—but Mal was just too damned tired. They'd been celebrating for hours, ever since Edward Leeland had accepted Malcolm's partnership offer for the Kingston Shipping Line.

Mal had worked his arse off for six months to convince Leeland that he was the perfect man to take over his family's shipping company—one of the largest in the world. The shipping line was Mal's first *completely* legitimate endeavor. Oh, he owned the dry goods shops and the shipyard, of course, but neither of those had operated entirely within the law. But Leeland was notorious for his strict morality, so Malcolm had deemed it wise to keep his hands clean with this deal.

He'd also needed to hide his sexual proclivities from the wealthy old man. These past months had been hard on him, Sukey, and Bri, but it had been especially difficult for Brian since he'd temporarily moved into lodgings of his own, away from their cozy nest at the shipyard.

It wouldn't have done for Leeland to learn that his partner-to-be lived in sin with his wife and a male lover.

But tomorrow, once the papers were filed with the bank, he, Sukey, and Bri could go back to living their lives.

The first thing he'd do is move them into a nice house far away from the shipyards. Living surrounded by his business—essentially in part of the massive warehouse—had been necessary while he'd supervised the building of the great iron hull ship that would revolutionize the industry, but now he was ready to move to a proper house in a good part of the city.

It had been the big ship—designed by the brilliant engineer Isambard Brunel but funded by Malcolm—that had finally convinced Leeland to merge with Malcolm's small company.

The venture with Brunel had been expensive and risky, but it had paid off now that he'd hooked Leeland.

Malcolm smirked; soon he'd be making so much money that nobody—not even his strict new partner—could tell him what to do.

Brian's finger circled his arsehole, jarring Malcolm from his triumphant thoughts. He spread his thighs wider to give the other man better access, reveling in the way the other man licked and probed his tight pucker, lovingly preparing it for penetration.

Malcolm had never pictured himself having more than one lover— at least not at the same time—and he wouldn't have believed it was possible for three people to live together harmoniously.

It had been Sukey who'd convinced him the arrangement would work.

Malcolm knew he was so besotted with his wife that he would have agreed to anything or anyone to keep her happy and satisfied.

And what Sukey wanted was Malcolm *and* Brian Harlow.

Sukey and Brian had been living together and putting themselves forward as husband and wife when he'd first met them. Malcolm had been surprised to discover they weren't actually married. Not because they hadn't wanted to marry, but because Brian already had a wife, a woman who'd run off years before.

When Sukey asked Mal to marry her—because she was a woman who never waited for what she wanted—Mal had accepted in an instant. Rather than be jealous, Bri had appeared delighted to move in with them after they'd married.

In the three years since, Malcolm had come to appreciate Brian's calm temperament and boundless sexual energy. It had surprised him how much he liked having the other man in the house, not just for sex, but also for a sense of family—something Mal hadn't had growing up in an orphanage. Now that he was so accustomed to having both Bri and Sukey, he wondered how he'd ever lived without them.

And soon he would be rich enough to buy his two lovers anything their hearts desired.

All in all, his life was bloody grand. The only person missing from his debauched celebration was his mate Smith—Malcolm's oldest friend, mentor, and occasional lover.

He grinned as he imagined Smith's reaction to the news that Malcolm was now a respectable shipping magnate. He would have told Smith about the deal already if the other man hadn't been away on business—not that Malcolm knew *what* business or where he'd gone.

Although Smith remained an enigma to him, Malcolm considered him his closest friend.

They'd met more than twenty years ago, back when they'd been bully boys for Chaz Greene, the once powerful—now dead—king of the London underworld.

Smith had been a jaded, weary sixteen to Mal's eager but ignorant thirteen and had, over the years, encouraged Mal to build something for himself. The older man had taught him everything he knew about business—both legal and illegal.

Smith had also been the one to introduce Mal to those exclusive brothels that catered to men and women with unusual, some might say *extreme,* sexual proclivities.

Before Malcolm had accepted Sukey's marriage proposal, he'd told her about Smith's special place in his life and introduced the two.

Sukey being Sukey—which was to say voracious and adventurous when it came to sex—she'd instantly adored Smith's hard body, filthy mouth, and utter lack of inhibition. Indeed, it had been her idea to invite Smith into their bed, both before and after their marriage.

It had been months since the three of them had last been together. Smith had engaged a house for them in Brighton and it had just been the three of them for five glorious days and nights of fucking.

They'd invited Brian to join them, but he had never warmed up to Smith.

"That man terrifies me," Brian had said after meeting Smith the first time.

Smith *was* terrifying—if you crossed him. But when it came to friendship, he was the best damned mate Mal had ever had.

And he was also one hell of a fuck.

Just thinking about that last time with Sukey and Smith made Mal's balls clench and caused his already hard cock to swell and leak even more.

Brian groaned and intensified his sucking.

Malcolm felt a fleeting—very fleeting—twinge of guilt that he was fantasizing about Smith and Sukey while Bri was working so very diligently to please him.

Still, what Brian didn't know wouldn't hurt him, would it?

He blinked his bleary eyes and stared down at the other man, flexing his cock, and making it dance. "It's all for you," he lied, his carefully cultivated accent slipping as he relinquished his usual iron-control.

Bri's answer was to push a slick finger up Malcolm's arse and drive all other thoughts from his mind.

He groaned and pulsed his hips, fucking himself on Brian's finger. "So good, Bri. Suck me harder." His lips felt strangely numb and it was difficult to get the words out. God, he was bloody drunk.

Brian swallowed him deeper, working him with renewed vigor.

Malcolm had never met a man—or a woman, for that matter— who enjoyed sucking cock as much as Brian Harlow. He'd thought the man was stark staring mad the first time he'd asked Malcolm if he could come to his office and pleasure him while he worked.

Of course, he'd allowed it—what man could say *no* to getting his knob polished, no matter where or when?

He'd not believed that he'd actually get any work done, but it had turned out that Bri's attentions were almost... soothing.

"I think Bri would sit under your desk all day long if you allowed it," Sukey had teased.

Malcolm allowed it plenty, but he'd put his foot down when it came to business meetings, no matter how much his wife had begged.

"It would be a great lark, Mal! You gettin' a proper suck with none of them the wiser. Let him do it when you're talkin' to those toffy-nosed arseholes with handles on their names."

It *would* be amusing to have Brian under his desk while Malcolm met with the condescending aristocrats he often needed to placate and flatter in the course of his business.

But as arrogant as Malcolm was—and he was *extremely* arrogant—he needed to keep his wits about him when dealing with men who could destroy him or buy him and sell him many times over.

Someday, when he was rich and powerful, he'd do whatever the hell he wanted.

Speaking of what he wanted ...

He glanced down at the man who'd been patiently working him for at least three-quarters of an hour. He normally allowed Brian to tease and play as long as he wanted—which was a long bloody time. The other man liked nothing more than to keep Malcolm skating on the edge of his climax for hours, but Malcolm was too damned tired to deny himself any longer.

He grabbed a fistful of Brian's silky blond curls and forced his head down. "Finish me," he ordered.

Brian opened his throat and took him deeper, his posture instantly submissive.

"Good little bitch," Mal praised, amused by the way his coarse words made the other man shudder and suck harder.

Being vulgar came easily to Mal. So, if crudity made Bri's cock hard, then Mal was thrilled to oblige.

"Open your throat for me, whore," he ordered in a voice gruff with need. "And take every inch this time."

Bri's sucking became frantic and he repeatedly gagged himself in his effort to take more.

Malcolm used him hard, his hips snapping with increasingly brutal thrusts, fucking Bri's throat the way they both liked it: rough and deep.

"Good, you're so good—*fuck!*" Mal shouted as Brian shoved a second finger in alongside the first, hitting the magical part inside his arse that Sukey called his *joy button.*

Malcolm tightened his fists in Brian's hair, holding his head immobile while he bucked into him. "Gonna come—gonna—*ungh*," he rasped as he rammed himself deep.

The orgasm felt as if it originated in his soul and Mal gave himself up to his long-denied release as his shaft thickened and flooded Bri's throat with jet after jet of hot spend.

Brian whimpered and choked, his throat working convulsively, but he didn't try to pull away.

"Swallow it all," Mal ground out, thrilling to the feeling of Brian's throat tightening around him. "So good," he muttered thickly as the other man milked his sensitive crown, sucking until his balls were empty.

"'nough," Malcolm mumbled, shoving Bri's head away when his touch became uncomfortable.

Brian gave a discontented whine but released him, his hot mouth moving to Malcolm's sac, which he began to lick clean.

Malcolm drifted into a half-doze, lulled by the sensation of a soft, warm tongue caressing him.

"Mal? *Mal?*"

His fuzzy brain distantly registered the sound. "Huh?"

Malcolm forced up his heavy eyelids, grimacing as the room spun around him, slanting from side to side, his guts sloshing along with it.

"Bloody hell," he muttered, trying to shake away the fog. But moving his head only made his stomach pitch so he remained still, cudgeling his brain to remember what was going on.

Ah, yes, now he remembered: they'd been celebrating. With champagne.

Christ! Champagne always made him feel like shite, but this was… bad.

"Mal?" A hand rubbed his bare thigh. "You awake?"

The room was dim, but he could see Brian peering at him.

"Time?" he croaked.

"It's after three. I'd better go if I'm leaving."

Malcolm's brain struggled to come up with an answer. Bri was leaving? But he lived there, didn't he? Why was he—

"Mal?"

He must have fallen asleep again because the voice jolted him. His body was so bloody heavy. *So* heavy.

Brian said something else but Malcolm just shook his head, and then grimaced at the lurching in his belly.

"—going now, Mal."

"Yeah," he slurred, sinking down and down into the welcoming darkness.

Her Beast

***

Crack!

Malcolm's eyes snapped open and he jerked upright in his chair.

Hot smoke seared his eyes and his lungs convulsed when he tried to breathe. He flung a hand over his mouth and squeezed his tearing eyes shut, struggling against a mental fug that was almost as thick as the one in the room.

One thought sliced through the confusion: *Sukey!*

Malcolm sucked in a lungful of air to call for his wife but doubled over as smoke scorched his throat and nose, his eyes steaming as he struggled for breath.

The air was slightly clearer closer to the floor so he sucked in a shallow breath. "Sukey!" he yelled. Except it wasn't a yell, it was a scratchy whisper, like the sound of a leaf skittering over cobbles.

Still coughing, Malcolm lurched through the smoke, stumbling over bottles and clothing and furniture.

"Sukey!" he yelled. His voice was louder, but still inaudible above the roar of the train.

Train?

No, not the train… the fire.

Malcolm staggered around the smoke-filled room like the terrified drunk he was, flailing his limbs, his hands and fingers questing over chairs, settees, the desk surface—*everywhere*—seeking the warm living flesh of his wife.

The goddamned office was *huge* and by the time he'd done one circuit, the glow had shifted to live, licking flames coming in through the door to the hallway.

Shut the bloody door and then check the bedchamber, a voice screamed inside his head.

Malcolm lifted his arms to shield against the heat and lunged toward the door, slamming against the roaring fire in the corridor. Pain seared his left arm and he gritted his teeth, slapping out the flames as he stumbled toward the connecting door to the bedchamber. His burning eyes flickered over the big room and landed on the motionless form on the bed.

"Sukey!"

But she didn't move.

Malcolm crouched low as he ran to the bed, but still his lungs were on fire by the time he reached it. He lowered his head to her naked chest and listened; her heart was beating, her chest rising and falling.

8

A half-full glass and a jug of water stood on the nightstand. Malcolm emptied both over her head and face, but Sukey didn't even twitch.

He shoved down the jagged bolt of terror at the lack of response. *Calm down*, he ordered himself. *She's breathing.*

She was alive. Malcolm just needed to keep her that way.

Water, I need more water.

But one glance at their bathing chamber showed a hellish whorl of dancing red and orange, the flames darting out through the doorway like tongues.

There would be no more water.

Instead, Malcolm wrapped the counterpane around Sukey, covering every inch of her. He yanked a bed curtain off and wrapped that around his waist and then pulled down a second drape and covered his head and shoulders.

A deafening *pop* came from the room behind him. And another and another, as the windows exploded from the heat, bringing in more air, feeding the fire.

There was no more time.

Malcolm scooped Sukey up, hissing with agony as her bundled body slid over the burnt skin on his left side. He inhaled what felt like a lungful of broken glass and leaned close to his wife. "I love you, Susan Elizabeth Barton," he whispered into the cloth covering head. "You'll be all right, darling. I swear on my life."

And then Malcolm plunged into the flames.

Chapter 1

15 Years Later
October 1872

Julia winced as she cleaned her tender skin with the cool, wet cloth.

"Did I hurt you, Julia?" Solomon asked, anxiety pulsing in his voice.

She fought down a twinge of irritation, tossed the cloth back into the tepid water, and then pulled up her drawers.

Once they were tied at the waist, she fiddled with her pearl bracelet rather than step out from behind the dressing screen and face Solomon.

Although the bracelet was neither expensive nor especially striking, it was her favorite piece of jewelry and the only time Julia ever took it off was while bathing. Usually just looking at the bracelet—which had once belonged to her mother—was enough to cheer her. Today it didn't appear to be working.

"Julia?"

"One moment." She sighed. While the last half hour hadn't been horrible, neither had it been rewarding. She forced her face into a pleasant expression and stepped out from behind the screen.

Solomon was perched on the edge of the bed, fully clothed.

He'd been too afraid to take off his clothes, removing only his coat and shoes, and opening his trouser placket.

Julia, meanwhile, had stripped down to her chemise.

Because you're a whore like your mother! a voice in her mind shrieked. A voice that sounded remarkably like her stepmother, Nadine.

Julia shrugged off the voice—she'd had lots of practice.

"Is something wrong?" Solomon asked.

"No, nothing." Julia's smile became less brittle when she met Solomon's concerned blue gaze. He was so sweet that she couldn't stay annoyed with him.

"Did it hurt?" he asked again.

"Only for a moment." That was something of a lie; it had barely hurt at all, but she could hardly tell Solomon that he hadn't been her first.

Matthew—Nadine's personal footman—had been the one who'd relieved Julia of her bothersome virginity almost three years ago, after she'd been sent home in disgrace from school.

It had been her best friend Lily who'd told Julia all about the joys of sexual intercourse. Lily had also been the reason Julia had been ejected from school.

Although they were the same age, Lily always seemed to know everything, at least when it came to things like men and sex. Her friend had orchestrated her own deflowering with one of her father's grooms when she'd been fifteen. She'd then methodically worked her way through the rest of his servants over the next three years.

Unfortunately for Julia, her father's servants were far too terrified of his wrath to bed his daughter, no matter how much Julia had wheedled and manipulated.

She'd barely been home a week—confined to the house and forced to dine on bread and water—when Matthew came to work for Nadine.

Matthew had been different.

Oh, how very, very different.

Julia had discovered just *how* different when she'd pried into her stepmother's private sitting room and had discovered Nadine seated in a wingchair with her gown over her thighs and Matthew busily at work between his mistress's spread knees.

Julia had been stunned—mainly because her moralizing stepmother had always appeared devoted to Julia's father. But perhaps her Papa didn't mind sharing his wife with the servants?

In any case, it was fortunate that Nadine had been facing the other direction and it had been Matthew who'd looked up and spotted Julia. He'd winked, smirked—his lips and chin slick and flushed—and then resumed his labors.

She'd decided on the spot that Matthew would be her first.

First, she had written a letter to Lily to ask her advice on the matter. Although Julia's father had forbidden contact between them after the debacle at school, she'd found a way around his ban by sending letters through her old nanny.

Lily had written back immediately with detailed instructions. "Drink a glass of sherry beforehand. It will hurt no matter what you do, but this will mitigate the discomfort. Most importantly, make sure that he gets you wet *before* he puts himself inside you as it will make penetration bearable. Lastly, insist that you do it somewhere with enough light to *see* everything, because it is most educational."

The idea of demanding advance stimulation from the handsome footman had been daunting, too say the least. Instead, Julia had taken care of *that* part herself, giving herself not one, but two climaxes, prior to summoning him to the sitting room.

It hadn't taken much to convince Matthew—who was very pretty, very vain, but not very smart—to risk his job and take his employer's daughter's maidenhood.

Unfortunately, neither her earlier climaxes nor the sherry had been enough to mask the sharp stab of pain when Matthew had shoved his thick tool inside her. He'd felt as big as a wine bottle and the entire ordeal—which had lasted less than a minute—had been agonizing.

Not only that, but she hadn't seen a thing, even though it had been the middle of the day.

When Julia had suggested removing their clothing, Matthew had gawked at her as if she were mad.

"I've got five minutes before that old rooster Dowling comes hunting me—he hates me, Miss Julia—so there's no time to be shucking our kit."

Julia had to admit that Dowling, her father's butler, did seem to bear an excessive grudge against the attractive footman.

And so Matthew had lifted her skirts and mounted her against the sitting room door.

The most disappointing part hadn't been the pain, but the fact that Julia hadn't experienced an orgasm—a wicked word that Lily had taught her.

Her friend hadn't just taught her the word; she'd also been the one who'd showed Julia how to give herself an orgasm whenever she wanted. "A woman doesn't need a man to do it; she can do it for herself."

It had been Lily's scandalous aunt—a woman who lived openly with her female lover—who'd shared that interesting information with her. "They believe in the demystification of sexual intercourse and argue that women should be mistresses of their own pleasure."

It had sounded revolutionary to Julia, especially since her own female role model—Nadine—had always behaved as if women didn't even *have* bodies below the neck.

Of course, Julia now knew what a hypocrite her stepmother was after spying on her afternoon trysts with Matthew.

Thanks to Lily's careful instruction at school Julia was quite skilled at bringing herself pleasure with her own hand, but it still wasn't as wonderful as the things Lily had done to her using her lips, tongue, and fingers.

Unfortunately, Julia was no longer a schoolgirl, sharing a room and a bed with her best friend every night. Instead, Lily was now far away and married to the Earl of Bankton, a man more than twice her age.

The earl had bought Lily a slapping string of hunters for her wedding gift and then he'd dragged her all the way up North to live. In Julia's opinion even fourteen prime goers and nearly year-round hunting couldn't make up for being married to a man older than her father. But Lily seemed happy and insisted that the earl did everything he could to please her—underlining the word *everything* five times in her letter. Annoyingly, her friend had not explained what *everything* meant. Julia suspected that the mysterious comment had something to do with sexual intercourse and that Lily was, for the first time in their friendship, withholding valuable information.

"Julia?" Solomon said, reminding her that she wasn't alone.

"Hmm?"

Solomon patted the bed beside him. "Come sit with me for a moment."

There was no denying that her stepbrothers' tutor was the most beautiful man she'd ever seen. But, for all his beauty, Solomon didn't make her heart pound or cause any tingling in her sex.

He was just too… perfect.

Julia felt a pang of guilt. All her life she'd heard the same thing: that she was perfect, that she looked like an angel, that she was the sort of beauty who came along only once in a generation. It had always annoyed her and yet here she was thinking the same thing about somebody else.

"Are you sure you're… er, alright?" he asked.

"I'm fine, Solomon."

Julia didn't tell him that the experience had been underwhelming and bland. Solomon had a tender heart and was a good person and Julia was a slut to want him to do the sort of vulgar, rough things she'd read about in the dirty stories that Lily had sent to her.

Solomon gave her a tremulous smile. "It was a magnificent experience, Julia, and I'm privileged that you chose me to receive such an honor."

It was difficult not to roll her eyes. Julia knew she'd get a poem about the *experience* from Solomon in a few days. He didn't just resemble a poet, he *was* one. Albeit not a very good one.

"We can do it again on Saturday," Julia said.

Maybe she would enjoy it more with him a second time. Especially if she could persuade him to keep at it a bit longer than he had. Or maybe she could convince him to allow her to inspect his penis this time, maybe even take him in her mouth, although he'd just about fainted when she'd suggested it once before.

His sky-blue eyes clouded with concern. "I'm—I'm not sure doing it again is a good idea."

Julia wasn't surprised by his words, nor was she put off by them. It had taken her months to convince Solomon to come to this unused bedchamber with her today; he might resemble a fearless hero from a fairytale, but he was timid and cautious.

When Julia didn't respond to his rejection, his alabaster cheeks flushed—as if he could read her mind and was embarrassed to be thought such a chicken-heart.

"It's not that I don't want you," he assured her. "But if your father catches us, he'll kill me, Julia. You are betrothed to Lord Basingstoke," he whispered, as if Julia didn't already know that.

"Yes, but I'm not married yet, so it isn't really a sin."

His brow furrowed at her reasoning.

"Besides, Sebastian has a mistress so why should he care what I do?"

"It's, er, not quite the same thing, Julia."

"Why not?"

"Have you thought about what will happen on your wedding night when Lord Basingstoke learns you aren't a maiden?"

"It will be too late for him to do anything about it by then, won't it?"

Solomon blanched at her response. "You are too innocent—you don't understand. He will be furious when he learns that you're no longer, er…"

"A virgin?" Julia didn't bother to point out that Solomon was not the man responsible for that condition.

His cheeks turned a fiery red at the word. Really, how had Solomon managed to make it to twenty-six with his innocence intact?

"Everyone knows I'm mad for hunting and that my father allows me to ride astride. Sebastian will just think that is how I lost my maidenhead."

Indeed, many parents forbade their daughters from wear split riding habits and riding astride for that very reason, preferring to jeopardize their daughters' lives riding sidesaddle rather than cause prospective husbands to question their virginity.

Julia suspected her own father would have done the same if not for the fact he was too terrified she might kill herself before he could marry her off.

Solomon's lips wrinkled in distaste—either at the indelicate subject of hymens or hunting. Not only did he have the appearance of a poet, but he had the sensibilities of one, too. He'd gone into a swoon a few weeks ago when her twin stepbrothers had been blooded after their first hunt.

Julia thought blooding was a stupid, disgusting ritual but it didn't make her faint. To be honest, she was a bit scornful of Solomon's over-sensitivity, but—

The door banged open, and they both shot to their feet.

"Oh God," Solomon moaned at the sight of Thomas Harlow.

Right behind her father was the loathsome Carl, or *Uncle* Carl as she'd been commanded to call him.

"Papa," Julia said, intensely aware that she was wearing nothing other than a thin chemise and drawers.

"Take the boy," her father snapped at his brother-in-law, his cold gaze on Julia.

"It's not his fault," Julia said as Carl stalked toward Solomon, an expression of brutal anticipation coloring his harsh features. "Papa, what are you going to—"

"He won't be hurt if you obey me, Julia."

Julia exchanged a quick look with Solomon, who was so pale she worried he might faint.

She gave him a tremulous smile. "It will be all right."

Uncle Carl closed one huge paw around Solomon's slender biceps and frog-marched him from the room, pulling the door shut behind him.

"Papa—"

"Shut your mouth!"

She clamped her jaws tight at the quiet menace in his voice.

"You are a whore, Julia, just like your mother was."

It infuriated her that her eyes prickled with tears even though he'd accused Julia of the very same thing when she'd been caught in bed with Lily.

"A whore," he repeated. His hand moved like a blur, the slap hard enough to knock her to the floor.

It wasn't the first time he'd done that, either.

Julia tasted blood and lifted her hand, wincing at the split on her lip.

"Get up," he ordered.

The room tilted as Julia scrambled to her feet and she clutched the nearby bedpost for support. Terror vied with fury when she met her father's gaze. Thomas Harlow had never looked at her with love, but neither had he looked at her with such revulsion.

Julia wiped the blood from her mouth with her shaking hand.

His arm twitched, and she flinched, expecting more—much more. After she'd been expelled, he had beaten her so badly that she'd not been able to show her face in public for weeks.

Instead of striking her again, he closed his hand into a fist and lowered it to his side, his eyes pulsing with something stronger than loathing. Something that looked almost like... hatred.

"What do you think would happen if Lord Basingstoke learned you've been fucking my servants?"

Julia flinched harder at the unexpected word than when he'd struck her. Thomas Harlow was intensely aware of his humble background and had never used vulgar language in her presence. Julia feared his change in behavior could only bode ill for her.

He nodded, as if she'd spoken out loud. "Yes, you are a whore, so from now on I'll treat you like one. You had better hope that Basingstoke doesn't hear of this."

It was on the tip of her tongue to mention that her fiancé kept a mistress, himself, so he'd be a hypocrite to point a finger at her.

Wisely, she kept her mouth shut.

"He is not pleased about this marriage and has only consented thanks to my *considerable* efforts on your behalf, not to mention a great deal of my money."

Julia already knew all that, and it rankled beyond belief that she was betrothed to a man who despised her. She would have loved nothing more than to refuse to marry the conceited peer, but she *needed* their marriage because it was the only way she could secure her brother Richard's future.

There was no denying that her future with such a man would be grim, but at least marrying a duke's heir would put her above most of the *ton*—a group who'd done nothing but disdain her. As a duchess, the *ton* would have to respect her and so would her father and Nadine.

"You had better *pray* that you are not with child—"

"I'm still intact, Papa," Julia lied. "Solomon and I did nothing but—"

"Because that is all you are to Basingstoke," her father continued, unheeding. "Nothing but a broodmare—a *cunt* to be bred—and not one with any bloodline to speak of, either." His lips twisted with distaste as he looked down on her. "If you destroy this arrangement—after all the work I've done—you will spend the remainder of your miserable life locked away somewhere remote and unpleasant. Do you understand?"

"Yes, Papa."

"Your mother—"

"She's *not* my moth—"

This time Julia managed to stay on her feet but her vision doubled from the pain of the blow.

"You don't deserve to call her *mother*," her father thundered, towering over her.

Only when she felt the hot tears on her cheeks did Julia realize that she was crying. But they were tears of rage; one day she would make him pay for each and every blow.

Unfortunately, today was not that day, so Julia kept her head bowed and her blazing eyes downcast.

"It is only because of your *mother's* unfailing kindness that I've allowed you so much freedom."

She bit her lip to keep from snorting.

"But after today she will wash her hands of you, and I won't blame her."

Julia wanted to jump and cheer; Nadine was the person she loathed most in the world.

"I am sending you to London immediately."

Julia's head whipped up. "But—"

"Your hunting season is at an end. In fact, I'm selling all your hunters." He gave her an ugly smile. "If your new husband wants you to hunt then he may mount you."

Julia opened her mouth.

"One more word and I will sell your hacks, too."

She clamped her jaws shut.

He nodded with grim satisfaction. "Your Uncle Carl and Netta will accompany you. They will go with you *everywhere* until the wedding to make sure you behave yourself. Every. Where. Do you understand me?"

She nodded.

"No, say it."

"I understand," she forced the words through clenched teeth.

"You will be permitted to dine with your betrothed when Basingstoke goes to town to visit his grandmother; you will be allowed to shop with Netta; and the *only* riding you will do in the park will include a proper sidesaddle with Carl in attendance. Understood?"

"Yes, Father."

"You will obey your uncle in all things. I have given him complete authority to discipline you however he deems fit."

Revulsion pulsed through her body at the thought of *Uncle Carl* having such power over her.

Carl Sheehan was Nadine's brother and no blood relative of hers. In fact, Julia had met him for the first time a few months ago, after he'd returned from New York City where he'd been living for the past fifteen years.

He was a huge man—tall, raw-boned, and brutishly handsome— who towered over her. And the way his light green eyes crept over her body whenever he was nearby made Julia deeply uncomfortable.

"Do you understand me, Julia?" her father demanded.

"Yes, I understand."

He strode to the door and jerked it open to expose Netta Riley, her Nadine's old nurse, a woman who despised Julia almost as much as Nadine did.

Netta crooked a finger at Julia, as if she were a dog, her dark eyes glittering with malice.

"Go," her father barked when Julia hesitated.

But before she reached the door, her father's hand whipped out and caught her upper arm in a cruel grip. "One last thing." He jerked her close and hissed in her ear, "I want you to think about your idiot twin, Julia."

Fear, as cold and sharp as a blade, stabbed her. "Wh-what do you mean, Papa?"

"You know exactly what I mean. We had a bargain and you are trying to destroy it."

"I'm *not!* I'm still betrothed to Basingstoke. What happened today hasn't changed that."

"Not for a lack of trying on your part." His eyes narrowed. "What do you think I will do about your precious Richard if you don't hold up your end of the bargain?"

"You *promised* he would get to stay at Brookfield, Papa."

"And *you* promised me that you would behave like a young lady, not a back-alley whore."

She opened her mouth to beg and plead, but he wasn't finished.

"Richard is happy where he is right now, isn't he?"

"Yes, Papa, he loves it at Brookfield."

"Your mother believes Richard would be happier somewhere more… structured."

His words were far more stunning than his slaps had been and Julia's belly roiled the way it did when she felt ill. She clutched at his coat. "Please, Papa! Richard would *hate* it if you took him away from Brookfield. He'd *die* if—"

"It's probably time to pension off that old woman, too." Thomas Harlow smirked down at her, roughly plucking her fingers off his coat. "That is exactly what I will do if you force my hand, Julia."

Julia squeezed her eyes shut, but a hot tear escaped and trickled down her cheek. Her father was talking about Nanny Potter, the person her twin loved most in the world. It would kill Richard to be separated from their old nurse.

Julia opened her eyes to see her father glaring smugly down at her, his face as hard as granite.

"*Please*, Papa," she whispered. "I'll be good. You'll see. I'll be perfect."

"Just think about Richard the next time you consider disobeying me." He shoved her out the door. "Now get out of my sight."

Chapter 2

London

"Mr. Barton?"

Malcolm ignored the voice, his single eye riveted to the spot where the angel had stood before she'd disappeared into the exclusive bridal salon.

Plenty of women bought their trousseaux at Barton's Emporium—it was a supplier for the House of Worth, among other exclusive ateliers—but the bridal salon was reserved for those customers who paid enough money to merit both luxury *and* privacy.

"Um, Mr. Barton?"

Malcolm scowled and whipped around. "What the hell are you jabbering about, Butkins?"

To his credit, John Butkins held his ground where bigger, richer, and braver men would have recoiled. But then Butkins had been tolerating Malcolm's foul temper for over a decade.

The poor bastard.

"I've received the telegram from the New York store, sir. You said—"

Malcolm waved his left hand—or claw, rather—dismissively. "Later. Right now, I want you to go down to bridal and find out who that woman is."

Butkins came closer and peered out the window. "Er, what woman?"

"She's just gone into the private salon with one of the mannequins—a tall, buxom brunette."

Butkins's thin, homely face creased into a shy smile. "Ah, that would be Miss Amelia Brown, sir. She's quite—"

"Whatever," Malcolm snapped. "Get down there and find out that woman's name *now*."

Butkins fled, not bothering to ask foolish questions or dally—part of the reason he'd lasted so long in Malcolm's employ. If there was one thing Malcolm didn't tolerate, it was employees or servants who didn't obey orders quickly and efficiently.

You never did like anyone disobeying you, Mal—not even before you were swimmin' in lard.

He smirked at Sukey's mocking, but accurate, observation.

Back before Malcolm was *swimmin' in lard* he'd used his huge body and hard fists to intimidate people to do his bidding; now he used money and power.

Neither behavior had earned him friends and every employee and servant in this building either disliked or feared him—or perhaps both—thanks to his brusque behavior.

Fortunately for Malcolm, he wasn't in the friend-making business.

He turned back to the window, one of many that lined the four corridors that made up Malcolm's world and overlooked his London department store.

Each of his other six stores—soon to be eight—were constructed the same way. They were marvels of modern architecture that rose five stories, with his apartments occupying the top floor. A massive dome in the style of St. Paul's held up the four walls and allowed for a cathedral-like, awe-inducing openness within. Only the ground floor was complete, the other levels, and Malcolm's lair, were mezzanines.

In addition to providing a stunning environment for his wealthy clientele to spend their money, the cunning construction meant Malcolm could observe every part of his domain without leaving his perch.

Well, *almost* every part.

As much of a voyeur as Malcolm was, even he drew the line at spying into the female dressing areas.

The statuesque brunette—Amelia, Butkins had called her—came out of the salon door and headed toward a matron with two younger women.

As Malcolm watched and waited for Butkins to return, Miss Brown managed to sell not three, but five hats to the proud mama. Malcolm made a mental note to look at Miss Brown's commission report; a saleswoman that skilled deserved a bonus.

The door he'd been glancing at repeatedly for the past thirty minutes finally opened and the head of his bridal department, Miss Clemmons, exited the exclusive salon. Right beside her was the young woman he'd already christened *Angel.*

Malcolm removed his tinted spectacles and raised his gold-chased, single draw opera glass—which had once belonged to the Empress Josephine—to get a better view of the angel.

"Fuck me," he muttered, gorging on the exquisite face beneath the foolish twist of straw and net that counted for a woman's hat.

He could see her bloody eyelashes even from this distance!

The angel also possessed creamy, flawless skin; plush, pouty pink lips; a perfect retroussé nose; enormous blue pools for eyes; a determined chin; and a rounded jaw that Malcolm's palm itched to cup.

The young woman nodded at something Miss Clemmons said and then turned, her smile shifting into a scowl as she glared at an old crone who was hurrying across the store toward her.

Miss Clemmons wisely melted away as the two women commenced to bicker.

The older woman made a chopping motion with one hand and the angel turned away and flounced toward the east exit.

Not for the first time Malcolm cursed the fashion for bustles and cages and every other manner of frippery that hid a woman's body from a man's view.

But although her lower half was concealed from him, her flaring skirts led to a waist that could not be far off the current ideal of nineteen inches, making Malcolm's fingers—both real and phantom—twitch to span her slender body.

He loved the feel of a warm female body snugly encased in tight stays. If there was one garment he adored, it would be a corset. There was something unspeakably erotic about binding a woman's body into the masculine ideal of femininity, sculpting her for no reason other than male pleasure.

Just looking at the angel's snugly corseted body made him harden.

Still, as shapely as she undoubtedly was, she was also a very tiny woman. Malcolm estimated that she was roughly the same height as the current Queen of England, who had—at barely five feet tall—always looked bloody ludicrous whenever she'd stood next to her dearly departed Albert, a foot difference between them.

Malcolm was a huge man—even bigger than the Royal Consort—and he had a penchant for rough sex, so he'd never gravitated to small or fragile-looking women. Indeed, he had always believed that Sukey—who stood five feet and eleven inches in her stocking feet—had possessed the perfect female figure.

But, as much as he'd loved her, even Malcolm had to acknowledge that Sukey had not been a beauty like the woman four floors below. That hadn't mattered a whit to Malcolm, who'd valued and adored his wife's fire, brains, and liveliness far more than classically perfect features.

And yet here he was entranced by the perfect face of a stranger after merely gazing at her for ten seconds!

What was wrong with him? Why did he find this woman so bloody riveting?

Was it because he was a nightmare in human form who could never attract a woman like her, so now he suddenly yearned for the unattainable?

Or was it just her sheer physical perfection that drew him? After all, what man *wouldn't* find her desirable?

Just as his angel reached the door to the outside world a towering ginger-headed bloke approached her.

Malcolm lifted his glass again.

Christ! The man was massive—easily a foot taller than the girl and her chaperone—with a prodigious belly to go with his large build.

Running to fat was one thing Malcolm could not be accused of.

As hideous and scarred as he was, he'd never been more physically fit in his entire life. Not that any woman would notice his body after one look at his face.

The ginger-headed giant shook his head at the angel and whatever he said made her fling up her hands.

The man's posture stiffened and then he grabbed her upper arm and propelled her out of the store and into the hazy, polluted afternoon.

And that was the end of *that*.

Malcolm slowly lowered the opera glass as he pondered the strange trio, his mind lingering not on his angel but on the oversized man with her.

At six feet four inches Malcolm didn't see many men as tall as he was. And that red hair was more than a little distinctive. Why did Malcolm feel like he'd seen the man before?

He closed his eye, as if that might help him remember.

A faded image flitted through his mind, but when he tried to pin it down, the memory flickered and was gone, like a flash of light on water.

He opened his eye and stared at the huge glass doors far below.

He couldn't see outside the doors from this distance, but gray light filtered through the leaded glass panes into the store from the world beyond—a world Malcolm had not been a part of for many years.

Oh, he left the store, of course—he inspected all his stores annually—but he never moved among the crowds that filled the streets.

No, Malcolm did all his traveling in luxurious privacy.

His custom coach with darkened windows collected him at his *private* entrance. And then his *private* yacht took him in opulence and comfort across the channel. Or sometimes his *private* rail carriage took him to the various cities within Britain.

At the end of each of his journeys was a Barton's Emporium with a fifth floor that was identical to the original in London, complete with his special transparent mirrors, personal gymnasiums, and pleasure chambers that mimicked those at the Birch Palace, Malcolm's favorite London brothel—back in the days when he actually visited such places.

Malcolm turned away from the store when he heard the low, distinctive hum of the lift. A few seconds later the heavy bronze door slid open and his secretary emerged.

"Ah, Butkins. I'd begun to think you ran off with Miss Amelia Brown."

His secretary flushed as brightly as a schoolgirl at Malcolm's teasing. "I beg your pardon for the delay but both sales ladies were engaged with customers and I thought it best to wait until they were finished."

Malcolm approved of Butkins' actions wholeheartedly. He should do because it was his policy: the customer *always* came first at Barton's. He had only twitted Butkins because it was so amusing to make the other man blush and stammer.

"So, who is she?"

"Her name is Julia Harlow."

"Harlow?" Malcolm repeated.

"Thomas Harlow's daughter. She is engaged to marry the Duke of Angleton's heir, the Marquess of Basingstoke. The wedding is set for the end of January."

Malcolm slumped back in his chair, shocked. *That* was Brian's niece? Why, the girl couldn't be more than five years old!

That was fifteen years ago, Mal—the lass is a woman now, Sukey reminded him.

Christ. Had it really been so long ago?

"Sir?"

Malcolm blinked and looked up at Butkins. "Are you sure it's her?"

"Er, yes sir, I'm positive."

Malcolm summoned a mental image of the angel and compared it with what he could recall of her father. Yes, he saw a resemblance to

Tommy Harlow—both were fair and blue-eyed—but Julia took after her uncle Brian far more than her father. Brian had always been the more handsome of the two brothers, his hair blonder, his eyes bluer, and his features finer.

"How old is she?" he asked Butkins.

"Miss Clemmons mentioned that she was twenty, sir."

So, not a girl, but a woman.

Malcolm's damaged mouth pulled into a wry smirk at the twisted situation. What a fucking dog he was to be lusting after a woman twenty-four years his junior who was also the niece of his former lover.

It's a relief to know you're still alive, Mal. I've not seen your cock get so hard so fast since—well, not since that last time with me and Bri.

Malcolm shook his head at phantom Sukey. He knew the voice didn't *really* belong to his dead wife, but it was hard to remember that when she said things that she *would* have said if Malcolm hadn't failed her that night fifteen years ago.

Oh, Mal. How long will you punish yourself for something that wasn't your fault?

"Sir?" Butkins asked.

Malcolm shook himself. "Hmm?"

"I asked if there was anything else."

"What was the Harlow chit doing here?"

"Mrs. Clemmons said she had some questions about wedding clothes, sir."

"Obviously she was here about bridal clothes if she went into the bridal salon," he said icily. "But something must have happened for her to be ordering a gown at such a late date."

Not to mention the fact that Tommy had always hated Malcolm and Sukey and what Bri did with them, so he couldn't see Harlow allowing his daughter to shop at Barton's.

"She wasn't here to order a gown—she went to Worth's Paris store, sir. She was here to inquire about altering the gown."

Malcolm snorted at the pretentious poppycock. Barton's carried exclusive Worth designs—dresses even the atelier himself didn't sell in his Paris store as part of his agreement to get his clothing into Barton's. Why the hell would anyone go to Paris when there was a bigger selection only a few miles away?

Nothing but pure snobbery. Or the fact that Julia's father hated Malcolm. Or both.

An unwanted image of the red-haired man flickered through his mind.

He scowled. *Who the fuck is that big bloke and why is he tickling my memory like a feather up my arse?*

But there was no Sukey in his head to answer his question.

Malcolm saw that Butkins was still waiting and said, "Go to Joe Bacon and tell him to find out where Thomas Harlow's house is and who is living in it."

Butkins adjusted to the sudden change in subject with admirable swiftness. "Er, very good, sir."

"I want to know about *everyone* living in the house—servants and family. If Joe can locate photographs of the occupants, I want those, too. I'm especially interested in a huge bloke—maybe family, maybe an upper servant. Tell Joe to make this a priority. I want something by the end of next week."

"Yes, sir." Butkins looked unhappy at the prospect of talking to Joe Bacon, who was Malcolm's intimidating enforcer.

Just because Malcolm had gone legitimate—mostly—didn't mean he no longer needed muscle. Indeed, he seemed to need Joe more and more every year.

"Oh, and another thing," Malcolm said as the other man turned to leave.

Butkins's eyes filled with dread, as if wondering what fresh Hell awaited him. "Yes, sir?"

"Dora is set to arrive tonight?"

Butkins's face flamed. "Er, yes sir, at the normal time." He hesitated, flicked at gaze at Malcolm's crotch—as if afraid of what he'd see there—and then raised his eyes. "Did you, er, need her earlier?"

Malcolm laughed. "No, I can wait that long. But tell Madam Sylvie I don't want Dora. Tell her to send somebody new."

Malcolm usually employed whores for two weeks at a stretch, accommodating them in one of the luxurious guest suites he'd built for precisely that purpose.

"Any specific instructions?" Butkins asked, squirming under Malcolm's amused stare.

"You saw the Harlow chit—tell her that I want somebody who resembles Julia Harlow: blond, small, but not too thin."

Poor Butkins looked like he might faint from mortification. "Yes, sir. Is that all?"

"Yes. You can go," he said, smirking at Butkins's fleeing back.

Malcolm really was a pig to use the other man as his procurer, but it was his secretary's fault for reacting in such an amusing way even after all these years. It wouldn't surprise Malcolm to learn that Butkins was still a virgin.

As for the whore he'd just requested… Well, Malcolm knew he would never get anyone as beautiful as Julia Harlow, but a man could dream, couldn't he?

Chapter 3

That Same Night, Across Town

Julia entered her room and yelped at the figure lurking inside her dressing room.

"What are you doing in my chambers, Netta?" she demanded, cutting an accusing look at her maid, Mary, who was cowering behind the older woman and wringing her hands, a guilty expression on her pretty face.

"Why were you flittin' about the house all but naked?" Netta retorted.

Julia's face heated. "I'm *not* naked! I'm wearing my dressing gown. As to what I was doing, I went to fetch a book from the library, not that it's any of your concern. Now, I'm tired. So, tell me what you want and then get out."

The older woman's mouth tightened at her rudeness. "I'm here to discuss your willful behavior today."

"Oh, what behavior is that?"

"You sneakin' off to Barton's and then makin' a scene when I told you to leave."

For reasons beyond Julia's ken, both her father and Nadine refused to patronize the upscale department store, even though everyone *knew* they had Worth gowns so exclusive that even Worth didn't sell them at his own store.

"So what if I went into Barton's? As for making a *scene*, I merely disagreed with you—does that now qualify as a scene?"

Netta held up the distinctive white and pink box that Mary had smuggled into Julia's room earlier that day. "Just what is this, Miss Julia?"

Julia cut her maid—who was supposed to have hidden the box—a look of disbelief. Once again, Mary shrugged, her expression aggrieved and pitiful.

Well, Julia could hardly blame the girl; Netta was a force of nature. Like locusts or a plague of toads.

She forced a smile. "Why, that is a pastry box and those are called pastries, Netta. I'm surprised you've never seen such a thing before. Please help yourself. I recommend the cream cakes."

"You know you're not supposed to be eating sweets." Netta raked Julia with a scornful look. "You're fat, Julia. So fat that we'll have to alter your wedding dress to fit you—if that is even possible."

"For your information it *is* possible to alter that particular gown in time for the wedding. That's why I spoke to the woman at Barton's."

"You wouldn't need an alteration if you weren't such a piggy."

"I'm still lacing to twenty just as I have for a year, Netta. As for being a pig? I ate a piece of bread, an apple, and one miserly slice of ham for dinner. I'm so hungry I can scarcely see straight."

"You know the mistress ordered your gown to fit eighteen inches."

"Well then *she* can wear the vile thing!"

Nadine's mania for an hourglass figure had gone past the point of sanity and Julia's father did nothing to stop her tyranny.

"It is my job to see that you can fit into that gown. Your father paid—"

"Shut. Up. You. Horrid. Old. Hag."

Netta gasped. "Why you little—"

The bedroom door swung open and Carl stood on the threshold.

Julia gave an astonished squawk. "How dare you just walk into my chambers?"

"You needed me?" Carl asked Netta, ignoring Julia as if she'd never spoken.

Netta nodded grimly. "I'm at the end of my tether, Master Carl. Nothing I've done works and—"

"You mean starving me?" Julia spat. "Or do you mean boring me? Or perhaps you mean tying me to that *bloody* board so that—"

Carl closed the distance between them with only a few strides and slid a huge hand over Julia's mouth, while his other snaked around her waist and pulled her tight to his body.

Julia's screams were muffled by his meaty paw and when she tried to push away from him it was like attempting to shove an omnibus.

Netta marched toward her, the pastry box still in her hands, a nasty smirk on her ugly face. She spoke to Carl, but her gaze never left Julia. "Do whatever you must, Master Carl. I wash my hands of her. Mary," she barked at the cowering maid, making her jump. "You come with me."

Once the door shut behind the two women Carl turned Julia around as easily as he might position a doll, pressing his body against hers, his huge hand splayed across her lower back, his fingers dangerously close to her buttocks. He took her chin with his other hand and tilted her head back so sharply that pain shot down her spine.

"You listen, girlie," he said, staring in a way that sent a bolt of fear—as well as a darker, even more concerning emotion—ricocheting through her body. "Your father left me in charge of you—body and soul. I can tie you to your bed and give you nothin' but bread and water and nobody would stop me."

Julia knew that was no empty threat.

"Or I can bring you tasty little treats and make your life all around sweeter. It's up to you, luv."

As much as Nadine and Carl resembled each other physically, their speech and behavior couldn't be more different.

Nadine spoke with the cut glass accents of a social climbing cit while Carl sounded like an Irish lad from the stews.

"Well, girlie? If I remove my hand, will you scream?"

Julia gave a minute shake of her head and staggered back when he released her.

Rather than leave, as she'd hoped, he stood his ground and stared down at her.

"Wh-What else do you want?"

A slow, oily grin spread across his face. "You need to be punished."

"But you just said—"

"I'm going to punish you for bein' mouthy in the store today, *and* for goin' into the store after Netta told you not to."

"Punish me how?"

His eyes fondled her body like small, groping hands. "I think you'll like what Uncle Carl does to you."

Julia swallowed down her bile, but wisely kept her mouth shut.

He sat down on the padded bench at the foot of her bed. "Take off your dressing gown."

Her jaw sagged. "Absolutely *not*."

"Strip off your robe or I'll tear *all* your clothes off you."

Julia's mind staggered like a syphilitic man she'd once seen wandering down Oxford Street. How could this be happening? Surely this couldn't be what her father meant? But if she screamed for Netta would she—

Carl began to stand and Julia squeaked and hastily pulled the sash at her waist.

Carl sat back down and nodded. "Go on."

She fumbled with the buttons that ran down the front of the robe, her hand shaking so badly by the time she got to the last button that it took her four tries. She reflexively clutched the two edges of the dressing gown together once it was unbuttoned.

"I won't tell you again: Take it off."

She hastily shrugged the garment off, letting it slide to the floor.

Carl's eyes dropped to her chest and stayed there. He made a disgusting grunting sound and his lips parted, his expression ravenous as he stared at her ridiculously large breasts, which were rising and falling faster than usual.

Even though she hated Carl with a passion, her body responded to his hungry gaze and her nipples hardened against the whisper thin lawn of her nightgown.

Worse than that was the way her sex swelled and slicked the longer he looked, her body's response to masculine admiration making her hate herself even more than the man across from her.

Her father was right: she *was* a whore.

Carl shifted on the bench, looking poleaxed, his mouth agape as if he needed more air.

Julia didn't want to feel flattered—she hated Carl—but it was difficult to ignore such naked desire. The last person to look at her with such yearning hadn't been Solomon or Matthew, but Lily, whose gaze had always consumed Julia as if she were dessert.

"Come here," he ordered, his voice gruff.

Julia hesitated.

"*Now!*"

She jolted and took a small, shaky step toward him.

Carl's arm lashed out as quickly as a frog's tongue snagging a fly. His huge hand closed around her wrist and he yanked her down onto his lap.

"What are you—"

"Shut up," he ordered, effortlessly positioning her face-down over his thighs, her buttocks in the air.

When she tried to cover her bottom with her hands, he grabbed both her wrists with one hand and imprisoned them against her back. "I want you to count," he said.

"Count wha—*ow!*" Julia yelped when his flat hand struck her bottom.

He squeezed her wrists. "Count or I'll just give you more."

"One!"

"Good girl." He swirled his palm lightly over her cheeks, the gesture strangely … soothing.

"You can't do this to me!" she shouted. "I'm no child to be spanked, I'm *twenty!*"

"Twenty is what you'll get, then."

"What?" she shrieked.

Smack!

This time he struck her on only the left cheek. "Count!" he growled.

"T-Two!"

He struck her again, but on the other side. And far harder.

"Three," she whimpered.

Smack!

By the time he reached twenty the tears were streaming down her cheeks and she could barely force the words out.

Her bottom was on fire and throbbing with pain.

And she was aroused.

"Shhh," he murmured. His gentle rubbing on the enflamed skin was no longer soothing, instead it caused as much pain as the swats. "That's a good girl." He shifted beneath her, moving her higher on his lap.

And that was when she felt it: his erect penis.

Julia yelped and jerked back.

He chuckled evilly, holding her pressed tightly against the loathsome thing. "Feel that, do ye?"

"No, don't—please—"

"Shut up," he ordered, but the words lacked any real heat and he continued to stroke from her burning bottom down to the back of her knees, and then up again.

He pressed the heel of his hand against the split between her legs hard enough to nudge her clenched thighs apart, managing to stimulate her female parts even though he wasn't touching her directly.

Julia whimpered.

"Like that, eh?"

"No!"

He chuckled. "Liar. I bet if I shoved a finger up your tight little cunt it would be wet and swollen."

Julia shuddered at his vulgar, horrifying words.

But there was no denying the truth of them: she had rarely become so wet and swollen so fast, even with Lily.

His caressing hand hovered over her agonized backside before stroking against the seam of her legs, lingering over the place where her swollen lower lips were crushed between her thighs.

"I could do that for you—girl, give you what you need." His soft, wheedling tone was one she'd never heard from him before.

"Wh-What do you mean?"

Smack!

"You already gave me twenty!"

"Don't play stupid with me. You know what I mean. I've been watching you for months as you tried to get that little pansy to be a man and fuck you hard the way you need it. Christ! Every bloke for miles can smell that ripe cunny of yours." He lightly traced a finger down the fabric stretched over her back cleft. "Damned sweet it is, too."

When Julia tried to push herself up, he held her down with terrifying ease, laughing.

"Let me up." She'd meant to demand it, but sounded whiney and weak, instead.

"When I'm good and ready."

Julia gave up her pointless squirming since she suspected he actually liked it.

"You know what you are?"

Julia refused to answer.

"You're a filthy little slut who needs her cunt stuffed with something big and hard."

Julia's head spun at his vile words but the wicked throbbing deep within her womb intensified. The sensation was a familiar one—it was what she felt right before she climaxed from her hand—but this feeling was so much rawer.

Unwanted, Carl's words came back to her like a slap in the face. *You're a filthy little slut who needs her cunt stuffed with something big and hard.*

That's not true. That isn't what I want.

But even in the privacy of her own mind the protestation sounded unconvincing and pathetic.

Oh God. What is wrong with me? Why would I like such a thing—and from such an odious—

Smack!

Julia yelped again. "*Why*? You said you were only giving me twenty."

"I changed my mind. Now, *count*."

"Twenty-two, you—you *pig*."

He laughed and rubbed her bottom, his erection digging into her side. "I can give you what you want without puttin' a babe in yer belly, if that's what's worrying you." His voice pulsed with an animal need so desperate that it made her entire body flush. "You should take what I'm offerin' now. After you marry that cold fish you'll come beggin' for my cock. I know your sort."

"If you so much as touch my—my—"

"Go on, if I so much as touch your *what*?" he asked, his voice thick with amusement.

"My *body* that way I shall tell my father that you forced me!"

Smack!

Julia's vision darkened at the bolt of pain and pleasure that washed through her at the vicious blow.

"Shut your nasty little mouth," he snarled. "You think anyone would believe what you said? I could fuck you seven ways to Sunday and everybody would call you a liar."

Impotent rage and unwanted desire threatened to choke her.

"Don't worry about me forcin' you, lass. I don't waste myself on ungrateful, horny little jades. By the time I'm done you'll fookin' beg for my jack."

"I *hate* you!"

He laughed.

Smack!

"Now count, goddammit!"

"Twenty-four!" It was more a sob than a word.

"I knew yer Ma, did you know that?"

Please God, make him shut up, Julia prayed.

As usual, God ignored her.

"Yeah, I fucked her, too. Back when she was married to yer Da." He gave a filthy laugh. "She was a randy piece—there wasn't anyone she didn't take for a ride. Even yer own uncle, that sick twist Brian. She couldn't get enough—"

"Shut up you lying swine!"

"She liked it rough—"

"You're a liar!"

He just laughed.
Smack!
"Count," he ordered.
Julia counted.

Chapter 4

Come in," Malcolm called out at the knock on his study door. He removed his spectacles and set them beside the latest sales report from his second Paris store. The reports came to him twice weekly in a telegram that cost a fortune to send, so he went over them with a fine-toothed comb.

Butkins opened the door. "Mr. Bacon is here, sir."

"Show him in," Malcolm muttered, tossing down his pen and rubbing his eye before glancing at the clock: it was just before midnight.

He leaned back in his chair and looked down at the woman kneeling beneath his desk. Maisie's big blue eyes met his and she smiled around his prick. Or at least she tried to.

"We're done here, sweetheart," Malcolm said.

He waited until she'd lifted her mouth off him before tucking his cock—half-hard and smeared with scarlet paint from her lips— back into his trousers. And then he stood and extended a hand to help her up from her cushion.

She was small and shapely—just like he'd asked for—and barely came up to his chest. She'd been with him for almost a week but he'd not fucked her yet, only using her mouth.

He was saving her cunt and arse for when he could concentrate and appreciate it—something he'd not been able to do since seeing Julia Harlow and that big red-headed bastard in his store. Hopefully his mind would be his own again after Joe's visit tonight.

Maisie's hand shook when she offered it up to him. Even though she'd spent most of her stay being pampered by his superlative staff—massaged, bathed, fed the best food, wines, and champagne, and dressed in the most expensive lingerie, gowns, and jewels, all of which she'd get to keep when he was done with her—it was clear that she wasn't comfortable with the arrangement.

Or perhaps it was just Malcolm that she was skittish around.

No surprise, there.

Most women—and a good many men, for that matter— became nervous in his presence. No doubt she was wondering—

dreading—when he would finally use something other than her sweet mouth. He suspected she was terrified of what he kept hidden beneath his mask, gloves, and clothing and was worried that she'd have to look at his burnt, deformed body when he finally fucked her.

Malcolm put a finger beneath her chin and tilted her heart-shaped face toward him, desire pulsing through his body at the sight of her swollen, reddened mouth. He grazed her slick lower lip with his thumb, amused by the wide-eyed way she was staring at the half of his face sheathed in black leather. "You pleased me tonight, Maisie."

Her breathing quickened at his quiet words and her pupils swelled slightly at his praise.

It wasn't hyperbole: she had a mouth like hot wet velvet and knew how to keep him balancing on the razor-fine edge of desire for hours.

She swallowed hard. "But you didn't … er …"

"No, I didn't come," he agreed, his disfigured mouth twisting into a carnal grin that wasn't pretty—at least judging by the poorly suppressed revulsion in her blue gaze. "But I will shortly. Tonight, I'll visit you in your room and fuck you."

A shudder wracked her slender form.

Malcolm decided to pretend that it was passion.

He released her chin and took the flaps of her silk robe and pulled them open to feast on her petite but lush body.

"Mmm," he hummed, delighted with what he saw.

Maisie didn't look as fresh and natural as Julia Harlow, but she was close enough. Her breasts were over-large for her slender ribcage, her waist impossibly tiny, her hips the sort that begged for a man's hands to grip them.

The neatly trimmed patch of brown hair covering her sex didn't match the improbably golden hair on her head and he fought down a twinge of annoyance. He despised such artifice, but at least her hair was clean, healthy, and fell to her waist.

There was also a certain harshness to her skin—he suspected she owed the creamy color to cosmetics rather than nature—and he saw some scarring and imperfections, but in the low lighting she looked good enough.

He reluctantly closed her robe and tied the sash, looking up from her luscious body to meet her vapid gaze. "Mr. Butkins will take you to your room, where you'll find food and drink waiting. After you've eaten, Kemp will help you bathe and change into something special."

She nodded jerkily. "Yes, sir."

Malcolm ran the gloved knuckles of his right hand over the curve of her jaw. "So pretty," he murmured, his nostrils flaring when she flinched away.

"I'm sorry, sir," she said.

He smiled, even knowing how it twisted his damaged mouth. "It's all right, kitten." And it was, too. It didn't hurt Malcolm's feelings that she found him hideous; he *was* hideous. It was just a fact of life.

For her sake Malcolm wished she weren't so revolted by him, but he always blindfolded his women and usually only mounted them from behind, so she'd not have to look at or touch any part of him when he fucked her.

He turned to his hovering employee. "Show the lady to her room, Butkins."

Butkins gestured to the door. "This way, ma'am."

Malcolm couldn't help smirking at his secretary's visible mortification. He'd have thought Butkins would be comfortable around ladies of the night after working for Malcolm for so long, but he looked as shocked now as he'd done the very first time he'd seen a woman crawl out from under Malcolm's desk.

Thanks to Brian, Malcolm loved getting sucked off while he worked. But then who wouldn't?

While Maisie was no Brian Harlow—still the best gamahucher Malcolm had ever known—she still had superlative skills. For at least two hours she'd brought him to the edge of release and then eased him down, just the way he liked it.

As a result of her fine work his bollocks were heavy and full, his sac so tight he felt like he might explode just from the pressure of his trousers. But as primed as he was to empty his load into her, he'd still held back.

Mainly because he liked the sharp edge that such restraint gave him.

But he also enjoyed denying himself pleasure, punishing himself for being alive to enjoy such earthly delights while his wife was nothing but bones in a box.

That didn't mean Malcolm was a martyr to his guilt. No, not at all. Not only would he fuck Maisie tonight, but he'd been watching her every day this past week.

Indeed, sometimes he liked that—spying on the whores he hired—better than having sex with them.

A *voyeur* was the word he'd recently heard for what he did. At the orphanage they'd just called them *peepers*: perverts who enjoyed watching others engage in sex.

Malcolm refused to be ashamed of his prurient proclivities; when a man's face was enough to make women vomit or scream that man had to take his pleasure when and how he could find it.

A huge man appeared in the open doorway Butkins had just passed through.

Malcolm nodded his greeting. "Come in, Joe."

"Evenin', guv." Joe moved with the grace of a boxer, light on his feet for a man who weighed at least twenty stone. He was pure muscle, bone, and gristle; one tough bastard. He was also as smart as a whip and a hard worker.

"What do you have for me?" Malcolm asked.

Joe handed him a stack of papers and then lowered himself into the oversized leather chair across from Malcolm's desk and pulled out a small notebook, ready to report.

"Go ahead," Malcolm said.

"The Marquess of Basingstoke—heir to the Duke of Angleton—announced his betrothal to Julia Harlow two years ago. That top picture is from the announcement that was in the newspapers."

Malcolm greedily studied the photograph. Bloody hell she was gorgeous. Seeing a picture of her right after looking at Maisie made him realize there really was no comparison. Maisie was the proverbial mutton dressed as lamb.

As for Basingstoke?

Well, Malcolm knew women would find him attractive with his tall, elegant gentleman's body and fine-boned classical features. Not to mention his impressive title.

Malcolm thought he looked like a bloody tosser.

But *her*.

Christ. She was unlike anything he'd ever seen. The feeling in his chest when he looked at her was …

Hell, he didn't know what the fuck was clawing at him so painfully.

It's longing, Mal. You've been alone far too long.

Malcolm shoved Sukey's voice away, not interested in chatting with his dead wife at the moment.

He looked up at Joe. "Why the long engagement?"

"They were actually supposed to marry two years ago—when the girl left school—but a death in each family put the date off, twice. Also, from what I could learn, his lordship—Sebastian, his name is—wasn't exactly eager for the union."

Sebastian. Malcolm hated that poncy name; just hearing it made him want to punch the man in the face.

"Why is Basingstoke dragging his heels? I assume Harlow will pay generously for a duke's heir and marrying a woman who looks like her can't be any hardship."

Joe flipped a page. "Apparently he had his mind set on marryin' Lady Cynthia Beasley, the Earl of Carlton's daughter. In fact, everyone thought the two had an agreement. But Sebastian's papa is skint and the estates aren't entailed. So, if somebody don't pour some brass into His Grace's coffers there won't be nothin' left to inherit.

"So, Harlow's money talked louder than his lordship's love, did it?"

"That's about right."

"What's Harlow getting out of this—other than a title for his daughter and a son-in-law who will despise him?"

"The duke sits on an important tariff commission."

"Ah." Harlow made his money in shipping; it didn't take a genius to put two and two together.

"So, papa duke needs blunt," Malcolm mused. "What about the dukeling?"

"Sebastian don't have his pa's fever for the tables, but he's mighty expensive. Keeps two hunting lodges and some of the best horseflesh in the entire country. He fought the duke tooth and nail about the marriage even knowin' how badly dipped the family is. Neither of them was too keen to form a connection with a girl who has Harlow's blood in her veins."

Malcolm scowled. Fucking aristocrats and their tedious bloodline fuckery. "But they obviously changed their minds."

Joe nodded. "Harlow finally tipped the scales in his daughter's favor by offering Sebastian a horse breeding operation. Apparently, the stud is worth a fortune and produces the finest hunters in the country."

Malcolm snorted. "I don't suppose you know if the girl wanted a toff for a husband?"

"Miss Harlow's ex-maid said the lass would do just about anything to get out from under Mrs. Harlow's thumb. Besides," Joe scratched his head and shrugged, "Lord Sebastian Basingstoke is considered quite a prize in the marriage market."

Malcolm kept his thoughts on that subject to himself. Instead, he flipped through the papers and photographs, pausing at a large envelope. He opened it and several photographs slid out.

The first was of Julia Harlow, the sort of picture you could get taken at studios anywhere in the city. It was far less formal than the betrothal picture and had been tinted. She wore a frothy pale pink gown and the artist had done an amazing job coloring her eyes and adding a faint blush to her skin.

Malcolm couldn't stop looking at her face and it was a struggle to flip the picture over and set it face down on the desk.

Get control of yourself, man, he ordered, more than a little disturbed by his rampant obsession for a woman he'd never even spoken to.

The second picture was of the old woman who'd been with Julia. The name *Annette Fowler* was written in Joe's small, neat handwriting on the back. There were strange indentations around the edges of the photo.

"Did you take this picture from a frame?" he asked.

"Aye, right beside her bed. Wasn't no other way, sir." Joe gave him a sheepish smile.

Malcolm chuckled at the man's brazenness. "Tell me about Fowler."

"She claims that she was Mrs. Harlow's—formerly Nadine Sheehan's—childhood nurse, but she's actually Mrs. Harlow's aunt on mother's side, although hardly anyone knows."

"Nadine Harlow keeps her own aunt working as a maid?"

"Aye."

Malcolm gave a low whistle. "There is a new low in family relations. How long has this been going on?"

"Mrs. Fowler has worked Nadine's servant ever since Nadine married Harlow over fifteen years ago"

Huh. Malcolm had never heard the like.

"Anyhow," Joe continued, "About five weeks ago, Mrs. Fowler came to London with Miss Julia to keep her out of trouble before the wedding."

"Out of trouble?" Malcolm repeated.

"Aye, it appears the lass is a bit of a terror. Miss Julia is horse-mad, loves to ride to hounds, and is reckless."

Malcolm would never understand the aristocracy's fascination with chasing a fox with a pack of bloodthirsty dogs. Still, he was amused—albeit darkly—that the daughter of Tommy Harlow, a rookery lad, engaged in such rarified sport. Tommy had always been a pretentious git so he must be thrilled to bits by his daughter's toff pastime.

"How did hunting and horses get her in trouble?" Malcolm asked. "I would have thought her prospective bridegroom loved that about her."

"Oh, aye, it might be the one area they see eye-to-eye. But, er, she wasn't seeing eye-to-eye with only his lordship, beggin' your pardon."

Malcolm sighed. "In plain language, Joe."

"Er, Miss Harlow was caught in bed with the family tutor." He cleared his throat. "Before that—although her father and stepmother aren't aware—she gave her maidenhood to a footman named Matthew Miller. Miller told me he thought there might be others but had no names."

Something hot, fierce, and possessive pooled in Malcolm's belly.

Christ! Was he … *jealous* of a footman? Over a woman he'd never even met?

That's what it feels like to me, his dead wife piped up, her laughter echoing inside his head.

You're wrong, Sukey. If I wasn't jealous about you fucking other men, then I'm not likely to be feeling it now, am I?

But his wife was gone.

Long gone.

"Sir?"

Malcolm looked up to find Joe giving him a quizzical look.

"Go on," he said.

"The next photograph is of Mr. and Mrs. Harlow was taken about five years ago."

Malcolm recognized Tommy even though he'd not seen him in ages—not since he'd been fucking his brother.

He'd grown portly and his hair had thinned, making him look far older than his age.

Malcolm couldn't help wondering if Brian had aged as badly.

Brian Harlow had been one of the vainest people Malcolm had ever met and would hate losing his looks and getting old. He was the sort of bloke who couldn't bear anything that was ugly or broken or imperfect—hence the reason he'd scarpered to Paris so quickly after seeing Malcolm's badly burned face all those years ago.

Malcolm still felt a twinge of anger and betrayal when he remembered Brian's look of horror the few times his lover had visited him after the fire. He'd been hurt—but not surprised—when Brian had run away and left him lying in a hospital bed, but mostly, Malcolm had felt relieved. The last thing he'd wanted was to force anyone to stay with him. Especially somebody who openly loathed him.

Malcolm shook himself, pulling his thoughts from his old lover and looking at the photograph in front of him.

The sour-looking, bone-thin woman beside Tommy was a stranger to him.

"I've never met Harlow's wife—at least not this one," Malcolm said. "Back when I knew him, he was married to Jenny McQueen."

"Aye, sir, that was Miss Julia's mother. She died when the girl wasn't quite five and Harlow married Nadine Sheehan three months after."

Which meant they'd been married when he'd been living with Bri and Sukey—sometime around the time of the fire, in fact.

"Didn't let his first wife's bones grow cold, did he?" Malcolm muttered, staring at the photo. "Where is she from?"

"Mrs. Harlow likes to put it about that she's genteel, but she grew up in Whitechapel with her brother and was raised by her widowed mother and aunt—the same one who is now her maid."

Malcolm barked a laugh. "There's thanks for you." He turned to the next picture, this one from a newspaper. It was the big bastard who'd been with Julia Harlow.

"That's Mrs. Harlow's brother Carl Sheehan. He's in town to look after Julia Harlow, along with the old woman."

Sheehan and his sister shared a similar bone structure although Nadine was as skinny and hard as a rail while her brother was well-padded.

"Tell me about Sheehan."

"I couldn't find much about him as he just got back from New York City."

"Why was he in New York?"

"He was workin' for Harlow's shipping line in some capacity."

Harlow's shipping line.

Malcolm shook his head in grim amusement. Well, he could hardly blame Harlow for stepping into the partnership with Leeland once the shipyard and iron hull ship had been destroyed and Malcolm was lying in a hospital bed on the verge of death.

"Why'd Sheehan come back to England?" he asked.

"About six months ago he got in trouble and Harlow brought him home."

Malcolm glanced up from the photo of Carl Sheehan to find Joe watching him with a pensive expression on his homely face.

"This picture of Sheehan is from a newspaper," Malcolm said. "Where'd you get it?"

"It's the only one of him I could find. It's from an American paper and was taken about two years ago when he joined some club or other."

Malcolm nodded, unable to tear his gaze away from the slightly blurry photograph.

Where have I seen you before, you big bastard?

Joe cleared his throat and Malcolm looked up. "What?"

"I found a story mentioning him. It was published about six months ago."

"And?" Malcolm prodded. "Is it in here somewhere?" He riffled through the photos and other bits of paper.

"Er, no, sir. It would 'ave drawn notice if I'd taken it, but I can get you a copy, it'll just take some time."

Malcolm lifted his eyebrow at that but didn't press the issue. Joe's sources were his own business.

"What was this article about?"

"It mentioned Sheehan in connection to a crime in New York and I reckon it's why he came back home."

Malcolm frowned. "Are you going to make me pull each piece of information from you, Joe? What crime?"

Joe's eyes flickered over Malcolm's mask. "It was an arson investigation, sir."

Even the word *arson* was enough to cause a spike of nausea. Malcolm swallowed down the bile and panic that rose in his throat and said, "Go on."

"Harlow's company made an offer for some warehouses on the waterfront in New York City but the seller refused. A month later the building went up in flames. It was supposed to be empty at the time, but there were squatters and a family of five died in the fire."

A bead of sweat trickled down the temple that wasn't covered by his mask as Malcolm stared at Sheehan's picture.

"So," he finally managed. "Sheehan's a fugitive from New York?"

"Ah, no, sir. Seems the charges were dismissed when Mr. Harlow gave him an alibi. Apparently, he and his wife go to visit once a year so she can see her brother and he can check on the business."

"How fortunate for Sheehan that his brother-in-law happened to be there just then." Malcolm turned back to the photograph of Tommy and Nadine Harlow. "Christ, she looks like a hatchet-faced bitch."

"By all accounts she is one, too, sir."

"Do her and Tommy have children?"

"Twin boys who are eleven, sir." He flipped through his notebook. "The boys split their time between some fancy school and Mrs. Harlow's mother's place in Brighton. Seems Mrs. Harlow takes after the aristocracy when it comes to child raising, so she doesn't see the brats but once or twice a year. Mrs. Harlow and her mother—Mrs. Sheehan—don't get along." He scratched his temple. "I've not yet learned why they fell out with each other, but it Mrs. Sheehan doesn't talk to her sister Annette, either. For some reason, Mrs. Harlow allows her mother to take the boys on holidays, which the servants say is strange given how much Mrs. Harlow despises her mother's common manners."

"What a charming woman," he muttered. "What's the relationship like between Julia and her stepmother?"

"Bad. Same with Julia and her father. Apparently, Julia's mother cheated on Harlow shortly before her death and he holds her behavior against their daughter. Mr. Harlow never showed much interest in Julia until her betrothal to Basingstoke."

"Arsehole," Malcolm muttered. And then he asked the question he told himself he wouldn't. "What about Harlow's brother Brian? Does he live with them?"

Joe turned back to his book. "No. He moved to Paris fifteen years ago and hasn't returned since."

So, Brian hadn't returned, even after all these years. Ah, well—water under the bridge.

"Tell me more about this tutor," Malcolm said. "What's his name?"

"Solomon Vance."

"Did the two actually fuck, or was it just a bit of flirtation that got blown out of proportion?"

"Mr. Harlow caught them in the act." Joe clucked his tongue. "The servants say Miss Harlow hounded the young gentleman like a bitch in heat." Joe looked disgusted that a well-brought up girl would be so interested in sex.

But Malcolm liked Julia Harlow more and more. Good for her getting what she wanted! It sounded like she was sensual and adventurous—more like her Uncle Brian than her humorless, passionless dry stick of a father.

Joe cleared his throat and even from across the dimly lighted room Malcolm could see that his face had darkened. "What is it?"

"The tutor wasn't the first time she was caught, sir. Miss Harlow got up to naughty doin's at her expensive school—polishing school, is it?"

"Finishing school," Malcolm corrected. "What sort of naughty doings?"

"Well, uh, seems her and another girl were, uh," Joe scratched his head, clearly searching for the right word.

"Engaging in Sapphic love?" Malcolm suggested.

"I don't know what that is, sir—but if it means bein' a rubster, then yeah, that's what they were caught doin'."

Malcolm burst out laughing. He laughed even harder when Joe's eyes went round at the unprecedented sight of his employer all but pissing himself with mirth.

"Oh, God," Malcolm said, once he could catch his breath, brushing tears from his cheek. "I've not laughed so hard in—hell, years. What a prude you are, Joe!"

"Glad to amuse you, sir," Joe said stiffly.

"Rubster—that's a term I've not heard since I was a lad. So, the young ladies were rubbing each other's pussies, were they? Seems harmless enough to me." Not to mention making his prick hard enough to pulverize boulders.

"Well, it didn't seem harmless to her parents, sir. Even though Miss Harlow was eighteen and would have left the school in two months, her parents took her out early and forbade her to have any contact with the other young lady."

"What a pair of moralizing prudes. Find out about the other girl for me, Joe—where she is, whether she married, and if the two really did break all contact." There was no reason to investigate Julia Harlow's girlhood lover, but Malcolm was suddenly insatiably curious and decided to indulge himself.

Joe made another note in his book.

"What next?" he asked, turning back to the diminishing pile of photos.

"Last spring the lass paid one of the grooms to get her some French postcards. He remembered what he bought on Holywell Street so I got copies for you—they're in that envelope."

Malcolm opened the fat envelope and shook the contents out onto his desk. "Why did she feel comfortable asking this groom to buy her such pictures?" he asked as he flicked through them.

"She caught him with a maid and threatened to tell her father about it if he didn't take the money and buy her the photographs. The young man said she told him exactly what she wanted." Joe cleared his throat. "She also blackmailed him to allow her to watch the next time he and his girl, er, went at it."

Malcolm laughed. Good God, no wonder he'd been attracted to her even from several floors away! She was bold, sensual, and took what she wanted. Not to mention being a fellow voyeur.

"Our Miss Harlow is a hellion," Malcolm said approvingly. He pitied her growing up in her staid, boring father's household.

"Wild-to-a-fault was the most frequent description I heard."

"If she's twenty then she must have had a few Seasons."

"No, those two deaths in the family—Thomas Harlow's mum and then his uncle about a year later—kept the family in mourning."

"I can see mourning a grandparent for a year, but a grand*uncle*?" Malcolm shook his head.

"The servants I spoke to said Harlow would have found a reason to keep her from having a Season regardless," Joe admitted.

"I take it he was concerned she might get up to more antics?"

"Aye, sir, he wants her married before she ends up with a babe in her belly."

Malcolm felt a pang of pity for the young woman. Anyone this curious about sex—especially a female—would have a hard time finding happiness within the strict confines of the *ton*. Julia Harlow might think her impending marriage to a duke's heir meant freedom and power, but she'd soon discover that her husband and his aristocratic family would control her just as surely as her parents ever had, if not more.

Well, it wasn't his concern, was it?

He turned to the postcards.

The first two were nothing special—just the usual naked, nervous-looking females, in unnatural poses, probably poor young women who were struggling to put food on the table the only way they knew how.

The third photograph had two pretty women naked in a bed together, touching parts of each other's bodies in ways it sounded like Miss Harlow could identify with.

The fourth was slightly more risqué. The woman wore a dark, lacy negligee, the sort a rich man might buy for his mistress. She also wore a mask to hide her identity. Her naked body was pleasingly plump in a way that only a healthy diet of good food could create. That meant this was a woman from the upper classes.

Very interesting.

The next picture was of a huge man, naked, with an erection.

He was one hell of a fine specimen, but, overall, it was a silly picture. He was standing in front of a stuffed tiger—as if he were going to wrestle the beast to the ground—his cock and balls dangling in front of a part of the tiger's anatomy that no man would ever get near.

It was the last picture that was the most titillating—at least to a debauched pervert like Malcolm.

It was one woman and three men, their bodies entwined in a tangle of limbs.

One man lay on the floor on his back, his cock presumably buried in the anus of the woman lying on top of him. Another man was crouched over her body in a particularly uncomfortable looking crab-like position, his cock filling her pussy.

A third man knelt over the woman's face, his cock deep inside her throat.

It was an arousing picture so long as a person didn't contemplate just how uncomfortable the position probably was for all the participants.

Although he and Sukey had engaged in such activities more than a few times, Malcolm personally wasn't a devotee of triple penetration. It was always plagued with too many logistical considerations, no matter how enticing it sounded.

Double penetration on the other hand, now that had been one of his favorite pastimes with Sukey and Smith as partners.

He pushed aside his fond memories and scraped the postcards into a neat pile before putting them back into their envelope and turning to Joe. "I want you to keep poking around—especially into Carl Sheehan's background." It bothered the hell out of Malcolm that he couldn't recall how he knew the man.

Joe nodded and jotted something down in his book.

"Look into Basingstoke as well. I want to know what sort of debts his family owes, where he gambles and whores, his sexual habits—that sort of thing."

Not that Malcolm knew *why* he wanted to know such things.

Liar.

Malcolm sighed. Yes, he was. The truth was that he was interested in anything to do with Julia Harlow, even if only tangentially.

"Oh, damn, sir!" said Joe, an embarrassed look on his homely face.

"What now?" Malcolm asked, more than a little impatient. Imagining Julia Harlow rubbing one off with a schoolmate had made him harder than iron; he wanted to go plow Maisie before the enchanting image faded.

"I must be goin' soft in the head. I can't believe I forgot this," Joe muttered, pulling a thick, gray envelope out of his inner coat and laying it on Malcolm's desk.

Written across the front in bold black handwriting were the words: *For Malcolm Barton Only*.

"You talked to Smith?" he said, dread building in his belly as he looked at the ominous words.

"I hope I didn't do wrong, sir. You always send me to him first if he's in town."

"No, no, of course you didn't do wrong. I would have talked to him myself but I thought he was up North somewhere."

"He was only in town for a day before he turned around and went back up to Liverpool. Er, anyhow, he told me to give him a week to talk to his contacts, but then today a messenger brought me this right before I came to see you. Sorry I didn't mention it first."

Malcolm nodded. "Check into the things I mentioned and let me know if you find anything interesting. That's all, Joe."

"Of course, sir. Good night."

He waited until the door shut behind Joe before picking up the envelope, which felt too heavy for its size.

Whatever Smith had found out must be important or he would have just waited until their meeting next week. The second of December was the one night of the year when Malcolm was sure of seeing his mysterious friend.

He turned the envelope over and over, a sick feeling growing in his belly. Did he really want to know what Smith had found?

Toss it into the fire and go shag Maisie silly, Mal, Sukey advised. *Or, better yet, go introduce yourself to Miss Julia Harlow since she is the first woman in fifteen years who's piqued your interest.*

Malcolm dismissed her foolish comment and turned to the black lacquer box on his desk, toggling the lever on the far right.

The box was part of a state-of-the-art system that used electricity, rather than mechanical means, to ring servant bells.

Norris opened his study door not even a minute later. "Yes, Mr. Barton?"

"Tell Maisie I won't be joining her tonight."

Malcolm suspected that fucking would be the last thing on his mind after he opened this envelope.

Chapter 5

Julia stared at the canopy over her head and squirmed beneath the blankets, her finger circling her slick, swollen nub as she chased her second orgasm of the morning. She hoped this would be enough to satisfy her seemingly insatiable body, although she had little faith that she could eradicate the reason for her current state of arousal.

Last night Carl had given her thirty swats and her bottom still ached so badly that she could hardly move without crying.

But that wasn't the worst of it.

The worst was what had happened around swat number twenty-six.

Actually, the worst was that Carl had *known* what happened, even though he'd not touched her *there* or even said vulgar, offensive things. He'd done nothing but spank her; it was her own treasonous body that had betrayed her.

Once he'd quit chortling like the odious swine he was, he'd looked at her with an almost feverish stare and grabbed his disgusting erection, which was thrusting against his trousers. "See this?"

Julia hadn't wanted to look, but it had been like trying to avoid staring at a carriage accident. The ridge pressing against the thin wool trousers had been shockingly huge—even his massive hand couldn't make it look small. And then he'd stroked his big thumb over the end and Julia's eyes had almost bulged out of her head: the cloth was *wet*.

She'd stared, entranced and revolted.

He'd sucked in a harsh breath as he'd caressed himself. "See what you do to me?"

Oh yes, she'd seen.

"Have you changed your mind?" he asked.

Julia knew what he'd meant. "No!"

Rather than make him angry—as she'd feared—he'd just laughed and stroked himself harder when she'd denied him. "You will… soon. Until then, I'll be thinkin' of you when I fist myself."

Just the memory of his words and his expression of desperate desire caused her inner muscles to clench and flutter, hurrying her toward yet another climax.

Masturbating to thoughts of Carl? You know you'll hate yourself afterward, a prissy voice in her head chided.

"I don't care," she muttered between clenched teeth. "I… *need* this." Her finger moved faster, harder, and her back began to arch off the bed, the tension ratcheting her muscles tighter and tighter.

The bedroom door flew open hard enough that it struck the wall with a loud *bang*.

Julia screamed and yanked her hand from between her thighs as Netta stormed into her chambers.

"What are you doin' still abed, girl?" she demanded in her abrasive voice.

Julia shoved up onto her elbows. "How did you even get in here? I locked the door!"

Netta held up a key and smirked.

Julia fell back onto her pillow with an angry huff and hastily pulled down her nightgown beneath the covers.

She was just in time, too, as Netta strode forward and yanked the blankets off her.

"What are you *doing?*"

"Time to get up and get dressed," Netta all but chirped.

"You horrid woman—why won't you leave me alone?"

"You missed dinner and breakfast, but your midday meal is ready."

"Why should I go downstairs? It's not as if I will be allowed to eat anything."

"You'll get up and go about your business like a lady, that's why. I won't have you going to Lord Basingstoke as if—"

"Fine. I'll do anything you want if you just stop talking." Listening to Netta's hectoring voice was enough to make her vomit. "Ring for Mary and then get out of my room."

"That slut is gone."

Julia sat up. "*What?* She never said anything to me about leaving."

Netta fussed around her room, gathering scattered clothing and *tutting* to herself.

"This is most irregular," Julia persisted. It was true that Mary was timid, lazy, and useless in a lot of ways, but Julia was fond of her. "Did she say anything to anyone about leaving?"

"No, she just left."

"How will she find another position without a letter to recommend her?"

"That is her concern, not yours. I'll engage a proper maid for you."

Julia glared. "I'll choose my own maid, thank you very much."

"The master already told me to do so."

Julia opened her mouth to argue but then, quite suddenly, lost all energy to do so. After all, what was the point?

Not only was she exhausted and weak with hunger, but she couldn't forget how her father had threatened Richard's future and his happiness. Julia never would have believed that a father would do such a thing to his own child. She'd always known that Thomas Harlow was ashamed of his oldest son—hiding him away, denying his existence, and calling him an idiot and lackwit when Julia had begged him to allow her twin to come and live with them—but to threaten to send him to a sanatorium was sickening.

Her father had always been coldblooded but had become even worse over the past few years and she was convinced his cruelty was Nadine's fault. If Nadine had her way. Julia wouldn't have been allowed to even visit Richard once a year or exchange letters with Nanny Potter.

In any case, arguing with Netta wasn't only pointless, it was dangerous. It would be wise to toe the line with both her parents until she was married. Until then, Richard's future wasn't secure.

"Well, you'd better engage somebody quickly, Netta," Julia said. "Don't forget I've got dinner with Sebastian and Lady Winthrop tomorrow night."

"I will dress you until we can get you a proper servant."

Julia grimaced but didn't argue. Instead, she scooted toward the edge of the bed on her bottom before she'd recalled how sore she was. She hissed and squeezed her eyes shut for a moment, not just against the pain, but also against the mortifying stab of arousal.

"Hurt, do you?" Netta snorted. "I reckon that's what you've been needing all along."

"What I need?" she repeated, the older woman's smug tone and even smugger expression catapulting her beyond mortification into rage. "To be *fondled* by a degenerate who is supposed to be my—"

Netta's hand flew and a loud *crack* filled the room.

Blood flooded her mouth and Julia raised her hand to her cheek, a red haze blurring her vision.

"I should write to your father and tell him—"

"No, don't!" Julia blurted, fear for Richard dousing her rage. "I'm—I'm sorry."

"Hmph. Not sorry enough." Netta gave her a venomous look. "You will *never* say such vile things about Master Carl. Why, he's worth ten of a brazen hussy like you." Her mouth screwed up until it looked like the back end of a pig. "I can see that you need a few more swats before you know your place. Perhaps a willow switch next time?"

As much as her mouth hurt, Julia had to bite back her amusement at *that* threat; Carl liked touching her bottom far too much to ever use a whip or paddle.

"Nothing to say to that, eh?" Netta goaded. "I think—"

A knock on the door interrupted her tirade.

"Who is it?" she snapped.

One of the parlor maids poked her head into the room. "A telegram for you Mrs. Fowler."

Netta snatched the paper from the girl's hand without a word of thanks.

"Thank you, Dora," Julia said in an exaggerated tone. But Netta was too consumed by the telegram to notice. Indeed, her ugly face had paled and her toadlike mouth had sagged open.

"What is it?" Julia asked.

"The mistress is ill and needs me," Netta said, visibly stricken.

It was a struggle to suppress her glee. "Oh? When are you leaving?"

"Immediately." Netta folded up the telegram, her expression distracted. "One of the maids will have to help you until I return."

Hopefully the nasty old hag wouldn't return until *after* Julia's marriage. Carl might be repellant, but at least he had no idea of her schedule or what was proper or improper for a young lady of her status. She'd be much freer without Netta. In fact, she might get to eat for a change.

Netta's expression sharpened, as if Julia had spoken aloud.

"Master Carl will go with you *everywhere*. You shall never be out of his sight."

Julia rolled her eyes, but the older woman was too flustered to notice.

"I'll send up a maid to help you dress."

"Yes, do that," Julia ordered, waiting until the door slammed to give full rein to her joyous grin.

Life, Julia suspected, would be a great deal less onerous with the worst of her gaolers gone from the city.

Now all she had to do was rid herself of Carl.

Chapter 6

Malcolm sat in the darkened room; his fist tight around his engorged cock as he stared at the trio of people on the other side of the large window.

A narrow corridor separated Malcolm's study from the other room. The hallway was part of Malcolm's private network of secret passages that he used to spy and sneak and lurk.

Instead of a window, the people in the other room would be staring at themselves in a mirror.

But it wasn't a regular mirror; it was something called a transparent mirror—a mirror on one side and a window when viewed from the other.

Malcolm had been overjoyed to discover such a miracle even existed. He'd been so impressed that he'd financed the inventor and they were now co-owners of a small factory that manufactured the cunning mirrors.

He'd had them installed in all his houses, using them strategically in numerous locations.

The woman and one of the men in the other room were prostitutes. The third person—Mr. Smith—was one of the richest men in Britain, although Malcolm doubted that more than a handful of people knew that.

Of course Malcolm hadn't paid Smith to come tonight, but the two prostitutes would be well-compensated.

Malcolm had employed the male whore—Samuel—several times in the past. He considered himself fortunate to find somebody who bore such a close resemblance to him since there weren't huge, hulking blokes in most brothels.

In addition to topping Malcolm's height by an inch, Samuel had a stone or two on him, and it was all muscle.

The female prostitute—Minette—bore a remarkable resemblance to Malcolm's dead wife in both face and body. But while Minette possessed similar blunt features, a voluptuous body, and thick chestnut hair, she lacked the intelligence and sparkle that had enlivened Sukey's brown eyes. His wife had possessed more zest for life than any ten people combined and had attracted men—and women—like moths to a flame.

Quit thinking about me when you've got real, live lovers right there, ya dafty.

Sukey's voice was so loud that Malcolm glanced behind him.

And immediately felt like a fool.

Why are you in this room alone, Mal? Get in there and tan Smith's delicious backside for him—and then ride him hard, just the way you used to do.

Malcolm didn't bother to argue with her. Sukey had no idea what he looked like now because she was dead.

But the voice was right in saying that Smith looked delicious.

His arms were stretched high above his head and his feet were spread wide and bound at the ankles. Samuel whipped him with a leather flail while the Sukey-lookalike knelt between his legs, doing her best to throat Smith's freakishly big cock, which had a leather thong wrapped around the base to delay ejaculation.

The three were angled in such a way as to afford Malcolm an excellent view of all participants.

This scenario had been Sukey's favorite among the many they'd acted out with Smith. Sometimes it was Smith bound, sometimes Malcolm, and sometimes Sukey.

As always, watching Smith brought memories flooding back. They only did this on Sukey's birthday. It was morbid, but Malcolm didn't give a damn. Instead, he reveled in the past and pumped himself with firm, unhurried strokes as he watched Smith take his beating. The other man's body was a work of art—hard and chiseled, like wood that had been dried in a kiln—and as close to perfection as anyone Malcolm had ever seen.

It had been Smith who'd shown Malcolm how to exercise and care for his wrecked body after the fire. He'd even designed Malcolm's private gymnasium for him.

Keeping his muscles limber and toned, no matter how horrific he might look, was the main reason that Malcolm didn't shove a pistol under his chin and blow off his head.

Sex was another thing that made life worth living.

The first few years after the fire he'd not wanted anyone to see him or touch him. He'd gone to brothels heavily cloaked, sat in the darkness, and paid for shows like the one he was watching now.

Later—after his first department store had become a resounding success and he'd begun to make more money than he could spend—

he'd built these private apartments so he didn't have to leave his home to enjoy the sight of beautiful men and women fucking for his pleasure.

But even that had begun to pall five or six years ago.

It had been Smith who'd pushed him to have physical contact with others. "You'll die without touch, Malcolm," he'd insisted. "Mask your face and cover yourself, if you must, but don't give up on sensory pleasure."

At the time, Malcolm had already begun to despair and knew the other man spoke the truth. And so he'd slowly broadened his horizons.

The first time he'd fucked a woman he'd removed his gloves and rolled up his shirtsleeves. Malcolm would never forget the disgust and horror on that poor whore's face at the sight of his ruined flesh.

After that, he'd never showed any part of his damaged body—not even his hands—to anyone again. The only person who was forced to look at him naked was Norris. If his valet found him sickening, he was paid well enough to hide it.

That whore's disgust had proved to Malcolm that not even his piles of money could buy the desire and admiration he'd seen in Minette's eyes when she'd dropped to her knees and taken Smith's cock in her mouth.

And so he kept on all his clothing, like some punter rutting in an alleyway rather than his own home.

But Smith had been right; just that little bit of human contact—his cock inside a warm body—was enough to keep him sane.

And of course there was always this: watching.

While voyeurism meant that Malcolm missed out on the taste and feel of a woman under his hands or mouth, it was also far less stressful because he didn't have to endure horror in a woman's eyes, something that was always present in his interaction with whores, even when he was masked, gloved, and clothed.

Was his fear of exposure pitiful?

Undoubtedly.

Did he care?

Not in the slightest.

The pained grunts from beyond the window drew his attention away from darker thoughts.

Tears rolled down Smith's blade-sharp cheekbones and his eyes had a blank look that said he'd left his body—carried away by the exquisite pain of a proper whipping.

Malcolm knew the feeling well.

Or at least he used to. With half his body covered in delicate scar-tissue his days under the lash were behind him.

But it still made him hard to watch or wield a whip himself on occasion.

Samuel's massive torso was gleaming with sweat, his muscles bulging from the sheer physicality of beating the other man. Malcolm's cock was so primed he could have come ages ago, but he liked to wait until the whipping was over, when he could imagine that he was the man who would bury his hard shaft in Smith's powerful body and then ride him for Sukey's viewing pleasure. There was something unspeakably primal about mounting another man in front of one's woman. Especially a fine male animal like Smith.

Beyond the glass Smith shuddered. "Now," he shouted hoarsely, every sinew, vein, and muscle in his body taut beneath his olive skin.

Samuel flung aside the whip and poured oil over his slab of a prick, slicking his shaft while his thick, glistening fingers probed Smith's hole. He opened him carefully, finger-fucking him with gradually increasing force, until his enormous biceps flexed with the power of his pumping.

Smith squeezed his eyes shut, his tightly bound body straining to buck and thrust and fuck. "*Now*, goddammit!"

Samuel positioned his cock at Smith's pucker and slammed into him, not stopping until his pelvis was flush against Smith's arse.

Smith groaned, his face a mask of pained bliss.

Minette removed the thong from around his cock and balls and swallowed him while Samuel fucked him.

It was beautiful.

Malcolm closed his eyes and imagined he was in the other room, but with Sukey and Smith.

In his mind's eye he saw them as they'd been all those years ago: Sukey vibrant and alive and laughing with pure sensual joy, Smith younger, but just as mysterious and fierce, and Malcolm—unscarred and unscathed, ignorant of the pain that awaited him just around the corner.

Happy birthday, Sukey. I love you, darling. I'll miss you until the day I die.

Malcolm's silent declaration echoed unanswered. A tear slipped from beneath the lid of his remaining eye before he could squeeze it shut. He pumped himself savagely enough to hurt, brutally driving himself toward a pleasure that he shouldn't be alive to enjoy. Not when he'd failed to save the only woman he'd ever loved.

Regardless of his shame, hot seed spilled over his fist and he came with the sound of sucking, moaning, and slapping flesh in the room beyond, tugging at himself until his body was sated.

But his heart was dry and barren and his mind was filled with Sukey.

Always Sukey.

***

Malcolm handed Smith a glass of the Armagnac he kept just for his friend's visits.

"Cheers," Smith said, sinking into the chair across from Malcolm's desk and heaving a contented sigh.

Malcolm smelled sex and sweat on the other man, and it made his prick perk up and his mouth water.

"You should have joined us," Smith said. His white silk robe gaped open, exposing a tantalizing strip of hard, smooth body.

"You didn't care for Samson?" Malcolm asked, his gaze lingering on the other man's taut, ridged abdomen before he reluctantly pulled it away.

"You know I did—thank you for such a treat. But nobody compares to you, Mal." He gave Malcolm a look that smoldered.

He shivered at the sound of his pet name on the other man's tongue; Smith was the last person to remember who Malcolm used to be, the poor, gangly street lad with feet and hands that were too big for his rangy body.

"It's a shame we only manage to get together a few times a year," Smith said.

"I'm sure you have many others clamoring to amuse you."

Smith swirled the golden-brown liquid around in his glass and gave Malcolm a faint smile, neither confirming nor denying his words. Instead, he asked, "How have you been occupying yourself since last we spoke?"

"I will never again open two stores at the same time as long as I live."

Smith chuckled. "It does seem like a big mouthful. And yet I don't think you would hesitate to do so again. You will never slow down."

"Will you?" he retorted. When Smith hesitated, Malcolm's eye widened. "Don't tell me you are considering slowing down, Smith?"

"Sometimes I think about it."

"I'm stunned." Smith was the only man Malcolm had ever met who was as driven, if not more so, than he was. "What would you do if you didn't work?"

"Oh, I'd never stop working, but I do wonder if there is not more to life."

"Such as?"

"Children, a family."

It was a night for surprises. "You've never mentioned wanting a family."

"Is it something you want?" Smith countered.

"It doesn't matter what I want. No woman would want me for anything other than my money. Even if she could stomach me long enough to fuck me and bear my child, what kind of life would a family have with a monster such as me?"

"Do you think Sukey would have felt that way if she'd survived?"

"No, of course not. But she loved me before *this*"—Malcolm waved a hand at his ruined face and body. "Anyone I meet *now* would have to possess a cast iron stomach and a reason to look beyond the wreckage."

"You don't think there are women who would do that?"

"No doubt there are a few, but I am not willing to put in the time and effort to find them. And quit trying to change the subject, Smith. Are you considering marriage after all these years?"

"No, not marriage."

"But there is somebody, isn't there? Is it that lad who lives with you—Charles?"

Smith sighed. "I'm afraid my time with Charles is at an end."

Malcolm wasn't surprised; Smith rarely kept his lovers for long, nor did he ever get very attached. He'd always held part of himself aloof even with Malcolm. Although they'd been friends and lovers for decades, he still knew nothing about the man's past before he came to England, and he'd long ago learned not to pry. The only time he'd pressed Smith on the issue the man had disappeared from his life for almost two years.

"Tell me something," Smith said, his expression almost pensive. "Sukey had other lovers—not only the ones you enjoyed together, but others you didn't meet or know?"

"Yes, she did."

"It never bothered you?"

Malcolm blinked at the change in topic. They'd not discussed much other than exercising, whores, or business, for years.

"I assume you're asking if I became jealous?" Malcolm finally said.

"Did you?"

"No."

"That's unusual, isn't it?"

Malcolm shrugged. "I suppose."

"You're not the jealous sort?"

Malcolm chuckled. "Oh, I'm capable of jealousy—plenty capable. The lass I was with before Sukey drove me half mad with it."

"Then what was different with her?"

"It certainly wasn't because I didn't love her."

Smith nodded. He knew better than anyone how much Malcolm had loved his wife.

Malcolm gave the matter some thought. "I think it was different because Sukey was already with Brian when we met, so I could hardly complain about her predilections when I'd known about them right from the start."

"I never did hear how the three of you first became intimately acquainted."

"That's because you never asked."

"No, I didn't—back when Sukey was alive, we were too busy enjoying ourselves to waste time on mere conversation."

Malcolm chuckled. "No, Sukey wasn't much for talking when she could be fucking."

"Tell me about it now."

"Why?" Malcolm stared hard at his friend for a long moment. Just what was the man up to delving into the ancient past?

"I'm just curious, Mal. I swear I've got no ulterior motives."

Malcolm snorted. "You without an ulterior motive? I'll believe it when I see it."

"Well, perhaps I should have said I have no ulterior motives that involve *you*. But I am very interested in how you managed your unusual arrangement with Sukey."

What could it hurt to share the story? Besides, Smith was the only person left he could talk to about his dead wife.

"I was living in a glorified broom closet above my first dry goods shop when I met Sukey and Brian. They lived above her glove store in the building next to mine. When they invited me to dinner the first time, I thought they were just taking pity on a poor, hungry bachelor. I thought they were happily married so I was proper gob-smacked when Sukey asked me to join them for, er, dessert."

Although Malcolm had been ten years younger than both Sukey and Brian, he'd had plenty of sexual experience by the time he met them. Even so, his his jaw had hit the floor when Sukey told him they wanted him in their bed.

He glanced at Smith, who was waiting patiently. "I was hesitant—not because I wasn't interested—but Sukey and Bri were neighbors and I worried what might happen if things went, er, badly."

"That could have become awkward," Smith agreed.

"That first night was—" Malcolm broke off and smiled fondly at the memory. "Well, let's just say it was the first of many." He shook away the past. "Anyhow, I quickly learned that she needed time to herself, time to have her little adventures, she called them."

"Adventures meaning other lovers," Smith said.

"Yes." Malcolm agreed. "So, you see, I knew what she was like before I married her."

"That wouldn't stop a lot of men from being jealous or putting a stop to her activities," Smith said.

"No, you're probably right."

"Could you have been satisfied with just her and no other lovers—not even Brian?"

"Aye," Malcolm said without hesitation. "She was always enough for me." He cut Smith a teasing look. "I'd even have given up *you* if Sukey had asked me to."

"But it never bothered you that she needed more?"

"No. I liked it."

Smith's eyebrows shot up.

"It's true. It made me hard to think of her taking what she wanted. Besides, after she was done with them she always came home to *me*. None of those others were competition. What we had was one-of-a-kind."

"Did you take lovers without her?"

Malcolm hooted. "Lord, no! My Sukey was fine sharing if *she* was part of the fun, but all Hell would've broken loose if I'd wanted to keep lovers on the side."

Smith looked bemused. "And that inequity never bothered you?"

Malcolm narrowed his eye at the other man. "I might be thick, Smith, but why do I feel this isn't about me?"

Smith chuckled. "See right through me, do you?" He sighed, the smile sliding from his lips. "I'm afraid the arrangement you had with Sukey must be very rare."

"Probably," Malcolm agreed. "Most people place a high value on sexual fidelity." He hesitated and then asked, "Is you being here tonight bothering your Charles?"

"Yes," Smith said without hesitation.

"But you're here, anyhow."

"Yes."

"If coming here is causing you trouble, then we can make this the last time you——"

"Absolutely not." Smith hadn't raised his voice, but his soft tone had been implacable. "These annual reunions are important to me and I don't wish to give them up."

Malcolm was surprised by the rush of relief he felt at the other man's words. As pitiful as it was, he enjoyed their debauches and knew Sukey would have liked that they honored her memory in such a way.

Smith was just like Sukey when it came to being sexually voracious and adventurous. He pitied poor Charles if the man thought he could ever tie Smith down.

"You've made up your mind, Malcolm?"

Malcolm blinked at Smith's change of subject but didn't need to ask what he meant. "Yes, I have."

Smith took another drink.

"You don't think I should do it?" Malcolm asked.

"No, I don't."

Malcolm gave an exasperated huff. "You're the one who gave me the information I needed. You could have withheld what you knew about Sheehan and Harlow and I probably never would have found out."

"Yes, I know." Smith caught his gaze and held it. "I told you what I knew because you asked me for it. I'm not your conscience, Malcolm, I'm your friend. And as your friend it is my duty to tell you that I think your plan is unwise."

"You think I should just go ahead and kill them and be done with it?"

"No, I think you should allow me to take care of the problem for you."

Malcolm bristled. "You think I'm not capable of doing my own killing?"

"I know you are entirely capable of that, Malcolm. However, this is… well, it will get ugly, won't it? Ugly and very personal. I would be honored to do this for you."

"I won't ask you to do my dirty work."

Smith shrugged. "If you won't let me handle it, so be it. I *will* say that I think it's a mistake to bring in an innocent."

"I won't hurt her."

Smith didn't look convinced, but he didn't argue. "Do you need any help?"

Malcolm gave a startled snort. "You just finished telling me that you don't agree with how I'm handling this."

"I don't."

"But you'd help me, anyhow?"

"That is what friends are for." Smith gave him a slight smile. "And you are perhaps my only friend."

Malcolm was deeply touched by both his offer and his words. "I appreciate the offer, but I don't need any help."

Smith nodded.

"It's too late to change things, in any case," Malcolm said—perhaps more for himself than Smith. "It's happening right now, as we sit here. The girl will be here in a few hours."

Smith's hand absently stroked his chest and he stared at nothing, his mind obviously elsewhere.

Malcolm's mouth flooded as he watched Smith's hand stroking down over the defined muscles of his chest to the sculpted ridges of his abdomen, hovering just above his half-slumbering cock.

As long as he'd known him, Smith had always shaved every part of his body except for his head. Sukey had loved the look and feel of such smoothness and so she and Malcolm had groomed each other, taking as much pleasure in the act as the result. Now Malcolm was as hairy as a bear. Or at least half a bear, since nothing grew from the burned side of his body.

Smith's fingers stopped caressing and Malcolm looked up to find the other man's eyes on him.

"I can feel your gaze on me even though I cannot see you over there in the gloom," Smith said.

Malcolm never lit the lamps around his desk, not even with Smith.

Smith pulled open the loose flaps of the robe, exposing more of his exquisite body to Malcolm's hungry gaze. "I don't think our show tonight satisfied your needs, Malcolm." His hand drifted to his smooth scrotum and he fondled his balls, the muscles in his forearm and biceps flexing, his shaft growing thick and long. He softly clucked his tongue. "How you like to hide yourself in the darkness, Malcolm. Even when I have already seen every inch of you, damaged or otherwise."

Malcolm's disfigured mouth tightened.

Smith *had* seen him, right after the fire, while Malcolm had been in too much pain to care or object, when all he had wanted was death.

He'd had no pride and had begged his friend and lover to kill him.

But Smith had refused.

Instead, he'd sat by Malcolm's bed for an hour or two every day, until his natural instinct for survival—no matter how miserable his existence—had reasserted itself.

Malcolm knew the cost of such time and effort and he loved Smith for his care even though he occasionally still hated him for denying Malcolm an easy escape all those years ago.

In the end, it had been Smith who'd kept him alive. And Smith who'd made sure he wasn't a vegetable. Smith was the one person in the world Malcolm really gave a damn about.

Smith stood, shrugged off his robe, caught it before it fell, and then neatly laid it over the chair he'd just vacated.

Amusement at the fastidious gesture pushed through Malcolm's raw desire; he had never met anyone as tidy as Smith.

Smith turned up the flame on the nearby gas lamp until the edge of the corona illuminated Malcolm, too.

Malcolm gritted his teeth but said nothing as Smith strode to him, his cock jutting thick and heavy. Smith had one of the biggest pricks Malcolm had ever seen, and it looked even bigger because Smith was not a large man.

He didn't stop until his bare legs brushed against Malcolm's trousers. An odd smile softened the stark planes of his face. "Do you wear your mask even when you are alone, my friend?"

"Always, except when I sleep or bathe."

Smith reached for it.

Malcolm grabbed his forearm, which was like grabbing a chunk of hot iron. "You don't want to see me."

"I *have* seen you." Smith tugged his arm lightly and Malcolm let him slip free.

Smith reached behind Malcolm's head and untied the leather cords that kept his mask in place.

Malcolm closed his eye and sighed with a combination of resignation and relief when Smith lifted the mask off. He heard it clatter to the desk and then felt Smith's fingers slide into the hair on Malcolm's undamaged right side while his other hand lightly stroked the raw whorls of flesh on his left.

It had been years since anyone other than his valet had seen or touched him and Smith's hand on his damaged cheek felt strange, but not unpleasant.

The skin-to-skin contact on his right side made him desperate for more and Malcolm pressed his undamaged cheek against Smith's palm, his tongue darting out to taste the salty skin.

Smith hummed with approval, his fingers tensing as he tilted Malcolm's head up and up, forcing Malcolm to meet his dark, raptor-like gaze.

"How long has it been since you've had my cock in your mouth?" he asked, his expression fierce and hungry

Malcolm gave a surprised huff of laughter and his groin throbbed. "Are you telling me you don't remember, Smith? I guess I couldn't have been that memorable." He was pleased that he sounded mocking rather than needy and desperate. Which is what he was feeling: so goddamned needy that he bled it from his pores.

Smith ignored his attempt at diversion, instead stroking Malcolm's lower lip with his thumb, the rough pad lingering on the burned, slightly puckered skin on the left corner. "I want you."

Malcolm's ballocks clenched and his half-hard prick stiffened the rest of the way.

Every single time they got together Smith said something similar.

Every single time, Malcolm refused.

This time, he nodded.

Surprise flickered across Smith's starkly handsome face and his slow smile was wicked and sensual. Rather than ask Malcolm why he'd finally changed his mind, he said, "Will it hurt if I fuck your mouth?"

Knowing Smith, it would. But Malcolm didn't care. "No."

Smith eyes darkened even more. "Take off your gloves. Both of them," he added, reading Malcolm's expressions far too easily for his comfort.

Malcolm gave an irritable sigh but obeyed, carefully peeling off the tight, tissue-thin leather of the Limerick gloves, which allowed him some degree of sensation in the fingers of his right hand and even a little in the three-fingered claw that was his left.

Smith strode over to the settee, brought back a cushion, and tossed it on the floor at his feet. "Kneel," he ordered, taking his thick shaft in his hand and working himself with slow, sensual strokes.

As Malcolm lowered to his knees, he couldn't help being grateful for the hours he spent in his gymnasium. Between the exercising, the many skin grafts, and the frequent oiling, he felt barely a twinge in his knee.

Smith's huge cock was now eye-level and he could smell his spunk as well as the faint hint of feminine musk from earlier in the evening, when he'd fucked Minette's cunny. Malcolm inhaled, filling his lungs to bursting with their mingled scent, gorging like a starving man.

"Look at me."

Malcolm obeyed without hesitation.

Smith's eyes were black in the low light, his face harsh and satanic. "You may take out your cock, but no coming until I say."

Malcolm fumbled with his trousers to comply, his prick already hard and leaking.

Once he was free, he looked up and met Smith's dark, hungry gaze. "Tongue my slit."

Malcolm swallowed convulsively at the familiar order—one he gave often to the whores who serviced him.

Smith's eyelids fluttered as Malcolm probed the tiny opening with the point of his tongue, his own cock hard and throbbing even though he'd ejaculated barely an hour before. The familiar masculine taste of semen sent blood roaring in his ears and Malcolm sucked on the little hole, desperate for more.

Smith groaned and carded his fingers into Malcolm's hair, pulling him onto his prick.

Malcolm had to stretch his jaws wide to take Smith's thick rod into his mouth and the skin at the burnt corner of his mouth cracked and split. He didn't give a damn about the pain and feasted on the silken flesh, making love to the fat crown.

"So good," Smith murmured, his hips pushing closer, urging Malcolm to take more. "Touch me."

Malcolm raised both hands to Smith's taut, narrow hips and cupped a muscular buttock in each hand, squeezing as hard as he could.

Smith gave an earthy chuckle. "Your hands are strong; you've been doing your exercises."

Indeed, he had.

Even though Malcolm could squeeze Smith's delectable arse and feel the muscle he couldn't feel the silken skin, at least not with his left hand, and barely with his right, which had suffered burns on the tips of his fingers. But he could appreciate the sheer artistry and shape of the other man and allowed his fingers to explore the defined musculature of his back and then around front to his favorite part of Smith's body—what painters and sculptors called the Adonis Belt.

As for Smith's cock? Well, Malcolm had never been able to take all of him but he took as much as he could, mouthing and licking and sucking while he reacquainted himself with the feel and taste of a thick, hard jack. It had been years, but sucking cock—just like swimming, it seemed—was a tricky skill to acquire but difficult to lose.

Smith's powerful hips were slow and easy at first, pushing deeper with each thrust and testing his limits. Malcolm opened wider, silently indicating his eagerness for more and Smith worked him with controlled pulses.

Malcolm tasted the coppery tang of blood and knew the injured corner of his mouth had torn from the girth of Smith's shaft, not to mention the increasing violence of his thrusts.

The pain incited rather than dampened his lust and he dug his fingers into Smith's rock-hard arse. It felt oddly liberating to be used—nothing more than a hole for Smith's pleasure, an empty vessel to be fucked and filled. As the thrusts grew more violent, Malcolm opened his throat, timing his breathing to each stroke.

Smith grunted. "Yes … good … so … fucking … *good*." He pistoned roughly, his thrusts savage and his fingers painful in Malcolm's hair. "Coming," he gasped, his cock thickening and spasming as he flooded Malcolm's throat with hot, bitter spunk.

Malcolm swallowed every drop, milking his balls dry before Smith opened his eyes and pulled out, his chest rising and falling as if he'd been running. He cupped Malcolm's jaw—the injured side this time—and brushed his thumb over Malcolm's lower lip, thumbing the bloody corner of his mouth, before lifting his hand to his mouth and sucking his finger clean.

He cut a glance down to where Malcolm's cock hung heavy, hard, and leaking. "Come for me, Mal."

Malcolm barely needed to stroke himself twice before he came off, hot spurts jetting onto his knuckles, the sensation in his overworked balls somewhere between pleasure and pain.

Spent and exhausted, he heaved a contented sigh and rested his head against Smith's hard belly as he caught his breath.

"I think you needed that," Smith said, his voice thick with humor.

Malcolm's throat and mouth already hurt—and they would be worse tomorrow—but Smith spoke the truth.

Why the hell had he waited so bloody long to take the other man up on his offer?

Because you're a stubborn fool. This time the voice was his own, rather than his dead wife's.

Smith's fingers slid under Malcolm's chin and he tilted his face until he met his gaze. "A man can't exist on his own, Malcolm." Something like desolation flickered across Smith's severe features. "Trust me—I've tried."

He helped Malcolm to his feet, pulling him up easily, even though Malcolm was at least six inches taller and three stone heavier.

Once he was standing Smith did something he had never done before: he embraced Malcolm.

They had engaged in every manner of debauchery over the years, but never this. Never just comfort.

Malcolm's arms rose slowly and he patted Smith, tentative at first, gradually tightening his hold.

Christ. Who knew this could feel so bloody good? So… comforting?

Only as he was standing there, the tension draining from his body, did Malcolm realize that he'd been in a silent, but lethal, state of rage for days—ever since Smith had given him the information about Harlow and Sheehan and what they'd done all those years ago. His revenge had barely begun and yet he was already exhausted.

Was he strong enough to do what needed to be done?

"Are you sure about what you are about to do, my friend?" Smith asked, easily reading the tension in Malcolm's body. "Once you take this step, you can't go back."

Malcolm hesitated and then said, "I'm sure."

He knew Smith heard the doubt just as strongly as Malcolm felt it. But that didn't mean he would change his mind. Malcolm wasn't even sure that he *could* change it at this point.

"I owe Sukey this much," he added.

Smith released him and stepped back. "Just don't forget what you owe yourself, Malcolm."

Chapter 7

Julia sat in the carriage alone and fumed.

At least Carl was riding on the box and Netta wasn't there to torment her on the drive home from her humiliating dinner with horrid Sebastian and his horridly condescending grandmother.

Julia was no stranger to condescension. How could she be? She was a cit's daughter who'd rubbed shoulders with aristocrats for years.

Before tonight, she would have said that she'd endured every snub known to womankind when she was at school, but the humiliating meal she'd just endured with Sebastian and Lady Winthrop took the cake.

Julia wasn't stupid; she knew Sebastian hated her and resented being forced to marry her. This was the quintessential marriage of convenience on both sides. Her father wanted the duke's status and political clout; the duke and Basingstoke wanted her father's money; and Julia wanted a safe harbor for her brother Richard and to be free of her father and Nadine's control.

Oh, and Basingstoke also wanted an heir, although she didn't think he was nearly as keen about that part as her father seemed to believe.

When papa had first told her that Lord Basingstoke had asked permission to court her Julia couldn't believe it. Sebastian had eluded matchmaking mamas for over a decade. At the age of thirty-eight he was, in the opinion of everyone who was anyone, the prize of the century.

Personally, Julia found Sebastian's golden-haired, blue-eyed looks insipid and thought he had as much sensual appeal as a box of cutlery. He was like a male version of her: golden and perfect and boring.

But as dismissive as she was of his person, she couldn't deny that she was looking forward to the power and freedom that marriage to him represented.

Not only that, but for the first time in her life her father had looked at her with something other than annoyance or dislike. For the first time in her life her father had almost smiled when he looked at her.

"Your marriage is the most important thing to happen to our family since I acquired the shipping line."

Julia had almost fainted from shock when he'd admitted that. According to her father, his purchase of the shipping company ranked up with the Second Coming in matters of importance, so she had certainly risen highly in his estimation. Indeed, for once in her life, she had actually managed to earn Thomas Harlow's respect.

And almost lost it again thanks to the disaster with Solomon.

Julia scowled at that unwanted thought. *My father will forget all about Solomon once he has the duke and his son firmly in his pocket.*

Normally that thought would have been enough to soothe any qualms she had about her betrothal, but after tonight… well, suffice it to say that this evening's dinner had surprised her, and not in a pleasant way.

Tonight had been the first time she'd been around her betrothed without having lots of other people as a buffer and Sebastian's usual manner toward her—cool and detached—had changed to something else entirely.

In fact, she thought it would be fair to say the man hated her. He and his supercilious grandmother had sharpened their claws on Julia the same way the barn cats in her father's stables scratched on a stall door.

They'd discussed people she didn't know, talked about places she'd never been, and generally made her feel like a gauche schoolgirl.

Julia supposed that is exactly what she was thanks to her father's *refusal* to give her a Season. And all because Thomas Harlow lived in fear that Julia's behavior would jeopardize her upcoming marriage.

Well, she thought with a reluctant smile, he was probably right about that. Julia was reckless and prone to impulsive behavior so she would have run amok if she'd had a Season.

Although she would always regret that she'd not been permitted to join Lily—who'd at least enjoyed a few months of freedom before she'd married her earl—she knew she'd have ample opportunity to socialize with the *ton* in the years to come, and as a duchess rather than a mere cit's daughter.

A duchess whose husband hates her.

So? Their arrangement didn't require that they like each other, all they had to do was tolerate one another. He could have his life and Julia could have hers and hopefully—after she'd done her wifely duty and delivered him sons—they'd see each other once or twice a year.

If she had her way about it—and she intended to—Julia would spend a goodly part of the year with Richard at Brookfield.

Julia's happy musing were shattered when the coach swayed wildly, as if something had knocked it off balance. She grabbed for the hand strap but her fingers fumbled when the carriage jolted to a stop so abruptly that she slid from the leather seat and landed on her knees hard enough to make her eyes water.

She'd barely scrambled up to her seat when the door swung open and a huge brutish man appeared in the opening.

"Who are you?" she demanded shrilly. "Where is Carl and what is—"

"Hush now, Miss," he soothed, reaching for her with gloved hands that were as big as shovels.

Julia scuttled to the far end of the bench seat. "This necklace is all I have—here, take it!" She yanked the slender chain and cross from her neck and flung it at him, but he kept coming.

"Help!" she screamed, fumbling for the door handle on the opposite side, not wanting to take her gaze off the giant. "Somebody help me!"

The door she'd been struggling to open suddenly did just that and an arm slid around her waist. "I got 'er!"

"Unhand me!" Julia shouted, squirming against her unseen captor while kicking at the brute coming toward her and tipping the carriage as he climbed inside.

"Shhh." Her assailant lifted what looked to be a large white handkerchief to her face. "You just have a whiff o'this and all will be fine."

"Please, stop—"

The cloth pushed over her mouth and nose and Julia gasped for breath, filling her lungs with air that was sweetly astringent.

"That's a good lass. Take another sniff. Just a few more, eh?"

"No!" she shouted, but the word was muffled.

Julia struggled but the four hands were too big—too strong. The interior of the carriage shimmered and somebody lifted her.

Up, up, up, up …

And then she floated away into darkness.

***

"She came without much of a fuss," Joe said, offering up the bundle in his cradled arms for Malcolm's inspection.

She was swathed from head to toe, no part of her showing. Malcolm lifted the corner of the blanket and stared at Julia Harlow's ethereally beautiful face.

He frowned. "Is she all right? She looks so white and still."

"Aye, sir. It's that drug—works like a charm it does, but it won't hurt her permanently."

Malcolm lowered the blanket and nodded to Norris, who hovered in the background. "Carry her to her chambers, Norris."

His valet complied with his usual aplomb, as if collecting unconscious girls at three in the morning was unexceptionable.

Once Norris had gone, Malcolm turned back to Joe. "And Sheehan?"

Joe chuckled. "Ahh, well, he was a scrapper. I'm afraid we mighta broke his arm."

Malcolm didn't care if he'd broken his damned head. Still, he wanted the man alive when he went to speak to him. "Fetch Doctor Cartwright to see to him."

"Already done, sir."

He should have known; Joe might look like an oaf, but he was sharp as a cobbler's awl.

"We've got him all right and tight at the cottage, sir. When'll you want to speak to him?"

"It will be a few days. I want him to spend some time wondering and worrying."

"No message for Harlow yet, sir?"

"No, I want him to stew." Malcolm planned to enjoy watching Tommy Harlow twist in the wind as he tore London apart looking for his daughter and brother-in-law.

"You want us to lay off Sheehan if his arm is broke?" Joe asked. "Or should we soften him up a bit?"

Malcolm's hands fisted at the thought of being in the same room with Sheehan. He knew he'd not be able to stop with a mere *softening* if he got his hands on the man right now. That was a job best left to less personally invested individuals.

"Do whatever it takes to break his will, short of killing him."

"Very good, sir."

He watched the big man leave before he drew the drapes that usually covered the large window that looked directly across a narrow corridor into another bedchamber.

Unlike the room where Smith had played with the two whores earlier, this bedroom did not resemble a torture chamber in a bordello.

Malcolm had ordered the room decorated especially with Julia in mind. The walls were hung with cream silk, the floor was a flat, milky white wood covered with ivory and gold carpets. The bed was a true masterpiece, the same milk-stained wood as the floors, the canopy, curtains, and bedding ivory silk that resembled a cloud. All that was lacking to complete the heavenly image was an angel and her harp.

Miss Harlow would be conveniently close so that Malcolm could observe her at all times. And she would never know it.

He told himself that was all he would do: look.

If he wanted a fuck, he had Maisie staying in the usual guest suite.

When Malcolm had first devised this plan, he'd considered going without a woman while he kept Julia Harlow. But the more he thought about her staying just on the other side of the corridor from his own room, the more he knew that doing without Maisie would be foolish and dangerous.

Yes, he had abducted Julia Harlow. Yes, he would spy on her without her permission. But he drew the line at touching her.

It wasn't the first time he'd had two women staying at the same time. The fifth floor had been arranged to suit Malcolm's peculiar desires so the corridors didn't follow the rules of a conventional house and were laid out for his convenience, not his guests. The women would never know that the other even existed.

Maisie had no curiosity about the house or Malcolm. All she'd done during her stay was lounge, consume expensive food and drink, and enjoy her pampering. Malcolm was probably the easiest and most generous client she would ever have. He hadn't even bothered spying on her after the first few days because she slept more than a cat and did nothing of interest while she was awake.

He suspected that Julia Harlow, on the other hand, would be a different kettle of fish. Given the little he'd learned about her from Joe, she would be curious and would test the bounds of her captivity.

Malcolm had already warned Butkins, Kemp, and Norris to make sure the other servants were especially vigilant about locking doors while she was in the house. The last thing he needed was to have her stumble on something that damaged her for life. A bit of innocent sensual exploration was one thing, but what Malcolm did with the whores he engaged was something else, entirely. Even hardened deviants found some of his activities distasteful.

Norris entered the room on the other side of the transparent mirror and laid Julia Harlow on the bed. Mrs. Kemp, a woman Malcolm employed full-time to wait on his female guests and manage his household, had a quiet conversation with the valet before Norris left.

And then Mrs. Kemp began to undress her newest charge.

If the older woman guessed that Malcolm was watching, she gave no sign of it. Malcolm never knew how much his upper employees had guessed about his proclivities. Oh, Norris knew everything about Malcolm's insomnia and how he roamed his secret corridors. It was also his valet's job to keep Malcolm's erotic playroom clean and orderly.

But what the others—like Kemp or Butkins—knew, he had no clue.

Nor did he care.

They were excellent, obedient servants who kept their mouths shut. In return, he paid them more than the average Harley Street physician made in a year.

Beneath the blanket and heavy velvet cloak Julia Harlow wore a magnificent Worth gown. The gown was a striking high-necked black and white stripe combination that radiated from her impossibly tiny waist, accentuating her hourglass figure.

Her only jewelry was a pair of crystal earbobs and a flimsy pearl bracelet, both of which looked cheap alongside the gown, which he knew for a fact cost more than a butler made in a decade.

Tommy Harlow was a wealthy man and could afford to dress his daughter in the finest. Why he didn't give her decent jewels, Malcolm didn't know.

Blood roared in his ears as Kemp peeled off her clothing, layer by layer by layer. He was a pig to watch as the servant stripped her, but he couldn't find the strength to make himself stop.

Beneath her expensive gown and luxuriant petticoats, she wore simple white cotton undergarments. Malcolm had not seen such virginal clothing since… well, perhaps he'd *never* seen underclothing like it. When he'd been younger, most of his lovers had either been working girls, most of whom wore sensual lingerie. Who would have guessed that a white corset and the plain combination beneath it could be so bloody alluring?

Then Kemp removed that final barrier to Julia's modesty and Malcolm's breath fogged the glass.

"Bloody hell," he whispered.

Julia Harlow was so perfect she didn't even look real.

She was paler even than the silk bedding, the blue veins pulsing beneath her skin like warm, living marble.

Her breasts were full and tipped with surprisingly large nipples that were a dark rose.

The whores Malcolm used were always shaved, or at least trimmed, so it had been ages since he'd seen a full bush. Unlike the corn silk hair on her head, the tangle of curls at the apex of her thighs was the color of ripe wheat, pale enough that he could see the shadow of her cleft.

Blood thundered to his cock as he gorged on her beauty. He was so damned hard that he could probably ejaculate without even touching himself.

But he denied himself that pleasure, instead reveling in his erotic suffering.

Kemp lifted the fine Irish bedding and silk blankets and covered Julia to her chin.

As per Malcolm's instructions, the lights concealed in the cornicing—the most advanced gaslighting of its sort—were left on, casting a soft, but not obtrusive, glow over the room. There were no windows out onto the world, so Malcolm controlled whatever light the inhabitant would have.

Kemp shut the door behind her and Malcolm was alone with his sleeping angel.

He knew he should be ashamed that he'd taken her, but he'd not felt so excited and invigorated since Sukey had been alive.

That feeling alone was worth the bother of abducting her.

He extinguished all the lights in his bedroom and lowered himself into the chair Norris had thoughtfully placed facing Miss Harlow's room.

And then he watched and waited.

Chapter 8

Malcolm didn't wake up until almost nine thirty the following morning, later than he'd slept in years.

Amazingly, he'd fallen asleep in the chair.

When he pushed himself to his feet his body reminded him that he'd abused it for almost three hours in his gymnasium the day before.

"Uhhgh," he groaned, gingerly stretching the kinks from his arms and legs, taking care not to overextend the limbs on his damaged left side.

He didn't usually exercise so strenuously, but it was the only activity that had calmed him after reading the information Smith had given him a week earlier.

And so every day he'd spent two and even three hours trying to work off his rage.

It was always a temptation to exercise only his healthy limbs, but the last thing he wanted was to end up with a mass of muscle on the right side of his body and nothing on the other—like a human fiddler crab—so he was consistent, even though there was always pain when he used his left side.

"Good morning, sir. Did you sleep well?" Norris asked, emerging from Malcolm's dressing room.

He grunted.

"Will you be exercising as usual, sir?"

Malcolm stared at the sleeping beauty in the next room and considered Norris's question.

He'd woken with his usual erection and was still hard. If he skipped his morning exercise, he could watch his angel wake up and enjoy a leisurely frig.

His cock twitched happily at the notion.

Malcolm snorted softly. He would have thought that last night's session with Smith—the first time he'd laid bare hands on another human being in years—would have sated him for a while, but instead it appeared that he'd opened the lid on a dangerous box because today he was hungrier than ever for more sex, more touch, more … well, just *more*.

Christ. He should have known it was a mistake. Smith might be able to tolerate his wreck of a body, but nobody else would.

Malcolm felt a sharp stab of anger at his friend. Oh, he knew Smith had just wanted to please him, but all last night did was create unreasonable expectations.

He frowned, grabbed his cock, and squeezed hard enough to quell his erection. He would go to the gymnasium and smother his arousal with exertion once Norris had slathered him in salve.

Later today, if he was still horny, he would use Maisie.

But first, exercise.

He turned to his patiently waiting servant. "I'll stay with my usual routine."

"Very good, sir," Norris said, turning away to fetch the salve for Malcolm's daily oiling.

Malcolm shrugged out of his silk robe and tossed it over the nearby chair before spreading his feet.

Norris returned with a hand towel and large tin of ointment and dropped to his knees. He started with Malcolm's foot, ignoring the half-erect shaft bobbing only inches from his face.

The salve Doctor Fowler prescribed for Malcolm's burns was a miracle that contained a substance called silver nitrate. Fowler had emphasized the importance of keeping his scar tissue supple in addition to regular, rigorous movement.

Jonathan Fowler had been a close associate of Jacques-Louis Reverdin—the doctor who'd pioneered skin grafts—and had used the relatively new Reverdin grafting technique on Malcolm's knee, elbow, and shoulder joints. It was Malcolm's opinion that the combination of exercise, skin grafts, and ointment were what made his life bearable.

Fowler had wanted to use the technique on his jaw and cheek, but Malcolm had declined. Although the grafted skin made movement easier, it was not especially attractive, nor would it make areas like his face look normal. Nothing would.

Norris finished Malcolm's outer thigh and hip and then stood. Malcolm held out his arm, impatient for the man to finish, but aware he couldn't rush him. His burned skin tightened without use, so it was always most uncomfortable in the mornings. If he didn't oil the skin that had no functioning oil ducts, it would tear and crack and bleed.

Five minutes later—slathered in grease like a suckling pig and garbed in a loose smock shirt and drawstring trousers—he entered his private gymnasium.

The room was almost an exact replica of Smith's, except with only two mirrors rather than Smith's eight.

When Malcolm had asked his friend about all the mirrors, he'd been stunned by the other man's answer.

"You exercise without *any* clothing at all?" Malcolm had repeated.

Smith had laughed. "For a sophisticated man you certainly have a parochial outlook on some things. Yes, Malcolm, I exercise nude now that I have the luxury of my own gymnasium. The mirrors help me keep my form." He'd smiled slyly. "Also, physical exertion makes me hard and I enjoy looking at myself."

It had made Malcolm hard just thinking about Smith hot, sweaty, and erect.

The thought of looking at his own burned body naked had the opposite effect.

"You would be well-advised to have at least one mirror, no matter how much you hate looking into them," Smith had advised, guessing the trend of Malcolm's thoughts. "You can damage yourself easily if you don't hold the correct form. Especially when you use the dumbbells."

Malcolm had seen the wisdom of Smith's advice the more he'd exercised. He found the activity strangely addictive. He rarely drank alcohol anymore—he never wanted to be as insensate as he'd been that long ago night—and he had no pastimes or vices other than whores and work, so honing his broken body had become his hobby.

Usually, exercise helped him focus his thoughts and prepared him to face the day.

But today, even two solid hours in the gymnasium didn't help exorcise Miss Julia Harlow from his thoughts. All he could think about was finishing up and getting back to his chambers to spy on his houseguest.

But when he finally returned to his chambers he saw that she was still fast asleep.

Indeed, she didn't appear to have moved since the night before. She was nothing but a small bump beneath the covers, her abundant pale blond hair spread across the pillow like silk.

By the time Malcolm had bathed, shaved, and dressed it was after noon and she was still sleeping.

"Have Kemp go check on her—make sure that drug Joe used didn't have any ill effects," he told Norris when he arrived with Malcolm's midday meal.

"Of course, sir."

Malcolm sipped his coffee and looked through the store reports that were delivered each day, pausing his work when Kemp entered Julia Harlow's room.

The maid checked her pulse, laid a hand on her forehead, and then settled the blankets around her before leaving the room.

So, the girl was fine.

Malcolm worried his lower lip as he stared through the mirror. Should he simply get on with his day or keep waiting?

It's not like you to dither, Mal, Sukey chided.

Oh, now you're back.

You've kidnapped an innocent young woman.

I'm not going to hurt her.

You're spying on her.

How is that hurting her?

As usual, Sukey disappeared after she'd had her say.

"It's not really Sukey." Malcolm said aloud, which made him feel like an even bigger idiot.

He stared through the glass, an uneasy feeling building in his belly.

Close it, his conscience ordered.

You're doing nothing wrong, just looking. It's not like you're fucking her… a base, greedy voice whispered.

Usually when Malcolm's conscience and cock argued his cock was the clear winner.

But not today.

"Bloody hell," he muttered, and then yanked the drapes closed, pulling so hard he was surprised he didn't jerk them off the wall.

Malcolm slammed his bedroom door and stalked toward his study. He was furious with himself for this missish lapse into—*what?* Morality? Guilt?

Since when had spying on a woman—or anyone—bothered him? Watching others was one of the few joys left in his life; he deserved some small measure of enjoyment from it, didn't he?

Malcolm scowled at the peevish, whiney tone of his thoughts; he sounded like a spoiled child.

Quit lying to yourself. You know exactly why you feel like a lascivious shit.

He sighed. Yes, he did. The girl wasn't one of his whores, she was just an innocent bystander who'd been caught up in the net of his revenge. Malcolm was using her, just like he'd use any other tool at his disposal.

He was despicable.

He dropped into his desk chair and stared at yet another transparent mirror—the one that looked onto the room where he'd watched Smith and the others perform for him last night.

Lord. Was that only last night? It felt like a hundred years ago.

Smith had warned him about going down this road and Malcolm was speedily realizing his friend was right. There was a cost for revenge and he was already feeling fatigued by the energy such hatred required to fuel it.

He drummed his fingers on his desk; he should just kill Harlow right now and forget about toying with the bastard—no matter how much he'd earned the right to inflict some suffering.

But he couldn't do that until he'd spoken to Sheehan. And if he spoke to Sheehan in his current state of mind, he'd kill him.

Malcolm's fists curled at the almost irresistible thought, and he began to sweat. Yes, why not kill him? He could go over there *right* now and—

Patience. Have patience and stay with your plan.

He ground his teeth until his jaws ached.

Patience.

Malcolm squeezed his eye shut and struggled with the violence that was threatening to tear him apart. Slowly and methodically, he regained control of his fraying temper, breathing deeply for several moments, until the rage storm had passed.

Smith had given him one of the people who'd murdered his wife, but Malcolm strongly suspected there was more. The only way to find out the entire truth was to wait until he had *all* the puzzle pieces.

Only then would he put them together.

Until that time, he'd keep Julia Harlow, but he'd respect her privacy and leave her alone.

All alone.

***

Julia opened her eyes and then whimpered and quickly closed them again as the pounding in her skull intensified.

The brief, blurry glance was enough to tell her that she wasn't in her own bedchamber.

Last night came back to her in jagged fragments: the wretched dinner, Sebastian's disdain, the carriage… Yes, she'd been in the carriage when it had stopped and a large man had opened the door and…

And that was all she recalled.

Her stomach gurgled loudly and she realized she was starving. But then, when was she not?

Still, this hunger was different, sharper and painful; she actually felt hollow inside.

Julia opened her eyes, but slowly this time. Although her head didn't stop pounding at least the light—which was quite muted—didn't stab at her.

Gradually she could see clearly enough to take in the large, exquisitely furnished room around her. It was comprised of celestial blue and soothing shades of ivory, cream, and white.

Julia felt as if she were reclining on a cloud. Was she dreaming? Dead?

"Hello?" she called out, her raspy voice echoing eerily in the cavernous chamber. "Is anyone there?" she asked a bit louder, even though it made her head pound.

She pushed herself up onto her elbow, which is when she discovered that she was naked. Blood pounded in her temples and her face heated; *somebody* had undressed her! Julia pulled the blankets up to her chest and glanced around the room. A garment that looked to be a dressing gown was draped over a nearby chair.

She flung back the covers and stalked over to the robe, her eyes opening wide when she held the garment up in front of her.

Nadine might have starved Julia, tied her to a posture board, and dressed her in frilly gowns that she despised, but her stepmother had never stinted when it came to fine clothing because that would have reflected poorly on *her*.

But nothing Julia possessed was as gorgeous or expensive looking as the dressing gown.

It was yards and yards and yards of gossamer-thin blush-colored silk, the material so light and soft that it felt like she was wearing down when she slipped it on.

She gasped when she caught sight of herself in the enormous mirror that took up most of the wall opposite. Julia's image briefly distracted her from her current predicament. Her hair, which was normally plaited before bed, had been unbound and hung in a riot of messy curls that fell to her waist. Anger had given her normally pale cheeks color and the robe clung to her overripe body like silken sin.

For once, she looked wild and sensual rather than blandly angelic.

A pair of pink slippers sat neatly by the leg of the chair and when she slid her feet into them, she discovered they fit perfectly.

Julia didn't want to ponder how her mysterious captors knew her sizes. Instead, she tried the door, unsurprised to find it locked. So she yanked on the velvet servant cord, pulling it repeatedly before turning to investigate her prison.

There were four rooms: bed chamber, sitting room, bathing chamber, and dressing room. Both the décor and room size made her suite at her father's house appear paltry by comparison. Everything was the finest of its sort—the furniture lovely, the fabrics exquisite, the art on the walls looked fit to grace a museum.

The door open and Julia spun around to find an older woman dressed in the sedate garb clothing of an upper servant.

"Good morning, Miss Harl—"

"Where am I? What am I doing here?"

The woman smiled politely at her rude interruption. "I am Kemp. If you'll allow me to help you get dressed, you can come to breakfast, and those questions will be answered."

Julia opened her mouth to vent her spleen, but one look at the older woman's opaque expression convinced her that arguing was pointless.

"Fine," she said.

"Shall I fill the tub or would you like a shower-bath?"

"Neither. I will wash my face, you may brush and plait my hair, and then I will get dressed."

"As you wish."

The next ten minutes passed in tense silence.

Once Julia's hair was coiled into a neat and tidy crown Kemp opened one of the cupboard doors in the enormous dressing room, exposing built-in racks of clothing, shoes, hats, coats, and every other garment a woman could need or desire.

"Would you like to wear a—"

"I want my clothing. *Mine.*"

The maid hesitated and, for a moment, Julia thought she might argue.

Julia would have relished some open conflict.

But Kemp merely opened another door. Inside were only her dress, underthings, velvet cloak, and slippers.

Julia felt far more herself once she was garbed in her familiar dinner gown, no matter how inappropriate it might be. The dress was her favorite, not just because it was beautiful, but because she'd had to fight Nadine to have it. Her stepmother had believed the black and white pattern was too mature for a nineteen-year-old.

For once, her father had sided with Julia. "It's far better than all those frills and bows she usually wears, my dear. Let her have the gown."

Although her father hadn't known it, his words were a direct insult to his wife because it was Nadine, and not Julia, who was responsible for Julia's frilly, over-embellished gowns.

In any event, today her favorite gown felt like armor. "I'm ready," she said to Kemp.

The hallway outside her room was paneled in dark wood, the floor carpeted with a plush Aubusson runner, the lights covered with magnificent hand-blown glass shades in jewel tones.

They took several turns and she scrambled to memorize her way, using the landscape paintings they passed as markers. Several of the paintings looked so familiar that she supposed they must be well-executed reproductions of famous works.

Finally, Kemp stopped in front of a door that was larger than the others and opened it.

Julia hesitated, looking at the older woman rather than into the room. "Who will I be meeting?"

"He will tell you what you need to know." She hesitated, and then added in a warmer voice. "Don't be afraid, Miss Harlow, the master won't hurt you."

"I'm not afraid," Julia lied. And then she squared her shoulders and walked through the doorway.

Chapter 9

Julia didn't know what she'd been expecting, but it wasn't the fairytale she walked into.

Rather than a room, it was a greenhouse—the most magical one she'd ever seen.

"The greenhouse runs along the entire south side of the roof," Kemp said. "If you follow the path"—she gestured to a miniature tree-lined avenue—"it will lead you to the dining room." And then she gave a slight curtsey and exited the door they'd just come through.

Julia turned in a circle, gaping at the idyllic pond—complete with a miniature waterfall—trees that held dozens of tiny, brightly colored birds, and exotic blooms that looked twice as shocking in the middle of winter.

The air inside was humid and almost tropical, or at least what she imagined the tropics to feel like. The glass ceiling soared perhaps twenty feet above her head and outside was the gray London sky, but no snow clung to the peaked roof. Judging by the angle of the sun it was well after midday.

"Good afternoon, Miss Harlow."

Julia spun clumsily on her high-heeled evening slippers.

"I'm sorry to startle you," a handsome young man dressed in elegant livery said. "I'm James. If you'll step this way, I'll show you to the dining room."

He led her down the tree lined path toward another larger area like the one she'd just left.

French doors off to one side opened to what appeared to be a dining pavilion. An enormous man stood beside a table that was long enough to seat eight or ten people. He was dressed all in black—even his hands were gloved in black—and half his face was concealed by a black mask that looked to be closely contoured to his face.

He was… striking and his dramatic appearance added to the sense of unreality.

His mouth flexed into a crooked, mocking smile, making Julia realize that she'd been staring. "Please, come in, Miss Harlow."

Julia's feet propelled her forward as her eyes struggled to take everything in—the man, the elegant room, the magnificent foliage she was passing through.

She hovered on the threshold, glancing from the table—at which two places had been set, one at the head and one at the foot—and then back at the unusual man standing before her.

He gestured to the table. "Won't you have a seat?"

Julia suddenly noticed her wide-eyed reflection in the large mirror on the wall behind Mr. Barton.

Shame flooded her at her gauche behavior. But right on the heels of that shame was anger; why should she care if her reaction was rude? The man had *abducted* her.

"Who are you?" She crossed her arms and stayed exactly where she was.

He bowed. "Malcolm Edward Barton at your service."

Julia struggled to place the name. "Malcolm Barton? As in Barton's Emporium?"

"The very same. Come, won't you sit and eat. I know you must be hungry—you've been asleep for at least ten hours."

His accent was like her father's—that of a man who was trying to ape his social betters.

Julia had always thought it made her father sound desperate. From this man, however, the careful, cit accent sounded more like a foreign language, something he'd learned in order to converse with the natives, the natives in this case being the aristocracy.

"You can be angry with me far more effectively with a full belly," he said in a cajoling tone when Julia continued to stand and glare.

His pale blue eye twinkled with amusement, which only made her angrier.

What you underline should be feeling is fear, a voice whispered in her head.

Julia knew that was good advice, but it was difficult to be afraid when one was being treated like royalty.

And then there was the fact that she was so hungry she could barely think logically.

"Fine," she snapped, moving toward the foot of the table.

He took three long slides, arriving before her and pulling out her chair.

Julia had seen that he was tall but hadn't realized just *how* tall until she was standing beside him. Carl was the tallest man she'd ever met, but he was slope-shouldered and a bit doughy. Mr. Barton was like a wall that moved and his massive shoulders tapered to a narrow waist and tight, compact hips, judging by the fit of his coat.

Julia had to crane her neck to look up, but she made herself do it, purposely staring at the side of his face covered by the eerie black leather mask, forcing herself to be bold, no matter how discourteous such gawking might be

The mask *was* eerie but mainly because there was no opening for his eye. It covered part of his nose but exposed his mouth, the left corner of which was puckered, the skin darker pink and crepey. It covered the left side of his skull, with only a small hole over his ear.

The part of his face that she could see was handsome, his features chiseled and exceedingly masculine. His wavy black hair was unusually long, hanging almost to his shoulder on the right side and was shot through with thick strands of silver The way the mask fit told her he had little or no hair on his left side.

His heavy-lidded eye was the coldest shade of blue Julia had ever encountered and was fringed with spiky black lashes.

His silky sable eyebrow lifted, the small movement speaking volumes.

Julia refused to apologize for staring. Instead, she lowered herself into the chair.

Once she was seated, he said, "Allow me to serve you."

It wasn't a question, so she didn't speak. Instead, she stared at his broad back when he turned to fill a plate at the buffet.

Sebastian's clothing was expensive and exquisitely cut, but never had she seen garments so perfectly tailored to a man's figure.

His shirt was high-collared and snowy white, but everything else— his waistcoat, coat, and trousers—were black. He moved easily, but she noticed he favored one side of his body—his left. So, he must be damaged on more than just his face.

"I thought you might like to try some of all the dishes," he said as he turned back to her, setting down a plate that held more food than she'd been given in years.

The aroma of the rich food assaulted her nose, leaving her woozy.

"Coffee, or tea?" he asked.

"Tea, please."

He nodded to James. "Tea and fresh coffee."

"Right away, sir."

Julia's hands trembled as she picked up her utensils. She told herself it was hunger, but that was a lie. As politely as Mr. Barton was

behaving, the man had kidnapped her. Besides, he emanated…
something. Something unnerving.

She gripped her fork and knife hard to stop from shaking and cut a
miniscule piece from the thick, juicy slab of ham.

Last night—had it only been last night?—at Sebastian's
grandmother's house there had been no Netta or Nadine to starve her,
but Julia had been too anxious to eat, more than a little concerned she
might vomit all over her hostess and betrothed if she did so.

She raised her fork to her mouth and then paused when she saw
Mr. Barton was still and watchful, his icy gaze on her.

Julia lowered the fork back to her plate, food untouched. "Aren't
you eating?"

"I already ate."

"Oh."

He gave an encouraging nod. "Please, eat while I talk."

When she placed the tiny sliver of ham in her mouth smokey,
savory goodness exploded on her tongue.

It was so delicious Julia almost swooned.

He tracked her chewing the way a falcon stalked its prey, which
made it extremely difficult to swallow the morsel of food, no matter
how small.

Julia cleared her throat and set down her cutlery and his gaze
moved from her mouth to her eyes.

"You were going to talk," she reminded him, her voice
impressively firm considering how chaotic she was feeling inside.

"I swear I won't hurt you. I am only keeping you here to
encourage your father to cooperate with me." He spoke in an
inflectionless tone.

"You know my f-father?"

"Yes."

"Cooperate how?" She picked up her knife and fork, needing to do
something with her hands.

"You don't need to know the specifics."

"But I'm the one who has been abducted."

His lips twitched. "True. But this disagreement has nothing to do
with you."

"But *I'm* the one who has been abducted," she repeated, dropping
her cutlery with a clatter.

"Yes, we've established that."

"You don't think it's a bit unfair that I'm the one inconvenienced but I don't get to know why?"

The moment the word *unfair* left her mouth Julia wanted to kick herself. Could she sound more like a child if she tried?

He chuckled, the tolerant sound beyond grating. "You are young, so perhaps nobody has told you this yet: life isn't fair, Miss Harlow."

Julia's face scalded at his condescending tone. "Am I to know how long I will be kept?"

"As long as it takes."

"And I'm just to sit here and… *wait* until whatever happens?"

"Yes."

Julia was used to doing what she was told—mostly. She'd learned the hard way what happened when she circumvented authority to get something she wanted.

And yet something about Barton's calm, utterly arrogant demand rankled beyond bearing.

Julia's hands closed around her knife and fork and she gripped the heavy, ornate handles so tightly the metal cut into her flesh.

Did *everyone* in England believe they had the right to tell her what to do? Her father, Nadine, Netta, *Uncle* Carl, and now this stranger, too?

The fury she'd been feeling since the moment she'd found herself naked began to boil over and her entire body was suddenly hot and flushed.

"Miss Harlow?"

Her head whipped up and she glared at him. "What?"

"I will try to make your stay here as pleasant as possible." His tone was slightly softer, not necessarily kind, but at least not as dictatorial. "It is my understanding your father sent you to London to punish you because of an unfortunate episode involving your brother's tutor."

His words literally knocked the breath from her lungs and it took Julia several attempts before she could speak.

"How—how do you know such a thing?"

"That needn't concern you. What should—"

One moment Julia held the knife in her hand, the next it was sticking out of his left shoulder.

Julia shrieked, but Mr. Barton didn't make a sound as he carefully tugged out the blade and set it on the table.

James, who must have been lingering outside in the greenhouse, darted into the dining room. "My goodness, Mr. Barton! Are you—"

Malcolm Barton raised a hand in a *stop* gesture at his frantic servant. "It is fine, only the tip went in. Most of it was caught by my coat, waistcoat, and shirt."

The footman's handsome features twisted with concern. "Sir, I can see blood on your coat. You should—"

"Leave us." He didn't speak loudly, but his low voice was so cold Julia swore she saw frost.

The younger man left without another word.

"I'm so sorry," Julia said, beyond mortified at her behavior. "I didn't mean—"

"Apology accepted," he said in a cool, brisk tone that made her feel like an obstinate toddler who'd just been put in her place. His lips flexed into a faint smile at whatever he saw on her face. "I can see you find my company repellent, so I won't force my presence on you."

Julia's heart leapt. "Then you'll let me go?"

"No, I meant I won't force my company on you for the duration of your stay."

"But you refuse to tell me how long that will be?"

"I won't release you until you've served your purpose."

"Until I've served my purpose," Julia repeated flatly, any regret she felt about stabbing him quickly draining away. "A purpose you refuse to—"

"There is no point in continuing with this subject. I've already answered all the questions I will answer."

Julia's head buzzed she was so angry. Before she could do something else that she would regret—like throw her entire plate—she pushed to her feet and strode toward the door.

"You need to eat, Miss Harlow."

She whipped around at his words. "I'm afraid being held hostage has had a negative effect on my appetite," she lied.

"If the food is not to your liking, you must tell me what you want and you shall have it. I'm sure my chef can find something to tempt your appetite." His cold eye narrowed. "I will not have you starving yourself."

"Are you saying that you will *force* me to eat if I refuse, Mr. Barton?"

His lips twisted into an unpleasant smile that made the hair on her neck stand up. "If you are trying to test my patience you will quickly discover that I don't have any, Miss Harlow."

Julia wisely held her tongue.

"You don't need to eat *here* if you don't wish to, but you *will* eat. Understood?"

Self-preservation and rebellion roiled in her belly and self-preservation won out.

"I understand," she said through gritted teeth.

"Good. Kemp will inquire into your food preferences. You may ask my servants for anything you need—books, clothing, paints, musical instruments, a pet poodle—whatever it will take to keep you happy."

"A carriage ride home?"

"I'm afraid not."

"How about a loaded pistol?"

He gave a surprised-sounding chuckle. "Perhaps I should have said *anything within reason*. This part of my house is completely at your disposal; Kemp will give you a tour. If you need to ask me anything, you may send word by any of the servants."

Without further ado, he dropped a brief bow and strode from the dining room.

Julia stared after him.

How was it that *she* felt guilty when *he* was the one who'd abducted her?

***

"Bloody hell," Malcolm muttered beneath his breath as he made his way back to his office. Julia Harlow had been beautiful asleep, but she was incandescent awake and angry. Temptingly so.

It was a good thing she hated his guts—which was certainly what knife hurling had indicated—because it would be torment to be in the same room with her and not touch her.

She'd not flinched from him in horror or been afraid like most people when they were forced to look at him. No, she'd just glared right back at him.

And then thrown a knife.

Malcolm snickered to himself; she was bloody magnificent.

He shut the door to his office and then sank into the chair behind his desk with a sigh, his mouth pulling into a slow smile at the memory of her outburst. He reached up to rub his shoulder and encountered something wet and sticky. The cut didn't hurt, but the knife had punctured his damaged skin, which was prone to tearing, so he'd have to ring for Norris sooner rather than later to see to the wound.

He dropped his hand to his desk and considered the scene he'd just left, absently drumming his fingers.

Malcolm had—stupidly—hoped to enjoy Julia Harlow's company while he plotted and planned to destroy her family. Now he saw that would be impossible. Of course she was going to resist her captor and it was natural that she'd spent the entire time spitting and scratching like an infuriated kitten. It was his bloody luck that the first woman he'd met in fifteen years who'd not fainted at the sight of him was the same woman he was using as a weapon against her own family.

You could change that right now, Mal. There's still lots of time to do the right thing.

No there wasn't. That time had passed and he knew it.

Malcolm couldn't help grinning at the memory of her sharp tongue and hateful looks, although he could have done without the stabbing.

Indeed, he'd enjoyed being around her a great deal too much. Already visions of bending her over the breakfast table and fucking that adorably pouty look off her face were romping through his mind.

It would not be easy leaving her alone for the next few weeks—or longer if he couldn't get what he wanted quickly enough—but he suspected his body would soon overwhelm his reason if he was in her presence for too long.

Malcolm didn't *like* to deny himself sensual pleasure, but in this case, he could and he would.

Besides, he didn't need to go without entirely; Maisie was at hand.

Malcolm toggled the second lever on the black lacquer box on his desk.

He didn't have to wait long before the door to his study opened.

"Yes, sir?" Butkins said.

"I want the estimates from the Brussels store and send Maisie to me."

"Right away, sir."

The door closed and Malcolm's fingers resumed their drumming on the desk.

It would take some effort, but he would put the Harlow chit from his mind using the time-honored methods of hard work and whores. It wouldn't be difficult.

No, it wouldn't be difficult to forget her, at all.

Chapter 10

It took Malcolm five full days before he felt he could trust himself around Carl Sheehan without killing him. Those five days had felt like fifty as he'd endeavored to keep his mind—and spying eye—off his houseguest.

For once, poor Maisie was earning her keep.

Although he'd not yet heard anything from Harlow—meaning the man was probably tearing his hair out by now—it was time to confront the first of his victims.

It was just past midnight and Joe was waiting for him when Malcolm arrived at the cottage where Sheehan was being held.

"We've got him tied to a chair, sir," Joe said, after taking Malcolm's overcoat and hat. "You need any help with him?"

"No. Stay out of the room unless I call for you."

Joe nodded.

Sheehan had fallen asleep, which gave Malcolm a moment to observe him.

He was Malcolm's age with more gray threaded through his red hair, his big body overflowing the heavy wooden chair. There were bruises darkening his handsome face and smudges beneath his eyes, hinting at sleep deprivation. In Malcolm's experience, there was no better torture than a lack of sleep.

A normal human response would have been to feel pity for a human being who was so battered and strained.

Malcolm wanted to cut Sheehan's throat. Or set him on fire.

Or maybe both.

Instead, he punched him in the face hard enough to knock the chair onto its side. If there hadn't been a rug on the floor Sheehan's skull would have split open. As it was, he groaned, proving he was still among the living.

Sheehan blinked his eyes and licked the split in his lip as Malcolm loomed over him.

The Irishman stared for a long moment and then gave a huff of laughter. "Bloody hell! *You*?" He shook his head in genuine amazement. "Fucking impossible! After all these years. Who would have guessed?"

Malcolm bent over, grabbed Sheehan's chair, and set it on its feet. "It took you seeing me again to figure it out, did it? A lot of people want to abduct, beat, and kill you?" he asked, massaging his aching knuckles with his damaged left hand.

"Aye, more than a few," Sheehan conceded, his insouciance forced. "You saw me when I came into your store, didn't you?" He made a noise of disgust. "This is all that little bitch's fault! If she'd not gone in there—"

Malcolm hit him again. "Watch your mouth."

Sheehan blinked, shook away the pain, and then smirked up at him. "You've fallen under her spell, haven't you?" He gave a filthy laugh at whatever he saw on Malcolm's face. "She's like her ma, that one—a regular little bitch in he—"

This time Malcolm kicked Sheehan in the chest hard enough to knock the chair over.

It took a basin of water to wake the bastard up again.

"I knew I'd seen you before," Malcolm said, before he could open his mouth. "But it took me a while to place your face. You came to my shipyard the day before the fire—you were there to repair the big furnace."

Sheehan laughed, but his eyes were afraid. "Took you long enough to remember me, eh? Fifteen years!"

Malcolm ignored him. "It must have been easy for you to rig up a fire with all those solvents and pitch and other flammables."

Sheehan had no smart answer for that.

"The insurance finding was negligence on our part," Malcolm said, although he suspected the other man already knew that. "Their investigator said we should have faced criminal charges for storing such items so close to a raging fire. He said we were fortunate the entire waterfront didn't burn to the ground. I wasn't there during the inquest to hear all that, of course. I had to read about it months later, when I finally left my hospital bed."

Sheehan swallowed, his Adam's apple bobbing wildly.

Malcolm clucked his tongue at the other man. "All of this would have stayed buried if you'd remained in America."

Sheehan forced a grin, sweat rolling down his forehead even though the room was cold enough that Malcolm could see his own breath. "I was homesick."

"Why *did* you leave New York, Carl?"

Sheehan's green gaze flickered nervously over Malcolm's mask. "I guess you could say things got too *hot* for me there."

This time, Malcolm hit him in the stomach, which was a lot easier on his hand.

While Sheehan was gasping for breath, Malcolm closed his hands around his throat. "You think burning alive is amusing?" he asked, squeezing the man's throat too hard for him to answer. "That's seven people, by my count, that you've murdered with fire."

Malcolm watched as confusion bloomed in the other man's terrified gaze.

"Yes, *seven—two* people died in that warehouse." He pressed both thumbs against Sheehan's larynx. "Do you have any idea how much pain you've caused?"

Malcolm squeezed until Sheehan's eyes bulged.

As he stared into the other man's hateful green gaze, he saw the truth: Sheehan was hoping to goad him into killing him quickly and Malcolm, stupidly, had almost given the other man what he wanted.

He yanked back his hands back as if Sheehan had suddenly burst into flame. "No. You won't get off so easily."

As the other man coughed and gasped for breath Malcolm reached behind his head and pulled the leather cords before removing his mask and tossing it onto a nearby table.

"Now, tell me who came up with the idea to set the fire, who knew about it, and who helped?"

Sheehan's eyes widened in horror when he saw Malcolm's face. "Jesus Christ! You're a fucking monster. Why didn't you just kill yourself?"

"Who came up with the idea, who knew about it, and who helped?"

"Fuck yourself, Barton."

Malcolm felt an unpleasant smile take control of his face. "I was hoping you'd say that. Let's see what I can do to convince you to cooperate." He removed a photograph from his breast pocket and held it up in front of Sheehan's bruised and battered face.

"Why are you showing me that?" the other man blustered, the attempt feeble.

Malcolm just stared, pleased when all the blood drained from Sheehan's face.

"Please," he finally croaked.

"Please?" Malcolm cocked his head, as if he couldn't hear him. "Please what? Please kill them quickly? Please don't burn them alive? Please *what*, you repugnant piece of shit?"

Sheehan gulped convulsively. "How—who told you about them?"

"I have heaps of money and heaps of time," Malcolm said, enjoying the look of misery on the other man's face far too much. "And—thanks to you—I have nobody in my life to spend either on. So you, my dear Carl, have become my new hobby. Or perhaps obsession would be a better word." He glanced down at the photograph in his hand. It had been tinted, so he could see how both the woman and the twin boys she held were all gingers.

"They look a great deal like you, don't they?" he mused aloud, and then laughed. "But I suppose that's not surprising given that you're their father *and* their uncle."

"What are you going to do, Barton?"

Malcolm grabbed his mask off the table and quickly tied it onto his head.

"Please," Carl begged, "I'll tell you everything I know. Everything. Please—*please* don't hurt them."

"Start talking. And you'd better make sure what you tell me is the truth, Carl. Because I will check the veracity of every single word."

"I swear to you on my children's lives that I'll tell you every single thing. Just don't hurt them."

Malcolm smiled, enjoying the way the other man winced at his expression. "Tell me everything. And be thorough."

***

Malcolm washed the blood from his gloved hands, his mind on what he'd just heard.

His ears rang from Sheehan's screaming—and begging—but it was his heart that truly hurt.

Not because he'd just tortured a man. He and Smith—back in the day—had done far worse to less deserving victims than what he'd just done to Sheehan.

No, he was sick because of what he now knew.

You always wanted to know all of it, Mal—you wanted the truth. Be careful what you ask for.

He lifted his hands from the water and Joe stepped forward with a clean cloth. "Here you go, sir."

Malcolm stared at the other man as he dried his hands.

Joe's expression was unreadable. Torturing another human being—especially what Malcolm had just done to Sheehan to ensure the man had told him the entire truth—was disgusting business but Joe had been in the bully business a long, long time.

He wasn't a bent man, so he didn't enjoy inflicting pain. But he was practical, so he wouldn't judge Malcolm for doing what had been necessary.

Joe would have taken care of Sheehan if Malcolm had asked, but he'd wanted to handle the man himself.

On one hand, Malcolm was sickened by what he'd just done.

On the other—he wanted to go back into that blood, piss, and shit-stained room and do it over again and again and again.

It won't bring me back, Mal.

He knew that. He wasn't even sure that causing Sheehan pain had vented any of his wrath. If anything, what he'd learned tonight had only left him more enraged.

Not to mention conflicted and confused.

"Should we finish him, sir?"

"No. I'm not done with him yet." Malcolm handed Joe the towel and flexed his hands, wincing at the pain. He'd been foolish to damage his hands on the human rubbish in the other room.

"Get Doc Cartwright in here to fix him up."

"Aye, sir." Joe scratched his head, clearly confused as to why Malcolm would doctor a man he'd just tortured half to death, but he was a good enough employee that he never questioned Malcolm's orders.

Malcolm pulled on a second, fur-lined, pair of gloves with a pained wince. "Where are the Harlow twins right now?"

"Most holidays they spend with their grandmother when they're not away at school."

Malcolm snorted. "That's right—I'd forgotten that their mother proudly apes the aristocracy when it comes to childrearing. I want you to go get them."

Joe inhaled deeply and then let it out slowly, his normally ruddy face going pale.

Malcolm sighed. "I don't want you to hurt them, Joe. Use my private rail carriage and coach and take them and their grandmother on a holiday journey to Paris. Put them up in my apartment there. If the grandmother kicks up a fuss convince her that her cooperation is… critical."

"What should I say?"

"Tell her that Harlow is treating her to an all-expenses paid holiday."

"Er, Mrs. Sheehan don't get along with her son-in-law, sir."

Malcolm sighed. "Then tell her she has a secret admirer who paid for the holiday. Tell her anything you want except the truth—I don't care. Just don't upset her or the boys."

"Yes, sir. Any idea how long this will be?"

Malcolm thought about what Sheehan had just divulged.

"This might take a bit longer than I'd expected."

Chapter 11

Julia thought she had been bored while locked up with only Netta and Carl for company.

After six full days of her own company, she would have welcomed even Netta with open arms.

On her seventh morning of captivity—after she'd woken with another day of boredom stretching before her like eternity—Julia finally admitted that it might have been foolish to hurl cutlery at her host.

She could be very charming when she put her mind to it, and now was as good a time as any to exercise that charm. Besides, not only would seeing Barton alleviate her boredom, but he was her only source of information. After almost a week in his household she'd learned that *none* of his servants would tell her anything. If she was going to learn anything at all it would have to come from the man, himself.

Julia pulled the bell for Kemp.

"He's not available to come to breakfast?" she repeated, a few minutes later. "Then what about nuncheon?"

"Mr. Barton doesn't usually sit down to a midday meal, Miss."

"Tea?"

Kemp looked pained. "He is not in the habit of taking tea, I'm afraid."

"Dinner, then," Julia said flatly. "Or does he not eat that meal, either?" As soon as the snappish question was out of her mouth, she felt like a shrew for using such a tone. "I'm sorry," she said before Kemp could answer. "I shouldn't use that tone on you."

"It's fine, Miss."

"No, it's not. It's rude."

Kemp didn't deserve her tantrum; she was just a servant, doing her job. She was kind, thoughtful, and worked hard to please Julia.

Thanks to Kemp, Julia had her favorite foods three meals a day and at tea, the finest painting supplies—undeserved given that she was a mediocre painter at best—the most beautiful piano she had ever played, which was truly undeserved as she was horrific pianist—more books than she'd read in a year, a ridiculous amount of clothing, and anything else that crossed her mind.

Well, except the poodle.

Julia had been tempted to fill her room with dogs, parrots, and monkeys—just to show the arrogant Mr. Barton—but then she'd thought about the poor animals that she'd have to leave behind when he released her. Nadine said indoor animals were filthy and disgusting and Julia suspected Sebastian held a similar opinion on anything except dogs.

Julia really had very few complaints about her situation. In fact, other than a menagerie, she had everything except her freedom.

Oh, and companionship.

"I'll ask Mr. Barton's secretary about dinner, miss. He will be the one who can tell me if the master is free for dinner."

"Who is his secretary? Does he live here?" Julia blurted before she could stop herself. "I know, I know," she said before Kemp could speak. "You can't tell me."

"Those are questions you should ask Mr. Barton, Miss Harlow."

"Of course, I know that. It's just"—she broke off and chewed her lip.

Kemp looked genuinely concerned. "What is it, Miss Harlow?"

It was the other woman's kindness that shattered Julia's resolve to be strong. "I'm lonely." Her face scalded at the childish confession, but she couldn't bring herself to care.

Kemp hesitated a long moment, and then surprised Julia by saying, "Perhaps I might join you while I do my mending—if you do not mind?"

Julia was touched by her offer. "That would be lovely. Perhaps I could help? I'm a competent needlewoman, if not exactly inspired."

"I would appreciate that. First, let me send somebody with your question about dinner, and then I will come back and sit for a while."

Julia nodded, not trusting herself to speak without getting teary. "Thank you."

Once Kemp left, Julia sagged back against her pillows. A rational person would have been frightened and worried rather than bored, lonely, and actively seeking her captor's company. She knew that being lonely was a sign of weakness, but she couldn't help it. She'd spoken to nobody besides Kemp and two footmen for almost a week. When she'd tried to strike up a conversation with Mr. Bobbitt, the gardener who maintained the greenhouse, he'd looked terrified and fled, almost as if he'd been warned away from her.

Yes, she had every material item she could imagine, but Julia had discovered something important over the last week: lovely things were far less exciting when there was nobody to share them with.

And while it was wonderful to spend one's afternoons sipping lemonade and reading in the magical rooftop greenhouse, the enjoyment palled when one was all alone.

Julia chewed her lip, regretting that she'd not sent a message of formal apology about the knife incident. Yes, Mr. Barton *had* abducted her, but he'd not hurt her—not even after she'd stabbed him.

For the first few days she'd worried he'd punish her for her actions, or perhaps try to torture answers from her—not that she actually knew anything of value.

Instead, he'd just *ignored* her!

Perhaps he'd done so because the knife had hurt him more than he'd said? Or what if she'd damaged his pride by gawking at his masked face in such a discourteous manner?

Julia sighed. Barton had been kind—other than the abduction itself, of course—and she had repaid him by stabbing him.

She hated to admit it, but it frightened her how much she hoped Mr. Barton would agree to share a meal with her.

A person couldn't *die* of loneliness, could they?

***

"Yes, what is it?" Malcolm called out irritably at the knock on his door.

The door opened a crack and Butkins's face appeared in the gap. "I'm sorry, sir, I know you said you didn't wish to be disturbed—"

"You have already disturbed me, so what is it?" Malcolm tossed his pen onto the desk, pinched the bridge of his nose between his thumb and index finger, and closed his overworked eye.

"Er, it's about Miss Harlow, sir."

His eye popped open. "What about her?"

"Kemp says she's asked if you will join her for dinner"—he coughed—"actually, Kemp said she asked if you'd join her for breakfast, nuncheon, tea, and/or dinner."

Malcolm sat back in his chair. Well, this was... unexpected. "Is there something she wants?"

"Erm, apparently she is lonely, sir."

Malcolm's eyebrow shot up. "Lonely?"

"Yes, sir. That is what Kemp said."

Well.

"Kemp told her you generally didn't stop for nuncheon or tea."

Malcolm gave his employee a hard look. "I see—which means I *do* stop for breakfast and dinner."

Rather than cringe at his cold tone—as he normally would—Butkins unflinchingly stood his ground.

"I would have thought you, of all people, would have rejoiced at me leaving her alone, Butkins."

Butkins opened his mouth, hesitated, and then said, "Kemp and the other servants who've waited on her say she is a very nice, pleasant, and polite young woman. They also say she seems to be… wilting the longer she is here. I think it would be a kindness to dine with her, sir."

Malcolm hated how pleased the invitation made him. What sort of pathetic creature was he to take comfort in a lonely young woman's invitation?

"Sir?" Butkins prodded.

"Fine," he snapped. "You may tell her that I shall eat breakfast and dinner with her unless I am otherwise engaged."

"Very good, sir."

Malcolm squinted; was that a smirk on the other man's face?

"Oh, Butkins," he said, when the man turned to leave.

"Yes, sir?"

"Send Maisie to me."

Butkins blinked owlishly behind his spectacles. "Erm, right now?"

"Yes, *right now*. And also send a message to Madame Sylvie and let her know I'll be keeping Maisie for the foreseeable future."

Chapter 12

J ulia gasped when she opened the door to the greenhouse. It always looked lovely but tonight it had been transformed into a fairy wonderland.

She was still standing and admiring the dozens of colorful paper lanterns a few minutes later when the door opened.

Julia had convinced herself that her memory had exaggerated Mr. Barton's size.

It turned out he was actually larger than she remembered.

Or maybe that was the effect of his evening blacks. He'd looked impressive in his day suit, but there was no denying that a tailcoat was the perfect cut for such a magnificent physique. His shoulders filled the doorway so completely that he looked like a second, more impressive, door. His long, powerful legs were encased in narrow trousers that made him seem seven feet tall.

Even wearing three-inch evening heels Julia had to look up.

Although he was dressed in the most elegant evening garments she'd ever seen on a man, he did not look entirely civilized. That had to be the effect of the black leather mask. Julia knew he was wearing it to hide his scars but that was the least of what it managed to do.

His undamaged face was undeniably handsome, but the other side—the cold, featureless void—somehow enhanced his appeal. At least for her. Her attraction to such a dangerous man appalled her; she was no better than a moth courting a flame.

"Good evening, Miss Harlow." His mouth pulled up on the right side, forming a slight smile as he gestured to the paper lanterns. "Do you like it?"

"It is magical." She hesitated and added, "Thank you."

"I can't claim responsibility. It was my secretary's idea to make the garden both festive and easily navigable."

"He did a splendid job."

"I shall pass along your appreciation. You look exquisite," he said, his pale gaze moving over her in a way that quickened her breathing. "That dress might have been designed with you in mind."

Julia had received compliments all her life, but his words—accompanied by such an intense assessing look from his flame-blue eye—rendered her speechless.

She had dithered about whether to wear one of the dozens of new gowns in her dressing room or the one she'd arrived in.

While it had been difficult to resist the brand-new clothing, for tonight, at least, she had needed the strength she drew from her own garments. Besides, the Worth gown was exquisite, the sort of garment that would make any woman look astounding.

"Thank you," she said.

He offered his arm. "May I escort you into dinner?"

Julia laid her gloved hand on his forearm and they walked the short distance in silence to the dining room, which was magnificent illuminated by the massive chandelier.

Mr. Barton waved away the footman and seated her himself.

"Wine?" he asked.

"Please."

Once he'd taken his seat he nodded at the footman. "You may begin serving, Charles."

After the servant left Julia forced herself to say, "Thank you for agreeing to have dinner with me, Mr. Barton."

"The honor is all mine. I would have asked you sooner but didn't think you wanted my company."

"I'm sor—"

"That wasn't my way of asking for another apology, Miss Harlow. You are already forgiven."

"Thank you. Did you suffer much damage?"

"Very little."

"I am relieved to hear it."

A not entirely comfortable silence inserted itself, and he seemed disinclined to do anything but sip his wine.

"Do you live here?" she blurted.

"I do."

"But I never see anyone else—not even in the delightful greenhouse."

"No, this entire area is all yours."

"Do you have a private greenhouse, too?"

Humor glinted in his eye. "No, I'm afraid there is only one of those."

"And I have driven you from it."

"Not at all." He hesitated, and then said, "To be honest, I've rarely used it."

"That is a shame. It is quite the nicest I've ever seen. Your gardener is superlative."

"Indeed, he is."

Again, the silence stretched.

"This must be a very odd house."

His eyebrow lifted.

"I didn't mean that in a negative way," she hastened to assure him. "I just meant that my rooms seem to be in the middle of the house, which appears to be almost entirely contained by the rest of the house." She gave a small laugh. "I'm not really describing it very well."

"You are correct; it is… unusual. I designed it specifically to suit my needs."

She perked up at this interesting tidbit. "What needs?"

Again, he hesitated. "It serves both as my home and business office so I need to compartmentalize those two areas."

Julia wasn't sure what he meant, but three servants entered bearing trays just then, and there was no opportunity to pursue the matter.

Once everything had been set out Barton dismissed the servants and looked across the dozen dishes at her. "I thought we might enjoy dining more simply tonight."

Julia laughed. "Your notion of simple is interesting."

"What do you mean?"

"I've eaten better here than I have anywhere else in my life."

"I'm pleased to hear it. Although I'm surprised to hear Tommy Harlow keeps such a meager board. Back when I knew him, he enjoyed a good meal."

Julia suspected Nadine—who was thin to the point of emaciation—was responsible for her father's almost spartan habits, but that was hardly proper conversation. Instead, she said, "That must have been a long time ago."

"It was a lifetime ago—yours, to be precise. When I knew him, he was married to his first wife."

Julia lowered the spoonful of consommé she'd just lifted to her mouth. "You knew my mother?"

"I did, but not well. We all came from the same area—me, your mother, father, and of course your Uncle Brian."

"My father never talks about where he came from."

"What about your uncle?" he asked, his gaze almost intense. "Does he ever tell stories of his past?"

"My Uncle Brian? I haven't seen him for years—not since I was little. He left England not long after my mother died. I scarcely remember him as I was barely five at the time. He lives in Paris and must love it there because he never visits."

Julia ate in silence for a while, arguing with herself before once again setting aside her spoon. "Will you tell me what it was like growing up?"

He wiped his mouth with his linen and sat back in his chair. "What do you want to know?"

***

Malcolm knew he was a bastard for what he was about to tell her, but then what had Tommy Harlow ever done to deserve his protection?

"What do you want to know?" he asked.

The open delight on her face was more brilliant than a pyrotechnic display.

"Why is my father so ashamed of his past? Just because everyone was so poor?"

"The more successful some people are, the more they struggle to hide their roots. But it's not just poverty that your father is trying to forget."

Her forehead furrowed. "What do you mean?"

Malcolm looked across into her huge innocent blue eyes and felt like he was corrupting a toddler. "Are you sure you want to know what I mean, Miss Harlow?"

She scowled. "I wouldn't have asked if I didn't."

"Fair enough. Your father hasn't always been a legitimate businessman."

"Go on," she said, not looking especially surprised.

"Once upon a time we both worked for the same man—a criminal named Charles Greene."

"Doing what?"

"Whatever Greene wanted us to do." He watched as she absorbed his words and wondered what she was concluding.

She pressed her lips into a tight frown and nodded. "I think I can imagine what you mean."

Malcolm seriously doubted that, but he wasn't about to enlighten her on the specifics.

107

"In your father's defense"—he snorted—"well, and my own, too, I suppose, working for Greene was the only way to get out of the Dials other than a cheap pine box. Greene held out that rarest of rare offers to young men like us: opportunity."

"You worked together and yet you are enemies with my father?"

"Not back then. Back then I barely knew him. I knew your Uncle Brian much better."

"You were friends with my uncle?"

Malcolm hesitated, and then nodded. "Yes, we were friends."

She cocked her head. "Why do I feel as if there is something you aren't telling me?"

He couldn't help smiling at that. "There are a *lot* of things I'm not telling you, Miss Harlow."

For a moment she looked offended, but then she laughed. "I suppose that is true. So, you've kidnapped me for something my father has done recently, then?"

"I won't answer questions about that."

She flinched at his cold tone and Malcolm felt a surge of guilt for suppressing her naturally curious nature so abruptly, so he said, "To be honest, I only worked with your father for a short time before Greene lost control of his… organization. Half the people who worked for Greene shifted their allegiance to the man who took his place and the rest of us moved on to other things."

"I'm assuming when you say *lost control* you mean he died—or was killed, rather?"

Malcolm eyed her with respect; it wasn't what the average debutante would have said.

"Yes, a competitor killed him and took what he had. That was the way things worked in the Dials—probably still do. You see the government wants nothing to do with areas like that, so criminals step in and provide things the people need. Of course, those criminals are not altruistic so there is always a cost for those services. In any case, a man needs to be strong to hold that position. Greene grew lazy and placed too much faith in somebody young and hungry; somebody who eventually took what he had."

"And my father worked for the other man?"

Again, he hesitated, but then said, "He did."

Malcolm could see she was struggling to adjust to the thought of her father engaging in criminal activities and was glad he'd not told her the truth: that her father had betrayed Greene's trust and carved up his empire *with* Greene's successor.

Or maybe it was just hard for her to imagine her father—a man who'd become one of England's leading industrialists—working for anyone.

Either way, he was tired of talking about Tommy.

"It's my turn to ask some questions."

She narrowed her eyes at him. "The way you talked my first morning led me to believe you knew a great many things about me already."

Malcolm knew they were both thinking about the comment which had triggered the knife throwing.

"I actually know very little," he lied, for the second time in as many minutes.

She chewed her plush lower lip, her expression thoughtful. Malcolm suspected she was weighing answering his questions against her recent boredom and wasn't surprised when she capitulated to his request.

"Very well, what do you wish to know?"

The wicked things.

Instead, he said, "Tell me about life at your father's house in— where was it, again?" Not that he didn't know *exactly*.

"You want to know about life in Dorset?"

"Isn't that where you've lived since leaving school?"

"We spent a good deal of time there as we've been in mourning for almost two solid years." Her face briefly flexed into a frown.

"You don't like the country?"

"I *love* the country," she said, "Why do you ask?"

"Because of the way you said it."

"Oh. That's because I would much rather be at my father's other house, Brookfield, but…" She shrugged her shoulders.

Malcolm's antennae twitched at her answer. "Why is that?"

Her mouth twisted strangely. "I just like it better."

She was a terrible liar, but he decided not to probe.

"I enjoyed being in Dorset when it was hunting season. It was smashing," she added, her smile blinding.

"You like to hunt?"

"I love it."

"You feel you are ridding the country of vermin?"

She looked momentarily perplexed. "Oh, the foxes. Well, actually they are quite adorable—although they do lay waste to game birds—but I like the opportunity to run neck-or-nothing. *That* is what I crave about hunting."

"And you can't do that just anytime?"

"Not in our household." She saw his questioning look and explained. "My stepmother *despises* all things having to do with horses. Well, other than the ones pulling her carriage. She doesn't think it a fitting activity for a female. If not for the fact that *all* the best people hunt—and Basingstoke is especially mad for it—she would have forbidden me to ride at all."

"And your father? Does he feel the same way?"

"Papa hates hunting, too. Not because he thinks it is savage but"—she smothered a laugh and gave him a shy look.

"What?" he prodded.

"Papa has the world's *worst* seat and rode once with the local pack and was thrown off at the first coop." She chortled at this.

"Coop? Er, what do chicken coops have to do with fox hunting?"

Her eyes widened for an instant and then she collapsed in a fit of laughter.

Malcolm just drank in her pure, unadulterated joy like the obsessed fool he was.

***

"I'm sorry," Julia said when she could speak again, wiping the tears from her eyes. "I hope I didn't offend you by laughing, it's just that the idea of jumping hen houses was too amusing."

"So, what is a coop, then?"

"It is just wood braced over an area that might be too dangerous to jump. This particular section was something stupid my father erected—metal railing like the sort you'd find in town. He took it down after that hunt. Anyhow, he was so mortified that he's not been on a horse since." Julia speculatively eyed Mr. Barton's huge body.

"No," he said.

"No, what?"

"You were going to ask if I rode. I do not. I'm afraid that—like your father—it wasn't something one did when we were young. By the time I could afford a mount I valued an intact skull too much."

She laughed. "So, no riding, then. What *do* you do for entertainment, Mr. Barton?"

"I work."

"I meant for pleasure."

He hesitated so long she thought he wouldn't answer. "I have a gymnasium."

"It seems like I've heard that word, but I'm afraid I don't know what it means."

"You've probably heard about the public gymnasium built here in London a few years ago. It was built as part of a credo—Muscular Christianity—by the founders of the Young Men's Christian Association."

Julia laughed. "What is Muscular Christianity? It sounds rather— er, daunting."

"It is merely a movement embracing physical fitness."

"And you, er, practice that?"

"No. I just have a private gymnasium."

"I still don't understand what it is for."

"It is a room built to accommodate dumb bells, sparring bags, and other items that one uses to train one's body to be, er... well, stronger."

Julia couldn't help but look at his shoulders and chest—the only part of him visible above the table—and knew she'd be red-faced, yet again. "It seems to be working."

His lips parted as a surprised look flickered quickly across his face. He laughed, the sound low, masculine, and pleasing. "I'll take that as a compliment."

Julia suddenly felt uncomfortable meeting his direct blue gaze. "So, er," she babbled, "that is all you do? Work and spend time in your gymnasium? Do you read fiction? Play cards? Fence? Shoot guns?" Julia scrambled to think of other masculine pursuits, and then recalled her brother Richard's latest, disgusting hobby. "Taxidermy animals?"

His eye widened. "*What?*"

"You've not heard of it?"

He gave a faint shudder of revulsion. "I've not only heard of the disgusting hobby, I've seen the repulsive results. No, thank you very much, I am *not* a stuffer."

She laughed. "What about cards?"

"I used to play cards—a long, long time ago."

Julia latched onto that. "I adore playing all sorts of games." She pulled a wry face. "Perhaps not the sillier ones I play with my younger brothers, but I do love cards. Why did you stop?"

"I suppose I just became too busy with work."

She somehow suspected he used that excuse for a great many things. "Perhaps we might play after dinner one night?"

His brow furrowed. "You want to play cards with me?"

"Why do you sound so shocked? It is what people generally do in the evenings. Either that or go to parties or balls or"—she couldn't help laughing—"you should see your face!"

Almost immediately, she realized how he might have taken her words. "Oh, I didn't mean—"

"I know what you meant," he assured her.

She gave a relieved, nervous laugh. "You looked quite horrified. Do you hate socializing that much?"

"Yes."

He hadn't raised his voice, but his abrupt answer dampened the mood. Well, at least it dampened *her* mood.

"I'll have the servants set up a table for us to play tomorrow—after our meal," he said.

"Oh, lovely!"

"What do you like to play?"

"My favorite two-player game is cribbage, but we will need a board for that. Do you have one?"

He smiled "I suspect I know where I can locate one."

"Of course, you have an entire department store below! Have you played cribbage before?"

"It has been many years but I'm sure you can refresh my memory." His gaze settled on her and the air between them felt strangely heavy.

Why did his words sound so… suggestive?

Julia suddenly realized they'd both finished eating some time ago. "Oh dear, here I've been yammering at you when you must want your port."

He gave her a faint smirk. "I'm not especially keen on port and cigars after dinner."

She glanced at the clock; it wasn't even eleven yet.

While she was struggling for some way of asking if he'd like to continue their conversation, he said, "Would you like to retire to the library? I can ring for tea."

"Yes, that would be lovely," she said, pulling on her gloves and wishing she'd not sounded quite so *thrilled.* He must think she was a desperate little schoolgirl. Thank goodness he'd not heard her pitiful confession to Kemp, about being lonely.

He came to her end of the table and held out his arm, towering over her. "May I escort you, Miss Harlow?"

She glanced up into his pale eye and then couldn't look away.

"What happened?" The impolite question was out before she could stop it. "I'm sorry. I shouldn't have—"

"A fire," he said quietly, his expression unreadable.

"Is it—are you, er, does it still hurt?" she finally managed—not what she'd really wanted to ask, which was how much of him had been damaged.

"No, it was a long time ago. Fifteen years."

Julia had a dozen more questions, but she'd already overstepped dreadfully. So, instead, she said, "I wish you'd call me Julia."

He looked momentarily startled, but then a smile ghosted across his full lips. "I'd be honored. Please call me Malcolm."

Chapter 13

Mr. Barton joined Julia at breakfast the next morning, without her even having to ask. Indeed, he was there when she arrived.

He stood when she entered, dressed to perfection in what she assumed was his normal black attire.

"I hope you don't mind if I join you, Julia?"

She jolted; she'd forgotten they'd reverted to Christian names last night. Hearing him say her name in the bright light of day felt oddly… intimate. And had she imagined the slightly caressing way he'd pronounced it?

Julia saw he was waiting for a response. "It's kind of you to join me—especially given that I stabbed you at our last breakfast."

He barked a startled laugh. "I had the servants leave the knife out of your place setting—just as a precaution."

Julia glanced down at his words and then rolled her eyes when she saw the knife was right where it was supposed to be.

"Sorry, I couldn't resist," he teased when she looked up. He stood and moved toward the buffet.

"I will serve myself," Julia said hastily, recalling the last time she'd eaten breakfast and he'd loaded a plate for her.

He bowed. "As you wish. "

Julia felt the weight of his gaze on her back while she stood at the buffet and was glad that she'd worn the day dress that Kemp had just brought up from the store that morning, a peacock blue velvet with dark-raspberry trim. There were no tiresome ruffles, as Nadine would insist on, just the contrasting piping on the fitted bodice, tight sleeves, and the modish new style of bustle which Julia thought made her appear taller.

She'd been eating better than she had in years and suspected that she would not be close to fitting into the vile eighteen-inch waist wedding gown Nadine had chosen.

Julia couldn't bring herself to care.

Besides, if Mr. Barton—er, Malcolm—kept her captive long enough there would *be* no ceremony.

She found herself smiling at the thought of never having to see Sebastian's smug face again. Of never having to see his hateful grandmother or any of his other loathsome, superior relatives.

Or Nadine or Carl.

Perhaps Malcolm might just keep her forever? If she could only have Richard come and stay with her and was permitted to ride in the park a morning or two a week she might even want to stay. After all, what was there to dislike? She was permitted to eat, she spent her days painting and reading books she borrowed from the marvelous library and now she had the company of a mysterious, fascinating man.

She was still grinning at the thought when she turned away from the buffet.

And caught Malcolm staring.

He didn't look away, his frosty blue eye darker this morning.

Her face heated under his speculative, knowing stare—almost as if he knew what she had been thinking.

Foolishness.

***

Malcolm was an idiot to join her at meals—or anywhere else, for that matter.

Last night he'd not been able to resist sitting with her for an hour after dinner in the library. They'd chatted about nothing in particular and then played two games of chess with the antique ivory set he'd forgotten he owned. Neither of them was especially good, so they were well-matched and had ended the evening with one win each. Before taking her leave for the evening Julia had thrown down a gauntlet, demanding they have a tie-breaking game tonight.

Malcolm had been thrilled to agree.

As he looked at her now—no, as he *feasted* on her blushing, beautiful face—Malcolm couldn't recall meeting a more adorable, appealing young woman.

Were you ever that young, Sukey?

But his wife had been scarce these past few days.

Besides, he already knew the answer; Sukey wouldn't have been as naïve as Miss Harlow even when she'd been thirteen—which is how old she'd been when she'd lost her virginity. Or *got rid of the wretched thing*, as Sukey had once described the event.

Like Malcolm, she'd come from a part of the city where people had no childhood—or precious little—and she'd worked from the age of ten.

Malcolm hadn't associated with twenty-year-olds even when he'd been twenty. He'd had his first lover when he'd been fourteen—a bar wench who'd probably been in her middle twenties—and he'd always sought out experienced lovers, not virgins or girls his own age.

It struck him—along with a slight pang of guilt—that he didn't know how old Maisie was because he'd never asked. Indeed, he'd not asked the woman a single personal question—a fact for which she was probably grateful. But it stood to reason she was probably Julia's age since expensive whores didn't usually last much beyond five-and-twenty.

Malcolm studied the object of his obsession, who was blissfully unaware of his scrutiny as she savored a strawberry tart with a rapturous expression.

I used to wear that same look while sucking your cock, Mal.

Malcolm jolted at the far too erotic image his dead wife's voice summoned.

Ah, you're back now, are you?

Nah, darlin' I'm long gone. You're talkin' to yerself again, when you should be talkin' to the lovely young woman across from you.

I shouldn't even be sitting in the same room with the lovely young woman, not if I want to behave myself.

Why behave? Sukey whispered slyly.

Malcolm ignored the taunt, shook away his prurient thoughts, and poured himself more coffee.

"Kemp says you will soon have eight stores," Julia said.

"That is true."

"Do you ever visit them?"

"I try to go once a year."

In fact, if not for the delectable Miss Harlow's presence he'd be in Paris right then—and stay there until the New Year to avoid spending Christmas in London because he found the holidays an extremely depressing reminder of what he no longer had.

He kept that last part to himself.

Her pink tongue peeked out as she licked a bit of something—jam, perhaps—from her thumb, her actions as dainty and particular as a cat.

And also as arousing as hell.

Malcolm felt as though he'd tied his necktie too tight.

He cleared his throat and tried to think of something other than the erection in his trousers and how good her lips would look and feel wrapped around it.

"What about you, Julia." He savored her name every bit as much as she was savoring her pastry.

"What about me?"

"Will you travel when you are married?"

She gave a short, bitter laugh. "To Scotland or Wales, probably."

"Oh?"

"Basingstoke's family has estates in both places. Nice and remote."

Malcolm didn't like the sound of the other man's name on her tongue, not that he had any right to feel proprietary about her tongue or any other part of her body.

You could change all that, Mal…

Malcolm ignored Sukey and asked, "And that is where you would like to go—Scotland and Wales?'

"What I like will have no part of it."

Malcolm paused, opened his mouth, then closed it.

"What?" she asked, pausing in the act of slathering strawberry jam on a slice of bread. "You look like you wanted to say something."

He wanted to demand why the hell she would marry such a toffee-nosed stuffed shirt. Instead, he said, "Are you eager to marry Lord Basingstoke?"

"Eager?" She repeated, her expression uncharacteristically jaded. "I wouldn't use that word."

"What word would you use?"

She shrugged, looking ten years older than she'd looked a mere five minutes earlier. "It is an excellent union—for both of us."

"I know what he gets from marrying you," Malcolm persisted, seething at the thought of the bastard putting his hands on the woman across from him. "But what do you get?"

"Most people would say that *I* am the one benefitting."

"Most people are idiots."

She gave a delighted chortle. "I appreciate the sentiment, but it isn't quite fair to his lordship."

Malcolm merely raised his eyebrow.

"Oh come! He will be a duke one day. Do you know how many there are—dukes, that is?"

"It seems to have slipped my mind," Malcolm said dryly.

"Fewer than twenty-five. Just think," she went on, "that is twenty-five people out of"—she frowned. "How many people are there in Britain?"

"I take your point."

She poured more tea into her cup, doused it with milk, and then licked the tip of one of her fingers.

Malcolm bit back a groan; watching her eat was more erotic than the Dance of the Seven Veils.

"Besides," she said, utterly unaware of the havoc she was causing in his trousers. "One marriage is much like the next."

Ah, now there she was exposing her youth.

Tell her, Mal! Tell her how marriage to the right person can be heaven on earth, Sukey piped up.

And should I also tell her how losing that person can be hell? he shot back.

Sukey had no answer for that.

"What about you… Malcolm?"

"What about me… Julia?"

Her lips flexed into a smile at his teasing manner. "I haven't met a Mrs. Barton. Are you married?"

"She died."

Her pale cheeks darkened at his abrupt response. "I'm so sorry. I didn't mean to—"

"It was a long time ago." He hesitated, and then did something exceptional: he spoke the dreaded words aloud. "She died in the fire fifteen years ago."

She nodded, clearly wrestling with herself over something.

"Yes?" he prodded.

"You've never wanted to remarry, to share all this"—she made a gesture that encompassed everything around them—"with some fortunate lady?"

"Aren't these rather personal questions to ask a mere acquaintance?"

She huffed. "You asked me about marriage, first."

"Touché," he said.

"Besides," she cut him an arch look, "I wasn't aware there was a particular etiquette for how one should speak to their captor."

Malcolm grinned at her "I'll tell you what—I'll answer a question for a question."

"What does that mean?"

"That means you can ask me *anything* and I'll answer you. And I get to do the same."

"You'd even tell me what my father did to make you so angry?"

"Anything," he repeated, putting faith in his ability to judge character.

Her brow furrowed more deeply the longer she stared at him. "It occurs to me," she finally said, "that perhaps I don't wish to know."

Julia Harlow was no fool, but then he'd known that already. Nobody in their right mind should want to meddle in a dispute that was serious enough to kidnap somebody about.

"Do you have any children?" she asked.

Now *that* question did surprise him.

But it was a subject he wanted to discuss even less than the question about her father.

"No," he answered shortly. "My turn. Was it your choice to marry Basingstoke?"

She pondered his question before answering. "It isn't *not* my choice."

Malcolm tried to wrap his mind around her answer and failed. "I don't take your meaning."

"If you are asking me if I'm in love with him, the answer is no. In fact, I don't even like him—"

Malcolm snorted.

"*However,*" she said, giving him a quelling look, "he will one day be a duke."

Malcolm snorted again. "One of only twenty-five."

"Scoff all you like, but you are a man of the world. You *know* what position in society I will enjoy as his duchess."

Malcolm could have told her about the only position that interested him when it came to her, but it would be like taunting a kitten.

"So, you are marrying him for his status, then?" He cocked his head. "Why do I not believe you? And remember you vowed to tell the truth."

Rather than point out that she had already answered his question, she absently pulled apart a piece of toast, considering his question.

Malcolm wasn't surprised; most people loved answering questions about themselves. Indeed, most people liked to talk about themselves, full stop.

"I made a bargain with my father," she admitted.

"What sort of bargain?"

She worried her lip, visibly conflicted. "I don't want—I'm sorry, but I can't talk about it."

Malcolm stared at her, transfixed. What in the *world* could she value so much that she'd bargain her life away to a man she admitted she didn't like?

Tell me, he silently willed her.

Suddenly, she looked up from her shredded toast, her expression accusatory. "I already answered your question—more than one question, in fact. It's *my* turn to ask a question."

"No, I'll only answer one per meal."

Her jaw dropped. "But that's not fair—you didn't tell me that and I've answered a heap of them!"

"We've discussed the issue of fairness before, Julia."

"Oh, was that a discussion? Because what I recall was more of a royal proclamation or a Papal bull."

Malcolm threw back his head and laughed. When he looked at her, he saw that she was startled. "What? Your abductor isn't allowed to laugh?"

"Of course you are, I just didn't—" she broke off and shrugged.

"You just didn't what?"

Her eyes narrowed and she gave him a quick, sly, smile. "If you want to know what I was going to say, you can ask me at our next meal."

Malcolm grinned; the expression so rare it hurt his face.

And judging by her expression, it was just as shocking as his laughter had been.

He tossed aside his napkin and stood; it was time to leave when he started laughing and grinning.

"It has been a pleasure." He bowed and then turned to go.

"Er, M-Malcolm?"

He turned back. "Yes… Julia?"

She swallowed, every emotion she was feeling—embarrassment, diffidence, nervousness, to name a few—flitting across her lovely face. "W-Will you be at dinner?"

"Yes, I will."

She *glowed*. There was no other word for it. And Malcolm was responsible for her glowing.

"Good. Remember that you promised to me a third game of chess *and* cribbage afterward."

Once again, he smiled like a fool. "I'm looking forward to it."

All the way from the dining room to his office Malcolm thought about the mysterious bargain Julia had made with her father to marry Basingstoke.

A bargain she didn't want to talk about.

What could Harlow give her to make her marry a man she clearly loathed?

Why do you care? Do you think that you might be able to offer her the same bargain and save her from a loveless marriage? a snide voice—not Sukey's—mocked.

He didn't think any such thing. He was just curious.

Insanely curious.

When he reached his office, he sat and stared at the second lever on the glossy black box on his desk, pondering what he was about to do: pry into her life just a little bit more.

What can it matter after everything else you've pried into?

He ignored the taunting and toggled the second lever.

The door to his study opened barely a minute later and Butkins hovered on the threshold. "You need me, sir?"

"Get me Joe Bacon. Tell him there is something I want him to look into—immediately."

Chapter 14

In the days that followed, Malcolm joined Julia for dinner every day and breakfast most days.

And every evening they played cribbage, the occasional game of chess, and talked about everything from the recent police strike to the Springwell Pit disaster—where eight coal miners had fallen to their death—to the meteorite that had struck ground near Banbury.

Some nights they spent several hours talking, but—after that first breakfast—they never spoke about themselves or why Julia was there.

Julia couldn't help feeling that neither of them wanted to disturb the fragile, and enjoyable, peace that grew between them as the first week passed in a blur.

For her part, Julia found him more fascinating with each hour that passed. She knew, instinctively, that personal questions would only make him close up tight, like an oyster that guarded its pearl.

But as he became less formal and more comfortable in her presence, he also dropped tantalizing tidbits of information about himself and his life. Indeed, by the seventh night they were conversing with the relaxed ease of friends.

You're dreaming, Julia. A clever, driven man like Malcolm Barton doesn't make friends with chits who are scarcely out of the schoolroom.

Then why is he spending all this time with me?

Boredom. Pity. A sense of obligation as he is the one who abducted you. Take your pick. Any or all those things or a dozen more reasons you can't know.

Julia refused to allow the hectoring voice to dim her pleasure in what was becoming not just a tolerable stay, but a delightful one.

What kind of idiot revels in the company of her captor?

"My kind!" she snapped, and then hastily looked around to assure that nobody was near enough to hear her talking to herself.

Fortunately, she was alone, working on a painting from one of the sketches she'd made a few days earlier—a sketch she didn't want anyone else to see.

Indeed, the whole reason she was painting in her sitting room—as opposed to her favorite location in the greenhouse—was because her subject was Malcolm Barton.

He hesitated, and then said, "Mr. Barton designed it specifically to suit his needs."

There was that word again: *needs.*

"What needs?"

Mr. Butkins's frank gaze shuttered quickly. "Er, you'd have to ask him, miss. He's an extremely private man."

"I know that. Everyone knows he's a recluse. And he was burned in a fire."

Again, he hesitated.

"He told me so."

"He did?"

"Why do you sound so surprised? Is it a secret?"

"No, but it isn't something he talks about."

Warmth bloomed in her belly at the thought that he'd talked about it with her.

You hardly left him a choice, did you?

She ignored the dig.

"How much of his body was burned?"

He gave a rather harassed grimace. "Er, I couldn't say."

"Couldn't or won't?"

"Uhm—"

"What does he look like beneath his mask?"

Butkins's jaw sagged.

"Is my curiosity so hard to understand?" She knew she was being rude by firing questions at him so rapidly, but it was an excellent way to put a person off balance. And when people were off balance they were far more likely to let the truth slip.

"Well, no, I suppose. But I have never seen Mr. Barton without his mask."

"Never?"

Butkins shook his head.

"Have you worked for him long?"

"A little over twelve years."

"Twelve years! And you've never seen him?"

"He is extremely private," he said again.

Julia thought it sounded like something more than that, but she let the subject drop. "Will you show me the rest of the house?"

He gave her such an agonized look she almost felt guilty. Almost. "I *can't*, Miss Harlow."

"Oh, come, how dangerous can it be? I'm not asking you to allow me into Mr. Barton's gunroom or his—his bedchamber, just the other rooms."

He blushed at the word *bedchamber* and she decided that he reminded her a bit of Solomon—so shy and timid and proper. He was exactly the sort of man she could bend to her will without much effort.

"He doesn't have a gunroom," he finally admitted.

Julia laughed. "Oh no! You've answered a question."

He smiled.

"What about the tour?" she persisted.

"I would have to ask Mr. Barton."

That was a *no*, then.

"When will you ask him?"

He laughed, a startled blurt of a laugh that seemed to surprise him more than it did her. "You are very good at getting what you want, aren't you, Miss Harlow?"

She gave him a smile she knew men liked: innocent with a dash of sauce, as Nanny Potter used to say. "What can it hurt to ask?" she said in a wheedling tone. "It's not like I'll do anything bad—like try to escape. I'll behave."

"Yes, after stabbing my employer you've been a model captive," he retorted.

Julia gave a gurgle of laughter and his eyes widened, as if she'd just done something shocking.

"Ah, here is Kemp," Julia said, spying the older woman over Mr. Butkins's shoulder.

Mr. Butkins whipped around, his expression guilty. "Oh! Mrs. Kemp. I was just telling Miss Harlow that Mr. Barton wouldn't be able to come to dinner tonight."

Kemp lifted her eyebrows. "That was kind of you."

"Mr. Butkins has graciously agreed to have dinner with me, Kemp."

Kemp's eyebrows crept even higher.

"But not if you think it improper, Mrs. Kemp," Butkins hastened to say.

"Of course she doesn't think it improper," Julia said, taking Mr. Butkins by the arm and gently moving him out of the open doorway so the maid could enter. "Do you, Kemp?"

The older woman gave Julia a stern, narrow-eyed look—as if wondering what she was up to—but finally said, "No, I don't imagine Mr. Barton would mind."

"There, you see?" Julia assured him. "If Kemp says it is fine, then there is nothing to worry about. Do you play cribbage or piquet, Mr. Butkins?"

"Erm—" his eyes darted frantically between Julia and Kemp, making him resemble an animal caught in a snare.

It was Kemp who came to his rescue.

"You play whist, don't you, Mr. Butkins?"

"Oooh, yes! I adore whist," Julia said before the poor man could answer. "Kemp and I were just discussing it and she said Mr. Norris will play sometime, too. Please say you play because we *desperately* need a fourth."

Butkins blinked under her assault and nodded. "Er, yes, Miss, I do play." He looked exceedingly guilty about the admission.

Well, some people thought cards were a frivolous pastime.

"Oh, how wonderful! Do join us! Playing pairs will be so much more fun than widow whist. We can play tonight after dinner, since Mr. Barton will not be here."

Mr. Butkins cut Kemp an uneasy glance. "Er…"

"I'll check with Mr. Norris," Kemp said, once again coming to his rescue. "But I shouldn't think that will be a problem."

Julia clapped her hands, genuinely enthused at the thought of getting Malcolm's three upper servants in the same room and picking their brains about their exceedingly private master.

Butkins's cheeks pinkened with pleasure. "If Kemp thinks it is unexceptionable then I would be delighted.

***

Although Julia enjoyed her dinner with Mr. Butkins and the two rubbers of whist with him, Norris, and Kemp, her hopes of prying information out of them had rapidly deflated.

All three servants were excessively polite but had been implacable when it came to answering questions about their employer.

After the first quarter of an hour—and meeting brick wall after brick wall—Julia had given up on her offensive and, instead, had greatly enjoyed the evening of cards with three excellent players.

They'd just begun another game when a footman entered the library. "Mr. Barton is looking for you, Mr. Butkins."

The secretary leapt up from his chair. "My apologies, Miss Harlow, but duty calls."

She smiled up at him. "Thank you so much for your company this evening."

"The pleasure was mine."

"I'd better be off as well," Mr. Norris said, giving her a graceful bow. "It was indeed a pleasure to partner with you Miss Harlow."

Julia chuckled at his kind lie; she was a middling player at best while the valet was one of the best she'd ever played with. "Perhaps Kemp and Mr. Butkins will give us the opportunity to regain some of our honor."

"I look forward to it." Norris—who was a handsome older man with salt-and-pepper hair—gave her a pleased smile and departed, leaving Julia and Kemp.

"Are you ready for bed, miss? Or might I see to a few matters before coming to undress you?" the maid asked after they'd put away the cards.

"I finished my book so I'm going to look for another. I shan't take longer than half an hour."

"Very good, miss."

"And Kemp," she said, stopping the other woman before she could leave. "Thank you *so* much for organizing our whist game."

Kemp's cheeks flushed and she dropped a quick curtsey and then sped from the room, clearly uncomfortable with gratitude.

Julia took a moment to enjoy the silence in the vast room. She would never have imagined finding a library this ancient looking in such a modern building. It was a huge room with high, arching windows covered in heavy blood red drapes. Other than the greenhouse, it was the only part of the building she'd been in that had windows to the outside world.

Although she'd teased poor John earlier—that was Mr. Butkins's name, although he'd refused to call her Julia—about taking her on a tour of Malcolm's strange house, she really was curious about the layout.

John would never consent to give her a tour, but Malcolm might. If she worked on him…

Smiling to herself at the thought, she toed off her evening shoes and stretched her liberated toes with a sigh.

There, now she was comfortable and ready to browse.

Unlike her father's libraries—which held mostly self-improving or educational tomes—here there were hundreds and hundreds of novels, many of which looked as though they'd never been opened.

"Mr. Barton has me choose them for him," Kemp had explained when Julia had asked about the new books.

"Doesn't he read them?"

"On occasion, but I don't think he has much time for fiction."

Julia *adored* novels, from scandalous gothic romances to more serious works of literature: she loved them all.

The books appeared to be organized by publication date rather than subject or author, and so she pulled a good many off the shelves and read the first page or so before she found one that piqued her interest, titled *Little Women*

The frontispiece was an illustration of a mother and four girls—Jo, Beth, Meg, and Amy—so she doubted it was naughty, like the last book she'd read, *The Wickedness of Count Ugolino*.

Julia flushed just recalling that book. For some reason, she'd imagined the dastardly, yet irresistible, count as looking exactly like Malcolm. Such imaginings had led to several sessions with her hand between her thighs.

This new book looked more wholesome. Maybe it would simply send her into a dreamless sleep, rather than stoking fantasies about her deliciously mysterious host.

I think you mean captor, her boring inner voice scolded.

Julia rolled her eyes, scooped up her shoes, and then padded her way back to her chambers. At this time of night, she'd be fine in her stocking feet as there was never anyone around.

She couldn't help wondering where Malcolm had gone tonight. Did he have a mistress—a lover—that he visited?

Julia found that she disliked that thought *exceedingly*

Why? Do you think he likes silly little girls.

She was busy bickering with herself when she rounded the corner to her hallway and almost collided with the very man obsessing her thoughts.

Julia stopped and gawked. Why, he appeared to be stepping into the wall itself!

Her mind spun as her brain struggled to put together what she was seeing: It was another entrance. Right *next* to her chambers.

As she watched, the door—or wall panel, rather—swung silently shut behind him, leaving a regular-looking section of wall in its place.

Julia stared, frozen.

Why in the world was there a secret door right beside her chambers?

And what was Malcolm doing using that doorway at one o'clock in the morning?

Chapter 15

hat are you waiting for, Julia? You'll never get a better time than right now to investigate!

Julia glanced at the clock—it was just after two—and chewed her lip, trying to keep her willful mind in check.

Don't do it, Julia, her wiser angel begged. *It's not right. If Malcolm wanted you to know about the doorway and whatever it leads to then he would have told you.*

If you don't look now, you'll always wonder what was behind that panel. the devil prodded, far louder.

Julia groaned, tossing and turning beneath the covers.

You know you're going to do it so you might as well get on with it.

This is a terrible idea, Julia. You should not—

"Shut up!" Julia hissed at the voices. She shoved back the blankets and slipped out of bed.

Kemp had finished undressing her about three quarters of an hour ago and Julia had told the older woman that she was going right to sleep and wouldn't be reading.

But just in case Kemp peeked inside later to check on her, Julia arranged some clothing and pillows beneath the blankets to make it look as if she were asleep, and then she turned off all the lights—the ones in the cornicing were controlled by some switch she'd not found—and then opened the door a crack and peered out.

Everything was quiet.

She stepped out and examined the wall panel she'd seen Malcolm use. On first glance it looked exactly like the one on the other side of her door.

It was composed of eight smaller panels, so Julia pressed on them, one at a time.

Nothing happened until she reached the very top left panel, which she had to stand on her toes to push.

The panel sank in an inch and then popped open, making a smooth *snick*.

Julia had to stand back a few feet in order to see what was beneath the panel: a bronze knob that looked like a miniature doorhandle.

She stood on her tiptoes and fumbled for the handle before she could get enough of a grip to turn it.

But it didn't turn.

So she pushed it.

Nothing happened.

But when she pulled it, the panel moved too, opening without a sound. Julia released the nob and peered around the door.

It was a narrow hallway—far smaller than the hall she stood in.

Julia felt strangely lightheaded and realized she'd been holding her breath. She filled her lungs and then stepped inside, studying the panel for a handle that would open the door from the inside.

Yes, there it was, in the same place as it was outside.

Satisfied that she could get out when she needed to, she turned and examined the corridor. It was plain and quite narrow—like the servant hallways in her father's country house—and there were recessed lights like those in her chambers, albeit much dimmer.

Is that what this was? Just a servant corridor, built to ensure the master and mistress weren't disturbed by having to *see* the dozens of people who waited on them?

Just leave… now.

Julia ignored the voice.

She'd only walked a few feet when she saw something on the righthand wall that robbed her of breath: it was a window. And it looked right into her room!

Her brain scrambled to comprehend what she was seeing, but she knew it could only be one thing: the unusually large gold-framed mirror across from her bed was actually some sort of window.

Julia touched it; it was cool and smooth just like glass.

Her mind, already reeling drunkenly, veered down another path: Were *all* mirrors like this—so you could see through them from one direction and they gave a reflection on the other? It sounded like a stupid question, but then she'd never seen the back of a mirror before.

Whether it was purposeful, or not, Malcolm would have seen into her room earlier tonight.

Was that the first time?

As she stared at the bed another thought struck her like the blow from a hammer: Did he *watch* her? Did the servants?

She shivered at the thought of his glacial blue gaze on her, shock mingling with something else—something far too familiar: titillation.

You're a whore! Just like your mother.

Her father's voice was so loud that Julia stupidly spun around. He wasn't there, of course, but another window—this one dark—was on the wall right behind her.

Julia pressed her face close to it and squinted, but she couldn't see anything.

What *was* all this?

Go back to your room. You can confront him in the morning.

No. Not until she explored a bit.

Julia cautiously made her way down the corridor, which was bisected by another hallway. She could go left or right.

She paused, trying to visualize the layout. To the right, she was pretty sure, would be her sitting room, bathroom, dressing room.

She turned right.

Only a smallish mirror looked into her sitting room, but she could see every part of the room through it.

With her heart thumping loudly enough that she could feel her pulse beating against the thin skin of her throat she moved slowly toward the next mirror, the one that would look into her bathing chamber.

Julia stopped in front of the floor to ceiling mirror across from her tub.

"Oh Lord." She pressed a hand against her mouth. You could see the sink, the showerbath, and the huge bathtub.

Thank *God* you couldn't see the commode, which was in a separate room.

A room with no mirrors.

Julia hurried down the corridors, not paying attention to where she was or where she'd been; there were windows—or mirrors—in every room she passed.

There was one in the room where the piano sat, one into the dining room off the lovely greenhouse—the huge mirror over the buffet—and several into empty bedchambers, and others looking into rooms she had never seen.

The hallways seemed to go on forever, twisting and turning until she was lost.

It was almost like a second house inside the first.

Thus far, every room had been either unoccupied or dark. Where were Malcolm's rooms? Or were there no windows into *his* chambers. After all, it was his house, would he put these strange mirrors in his own rooms?

Julia was still pondering the matter when she turned down another corridor, this one slightly brighter than the rest.

Julia eased up to a window that was glowing faintly. It was smallish—like a looking glass that might hang beside a door.

She looked through it, gasped, and then stepped back.

It was Malcolm, and he was sitting at a huge desk, looking at papers.

Julia hesitated, and then sidled closer to look.

It was clearly his study. He had taken off his coat but still wore his mask and gloves.

She was looking at him from the left side, his damaged side, so all she saw was the black leather profile.

The desk surface was covered with neat stacks of paper and his hand flew over a document as he added comments of some sort and then wrote something at the bottom with a flourish—a signature, perhaps. He turned over the page without pausing and went on to the next. And the next, until the pile was finished and then he moved it aside and pulled another pile in front of him.

Julia could watch him for hours. He radiated pure concentration, moving through the documents like some sort of automaton. Never had she seen anyone who looked so focused. Or alone. Who looked so—

Suddenly, he put his pen in the stand and glanced down toward his lap before rolling his chair back and back and—

Julia gasped and slapped a hand over her mouth; his trousers were open and his *huge* erect penis was jutting up from his lap.

And there was a hand on his thigh.

He rolled out a bit more and a woman emerged.

Good God! He had a woman under his desk!

Julia gawked, riveted, as one of his huge leather clad hands came to rest on the side of her face, lightly stroking her as she shuffled closer on her knees between his spread thighs. He reached for his erection with his other hand and then aimed it toward her, like a club.

Without hesitation the woman leaned forward.

Julia knew what she was doing because she'd once watched one of their housemaids—Cathy—do the very same thing to one of their grooms, a handsome young man named Kenneth.

Just like Kenneth had done, Malcolm cupped the woman's blond head and pulled her down.

Unlike Cathy—who'd laughingly slapped Kenneth's hands and told him to hold his horses—this woman's head went down and down and down.

"Oh my goodness," Julia whispered as the woman's head continued to sink until she must have come to rest in the trouser material at Malcolm's groin, because—unlike Kenneth, who'd stripped off his clothing—Malcolm was still fully clothed, his erection jutting out from his trouser placket.

Instead of pulling off again, the woman *stayed* where she was, Malcolm stroking her face and hair with one hand.

How could that even be possible? Wasn't she choking? Didn't that *hurt?*

It was positively obscene.

That might be so, but the thumping in her sex—from her swollen lower lips to her womb—told her that her body felt otherwise.

Finally, when Julia had begun to worry for the other woman's safety, she knelt up higher and lifted off him, but not all the way, her lips wrapped around Malcolm's monstrous shaft, her face flushed and sweaty.

Malcolm nodded and said something to her.

Was he saying nasty things like Carl did? It shamed her to admit that she'd enjoyed Carl's filthy comments almost as much as the spankings.

Julia ground a hand over her mound, unable to look away as Malcolm placed a second hand on the woman's head, his hand flexing as he held her head immobile, his hips lifting from the chair as he pushed the fat mushroom tip deeper and then pulled almost all the way, pulsing shallowly, giving her just the crown for a time.

He gradually thrust himself deeper and forced her to take more, his powerful chest rising and falling faster as he flexed his hips.

His big hands seemed to engulf the woman's head, pulling her down and filling her with a penis that looked easily twice as big as Solomon's.

His entire body began to jerk, his hips viciously pumping into her now, his hands caging her skull.

The woman's body was tense, her posture submissive. Julia didn't know how she was breathing, he was holding her so cruelly, his movements a simulation of an act she had experienced with two men, but never for even a fraction so long as this.

Suddenly, he thrust hard enough to lift his buttocks off the chair. He held her still while his body jerked, each spasm slightly less intense than the last, until he sagged into the chair, his hands sliding from her head.

Julia recalled the same reaction happened when she gave herself pleasure, the sensation similar to being squeezed in a big fist while her inner muscles contracted and a slick wetness coated her thighs.

That is what had happened; he'd ejaculated into the woman's mouth.

"Oh God," she whispered in a tremulous voice.

And then, as if he could hear her, he turned in her direction.

Julia spun around and ran.

Chapter 16

Julia tossed and turned in her bed for hours until she finally gave in to her body's lustful demands and worked an orgasm from her slick, swollen sex. She used the shocking images from the secret corridor and it took barely a minute before she climaxed.

Instead of making her sleepy, as such activities usually did, she laid awake for hours, her mind racing in twenty directions at once.

Not until the early hours of the morning did she finally sleep, waking far too late to join Malcolm for breakfast. That was probably just as well because Julia didn't know how she was going to face him again without blurting everything out. Or just staring at him and blushing.

Julia was no novice when it came to sexual activity, but what she'd witnessed last night had been in a far different league than all the playing she'd done with Lily. As for the few times she'd been with men? Well, those were laughable experiences compared to what Malcolm had done with—or to, rather—that woman.

She wasn't a fool, either. The woman had looked so much like her that she'd been taken aback by the resemblance.

Why? Who was she? *What* was she to him?

More importantly, will you venture down that corridor again? the taunting voice asked.

Julia couldn't think about that right now; she needed to get through the day, first.

Besides, she'd had the strangest feeling he'd seen her and known she was there—that he'd *looked* directly at her.

The feeling was so strong that all day long, as Julia read and painted and played the piano, at the back of her mind there lurked the fear that Malcolm would summon her and confront her.

But all that happened that afternoon was Mrs. Kemp delivered a new dress to her.

"I didn't ask for anything," Julia said.

"Mr. Barton sent this." She handed Julia a small envelope with the word *Julia* scrawled in an elegant script across the front.

Julia turned away to read it, her fingers fumbling as she opened the envelope. Inside was a plain card, *This color was made for you. I look forward to seeing you in it. Your servant, Malcolm Barton.*

Julia swallowed convulsively, crushing the card in her hand before she turned to the huge glossy black and gold Barton's Emporium box. Her hand shook s she lifted the lid and peeled back layers of tissue.

Julia sucked in a breath. "Oh, my goodness."

"That is a lovely color for you," Kemp said.

Julia reached out to stroke the deep red—an odd shade that was almost the color of a ripe tomato. "My stepmother says I can't wear red." She petted the rich velvet like it was an animal.

Kemp leaned back and gave her a contemplative look, her gaze lingering on her hair. "No, in general I'd say not." She glanced at the gown again. "But this isn't really *red*. It's…" she shook her head. "I don't know what shade I'd call it, but it's certainly unusual. See how it flatters your hand."

Indeed, Julia's skin looked warmer—a creamy white rather than pasty—against the luxurious material.

"And he sent this." Kemp lifted a black velvet box and opened the lid.

Julia gasped and again her fingers moved closer to touch and stroke. But she pulled back just shy of the satiny orbs. "These are black pearls, aren't they?"

"I believe so."

Julia dropped her hand, almost afraid to touch the necklace. "They must cost a *fortune*."

The maid shrugged. "Mr. Barton is an extremely wealthy man."

"I can't accept such expensive gifts."

"You will offend him if you do not."

Julia chewed her lip. "Why is he giving me these things?"

Kemp's narrow, pale face flushed slightly. "He means no insult; it is his nature to be generous."

"With gifts," Julia said. Because he certainly wasn't generous with information, or even with his attention. At least not with her.

And that was what she really wanted from the man. Especially after last night…

Kemp held her gaze for a long moment and Julia flushed at the understanding in the older woman's eyes, as if Kemp could see how infatuated she'd become with her captor.

"I don't believe he wishes to place you under an obligation to him, Miss Julia."

Unfortunately, Julia didn't think he did, either.

"Shall I run you a bath as you didn't have one this morning?"

Julia cut a quick look to the large mirror in her chamber. Was Malcolm in that corridor right now, watching as she opened his gift? Would he watch her take a bath?

"Miss Julia?"

She looked into Kemp's questioning gaze before brazenly turning to the mirror. Was he behind that mirror? Did she care?

You care; you _want_ him to watch you.

Julia couldn't argue with the accusation. Thinking of Malcolm watching her was causing such a riot of reactions in her body that her thighs were damp with wicked desire.

"Yes, please run me a bath."

***

Malcolm had just topped up his wineglass when Julia entered the room.

He'd heard the term *weak in the knees* but had never experienced the condition before.

He'd known the gown would suit her, but the way it clung to her curves and made her skin glow—as if she were a human pearl—made the air hot and hard to breathe.

She hesitated near the door, a fetching blush on her cheeks as she absorbed the changes to the dining room.

Malcolm was tired of dining so far away from her, so he'd had most of the table leaves removed, creating a far more intimate table for two. The chandelier had been lighted and cast a more romantic glow than gas light.

Sitting so close to her would mean that *she* could see him, too, and that was unfortunate. But, for once, Malcolm had decided that he'd rather see her more clearly than hide himself.

"Good evening, Julia." He pulled out her chair.

"Good evening, Malcolm." She sat, carefully adjusting the gown's bustle, her slender hands and forearms sheathed in the pearl kid leather gloves he'd selected to go with the gown.

Malcolm couldn't resist stealing a glance at where the snug leather hugged the unspeakably tender skin of her upper arm. Truly, that sensitive, sweet bit of skin had to be one of the most sensual spots on a woman's body. If she were his, he would—

She is not mine, he sternly reminded himself.

Julia smiled warmly at James, his handsome young footman, as he poured her a glass of wine and Malcolm struggled with the urge to throw the unwitting servant bodily out of the room.

He was greedy and wanted all her smiles for himself.

The knowledge left him chilled and uneasy.

Once James left the room, she met Malcolm's gaze. "Thank you for the gown. It is lovely."

"Thank you for wearing it."

"I have never seen a color like it."

"The shade is the result of a new dye process that yields far more brilliant hues. It suits you."

She dropped her gaze and played with the stem of her glass. "My stepmother says women with my coloring shouldn't wear red." She sat up a little straighter and met his gaze. "She said it makes me look like a p-p-prostitute."

Malcolm couldn't help smiling, relieved when she didn't cringe away from the twisted, crooked expression. "In general, I would agree that bold shades overwhelm fair-haired women, but this color has depth and warm undertones that make it less harsh."

"Warm, yes, that is the perfect word. I didn't realize colors could look so similar and yet have such profound differences in shades." She pulled a wry face. "I suspect my lack of understanding when it comes to color is clear in the paintings I've done."

"What do you paint?" He'd known that she ordered watercolors from the store because he looked at all her requests.

"Just still lifes from the greenhouse. I cannot capture people—I've not the skill."

"I would like to see them."

The flush on her cheeks was lovely to behold. "Oh. Well. I'm not sure—er, perhaps."

They turned to watch as four footmen entered, each bearing large platters.

"Thank you," he said to James several minutes later, once the food had been laid out. "I will ring if we need anything."

Malcolm uncovered a tureen, the mingled aroma of oysters, butter, and heavy cream teasing his nostrils. "Oyster bisque." He lifted the lid on a second tureen. "Or consommé."

"The oyster bisque looks delicious, but I really shouldn't."

"Whyever not?"

This time her father's accusation lacked any teeth.

Instead of running away in shame—as she should—Julia used her sweaty palm to clear the film that was obstructing her view, desperately wishing she were closer or the room brighter, or both.

Once the other woman sat all the way down, she wiggled her hips slightly.

That tiny movement, more than anything, made Julia's slick thighs tense and quiver, her inner muscles clenching with the need to be filled and stretched, raw, consuming *want* clawing at her so viciously that she trembled with need.

Malcolm slid his hands around the woman's slender shoulders and waist, urging her back, until she reclined in his arms.

And then he lowered his head over her chest.

Although she couldn't see it, Julia knew he would be touching her breasts with his mouth.

Her own nipples tightened painfully as she recalled the delicious sensation of Lily's lips and tongue on her breasts while her slender, skilled fingers thrust into Julia's body, her slippery thumb caressing and flicking the bundle of nerves that yielded so much pleasure.

A low grunt of frustrated desire slipped from between her parted lips and Julia's eyes popped open and she clapped a hand over her mouth, whirling away from the mirror and pressing her back against the wall, too afraid to even breathe.

Had he heard her?

She swallowed convulsively, her body frozen with indecision: should she run, or wait?

Go on! Take another look.

Julia was moving before her brain had registered her decision.

Disappointment vied with arousal at the view that met her gaze. Malcolm wasn't glaring at her accusingly—or looking her way, at all— instead, he was captivated by the woman in his arms.

As Julia watched and yearned, the two lovers began to move.

***

Malcolm's balls were so bloody full and hard that he'd been in agony while Maisie sucked him, her divinely skilled mouth, tongue, and throat bringing him to the edge of climax over and over again.

Was it wrong of him to be imagining another woman taking his cock into her tight body?

Probably.

Is that what he liked—small blond women?

Foolish hope leapt inside her.

Why would he want a gauche, unsophisticated woman—a girl, really—like you when he could have somebody who clearly knew what she was doing?

The thought was painful, probably because it was true. He didn't need Julia because he already had somebody.

Julia studied him harder than she'd ever looked at any picture, searching for any emotion or some reaction on his stark, unreadable face.

The changes in him were minute: a slight tightening of his jaw, his hands curling on the arms of the chair, and the increasing rising and falling of his broad chest.

She saw a flash of white teeth as his lips pulled back into a half-snarl right before he reached out for the woman. Instead of fisting her hair as he'd done last night, he set a hand on her shoulder and his lips moved.

The woman slowly pulled away from him and then gracefully rose to her feet. With a graceful shrug of her shoulders her robe slid to the floor and she stood before Malcolm naked, her back to Julia.

Julia had seen naked women—she'd done more than just *see* them with Lily—but this was a mature woman, not a schoolgirl, her figure ripe and voluptuous, her waist tiny without any corset to shape her.

Julia saw Malcolm's arm move, as if he were taking something from his coat, and he handed her a black scarf.

The woman took it from his hand and, without hesitating, tied it over her eyes.

She struggled to make sense of what she was seeing. Why would Malcolm have her cover her eyes? Did the woman want that? Did he?

Julia pushed the questions away when the woman knelt on the chair, straddling his thighs.

Malcolm's black-gloved hands spanned her waist, steadying her when she knelt up high, his thick shaft jutting out between her bare thighs.

Julia bit her lip hard at the erotic view.

The woman slid her small hand around his arousal and deftly positioned him before lowering herself slowly, his ruddy length disappearing into her body inch by inch.

Julia's nose pressed hard against the glass, her hot breath creating a dense fog that reminded her of what she was doing: spying.

You're a whore, just like your mother!

She laughed. "Very well. You've convinced me—I'll take the bisque, please."

He served them both and watched from beneath lowered lashes as she took a dainty sip and then sighed with a sensual contentment that guaranteed Maisie would be earning her keep later tonight.

"Why shouldn't you have oyster bisque?" he repeated.

"I've been eating far too much."

Malcolm thought back to the small portions he'd seen on her plate at their last breakfast. "What do you eat at home?"

"My usual meal consists of dry toast, a thin slice of ham, a bit of potato, and as much water as I care to consume."

He lowered his spoon without tasting the soup. "But … *why?*"

"My stepmother says I am fat." Her lips flexed into a wry smile.

Malcolm struggled to suppress the sudden blast of fury he felt toward an idiotic woman he'd never even met.

Once he'd regained control of his temper he said, "Do *you* think you are fat?"

"I'm not as thin as she is, but… no, I think her expectations are unreasonable. She has always been rigid about slimming me, but she is frantic lately, worried that I shan't fit into my wedding gown."

Malcolm's anger at Nadine Harlow boiled over into genuine loathing. What sort of vile bitch would starve a person under their care?

As for Tommy, what sort of father would allow it?

He glared down at his soup, grappling with his emotions. When he looked up, he found her watching him. "Not that my opinion matters, Julia, but I think you are perfection."

Her lips parted and a soft puff of air escaped. "Oh." A beautiful blush spread over her cheeks and she lowered her gaze, a shy smile curving her lips. "Thank you, Malcolm."

***

Dinner had been … illuminating.

Sitting so near him Julia had been able to see the corner of his mouth that was usually shadowed by the mask. The skin was puckered and dark pink and when he smiled, as he'd done several times, only the right side moved.

Julia decided his smile was quite charming. In fact, *he* was quite charming.

An image assaulted her like a slap: Malcolm as he'd been the night before—his eyeless mask facing her—his leather-clad hands buried in the woman's golden hair holding her immobile, his erection thrusting

141

up between his trousered thighs, red and hard and slick, his hips pumping—

Julia shook her head to banish the image. She felt as if he had reached into her mind and plucked out her darkest, deepest desires. Desires so deeply hidden that *Julia* hadn't known they existed.

If she went down that corridor again who knew what else she might see?

I never thought you were a coward!

That was what Lily would say if she were there.

Julia gave a soft snort of laughter. No, if Lily were in Julia's shoes, she would have rapped on the mirror last night and demanded to be invited in.

Do it.

She glanced at the clock; it was late, but no later than it had been last night.

Would he be there?

As if in a trance, Julia opened the door, checked the hallway, and then slipped out. When she pushed the panel, it opened almost soundlessly and she quickly stepped into the corridor and shut it behind her.

Rather than wander as she'd done last night, Julia retraced the path of her hasty exit, moving slowly, as if something were pulling her against her will. Something that would change her forever.

When she reached the small window, it was so faintly illuminated that she feared the room was unoccupied or that it was a night without wickedness.

She needn't have worried; the view tonight was even more shocking and erotic than last night.

He wasn't at his desk, but in a chair so big it made his huge body appear almost normal-sized by comparison.

And rather than sitting in profile, he was almost directly facing her.

He was fully dressed in his evening blacks and the woman knelt between his thighs again, her head already moving in a way that made Julia's stimulated sex pulse. His arms rested on the chair, rather than her head, and he gazed down at her.

The woman's body was covered by a loose garment that looked like an undressing gown and her wavy, golden hair rippled down her back.

From this angle, Julia might have been looking at herself, although the woman's hair was brighter than hers.

This time her father's accusation lacked any teeth.

Instead of running away in shame—as she should—Julia used her sweaty palm to clear the film that was obstructing her view, desperately wishing she were closer or the room brighter, or both.

Once the other woman sat all the way down, she wiggled her hips slightly.

That tiny movement, more than anything, made Julia's slick thighs tense and quiver, her inner muscles clenching with the need to be filled and stretched, raw, consuming *want* clawing at her so viciously that she trembled with need.

Malcolm slid his hands around the woman's slender shoulders and waist, urging her back, until she reclined in his arms.

And then he lowered his head over her chest.

Although she couldn't see it, Julia knew he would be touching her breasts with his mouth.

Her own nipples tightened painfully as she recalled the delicious sensation of Lily's lips and tongue on her breasts while her slender, skilled fingers thrust into Julia's body, her slippery thumb caressing and flicking the bundle of nerves that yielded so much pleasure.

A low grunt of frustrated desire slipped from between her parted lips and Julia's eyes popped open and she clapped a hand over her mouth, whirling away from the mirror and pressing her back against the wall, too afraid to even breathe.

Had he heard her?

She swallowed convulsively, her body frozen with indecision: should she run, or wait?

Go on! Take another look.

Julia was moving before her brain had registered her decision.

Disappointment vied with arousal at the view that met her gaze. Malcolm wasn't glaring at her accusingly—or looking her way, at all—instead, he was captivated by the woman in his arms.

As Julia watched and yearned, the two lovers began to move.

***

Malcolm's balls were so bloody full and hard that he'd been in agony while Maisie sucked him, her divinely skilled mouth, tongue, and throat bringing him to the edge of climax over and over again.

Was it wrong of him to be imagining another woman taking his cock into her tight body?

Probably.

Is that what he liked—small blond women?

Foolish hope leapt inside her.

Why would he want a gauche, unsophisticated woman—a girl, really—like you when he could have somebody who clearly knew what she was doing?

The thought was painful, probably because it was true. He didn't need Julia because he already had somebody.

Julia studied him harder than she'd ever looked at any picture, searching for any emotion or some reaction on his stark, unreadable face.

The changes in him were minute: a slight tightening of his jaw, his hands curling on the arms of the chair, and the increasing rising and falling of his broad chest.

She saw a flash of white teeth as his lips pulled back into a half-snarl right before he reached out for the woman. Instead of fisting her hair as he'd done last night, he set a hand on her shoulder and his lips moved.

The woman slowly pulled away from him and then gracefully rose to her feet. With a graceful shrug of her shoulders her robe slid to the floor and she stood before Malcolm naked, her back to Julia.

Julia had seen naked women—she'd done more than just *see* them with Lily—but this was a mature woman, not a schoolgirl, her figure ripe and voluptuous, her waist tiny without any corset to shape her.

Julia saw Malcolm's arm move, as if he were taking something from his coat, and he handed her a black scarf.

The woman took it from his hand and, without hesitating, tied it over her eyes.

She struggled to make sense of what she was seeing. Why would Malcolm have her cover her eyes? Did the woman want that? Did he?

Julia pushed the questions away when the woman knelt on the chair, straddling his thighs.

Malcolm's black-gloved hands spanned her waist, steadying her when she knelt up high, his thick shaft jutting out between her bare thighs.

Julia bit her lip hard at the erotic view.

The woman slid her small hand around his arousal and deftly positioned him before lowering herself slowly, his ruddy length disappearing into her body inch by inch.

Julia's nose pressed hard against the glass, her hot breath creating a dense fog that reminded her of what she was doing: spying.

You're a whore, just like your mother!

She laughed. "Very well. You've convinced me—I'll take the bisque, please."

He served them both and watched from beneath lowered lashes as she took a dainty sip and then sighed with a sensual contentment that guaranteed Maisie would be earning her keep later tonight.

"Why shouldn't you have oyster bisque?" he repeated.

"I've been eating far too much."

Malcolm thought back to the small portions he'd seen on her plate at their last breakfast. "What do you eat at home?"

"My usual meal consists of dry toast, a thin slice of ham, a bit of potato, and as much water as I care to consume."

He lowered his spoon without tasting the soup. "But ... *why?*"

"My stepmother says I am fat." Her lips flexed into a wry smile.

Malcolm struggled to suppress the sudden blast of fury he felt toward an idiotic woman he'd never even met.

Once he'd regained control of his temper he said, "Do *you* think you are fat?"

"I'm not as thin as she is, but… no, I think her expectations are unreasonable. She has always been rigid about slimming me, but she is frantic lately, worried that I shan't fit into my wedding gown."

Malcolm's anger at Nadine Harlow boiled over into genuine loathing. What sort of vile bitch would starve a person under their care?

As for Tommy, what sort of father would allow it?

He glared down at his soup, grappling with his emotions. When he looked up, he found her watching him. "Not that my opinion matters, Julia, but I think you are perfection."

Her lips parted and a soft puff of air escaped. "Oh." A beautiful blush spread over her cheeks and she lowered her gaze, a shy smile curving her lips. "Thank you, Malcolm."

***

Dinner had been … illuminating.

Sitting so near him Julia had been able to see the corner of his mouth that was usually shadowed by the mask. The skin was puckered and dark pink and when he smiled, as he'd done several times, only the right side moved.

Julia decided his smile was quite charming. In fact, *he* was quite charming.

An image assaulted her like a slap: Malcolm as he'd been the night before—his eyeless mask facing her—his leather-clad hands buried in the woman's golden hair holding her immobile, his erection thrusting

141

up between his trousered thighs, red and hard and slick, his hips pumping—

Julia shook her head to banish the image. She felt as if he had reached into her mind and plucked out her darkest, deepest desires. Desires so deeply hidden that *Julia* hadn't known they existed.

If she went down that corridor again who knew what else she might see?

I never thought you were a coward!

That was what Lily would say if she were there.

Julia gave a soft snort of laughter. No, if Lily were in Julia's shoes, she would have rapped on the mirror last night and demanded to be invited in.

Do it.

She glanced at the clock; it was late, but no later than it had been last night.

Would he be there?

As if in a trance, Julia opened the door, checked the hallway, and then slipped out. When she pushed the panel, it opened almost soundlessly and she quickly stepped into the corridor and shut it behind her.

Rather than wander as she'd done last night, Julia retraced the path of her hasty exit, moving slowly, as if something were pulling her against her will. Something that would change her forever.

When she reached the small window, it was so faintly illuminated that she feared the room was unoccupied or that it was a night without wickedness.

She needn't have worried; the view tonight was even more shocking and erotic than last night.

He wasn't at his desk, but in a chair so big it made his huge body appear almost normal-sized by comparison.

And rather than sitting in profile, he was almost directly facing her.

He was fully dressed in his evening blacks and the woman knelt between his thighs again, her head already moving in a way that made Julia's stimulated sex pulse. His arms rested on the chair, rather than her head, and he gazed down at her.

The woman's body was covered by a loose garment that looked like an undressing gown and her wavy, golden hair rippled down her back.

From this angle, Julia might have been looking at herself, although the woman's hair was brighter than hers.

Is that what he liked—small blond women?

Foolish hope leapt inside her.

Why would he want a gauche, unsophisticated woman—a girl, really—like you when he could have somebody who clearly knew what she was doing?

The thought was painful, probably because it was true. He didn't need Julia because he already had somebody.

Julia studied him harder than she'd ever looked at any picture, searching for any emotion or some reaction on his stark, unreadable face.

The changes in him were minute: a slight tightening of his jaw, his hands curling on the arms of the chair, and the increasing rising and falling of his broad chest.

She saw a flash of white teeth as his lips pulled back into a half-snarl right before he reached out for the woman. Instead of fisting her hair as he'd done last night, he set a hand on her shoulder and his lips moved.

The woman slowly pulled away from him and then gracefully rose to her feet. With a graceful shrug of her shoulders her robe slid to the floor and she stood before Malcolm naked, her back to Julia.

Julia had seen naked women—she'd done more than just *see* them with Lily—but this was a mature woman, not a schoolgirl, her figure ripe and voluptuous, her waist tiny without any corset to shape her.

Julia saw Malcolm's arm move, as if he were taking something from his coat, and he handed her a black scarf.

The woman took it from his hand and, without hesitating, tied it over her eyes.

She struggled to make sense of what she was seeing. Why would Malcolm have her cover her eyes? Did the woman want that? Did he?

Julia pushed the questions away when the woman knelt on the chair, straddling his thighs.

Malcolm's black-gloved hands spanned her waist, steadying her when she knelt up high, his thick shaft jutting out between her bare thighs.

Julia bit her lip hard at the erotic view.

The woman slid her small hand around his arousal and deftly positioned him before lowering herself slowly, his ruddy length disappearing into her body inch by inch.

Julia's nose pressed hard against the glass, her hot breath creating a dense fog that reminded her of what she was doing: spying.

You're a whore, just like your mother!

This time her father's accusation lacked any teeth.

Instead of running away in shame—as she should—Julia used her sweaty palm to clear the film that was obstructing her view, desperately wishing she were closer or the room brighter, or both.

Once the other woman sat all the way down, she wiggled her hips slightly.

That tiny movement, more than anything, made Julia's slick thighs tense and quiver, her inner muscles clenching with the need to be filled and stretched, raw, consuming *want* clawing at her so viciously that she trembled with need.

Malcolm slid his hands around the woman's slender shoulders and waist, urging her back, until she reclined in his arms.

And then he lowered his head over her chest.

Although she couldn't see it, Julia knew he would be touching her breasts with his mouth.

Her own nipples tightened painfully as she recalled the delicious sensation of Lily's lips and tongue on her breasts while her slender, skilled fingers thrust into Julia's body, her slippery thumb caressing and flicking the bundle of nerves that yielded so much pleasure.

A low grunt of frustrated desire slipped from between her parted lips and Julia's eyes popped open and she clapped a hand over her mouth, whirling away from the mirror and pressing her back against the wall, too afraid to even breathe.

Had he heard her?

She swallowed convulsively, her body frozen with indecision: should she run, or wait?

Go on! Take another look.

Julia was moving before her brain had registered her decision.

Disappointment vied with arousal at the view that met her gaze. Malcolm wasn't glaring at her accusingly—or looking her way, at all— instead, he was captivated by the woman in his arms.

As Julia watched and yearned, the two lovers began to move.

***

Malcolm's balls were so bloody full and hard that he'd been in agony while Maisie sucked him, her divinely skilled mouth, tongue, and throat bringing him to the edge of climax over and over again.

Was it wrong of him to be imagining another woman taking his cock into her tight body?

Probably.

She laughed. "Very well. You've convinced me—I'll take the bisque, please."

He served them both and watched from beneath lowered lashes as she took a dainty sip and then sighed with a sensual contentment that guaranteed Maisie would be earning her keep later tonight.

"Why shouldn't you have oyster bisque?" he repeated.

"I've been eating far too much."

Malcolm thought back to the small portions he'd seen on her plate at their last breakfast. "What do you eat at home?"

"My usual meal consists of dry toast, a thin slice of ham, a bit of potato, and as much water as I care to consume."

He lowered his spoon without tasting the soup. "But … *why?*"

"My stepmother says I am fat." Her lips flexed into a wry smile.

Malcolm struggled to suppress the sudden blast of fury he felt toward an idiotic woman he'd never even met.

Once he'd regained control of his temper he said, "Do *you* think you are fat?"

"I'm not as thin as she is, but… no, I think her expectations are unreasonable. She has always been rigid about slimming me, but she is frantic lately, worried that I shan't fit into my wedding gown."

Malcolm's anger at Nadine Harlow boiled over into genuine loathing. What sort of vile bitch would starve a person under their care?

As for Tommy, what sort of father would allow it?

He glared down at his soup, grappling with his emotions. When he looked up, he found her watching him. "Not that my opinion matters, Julia, but I think you are perfection."

Her lips parted and a soft puff of air escaped. "Oh." A beautiful blush spread over her cheeks and she lowered her gaze, a shy smile curving her lips. "Thank you, Malcolm."

***

Dinner had been … illuminating.

Sitting so near him Julia had been able to see the corner of his mouth that was usually shadowed by the mask. The skin was puckered and dark pink and when he smiled, as he'd done several times, only the right side moved.

Julia decided his smile was quite charming. In fact, *he* was quite charming.

An image assaulted her like a slap: Malcolm as he'd been the night before—his eyeless mask facing her—his leather-clad hands buried in the woman's golden hair holding her immobile, his erection thrusting

141

up between his trousered thighs, red and hard and slick, his hips pumping—

Julia shook her head to banish the image. She felt as if he had reached into her mind and plucked out her darkest, deepest desires. Desires so deeply hidden that *Julia* hadn't known they existed.

If she went down that corridor again who knew what else she might see?

I never thought you were a coward!

That was what Lily would say if she were there.

Julia gave a soft snort of laughter. No, if Lily were in Julia's shoes, she would have rapped on the mirror last night and demanded to be invited in.

Do it.

She glanced at the clock; it was late, but no later than it had been last night.

Would he be there?

As if in a trance, Julia opened the door, checked the hallway, and then slipped out. When she pushed the panel, it opened almost soundlessly and she quickly stepped into the corridor and shut it behind her.

Rather than wander as she'd done last night, Julia retraced the path of her hasty exit, moving slowly, as if something were pulling her against her will. Something that would change her forever.

When she reached the small window, it was so faintly illuminated that she feared the room was unoccupied or that it was a night without wickedness.

She needn't have worried; the view tonight was even more shocking and erotic than last night.

He wasn't at his desk, but in a chair so big it made his huge body appear almost normal-sized by comparison.

And rather than sitting in profile, he was almost directly facing her.

He was fully dressed in his evening blacks and the woman knelt between his thighs again, her head already moving in a way that made Julia's stimulated sex pulse. His arms rested on the chair, rather than her head, and he gazed down at her.

The woman's body was covered by a loose garment that looked like an undressing gown and her wavy, golden hair rippled down her back.

From this angle, Julia might have been looking at herself, although the woman's hair was brighter than hers.

Chapter 17

J ulia had decided that Mr. Barton wouldn't be joining her for breakfast when he appeared at the French doors without a sound.

"Oh, you startled me," she said, raising a hand to cover her pounding heart.

Only part of her racing pulse was due to surprise, the rest was the effect the man himself had on her—especially when she thought about what he'd looked like the last time she'd seen him, gleaming with sweat and more than a little feral.

"Good morning, Julia"

She watched from beneath lowered lashes as he approached the buffet, huge, dark, and menacing—like a bear or a tiger or some other dangerous, mysterious animal she should be running from rather than gravitating toward.

Her whole body was pulsing just *looking* at him, seeing him as he'd been last night, when he'd been thrusting into his lover so hard that Julia swore she could feel it in another room.

Malcolm turned from the buffet, took his seat at the head of the table—which had, unfortunately, been returned to its usual size—and then tucked into his meal.

Julia had already consumed more than enough tea, but she nodded at James's offer of a fresh pot.

"Did you sleep well last night?" Malcolm asked.

"Yes, very." She hesitated and then asked, "And you?"

He took a sip of black coffee before answering. "I have insomnia. I never sleep through the night."

"That must be terrible."

"I've always had it so I don't know any different."

"What do you do?"

He paused, his fork halfway to his mouth, and cocked an eyebrow at her, his lips twisted into a smile so faint she might have been imagining it.

But Julia knew she wasn't imagining it.

She *knew* they were both thinking about the sorts of things he did late at night—although she hoped to God that he didn't know that *she* knew.

"I—I mean do you read or work or—"

"I do a lot of work at night," he said shortly. "You're not hungry today?" he asked, cutting into a deviled kidney while Julia toyed with a piece of toast.

"I've had plenty." She hesitated, and then said, "Might we have another exchange of, er, questions?"

He paused, suddenly looking more… alert. "Of course. Ladies first," he said, and then popped a piece of kidney into his mouth.

"Are you going to hurt my father?" Julia felt guilty that she'd not asked it before—it should have been the first question she asked. The fact that it hadn't even occurred to her was more than a little bit mortifying. What sort of unnatural daughter must she be?

One who is tired of being hit in the face and used as a bargaining chip in business negotiations, an unhelpful part of her brain suggested.

Malcolm chewed, swallowed, and took a mouthful of coffee. "Not physically."

She stared, considering what that meant. While a plain *no* would have been better, *not physically* was good. Wasn't it?

He continued to work his way through his food.

"Aren't you going to ask your question?" she finally asked.

He took a sip of coffee, wiped his mouth with his napkin, and then tossed it on his plate. "You can have it."

Julia didn't know whether to be thrilled at having another question or offended that he was so incurious about her. But then he already seemed to know everything about her, so he probably didn't need questions.

Before Julia could decide which question to ask, James entered the dining room. "This just came for you, sir." He handed Malcolm something she recognized as a telegram, although she'd never personally received one.

Malcolm's eye moved over it quickly, his features shifting into an expression that was truly… chilling.

He folded it twice, threw back the rest of his coffee, and stood. "I'm afraid I must be off, Miss Harlow."

"Wait," she blurted. "I still have the question you gave me."

Rather than look annoyed, he seemed amused. "Go on, ask me."

"Who is that telegram from?"

Julia knew it was childish to enjoy his look of surprise—quickly followed by one of chagrin—but she didn't care.

"Brian Harlow."

It was her turned to look surprised.

"But why is he—"

"Dress warmly tonight, Miss Harlow."

"Warmly? Why?"

"You're all out of questions." He smiled. "I shall see you at dinner."

***

Julia spent her day painting and pondering Malcolm's cryptic answers from breakfast. She had no idea why her uncle would have sent a telegram. But then she had no idea what was going on, full stop. She told herself that the next time she had a question she would use it more sensibly.

But she knew that was a lie.

Whatever Malcolm was up to—and whatever her father had done to him—she simply didn't want to know.

By the time early evening came around, Julia had little to show for her endless mental dithering other than a slight headache and a ruined watercolor.

As she was evidently staying over Christmas, she had decided to paint pictures as gifts for Malcolm and her three card-playing partners.

But not today's painting, which had turned out so wretched that she'd finally torn it up in frustration.

"*Please* tell me where he is taking me, Kemp," Julia begged when the maid arrived to dress her for the evening.

The older woman smiled. "You know I can't do that."

"Can't you even give me a tiny hint? After all, how shall I know what to wear?"

Kemp gestured toward a huge Barton's garment box on one of the settees. "He's sent what you will need to wear, Miss Harlow."

Julia glared at the box, guilt and greed warring within her. "Oh, I really shouldn't. He's already given me too much."

"I think you should," Kemp said, giving her a steady gaze that made Julia's face heat, for some reason.

"Fine," she said.

Kemp smiled and brought her the box.

"Oh, my goodness," Julia breathed when she lifted the lid. "It's magnificent!"

It was a coat in her favorite shade of peacock blue, a sumptuous velvet with dark brown fur cuffs and collar, lined with dull gold silk.

Kemp took the garment from the box and held it aloft. "Try it on."

Julia slid her arms into unspeakably soft silk and hugged the luxurious velvet to her body. It fit like a proverbial glove and was so soft and warm.

"It's so lovely," she breathed, twirling in a circle, which made the heavy, full skirt flare around her calves.

"One more," Kemp said, lifting another box which had been tucked away behind the settee.

"You open it," Julia urged.

Kemp lifted the lid and took an enormous muff from the box, the fur the same dark chocolate as the trim on the coat

Julia thrust her hands into the huge puff and gazed at her reflection, enrapt. "Where could we be going?"

"You'll soon find out," Kemp said. "I'll run your bath."

Julia nodded absently, her mind spinning. Why was he doing all of this? It was almost like courtship. Perhaps he wanted her enough to—

Don't build castles in the air just because a man has given you a few gifts, Julia. This means nothing—it's just his way of keeping you occupied while he does whatever it is he is doing to your father. And apparently your uncle, too.

Julia scowled at her reflection. *He is angry with my father, not me. He likes* me.

Even if that is true you know your father will put Richard in an asylum if you don't give him what you promised.

The thought doused her excitement like a bucket of freezing water. It was also something she needed to keep at the forefront of her mind for those moments when her romantic urges threatened to overwhelm her common sense.

Julia only had one future ahead of her, and it didn't include Malcolm Barton, even if he *did* want her.

***

Malcolm must be an idiot.

Skating in the park, at his age? He'd be lucky to end this evening without cracking his skull open and obliterating what little dignity remained to him.

"Fool," he muttered under his breath as Norris helped him into his coat.

"I beg your pardon, sir?"

"Nothing."

There was a knock on the door. "Yes?" Malcolm called out, straightening his necktie and frowning at his reflection.

Butkins stepped inside his chambers. "This just came for you, sir." He handed Malcolm an envelope.

Malcolm tore it open and quickly scanned the few sentences.

"Tell the messenger I already sent my answer to his employer."

"Er, Mr. Harlow brought the message himself, sir. His is downstairs and he threatened to notify the authorities that you are holding Miss Harlow."

Malcolm couldn't help laughing. "Tell him to go ahead and summon the police. In the meantime, escort him off the premises. He can wait for the authorities on somebody else's property. If he decides against that course of action—which he will—tell him he can wait for the appointed time—he knows when that is. That will be his one and only chance to talk to me. I will not see him at any other time. Ever."

Butkins nodded and left without another word.

Malcolm smirked, enjoying Harlow's agitation far too much. He'd already received five messages from the man, each more frantic than the last. He'd sent him one message with a day and time. He would meet him on Christmas Eve and no sooner.

The visit would be Malcolm's early Christmas gift to himself.

Norris handed him his hat and a thicker pair of fur-lined gloves that he would pull over the Limerick gloves when he went outside.

He was stupid to be going out in freezing weather, but he had a desire to see Julia's lovely, rosy-cheeked face against the stars. At least the little you could see of them on a polluted London night.

Malcolm strode to her chambers through empty, quiet hallways rather than using the much shorter private corridor, not wanting to run the risk of popping out of the wall where she might see him.

Kemp opened the door at his knock and dropped a graceful curtsey. "Good evening, sir. She'll just be—"

"No, she is ready now!" Julia came rushing from the other room, her lips and eyes smiling.

Malcolm experienced the same feeling he always did when he saw her: as if he'd been kicked in the stomach.

"Do you like it?" she asked and then spun in a circle, sending the hem of the heavy coat flying and clipping one of the side tables. A knickknack of some sort *thudded* to the carpet.

"Whoops! I'm sorry," she said, biting her lower lip.

"You look magnificent, Julia." Malcolm's voice was so hoarse with suppressed desire that he sounded like an old man.

Fuck. She was bloody beautiful.

He offered his arm. "Shall we?"

"May I ask where we are going?" Julia asked when they came to the steam-operated lift.

Malcolm opened the door and ushered her inside. "You may ask," he said, smirking as he turned the dial to the third floor.

She rolled her eyes. "Very droll. You are as bad as my younger brothers. *Where* are we going?"

"First, we are going to an early dinner."

"And after?"

"It is a surprise."

"Malcolm, don't be cruel."

God, he liked the sound of his name on her tongue.

And he *loved* hearing her beg.

The soft bell dinged and the small room stopped moving. Malcolm opened both doors and waited for her to pass through.

"Ooh, you're taking me to Barton's. However did you get a table? I've heard it is very exclusive."

"I know the owner."

She laughed.

Malcolm nodded to the maître d who stepped out to welcome them. "Hello, William."

"Good evening, Mr. Barton, Miss Smith, your table is ready, sir."

"Smith?" Julia whispered as Malcolm waved away the attendant and helped her out of her coat.

"I thought it best to give you an alias," he whispered back, his tone as teasing as hers. "Our table is by the window," he added, allowing himself the luxury of laying a hand over the small of her back as he guided her across the room.

"There is nobody else here," she said, looking around her.

"I might have reserved the entire restaurant tonight," he admitted.

"Afraid I would try to escape?" she asked, cutting him an arch look that went straight to his cock.

"Not at all," he murmured, leaning closer than necessary as he seated her at their table. "I just wanted you all to myself."

Her startled look and accompanying blush were oddly satisfying.

Malcolm nodded at William to commence his spiel.

"Tonight Mr. Barton has put together a special menu for your enjoyment—"

He blocked out the man's voice, gazing at the young, lively, excited, gorgeous woman across from him.

She's good for you, Mal.

Where the hell have you been? He demanded, thankfully only in his head.

You don't need me so much anymore—you've got somebody who makes you smile and laugh.

I don't have *her. I'm sending her back to her father.* Sooner than he liked, in fact.

Don't do this, Mal. You could stop things now—before you hurt anyone—tell her how you feel about her and help her get out of this disastrous betrothal and—

Go away, Sukey.

The last thing he needed was encouragement in an area that would lead to nothing but misery.

To Malcolm's shock—and disappointment—Sukey obeyed him.

"Mr. Barton?"

He blinked up at the maître d'. "I'm sorry?"

"I asked if there was anything else, sir?"

Malcolm saw their wine—which he'd chosen beforehand—had already been decanted and poured. "No, that will be all."

William bowed and left.

Julia pulled off her peacock blue gloves before reaching for her glass. "You seem distracted."

"I am. By you."

She blushed. "Why do you always deflect any personal questions?"

"Is that your daily question?"

Her delicate nose wrinkled. "You know it isn't."

"Well, go ahead."

"Do you have any family?"

"I grew up in St. Mark's Asylum for Boys. I left there when I was twelve and apprenticed to a coal merchant, hauling and delivering coal." His lips flexed into a smile. "I can see by your expression that you are imagining all sorts of horrors. Don't, the couple who operated the orphanage—Mr. and Mrs. Thomas—were kind, after their own fashion. They neither starved nor beat their charges and I have no complaints about the treatment I received there."

"How did you get from hauling coal to all this?" She gestured to the opulent room around them.

I went to work for a monster, killed some men, maimed a good many others, and then spent the last decade and a half living for nothing but work.

"I saved my money and bought a failing dry goods shop. It turned out I was good at operating it. So, I bought another and another, until I had enough money to do something … grander."

"You mean your first emporium?"

"No, I meant shipping."

"Oh, like my father?"

"Yes, exactly like him."

"What happened to change that?"

Somebody in your family set my home and business on fire and killed my wife.

"I saw the error of my ways and decided I should stay with what I knew: buying and selling goods. My first emporium was far less grand than the name would suggest, but it was a smashing success and profitable enough that I could afford to build this store."

"And how many others?"

"There will soon to be eight."

Malcolm couldn't resist preening a little at her openly admiring gaze. After all, what man wouldn't allow himself to bask in such a glow? At least for one night.

"My turn," he said.

"But I'm not done."

"I already allowed you more than one question. Don't be greedy," he chided.

She gave a gurgle of laughter that was more intoxicating than whiskey.

"Tell me about your first kiss."

Her eyes widened and she glanced around the empty dining room as if somebody—her stepmother? Father?—might pop out of nowhere.

"Nobody else can hear us, Julia."

She swallowed, her slender white throat tightening in a way that fed his filthy thoughts.

"It's—well, it's a bit naughty," she admitted, her flush doing the impossible and making her even more lovely.

"My favorite sort of story," he said lightly, his response earning him another delightful laugh.

"Promise me that you won't be disgusted?"

"There is nothing you could do that would disgust me."

She looked a little surprised by his emphatic response but was obviously too concerned with what she was about to divulge to pursue the matter.

"It was with my schoolfriend… Lily."

"Ah," he murmured. "The best sort of schoolmate."

Her eyes widened. "You're not shocked? Or disgusted?"

"I'm not. And I already told you I wouldn't be disgusted."

"Yes, but that was before you knew what I'd say." Her cheeks went from pink to dark rose. "A woman kissing a woman is… scandalous."

"I've paid thousands of pounds over the years to watch women do a great deal more than kiss each other."

Her jaw dropped open. "*What?*" she squeaked.

"You heard me," he said, taking a sip of wine.

She sputtered. "But—you can't just—" She bit her lip and then said, "You're not going to explain that comment, are you?"

"No."

She huffed an exasperated laugh. "You don't find such a thing, erm, immoral?"

"No."

Julia swallowed. And then did it again. "Have you ever—" her voice broke and she cleared her throat.

"Have I kissed a man?" Malcolm supplied, putting her out of her obvious misery.

She nodded, her cheeks on fire.

"Yes."

She goggled at him. "You *have?*"

"Yes."

Her hand shook as she lifted her glass to her lips, took a fortifying swallow, then a second, and then lowered it carefully to the table.

"Did you like it?"

"Yes." Malcolm smiled slightly and added, "Very much." Indeed, Smith was a superlative kisser.

The waiter arrived just then with their oysters and they ate without speaking.

Malcolm entertained himself by wondering what she'd say next. He honestly could not recall the last time he'd had a conversation with a man or woman and couldn't predict most of what came out of their mouths.

She set aside her oyster fork, took a sip from her goblet, and asked, "How many times have you been in love?"

"Once."

She nodded slowly, as if working up to her next question. "Will you tell me about your wife?"

Malcolm opened his mouth to say *no*, but Sukey stopped him.

Ach, Mal—don't be that way!

My memories of you are for <u>me</u>—not for anyone else.

Talkin' about me is a way to keep my memory alive though, isn't it?

Malcolm pondered the thought as he looked at the young woman across from him.

Julia squirmed under his inspection. When she opened her mouth, he knew she'd apologize for the question.

"I'll tell you about her if you'll tell me about your friend—Lily, was it?"

She looked startled but nodded. "All right."

Their waiter appeared with a silver tureen and served their soup.

Malcolm wished they'd dined in his room, without servants. And preferably without clothing—at least on her part.

The moment the waiter left Julia turned to him; her soup forgotten. "What was her name?"

He hesitated, and then said, "Susan. But I called her Sukey."

Chapter 18

As Julia buttoned her coat and prepared to follow Malcolm out of the restaurant foyer, she marveled at how much Malcolm had shared with her over the past hour.

Indeed, he'd allowed Julia question after question, seemingly forgetting that he was owed some answers of his own about Lily.

Julia felt a pang of regret that she'd not been pressed to share her experiences with her best friend, even though talking about what she'd done with Lily—and how she felt about her—would have been difficult, not to mention embarrassing.

Still, she was thrilled that he'd opened up about his wife because she suspected it was a subject he did not often speak about.

Susan Barton had been ten years older than Malcolm and they'd barely had three years together before she'd died in the same fire that had left him scarred.

Every word he said about her—and the way he'd said them—made the truth more and more evident: Malcolm *still* loved Susan Barton, even though she'd been gone for fifteen years, more than half Julia's life.

She now saw how he must view her: as nothing more than a child. Julia had been a fool to think he might be interested in her. Or even that he would feel lust for her.

How could he feel anything about you when you barely know each other?

That wasn't true! Although they'd had so little time together—a week less than they might have had thanks to her childish behavior with the knife that first day—they'd spent hours talking over meals and their card games.

Besides, what was there to know about her? Julia was like a baby animal, unformed and inexperienced, while Malcolm was a man with a lifetime of experience.

Julia was so fascinated by him that she could hardly bear it.

He was bold, fearless, and utterly unconcerned with what anyone else thought about him.

In a way, he reminded her of Lily. Oh, they looked nothing alike, of course, but they were both so secure in who they were, so confident about what they wanted and unapologetic about taking it.

Julia had been heartbroken when her parents had taken her away from school because she had been in love with Lily.

"Love is nothing to be ashamed of," Lily had said when Julia had confessed her feelings. "And you know I love you, too, Julia."

But her friend hadn't been *in love* with her and Julia had known that.

That knowledge had hurt her at first but she'd finally admitted that getting part of Lily was better than getting none of her.

She felt the same way about Malcolm. Even a little bit of him was better than leaving his house without ever getting close to him.

Julia couldn't help wondering if her growing feelings for Malcolm meant that she fell in love easily. Or was it neediness she felt rather than love? If so, was that necessarily a bad thing?

Why are you thinking about all this right now? He doesn't love you and never will. And if you know what is best for you—and Richard—you won't allow yourself to fall in love with him, *either.*

Yes, yes, yes. She knew all that. It was just—

"Why are you scowling?"

Julia glanced up at him as they rode the odd little moving room down to the bottom of the store.

"I wasn't scowling. In fact, I'm… happy." That was true; she *was* happy, even though sadness simmered not far below. "I enjoyed dinner very much."

"So did I." He captured her gaze with his, his face as unreadable as the moon.

Julia startled when the lift door opened, breaking the strange spell.

A man in some sort of uniform opened the doors. "Good evening, sir."

"Good evening, Parker, this is Miss Smith."

"Miss." Parker bowed and then strode ahead, a huge ring of keys jingling as he unlocked a plain wooden door—not one of the main store doors—and then opened it.

Julia gasped at the frigid air. "Goodness! It's my first time outside in…" she paused, trying to count just how many days she'd been his captive.

"A while," Malcolm said, guiding her down a narrow alley, his hand on her back.

His right hand was dexterous, although the left seemed stiff, especially the two smallest fingers, which didn't appear to move. But he quickly buckled the skates onto her boots. Once the second boot was attached, he wrapped a hand around her ankle and held it for a moment, his hand warm even through two layers of leather.

He inhaled deeply and released her before looking up, his expression once again unreadable, the heat she'd seen earlier gone. Had she imagined it?

He stood and offered her his hand.

Pretty lights in colored baskets illuminated the hazy, frozen air as they stepped out onto the ice.

One of Julia's feet would have slipped out from under her if Malcolm hadn't caught her, his grasp firm but gentle around her upper arm.

"Steady on," he murmured. "Just stand and get your bearings—let me do the work for a bit."

She was glad to comply. Her ankles were wobbly and weak; she didn't recall this being so difficult.

They skated in silence. Or rather he skated and she just stood still.

"Thank you," she said.

"What for?"

"For tonight. For this. For—for answering my questions and treating me like I'm a grown woman."

"You are a grown woman."

"You would never know that by the way I am usually treated." She looked up but he was staring ahead, his mouth stern—almost grim. "What are you thinking right now?"

"About taking you to bed."

Julia's knees turned to water.

Malcolm slid an arm around her waist, holding her upright as he skated to a stop. He took her chin and forced her to look up at him. "Too much truth for you?"

Julia's blood was pounding in her ears. "No," she said in a raspy voice. "Just—well, you surprised me."

His eyebrow lifted. "You couldn't tell that I desire you?"

"I know you think I am pretty, but—"

He gave a derisive snort. "Pretty? No. I don't think you are *pretty*," he spat the word, his nostrils flaring. "I think you are bloody gorgeous."

She'd heard how beautiful she was all her life, but never had the words made her body respond in all the ways it was currently doing.

"But that doesn't matter."

His harsh words—which had been more of a snarl—yanked her from her pleasant daze. "What doesn't matter?"

"It doesn't matter how much I desire you because I won't be acting on it."

Julia flinched at his abrupt words, but then realized they sounded like something he'd said more for himself, than for her.

"Come, let's skate," he said, his tone final, almost… bleak.

Aside from the distant street noises the only sound was the soft *shushing* of his blades on the ice as he pulled her along.

"Why?" she finally asked. "Because I'm betrothed?"

"No."

Shush, shush, shush.

"Then why?"

He made an exasperated noise and she felt him turn to look at her, but she kept her eyes on the pond, concentrating on the soothing *shushing* rather than the bold questions she was asking and the answers she might not want to hear.

"There are many reasons," he finally said. "But it isn't your turn to ask questions. It is mine. Tell me about Lily."

"But I'm not—"

"Tell me about her."

Julia heaved a sigh, not caring how petulant it sounded. "What do you want to know?"

"How did you meet?"

"We were put into the same room my first year at school." Julia laughed just recalling their first meeting. "We despised each other on sight. I think we are too similar—we both like to be the center of attention."

"I never would have guessed."

Julia ignored his teasing. "We fought constantly and begged the headmistress to move one of us, but she wouldn't. All year long we squabbled."

"About what?"

"Anything and everything." Julia didn't want to tell him about the cruel, childish pranks they pulled on each other—she didn't even like to think about how hateful she'd been. Not that Lily hadn't given as good as she'd got.

"Why did things change?"

"At our first Easter break there were only a handful of girls who stayed at the school."

"Where was your school?"

"In France, an old chateau in the country. Anyhow, we were the only two English girls whose family didn't bring us home." That was thanks to Nadine and set the trend for the entire three-and-a-half years she was away.

"Once there was nobody else looking on for us to entertain, we discovered we had a lot in common. Her mother had died when she was born and it was only Lily and her father, the Earl of Danforth. She rarely saw him and his only interest in her was keeping her out of trouble until she married. She was already betrothed to a man twice her age." Julia cut him a quick glance to see his reaction to that information, but he was staring ahead. "They are married now and she is very happy. Extremely happy," she amended.

He laughed softly. "That is reassuring to hear. So the two of you became lovers?" he persisted.

Why did the word *lover* sound so mature and taboo when he said it in his deep voice?

Julia was suddenly glad that he was staring ahead rather than at her. "Lily thought we should practice kissing for the day when we'd both be married. Both of us knew we'd have little enough time between school ending and getting married—oh look," she blurted, "I'm skating!"

He stared down at her, a slight smile curving his lips. "You've been managing for several minutes now."

Her hand still clutched his sleeve, but she was pushing herself along—true, with a bit of a wobble—but still moving on her own.

"Was kissing all you did?" he asked, taking her elbow and steadying her when she jolted at his question.

"Erm, no."

"Tell me how you pleasured each other."

Julia gasped.

"What?"

"The things you say! They're—"

"Naughty?" he asked, smirking down at her.

"You do it on purpose, don't you?" she asked, raising a cooling hand to her cheek, which was scalding hot.

He chuckled.

"Why are you laughing?"

"Because I'm charmed by you, Julia. Now tell me about the things you and Lily did to one another."

It was her turn to laugh. "You are wicked!"

"Yes."

"And shameless about it, to boot!"

He merely smiled.

Julia chewed over his demand for a moment, and then said, "I'll tell you one thing if you tell me one thing."

"Quite the little haggler, aren't you?"

"I believe that *you* were the one who initially decided we should make such bargains."

"I believe you are right. It depends—what do you want to know? You tell me your question and I'll decide if I wish to bargain."

"That doesn't seem—"

"Fair," he finished for her. "I know. But that is the offer, take it or leave it."

"I'll take it," she hastily said. "I want to know what sorts of things you p-paid women thousands of pounds to do."

He looked startled, as if he'd been expecting some other question. "Are you sure you want to know?"

"I'm not a child," she retorted, not bothering to hide her irritation. "I've had three l-lovers, you know." She glared up at him, furious with herself for stumbling over the word *lover*.

He held up a hand in a placating gesture. "I'm sorry, I didn't mean to imply that you were. It's just that my tastes are rather, er, unconventional."

"How do you know that mine aren't, too?"

This time she saw a definite glint of humor when he looked at her. "That is an excellent point."

"Well?" she prodded. "Are you going to answer the question? Or are you—"

"I like to watch a woman be stripped naked, bound hand and foot, and then whipped. Sometimes I include another woman—or a man— kneeling between her thighs, servicing her. Sometimes I like to administer the whipping myself. Sometimes I like to be the one licking her pussy." They'd slowed to a crawl and he was staring down at her, his gaze so hot she was surprised he didn't melt the ice. "But sometimes I just like to watch while I am sucked to orgasm—slowly brought to the peak of pleasure and then deprived—over and over—"

He caught Julia before she even realized she was falling, scooping her up and holding her as easily as a babe in his arms.

"*Whoops*," he whispered, and then brushed his cold lips softly against hers—the touch so brief and delicate that she wondered if she imagined it.

He skated to a halt, still holding her. "Do you want to stop skating, Julia?" His deep voice rumbled through her body.

"No."

He smiled and set her on her feet.

Julia clung to his arm, her knees still wobbly. She swallowed. "I think perhaps we should talk about something a bit less, er—"

"Stimulating?"

"I was going to say *distracting*, but I suppose *stimulating* is more honest."

"Does that mean I have to wait for my answer?"

"Yes," she said, still trembling. "I think that would be best."

They glided together in silence.

"Feeling more stable?" he asked a few minutes later, keeping pace beside her but allowing her to skate on her own.

"Much. May I ask you another question?"

He cut her a sidelong glance.

"Not *that* sort of question. There are other things to talk about besides, er—"

"Sex?" he suggested.

Julia sucked in a breath.

"What?" he said, the innocent look he tried to assume not even remotely convincing. "I thought you needed help finding the right word."

Julia ignored his taunting. "Well? Will you answer me, or not?"

"Ask and find out."

"You said growing up in the orphanage wasn't awful—but were you happy there?"

"Happy?" He pondered for a moment as the skated. "I don't recall being especially unhappy," he said after a moment.

"Didn't you ever want to know who your mother and father were?"

He didn't speak for a moment.

"I'm sorry. You don't have to answ—"

"I did when I was little." His lips curved into a small, cold smile.

"What made you stop?"

He turned to her and gave her a long look.

"I'm just curious," she said lamely.

"You are," he agreed, and then turned to look ahead. "There was a boy at the orphanage named Robby Smith. He was convinced his father was a viscount and lots of the lads believed him—after all, who would make up a viscount? Why not a duke? Or at least an earl?" He gave her a darkly amused look. "If you are going to dream—why not make it a grand one?"

"Perhaps he was telling the truth?"

"That's what some of us came to think. But then his mother came to claim him—six years after she'd abandoned him. The first words out of poor Robby's mouth were where was his pa, the viscount. Mrs. Smith—if that was really her name—was a whore, who'd only come to fetch Robby back because he'd come to an age where he could be put out to work and she'd get some money out of him. She cuffed him upside the head and told him not to be daft, that his father had been just another drunken sailor on leave."

Julia struggled to control the prickling feeling behind her nose and eyes—the sensation that always presaged crying. "That's a *terrible* story."

He gave her an unsmiling look. "Yes, it is. But it is also an excellent lesson."

"A lesson for what, pray?" she demanded, brushing a freezing tear from her cheek.

"That sometimes it's better if you don't know the truth; sometimes it's better to hang on to the dream."

Chapter 19

The evening had been a magical one—the most wonderful night that Julia could remember.

Malcolm hadn't just kidnapped her body, he'd captivated the rest of her, as well.

Her desire—no, her *need*—to see past the wall of reserve that he'd erected around himself to the man within had become an obsession.

And you think you will learn more about him by spying?

Julia grimaced guiltily at the thought.

But that guilt didn't stop her from pressing the secret panel and slipping into the gloomy corridor like a sneak thief an hour and a half after Malcolm had delivered her back to her chambers.

Julia knew—even before she reached the small window into his study—that something was different tonight.

For one thing, the long rectangle of glass across from Malcolm's study was illuminated, allowing her to see into the room for the first time.

And oh, what a room it was. A huge black four-poster bed dominated the large space, with a woman standing slightly off to one side, her arms cuffed at the wrists and stretched high over her head.

That was unusual enough, but there were so many other things clambering for Julia's attention.

The wall of whips was self-explanatory—although never had she imagined there were so many different sorts in existence—but the furniture was unlike anything she'd ever seen: a huge black X made from wood and several benches and racks, one that even resembled a stockade.

Julia's wide-eyed gaze slid back to the woman.

She faced straight ahead and wore a loo mask with blood-red pouting lips, an aquiline nose with holes for breathing, and impossibly long curling black lashes projecting from closed eyelids, which meant the wearer wouldn't be able to see.

Her long blond hair fell in waves around her face, making the mask look eerily real.

The mask didn't just conceal her face, it erased her identity. When you combined that effect with her naked body the result was distinctly dehumanizing, making her resemble a life-sized doll.

It should have repulsed Julia, but was almost suffocatingly arousing, instead.

It was either the woman from the other night, or one very similar in build and coloring. Once again, Julia couldn't help noticing the resemblance between their bodies.

Other than the shocking lack of private hair and slightly smaller breasts, they were almost identical, which made it very easy to imagine that was *her* on the other side of the glass. A human doll for Malcolm's pleasure.

It was as if thinking his name had summoned him and he strode into sight and stopped behind the woman. He towered over her, his huge body clad in evening blacks, the juxtaposition of naked and clothed, delicate and massive, causing Julia's sex to ache unbearably.

Malcolm set his gloved hands on the woman's shoulder and she flinched

"Shhh," he soothed.

Julia startled and stepped back at the sound of his voice, which was so clear there must be some outlet, which meant she needed to be utterly silent.

He pulled back her hair and lowered his faintly smiling lips to her bare throat, trailing kisses down the skin of her neck, pausing at the juncture between throat and shoulder, while he cupped the woman's breasts with his huge hands.

Julia bit her lip, barely catching a soft grunt of desire, her own breasts heavy and aching for his touch, her nipples as hard as diamonds.

His tall, broad body seemed to curl around the woman's far smaller form, as if he could consume her, his fingers pinching, stroking, and teasing her breasts until the woman was moaning and straining against her tight bonds, her hips bucking, the skin of her spread thighs glistening with arousal.

Just like Julia's.

"Amanda," he murmured the name into the woman's throat and at first Julia thought that was her name.

She jumped, yet again, when a woman rose up between the bound woman's spread legs, as if she'd been there all along.

Two women! This was what he'd talked about earlier.

Her heart was pounding so loudly that she almost didn't hear his next words.

"Open her for me, Amanda," he ordered quietly.

The new woman, whose eyes were also covered, but with a simple black silk scarf, reached up and spread the bound woman's sex lips.

Malcolm's hands paused their teasing and he looked up, his pale blue eye gazing straight ahead.

Julia's chest froze in fear. *He sees me!*

She gritted her jaw and prepared for his wrath.

And then realized he must be looking in the mirror.

He couldn't see her—it was a mirror.

She exhaled shakily.

"So pretty," he muttered, his breathing quickening and his nostrils flaring as he stared at the reflection of the woman's spread sex. "Do you want Amanda to lick your cunt, Maisie?"

The bound woman—Maisie, it seemed—nodded vigorously

His smile was unspeakably wicked. "You know what that will cost you."

It wasn't a question, but Maisie again nodded.

He tweaked her nipple hard enough to make Maisie squeak, and then said to the kneeling woman. "You may begin, Amanda."

Amanda lowered her mouth over the other woman's sex without hesitation, her slim white fingers keeping Maisie's inner lips spread, exposing her delicate pink jewel. She was glistening with arousal, her bare sex flushed and swollen as the kneeling woman took her into her mouth.

Julia was so entranced by the female lovers that she'd forgotten about Malcolm until he stepped back into the visible area, something limp and black dangling from his fingers.

Her eyes widened; it was a whip.

***

Malcolm caressed Maisie's lush bottom, amused when she jolted at his touch. Oh, how she loathed him.

And he *must* be loathsome to enjoy fucking a woman who couldn't abide the sight or thought or feel of him.

Thank God for money, he thought with a vicious smirk, squeezing her cheek one last time before stepping back so he could warm up Maisie's backside.

It had been a long time since he'd delivered a whipping but talking about it tonight with Julia had made him hungry for it. Still, he was terribly out of practice, so he chosen the softest of the suede flails, a whip so delicate that it was impossible to hurt anyone with it.

Normally he'd switch to something more aggressive after warming her up, but given his state of sexual frustration, a harmless flail was best for all.

It took him a half dozen swings to get into the proper rhythm. Once he felt comfortable with the tool, he could spare more attention to watching the women in the mirror.

Maisie was a greedy, responsive little thing and Amanda—a gorgeous brunette with a mouth that was truly a national treasure—brought her to her first orgasm before Malcolm had even broken a sweat.

"No rest for the wicked," he grunted out when Amanda would have sat back on her heels to give Maisie time to recover.

The experienced whore knew what Malcolm meant and immediately fastened her lips around Maisie's sensitive bud, causing the other woman to whimper and beg.

"Please, Mr. Barton," she whined, trying to jerk her hips away from Amanda's expert lips. But she was bound too tightly to move. "It's too much."

Normally he would have enjoyed her pretty begging—even though she was laying it on a bit thick—but tonight it grated on his nerves.

He briefly considered pausing to gag her, but—to be honest—he wasn't sure he'd find the desire and energy to continue if he did.

So instead, he whipped her until his arm was tired and her arse was rosy. By then, Amanda had forced another three orgasms from her, and Malcolm knew he was just being cruel.

Besides, he was bored; whipping her was not proving as therapeutic as he'd hoped.

Malcolm tossed aside the flail, unbuttoned his placket, and took out his cock, needing to pump himself before he was hard enough to bury himself in her soaking wet cunt.

Well, at least one of them was enjoying a pleasurable evening.

He accidentally caught sight of himself in the glass—a brutish monster with his damaged half face twisted into a snarl—and squeezed his eyes shut, fucking her faster, as if he could outpace the hideous sight.

Unbidden, Julia entered his mind. It wasn't a prurient image, but how she'd looked earlier after thrashing him at their nightly game of cribbage, her eyes shining with mischievous joy, her grin beautiful and genuine.

Unsurprisingly, his cock hardened fully at the memory, his balls drawing up tight to his body.

He smiled and the image shifted, until his imaginary Julia wore a different expression—this one shy and shocked and titillated, after he'd admitted to the sort of sex he enjoyed, in lingering detail.

That memory was all it took to shove him over the brink.

Malcolm grunted and buried himself to his root, his body spasming as he found his release.

Of course he'd barely finished before reality descended on him, reminding him that the cunt milking his balls dry belonged to a woman who despised him.

Malcolm scowled as he pulled out of her body, tired of his own bloody thoughts.

He tucked his wilted cock back into his pants and dimmed the lights to their lowest setting before turning to the women.

"Take off your blindfold, Amanda."

She complied and tossed her hair, cutting him a come-hither smirk with her swollen lips before unbuckling Maisie's ankles while Malcolm worked on the wrist cuffs.

"Thank you, sir," Maisie whispered when she was free, turning her back on Malcolm before slipping off her mask.

Malcolm held out his hand to help Amanda to her feet.

Instead of taking his hand, she spread her thighs enough that he could see her slick skin, and then laid her hand over his placket, smiling up at him. "Are you sure I can't do *anything* else for you, sir?"

He mustered a faint smile for her effort. "Not tonight, sweetheart."

Malcolm left through the panel door that was set into the wall. The women would leave through the main door, which connected to the suites where his "guests" usually stayed.

All except Julia, the only guest he'd ever kept so close to him. The same woman he would stroke himself to later on tonight when sleep eluded him.

Malcolm never should have bothered with Amanda or Maisie tonight because he certainly didn't feel satisfied. If anything, he felt even more disgruntled than he'd felt *before* his session with the two women.

Her Beast

Could that be because neither of them looks at you the way I used to do, Mal? The same way Julia does now: like you're the most interesting and desirable man they've ever met.

Christ, Sukey, you must think I'm an idiot if you expect me to believe that!

I think you're an idiot, she agreed, *but for other reasons entirely.*

Instead of opening the panel to his study, Malcolm rested his forehead against the cool wood and sagged against the wall.

He squeezed his eye shut and wished like hell that he'd never seen Julia Harlow that day. Before her, his life had been—

Miserable, Mal—don't lie to yourself. Julia Harlow is the best thing to happen to you since me, and you know it.

Malcolm groaned. *Being obsessed with her is bad enough. Being obsessed with her and destroying her family is a fucking disaster.*

So don't do it, Mal. The cost of revenge is too high.

Those last words weren't Sukey's, but Smith's.

Malcolm admitted that his friend had been right—the cost was proving to be catastrophically high.

He suspected that he would be paying for a long, long time.

When Malcolm opened his eye, something glittered right beside his shoe.

Chapter 20

Are you sure it isn't in there?" Julia asked Kemp for the fifth or sixth time.

"I'm sorry, Miss, but the only jewelry in the safe is what Mr. Barton has given you." Kemp hesitated and then said, "I don't recall the last time I noticed the bracelet as you've never taken it off."

"I know, I know," Julia muttered, pacing back and forth, anxious and irritable—at herself, more than anyone. How could she have lost the bracelet without even noticing?

Kemp laid a hand on her shoulder, her expression kind and concerned. "I'm sure Mr. Barton could find you a similar one if you—"

"It was my mother's."

"Ah," Kemp dropped her hand.

Julia hadn't taken off the bracelet—other than to bathe—since her father had given it to her five years ago.

Well, *he'd* not given it, he'd sent a servant to give it to her—along with a few other trinkets that had belonged to her mother.

The bracelet wasn't expensive, but it had still been nice enough that Nadine hadn't complained—at least not too loudly—when Julia insisted on wearing it all the time.

Netta, on the other hand, had nagged her relentlessly. "It's just a cheap trifle and doesn't belong at a duke's dinner table."

Julia didn't care; it gave her strength to wear it, *especially* when she'd had dealings with Sebastian and his horrid family.

And now she'd lost it.

"Did you check the greenhouse?" Kemp asked.

"I already looked there."

"What about the dining room?"

"I looked first thing this morning when I woke up and realized it was gone. I've checked the library and the music room. I've looked everywhere."

Well, not *every*where.

The one place she hadn't been able to look was the secret corridor, although she'd been very, very tempted. But it was simply too risky to enter the hallway during the day when a servant might pop up at any moment.

Julia realized that Kemp was looking at her, waiting for further instructions. She gave her a weak smile. "I daresay it will turn up. I suppose I should go to breakfast now."

Kemp nodded and Julia made her way to the dining room, albeit slowly.

Honestly, how was she to face Malcolm after what she'd watched last night?

The same way you've faced him the last two times you spied on him.

No, last night had been… different. Maybe because she had asked him to articulate a fantasy earlier and then he'd acted it out. Why that should be so much more potent, she didn't know.

As it turned out, her worrying was for nothing because the only person in the dining room was James, the footman.

"Good morning, Miss Harlow."

"Good morning, James." She hesitated, and then asked, "Has Mr. Barton already eaten?"

A voice came from behind her before James could answer, "Mr. Barton has *not* eaten and he is famished."

Julia spun around at the sound of Malcolm's voice.

He smiled down at her. "Good morning, Julia. Were you looking for me?"

Julia knew her face was beat red. "Er, no. Just wondering."

"Wonder no further, here I am." He turned to James, but his gaze stayed fixed on her. "Coffee for me—Julia?"

"Yes, coffee is fine."

Julia escaped to the breakfront, but Malcolm was right beside her.

"Did you sleep well, Julia?" he asked, lifting the lid of the dish that usually contained coddled eggs and gesturing to it.

"Yes, I did. And yes, I would like some eggs—just a little, please."

He put a generous spoonful on her plate and smiled down at her, the expression charming, but rare—certainly not accusatory or angry, as if he'd caught her spying in his private hallway. "More?" he asked when Julia just gawked up at him.

"Er, no, thank you." Julia turned away and briefly closed her eyes with relief; obviously he'd not found her bracelet—at least not yet. She still had time.

Once James arrived with their coffee, Malcolm dismissed him.

Julia waited a moment before saying, "May I ask you a question?"

He took a sip of coffee, set down the cup, and gave her a look that made her squirm.

"Not *that* sort of question."

"That's too bad," he said mildly. "What do you want to know?"

"Do you know how much longer I will be here?"

He hesitated, and then said, "I should think you'll be home by the New Year."

"So soon?" she blurted, and then wanted to sink beneath the table in mortification at her obvious disappointment.

You are a whore, Julia! Just like your mother.

Julia gritted her teeth against the hated words and turned to Malcolm, who was watching her with a slightly furrowed brow.

"Do you think it is strange that I don't balk more at being held captive?"

He blinked—slowly—and then sat back in his chair. "What do you mean?"

"Shouldn't I be fighting you?"

His eyebrow lifted. "Physically?"

Julia made an exasperated noise. "I could hardly overpower you. I meant in other ways."

"You mean, should you make my life more miserable? Torment the servants? Break things? Make a ladder out of torn bed linen and try to escape?" He hesitated, smiled, and then added, "throw more knives?"

Julia ignored his gentle teasing. "I meant that I shouldn't be speaking civilly to you, playing chess and cribbage with you, skating with you."

He stared at her for a moment and then said, "Why do you think you aren't more resistant?" He sounded genuinely curious rather than mocking.

It was a subject that Julia had avoided thinking about ever since she'd capitulated and begged for his company.

"I know I should feel like a traitor and that I should hate you, but…"

"But?" he prodded.

"But I suspect that my father has done something horrid to you—something that means he deserves whatever you will do. Don't worry," she added hastily, even though he looked as inscrutable as ever, "I know better than to ask what he's done and I don't want to know. But I can't help feeling—" she struggled to find the right word.

"Disloyal?" he suggested.

It wasn't exactly the right word, but it was close enough. "Yes."

"Has your father done a great deal to earn your loyalty, Julia?"

"He is my father!" she retorted, more than a little scandalized by his question. "Shouldn't one naturally be loyal to one's parents?"

"I don't have parents, so I'm not the best person to ask about that."

Julia felt like an ignorant oaf; how could she have forgotten that? "I'm sorry. I didn't mean—"

"Don't worry, Julia, you didn't hurt my feelings." An odd expression flickered across his face and she thought he was going to say something more, but he merely shook his head.

"What is it?" she asked. "Tell me—is there something that I should know, Malcolm?" The question was inadequate when it came to expressing what she was feeling. The truth was that she both wanted to know and was afraid to know. Knowledge might be power, but it could also be painful—like that little boy Malcolm had told her about last night.

He sighed, suddenly looking tired ."There have been numerous scientific theories bandied about in recent years regarding human beings and their relation to animals."

Julia blinked; those were not words she'd been expecting. "Erm, you mean what Mr. Darwin said? About evolution?"

"It is connected to that. Some people assert there is a vestigial part of the human brain—left over from a time when our ancestors were closer to beasts—that warns us of threats and danger. As civilized beings, we don't always recognize the warning for what it is, or even accept that it exists."

"Are you saying that my lack of loyalty is my brain trying to warn me about something dangerous? About my father?"

"I'm suggesting that if you are not feeling especially loyal to Thomas Harlow, there might be a very good reason for it. As to your other question, my answer is *no*. I do not possess any information that I think would be helpful or relevant to you." He paused and then added, "If I were to learn anything important, I would tell you."

Strangely, Julia believed him.

***

Malcolm was teetering on the edge of throwing caution to the winds and warning Julia—in no uncertain terms—that her impending marriage was a disaster in the making when James entered the dining room and saved him from himself.

176

But Mrs. Harlow didn't care for that question, either. Instead, she answered his prior one, "Of course I spoke to Thomas! He is the one who told me you abducted my brother and that *useless slut.*"

Malcolm squeezed the arms of the chair to keep from grabbing the emaciated bitch and making her eat her words.

He squelched his rage and got to the point—before he really did hurt her. "I'll ask you the same question I asked your dear brother, Mrs. Harlow: whose idea was it?"

Her lips parted in shock and her eyelids fluttered as she searched for a convenient lie.

"You have one chance to tell me the truth. One." Malcolm held up one finger—making sure to use his damaged left hand—and pushed all the loathing he felt for her into his quiet words. "If you lie to me, I will make you the sorriest woman in Britain. Are we understood?"

Her righteous indignation leached away, leaving her looking pasty and shriveled, as if she were slowly collapsing on the inside.

"I'll tell you the truth."

"Get on with it."

"I didn't hear about any of it until it was all over and done and—"

Malcolm barked an ugly, humorless laugh.

"—neither did my brother. Or Thomas," she added hastily.

"Do tell, Mrs. Harlow."

"It was all that vile pervert's plan—Brian's."

Malcolm laughed again, louder this time.

She scowled. "I suppose you find it difficult to believe because you were *fucking* him—letting a murderer into your own house. Your own bed. That would make *you* culpable in your wife's death, wouldn't it?"

"Indeed it would."

She looked nonplussed at Malcolm's easy agreement.

"Tell me what Brian would get from masterminding such a plan, Mrs. Harlow?"

"Twenty percent of the company. How do you think he's managed to live in the lap of luxury in Paris all these years?"

Malcolm didn't dispute her claim, nor did he accept it. If there was one thing that he'd learned since commencing this investigation, it was not to rule out any possibility and not to believe anything that any of these people said. At least not until he had proof.

"That's an interesting idea," he said, earning another startled look from her. "But I'm not here to talk about Brian. I'm here to talk about *you* and what *you* knew."

"I already told you—I didn't know anything about it until afterward."

"What do you think your brother said when I asked him the same question?"

She tried to mask her fear with a sneer. "I assume he told you the truth. Why are you laughing?" she demanded

He ignored her question. "Your brother said it was all your husband's—"

"You are lying filth! He would never—"

"Would you like to know *exactly* what your brother said?" He gave her a quizzical look. "Or perhaps I should call him your lover?"

Mrs. Harlow shot to her feet, as he'd known she would. "How dare—"

"Sheehan said it was all Tommy's idea. He said he was told to ensure the entire warehouse was destroyed so that I wouldn't be able to fulfill any part of my new contract and Tommy could step into my shoes."

She glared down at him, the spitting image of one of the gargoyles on Notre Dame. "That is so asinine it doesn't even merit acknowledging."

"That is *exactly* what I told the father of your children!"

Her face sagged in horror at his words. "What—how—"

"Shhhhh. Don't worry, Mrs. Harlow, I've not told your husband about your lover. Yet." He smiled unpleasantly.

"You—that—" she spluttered, shaking her head. "There is no proof," she finally managed.

Malcolm stood and she flinched away from him. "Not to worry," he soothed, walking around to the front of his desk. "I'm just going to give you something you might find interesting."

He unlocked the top drawer, took out the piece of paper that was waiting for him, and slid it across to her.

She stared down at it as if it might bite and then her eyes widened when she recognized the handwriting and she snatched it up, her gaze flickering wildly over the words before dropping to the signature.

Her mouth opened but no sound came out. When she could finally wrench her gaze from the words and stare at him with hate-filled eyes he already knew what she would do.

Her hands moved so quickly they were a blur as she tore the letter into tiny pieces. "There is your proof!"

"No, that was *your* copy. I had your brother write out several copies of his confession just in case one of them was damaged."

Her loathing vanished in the blink of an eye and she clutched his sleeve. "Don't do this. Please. I beg of you."

"I'm not going to do anything, Mrs. Harlow, *you* are."

She stared at him, uncomprehending. "Me? What do you want from me," she whispered.

Malcolm pried her fingers from his sleeve and leaned toward her. "I'll tell you what I told your lover, Mrs. Harlow. "I want a life, for a life."

Chapter 21

You seem preoccupied this evening," Julia said, setting down her dessert fork and pushing her plate away. "Have you had a busy day?"

Irritation flickered across Malcolm's normally inscrutable features. "There have been numerous delays at the store we are building in New York." He gestured to the wine and she nodded. Once he'd refilled their glasses, he took a sip and then sat back with a sigh. "Trying to finish a building during Christmas is not wise"

"Why is that?"

"The entire city grinds to a halt for the better part of two weeks."

"And what about you?"

"Me?" he asked, his eyebrow raised.

"Yes. Do *you* take a day of rest on Christmas?"

He looked startled by the question. "Er, not usually."

"It is tomorrow, you know—Christmas."

He gave her a wry smile, but it quickly changed to an even more unusual expression: regret. "I am sorry to be keeping you from your family."

Julia shrugged.

"You won't miss them?" he asked.

"No."

He gave a sharp bark of laughter.

"What?" she asked, and then grimaced when she caught his meaning. "Oh, I suppose that didn't come out the way I meant it to. What I meant was that—well, you know why my father sent me away—" her face heated at the admission. "I assume you know other things—like how little love is lost between my father, stepmother, and me—" she pulled a face. "I shouldn't admit such a thing out loud, I suppose."

"Why not?"

"Because it is impolite to talk about one's family problems in public."

"It's not polite to abduct young women, either."

Julia laughed. "You make an excellent point."

"Besides, I'm not interested in what is polite. I'd much rather we exchange truths than platitudes, Julia."

That sentiment pleased her and she smiled. "Well, to own the truth, I would love to be around my little brothers at Christmas but Nadine believes that celebrating with one's children is something only rustics do, so she and my father are usually at some house party or other during the holidays and she sends the boys to her mother, even though they don't speak to each other."

"They don't get along?"

"Nadine loathes her mother because Mrs. Sheehan is… well, she isn't the sort to put on airs. And Mrs. Sheehan despises Nadine's pretension. In any case, there is nobody at home who will miss me this year." Her throat tightened at her lie, her eyes suddenly burning with unwanted tears. Before she could think better of it, she added defiantly, "But I *will* miss seeing my older brother."

He looked arrested. "I didn't know you had an older brother."

"So, it turns out that you don't know everything about me after all, do you?"

"Apparently not," he said, looking more than a little chagrined by the admission. "Is he a half-sibling?"

She snorted. "Hardly. He is my older brother by eighteen minutes." He stared, uncomprehending. "He is my twin, Malcolm."

"Oh."

"Why do you look so betwattled?"

"Because I've never heard about him—and I recall hearing about you all those years ago."

"You did?" she asked, intrigued by this new information. "How did you hear about me?"

"I knew Brian quite well. He mentioned that he had a niece by his older brother."

"Ah," Julia said, deflating. Not so intriguing after all, then.

"Your brother doesn't live in your family home?" Malcolm asked.

Julia was torn between the wish to talk about Richard and an ingrained fear of doing so because of her father. All her life Thomas Harlow had threatened all of them about keeping Richard's existence a secret.

Quite suddenly, defying her father seemed like an excellent reason to talk about her brother.

"My father keeps Richard hidden because he's… different."

"Different how?"

Julia thought about Richard's sweet, loving face and the way her father treated him and frowned. "He is simple—or at least that is what my father and Nadine call him." Actually, they called him worse names than that, but Julia didn't want to speak the words.

When you say *hidden*, what do you mean?"

"Richard lives with our old nurse at Brookfield—it's just outside St. Albans."

"Why does your father keep him a secret?"

"He says nobody would want to marry me if they learned that such a thing ran in our family. He is especially anxious that Basingstoke doesn't know about Richard given his family's mania for bloodlines." Julia's eyes narrowed. "Why are you so interested in him?"

"No particular reason."

An unpleasant thought leapt to mind. "Please tell me you are not going to abduct Richard, too?"

"I won't abduct anyone else. Why would you think I would?"

She shrugged. "I've been here for quite a while, so I thought maybe my father was not, er, being cooperative and you needed another captive." She cut him an anxious glance. "Is he? Being cooperative, I mean?"

"Everything is fine, Julia."

"What does that mean?"

"Just what I said." He hesitated and added, "I'm sorry you won't get to see your twin over the holidays."

"Well, I wouldn't get to see him in any event. Don't feel badly on my account because I quite enjoy myself now that you've stopped ignoring me and I've got Kemp, Norris, and John to play cards with on the nights you're too busy for me."

His eyebrow—his most expressive feature—lifted. "John?"

"That's Mr. Butkins's first name." She smirked. "Or didn't you know that?"

"I am his employer and sign his cheques," he said dryly. "I know his Christian name. I'm just surprised you do."

"Why are you surprised? Did you expect me to sit here alone, talking to the walls when you leave to go off to do… whatever?"

He laughed. "It sounds like you miss me, Julia."

"I hardly noticed you were gone," she lied, the words sounding false to her own ears.

Judging by his smug smile, he thought so, too.

***

Malcolm moved his second peg into the last hole and sat back in his chair.

"Well, rats!" Julia muttered, glaring at the cribbage board as if it had personally offended her.

"That is twice in a row that I've lurched you, Julia. You are distracted tonight," Malcolm couldn't help teasing.

"I think you spend your days practicing cribbage rather than working," she accused.

He chuckled.

"You said you'd not played in years and yet you count faster than anyone I've ever met!"

And Julia was the most painstaking, methodical point calculator that Malcolm had ever met. It was bloody adorable.

"I've always been good with numbers," he admitted mildly.

"Did you learn everything you know at the, er, orphanage?"

He was amused by her hesitancy to say the word, as if it were not proper for polite company.

"If you mean schooling, then *yes*." He could have told her that his real education only began *after* he met Smith and started working for Charles Greene.

"How did you—" she broke off and chewed her lip. "I have a proposal."

"Yes?" he asked, intrigued.

"I propose we not be limited to one question at night."

He laughed. "Oh, is that only a breakfast tradition?"

"It makes conversation difficult," she pointed out.

"Ask whatever you like."

"But you won't necessarily answer, will you?"

"Ask and find out."

"Very well. Tell me what it was like at the orphanage. How long were you there? Why did you leave? Where did you go? Do you have close friends you grew up with?"

Malcolm cast his mind back a good thirty years. "I left when I was twelve—all the boys did—when I went to work for a coal merchant."

"That sounds rather dreadful. Did you hate it?"

"It was not my favorite job, but I liked my master at the time. Unfortunately, he died barely a year in and I did not like working for his son." That was putting it mildly. "So, I ended our association and that's when I went to work for Charles Greene."

"He was the crime lord?" She set her chin in her hand and stared up at him as if he were the most fascinating man alive.

Malcolm's cock highly approved of her expression.

"Tell me about him, what was he like?" she asked.

Before he could decide exactly what he was going to tell her the library door opened and Butkins appeared in the doorway.

"Hello, John," Julia piped up.

Malcolm's secretary blushed, as if Julia had said something wicked rather than just using his Christian name.

"Good evening, Miss Julia."

"What is it?" Malcolm said, inexplicably testy all of a sudden.

"Er, Mr. Smith is here, sir."

Malcolm blinked; Smith visiting? How unusual.

He turned to Julia, who'd perked up visibly at the prospect of a visitor.

"Did he need a word alone?" he asked.

"Actually, he indicated he'd like to meet your, er, guest, sir."

Why, the nosy bugger!

"He wants to meet me?" Julia demanded, wide-eyed.

Malcolm turned to Butkins. "Show him in."

"Very good, sir."

The door had barely closed when Julia said, "Who is Mr. Smith?"

"He is an old friend—my oldest friend, in fact." That was the truth and far easier than explaining *who* Smith was. Especially when Malcolm was never quite sure.

"Aren't you afraid I'll tell him you've kidnapped me?"

"He already knows."

Rather than look disappointed, she looked delighted. "Ah, a conspirator?"

Malcolm laughed. "No, I'm afraid this is all my doing."

"But he must be a *good* friend if you share your criminal activities with him?"

Fortunately, the door opened just then and the Smith himself entered, sparing Malcolm from further questioning.

Chapter 22

Julia knew that she should excuse herself so the men could socialize privately, but she was positively on fire with curiosity to know what Malcolm Barton's oldest friend was like.

You're burning to know <u>everything</u> about your captor.

That was true and she refused to be ashamed.

Julia's attention was riveted to Malcolm while he greeted his friend—whom he towered over, just like he did everyone—his open, affectionate smile filling her with a sense of almost unbearable yearning.

I want him to look at me that way, she suddenly realized.

Malcolm turned to Julia. "Julia, this is Mr. Smith. Smith, this is Miss Julia Harlow."

"It is a pleasure to meet you, Miss Harlow," Mr. Smith said, imbuing the common salutation with genuine meaning as he bowed over her hand, his dark eyes glinting with a knowing look that made her blush for some reason.

"Thank you," Julia mumbled, oddly flustered by the man.

"Can I get you something to drink, Smith?" Malcolm asked.

"I'll have whatever you're having."

Malcolm turned to Julia. "Shall I ring for more tea? Or would you like something else?"

"Nothing for me, thank you."

He turned to pour the other man's drink and Julia found herself the subject of Mr. Smith's silent scrutiny.

He was a handsome, if rather austere looking man, his face a collection of sharp angles that might have been intimidating if not for the warm, welcoming look in his lovely brown gaze. Strangely, there was something about him that seemed… familiar.

"Malcolm says you are his oldest friend," Julia said to break the silence.

Smith chuckled. "I wonder if he meant I am his *oldest* friend or his oldest friend."

"Both," Malcolm tossed over his shoulder.

Smith smiled at Julia. "We have known each other a very long time. I think Malcolm was fourteen, isn't that right?" he asked as Malcolm handed him a glass of golden liquid.

"Thirteen."

"So you didn't grow up together, but met after you'd left your first apprenticeship with the coal merchant?" she asked, wondering about the lightening-fast look of surprise that Smith cut his friend.

"Yes, after that." A faint red stain darkened Malcolm's cheek, as if Smith had caught him at something naughty.

It didn't surprise her to learn that Mr. Smith had worked for the crime lord, too. For all his warm humor, he had the same sort of predatorial air as Malcolm.

"I understand you are quite a talented equestrienne," Smith said before she could pursue the subject of their early friendship.

Julia stared. "How do you know that?"

"I met an acquaintance of yours when I was last up north—Lady Bankton."

She gasped. "How remarkable! Where did you meet her?"

"I've known Bankton for some time but I only met his new countess a few weeks ago when I stayed with them at their house in Rydale."

"I'm terribly envious!" she said, not lying. "Did you hunt with the Bilsdale pack while you were there?"

"No, I'm afraid I don't hunt." He smiled slightly. "At least not foxes."

Julia opened her mouth to ask what he meant, but Malcolm cleared his throat, cut the other man a sharp look, and said, "Lady Bankton is your schoolfriend Lily?"

Julia knew she was blushing. "Yes, she married the earl two years ago—right after leaving school." She gave Mr. Smith a puzzled look. "How is it that my name came up in a conversation with Lady Bankton? Or did you just come right out and admit that your oldest friend had abducted me?"

He laughed, visibly delighted. "I'm afraid your abduction didn't come up. She mentioned she'd be coming to London with her husband when he visits later next month. When I asked her how she planned to spend her time, she mentioned visiting a school friend who was soon to marry." He smiled, the expression attractively crinkling the skin around his eyes. "That's how you came up. She lamented that you'd not seen each other in some time."

"Yes, far too long," Julia admitted, excited at the thought of a visit from Lily, something she would *ensure* happened, regardless of what her father or Nadine had to say about it.

"And she seemed… happy?"

"Very," Mr. Smith said. "The earl shares her passion for the sport and he bestowed quite a magnificent hunter on her while I was there—an anniversary present, I believe."

"I am glad to hear it." And she was. But she was also a little jealous of her friend. Her husband might be older and not especially handsome, but at least Lord Bankton appeared to care for Lily and dote on her, which was more than she could say for Sebastian.

"How did you say you knew the earl?" she asked.

"We met through business several years ago and discovered we shared an interest in art."

"What sort of art?"

"Primarily painting, although I've recently acquired a sculpture or two."

"Miss Harlow is a painter," Malcolm said. "Kemp tells me they are quite good although she won't show me any."

Julia laughed. "First, I would never be so arrogant as to call myself a *painter*; I dabble. Second, they are certainly not *art*. And third, you may see them any time you like." Well, all but the one she was going to surprise him with.

"I've actually seen one of Miss Harlow's paintings," Smith said.

"Where could—oh no!" Julia grimaced. "Please tell me Lily didn't show you that childish effort I gave her?"

"I thought it was a charming painting of Lady Bankton."

She snorted. "As long as you didn't look too closely at the hands."

"I have an artist friend who complains about ears," he said. "But every time I look at something that she is unhappy with, I cannot see it."

"Smith knows Mrs. Edward Fanshaw," Malcolm said. "Nora Hudson is the name she goes by in the art world."

"Nora Hudson? Why, I saw her work at an exhibition last spring. She is quite marvelous," Julia stammered, vividly recalling her body's reactions to the erotic and wicked paintings.

Judging by the way Smith's eyes glinted he knew what she was thinking.

"That must have been her show at the Roth gallery."

"It was," she admitted.

Mr. Smith grinned. "It was quite a spectacular display of her work before it was shuttered for public indecency."

Julia scowled. "I was disgusted when I read about that in the paper. Did she actually go to gaol?"

He chuckled. "No—her husband saw to that. And don't be angry on Nora's behalf because she was quite tickled to be at the center of such a storm. Her work is always in demand but that controversy catapulted her into an entirely new category."

"Smith has sat for Mrs. Fanshawe on multiple occasions," Malcolm said.

"*That* is why you look familiar," Julia said. "There was a section at the gallery with several of you, wasn't there? They were the ones that—" she broke off and bit her lip.

"Weren't nudes?" Smith said. "No, I was clothed in all those."

"Smith has purchased all Mrs. Fanshawe's more incriminating paintings," Malcolm added, grinning at his friend.

Julia's gaze slid over Mr. Smith and she had to admit he appeared to be a fine physical specimen.

When she looked up it was to see both men regarding her with amusement.

"Oh dear," Julia said, mortified to be caught in the act of examining a man's physique. "I think it is time for me to retire," she said, before she could embarrass herself any further.

Besides, now would be an excellent time to search the hallway for her bracelet seeing that Malcolm was occupied with his friend.

***

Malcolm turned to Smith once he'd shut the door behind Julia and scowled at the gloating expression on his friend's face. "What?" he snapped rudely.

Smith tried to assume an innocent expression and failed miserably. "Nothing. Nothing at all."

"Then why are you grinning in that obnoxious manner?"

"Because I am pleased to see you happy, my friend."

Malcolm tried to maintain his scowl, but, for once, his face refused to obey him. His lips twitched into a smile and he grunted.

"She is a lovely woman," Smith said.

The comment irritated him for some reason. "Yes, she is beautiful, but she is more than just her face and body," he said sharply. "She's also clever, witty, and so full of life that"—he broke off when the other man chuckled.

Malcolm groaned when he realized just how easily he'd risen to the bait. "Christ," he muttered, throwing himself into his chair.

"I only spoke to her for a few minutes but I could see all that and more. She's delightful."

Malcolm preened like an idiot at his friend's praise, as if *he* had anything to do with why Julia Harlow was the way she was.

"So, to what do I owe the honor of your presence tonight, my friend?"

"Curiosity," Smith admitted without any shame. He reached into his exquisitely cut evening coat and brought out a piece of paper. "I also wanted to give this to you."

Malcolm eyed the paper with no little apprehension. "Do I want to know what that is?"

"It's about Miss Harlow's brother—her twin."

Malcolm gave an undignified squawk. "How in hell do you know about him? *I* only found out about the man's existence tonight at dinner."

"Yes, well, my information gathering network is better than yours."

Malcolm snatched the paper out of his hand. It held several addresses, one for Richard Harlow and the other two for men he'd never heard of.

"What's this for?"

"Joe Bacon said you wanted to know about the girl's bargain with her father—the reason why she has agreed to marry Basingstoke."

"I asked him to find me something on that *days* ago and he's come up with nothing."

Smith gave him an insufferable smile. "You should have come to *me*, my dear Malcolm."

"What did you learn?" he asked grimly.

"Your Miss Harlow is marrying Basingstoke so her father will transfer ownership of the house where her brother has lived all his life."

Malcolm frowned. "*That's* what he promised her to make her marry that bastard?"

Smith nodded.

"And she's not *my* Miss Harlow," he added.

Smith merely smiled.

"What are the other two names for?"

"The girl isn't a fool and she insisted on having the agreement drawn up and signed—"

"Her brother lacks capacity to engage in a contract—not if what she says about him is true—and Harlow would know that!"

Smith nodded. "Yes. It will be easy for Harlow's lawyers to void the contract."

"Christ! The man is so crooked he can't even deal straight with his own daughter."

"It's worse than that. Are you sure you want to hear it?"

"No, I'm sure I don't. But, go ahead and tell me."

"He's already got a buyer for the property—Brookfield, it's called, a small but pleasant manor, apparently—and he's putting his son into the care of a man named Doctor Benjamin Patterson. Patterson operates several homes that hide society's, er, *secrets* for a premium price."

Malcolm let out a stream of choice curse words.

Smith went on, "Patterson doesn't engage in any sort of gothic quackery with his patients although he does adhere to the maxim that a heavily sedated patient is a tractable one."

Malcolm could only shake his head, too disgusted for words.

"The first name on the list is the solicitor who drew up the agreement." Smith's smile was unpleasant. "It seems to me that a man who didn't inform his own client of the law deserves some sort of… correction."

"I couldn't agree more. The second name?"

"Harlow's man of business. Just in case you were interested in doing something about the upcoming sale of Brookfield."

Malcolm smiled, and he knew it wouldn't be pretty. "Fortunately, there is just enough time to pay both men a visit and spread some Christmas joy."

"Will you say anything to Harlow?"

"I don't know—it might be better to surprise him. In any case, I'm going to see him tonight." When Smith merely nodded, Malcolm narrowed his eyes. "But you already knew that, didn't you?"

"Just keeping a helpful eye—and ear—out for you, Malcolm."

"*On* me, is more like it. Hasn't anyone ever told you that it's impolite to spy on your friends?"

Smith laughed, but the humor drained away quickly. "Be careful tonight, Malcolm. The man is a snake."

Malcolm smiled. "Yes, but I'm a *bigger* snake."

Chapter 23

An hour later Thomas Harlow opened the front door himself when Malcolm knocked.

"What an honor!" Malcolm mocked.

Tommy scowled. "Don't flatter yourself. All the servants are gone—I gave them the holiday off."

"Are you here all alone, then?

"No. My wife is here too, of course." His eyes narrowed. "She's too distraught about our sons to go to the house party we'd planned to attend."

Malcolm pulled a sad face. "Ah, I feel guilty about that."

Tommy snorted. "We can talk upstairs."

Malcolm followed the other man up a staircase with a garish carpet runner and then onto a landing with hideous art on the walls.

"Would you like a drink?" Tommy asked grudgingly.

"I'll have whatever you're having." Malcolm looked around Tommy's study as he faffed about with the drinks. It was what he would have expected of the man: expensive but tasteless furnishings that screamed *parvenu*, complete with an insufferable portrait of Harlow and his cadaverous wife hanging above the huge hearth.

He heard movement on his left side and turned to find Harlow staring at his mask, the glass extended half-way.

Malcolm smiled. "Sorry, I'm afraid you were in my blind—and deaf—spot." He took the glass and raised it. "Here is to two lads from the Dials who've made good."

"I actually am not from the Dials," Harlow stiffly corrected.

Malcolm knew that. "Oh. Where were you and Bri from, again?"

His jaw tightened at the sound of his brother's name. "Whitechapel."

Malcolm laughed at the faint distinction and set down his glass without taking a drink.

Harlow frowned at that but made no comment. Instead, he returned to the protection of his desk and set his own drink aside. "I don't suppose we should dance about the matter. I want my daughter back."

"Yes, I received a very surprising telegram from your brother Brian asking if I knew of her whereabouts. I thought it was quite out of the blue, to be honest. It was the first I've heard from Brian in over fifteen years, not since my tragic… accident. I can't imagine why he thinks that I know anything about your daughter."

The other man sighed. "Enough of your games. I know you have her—and Sheehan. I've torn the bloody city apart. You are the only one left."

"Only what left?"

"The only man who might—however unfairly—bear me a grudge."

"A grudge for what?"

"Quit toying with me, Barton. What do I have to do to get my daughter back before her bloody wedding?"

"That's what you care about? Not your daughter, but her wedding?"

"Don't act all sanctimonious to me—not after using her to get what you wanted."

"Whose idea was it?" Malcolm asked mildly.

Harlow hesitated.

"Do not play me for a fool, Tommy."

"It was Sheehan's," he said, sounding almost convincing. "He did it without asking me. The man has an unhealthy love of setting things on fire."

Malcolm smiled and Harlow recoiled. "You're telling me Sheehan conceived of the idea and executed it without your knowledge?"

"That's exactly what I'm saying."

Malcolm laughed.

"You could never prove anything against him or any of us. Ever."

"Funny, but that's what your wife said when she came to visit me. Of course, she was talking about something entirely—" Malcolm stopped, made a lazy, dismissive gesture, and then said, "But that is neither here, nor there. What matters is that I'm not after proof, I'm after answers, Tommy."

"Well, I just gave you one," he snapped. "And I'd like to know what you are insinuating about my wife?"

Malcolm ignored his question. "I'm sorry. I should have said I was after *honest* answers."

"I swear that it was Sheehan. I barely knew him then. I had only just offered for his sister. For reasons unknown to me, the man got a bee in his bonnet about the damned shipping company—I don't recall how he even found out about it. He said it was a once-in-a-lifetime chance, but then Leeland chose you and rejected my offer. Sheehan couldn't leave it alone. You have to believe me when I say I knew nothing about his plans."

Lies, lies, and more lies. And not even good ones.

"And so Sheehan took me out of the running so *you* could benefit—out of the kindness of his heart?"

"Well, he did it for his sister, of course."

Malcolm chuckled. "Now *that* I believe."

Harlow frowned. "What are you—"

"When did you find out what he'd done?" Malcolm interrupted.

Harlow's face creased with relief that Malcolm might prove stupid enough to buy his lies. "Not until after it was over, when Sheehan came to me and boasted."

Malcolm was sure some boasting went on, but he doubted Sheehan was the only one doing it.

When he didn't reply, Harlow said, "I couldn't do such a thing. You believe me, don't you?"

"I believe that you don't like to dirty your hands. And I believe that Sheehan and his sister wanted more."

Thomas's lips parted in surprise. "Wait—I never said Nadine was involved. The first she heard about it was the other day." He scowled at Malcolm. "Thanks to your arrangement with her bitch of a mother and that trick with my sons, by the way."

"So that is the first she knew about it all?"

"Yes. Absolutely."

Malcolm reached into his coat and Thomas flinched.

He laughed and raised his hand in a calming gesture. "Relax, Tommy! I'm just taking out a letter for you." He lifted it up and waved it back and forth. "See, nothing harmful in my hand," he lied.

"A letter? From whom?"

Malcolm tossed it onto the desk. "Go ahead and read it."

Tommy snatched it up and unfolded it, his face going as pale as his wife's had done when she read her copy.

When he looked up, Malcolm tossed a photograph onto the desk—the same one he'd shown Sheehan to make him so cooperative.

Tommy picked up and the photograph and Malcolm watched as shock and disbelief turned to white-hot rage.

"The resemblance is quite astounding when you look for it, isn't it?"

Tommy crumpled the photograph in his fist and then looked up. "Where is he?"

"Don't worry about Sheehan—you'll see him soon enough. Worry about this, instead." Malcolm pulled out a final piece of paper and threw that down.

"What's that?"

"A list of instructions."

"Instructions? What instructions?"

"The first item on the list I want delivered to my house tomorrow, the rest I'll give you until the end of next month to take care of." He smirked nastily. "After all, some of the items will take some… scheming—but you're good at that, aren't you?"

Tommy snatched up the paper, tearing it in his haste to claw it open.

His eyes threatened to bulge out of his head. "I can't do all these things! You're—you're mad! And this last thing"—he shoved the paper at Malcolm, as if he'd not been the one who wrote it. "A life for a life? What does that even mean?"

"You're a smart man, I'm sure you'll figure it out."

Tommy shook his head, his eyes wide and frantic. "But you already have Carl and *he's* the one who killed her! What more do you want?"

Malcolm dropped his hands onto the smooth, cool surface of the desk and leaned toward the other man, bleakly amused when he recoiled. "Two people died in that fire, Harlow. Perhaps you didn't know that?"

"Two? But I thought it was just"—his jaw dropped and horror flooded his eyes. "Your wife," he whispered, "she was—"

"Yes," Malcolm said, not wanting him to finish the sentence. "She was."

"But… I—I don't understand what you want."

"I want the truth."

Tommy breathed rapidly through his mouth, looking like a landed carp. "I—I—" He gulped. "You were right, Malcolm. It wasn't just Carl, it was Nadine, too. She was the one who came up with the idea. She's always been that way—pushing for more and more." His face twisted into a vicious snarl. "I gave her *everything* and the greedy whore was fucking her own brother!"

Malcolm laughed. "It sounds like you and Mrs. Harlow are going to have quite the conversation after I leave here tonight."

Tommy stared at him with pure hatred. "You vile, disgusting—"

"Come now, Tommy. You should be thanking me instead of cursing me. After all, I've made it easier for you to give me what I want." Malcolm stopped smiling. "What was it that I wanted, Tommy?"

Tommy's rage drained away, leaving him looking sick. "A life for a life," he whispered.

"Good," Malcolm said. His eye narrowed and he jabbed a finger in Tommy's stunned face. "Just remember: if you don't take care of it, I'll make the choice for you. And I don't care which of one of you will pay the price."

Chapter 24

Julia wanted to scream.

After leaving Malcolm and Mr. Smith in the library she'd hurried back to her rooms only to find Kemp pacing her chambers while two men did something that involved a lot of banging and clanging in her bathing chamber.

"What in the world is going on, Kemp?"

"I'm so sorry Miss Julia. I discovered a leak in your showerbath not long after I dressed you for dinner. These gentlemen," she scowled at the men, "*promised* me they would be gone by the time you came back."

"We're 'bout done, missus," one of them men said.

"That is what you said three hours ago." When the man didn't answer, Kemp pursed her lips and shook her head.

Julia looked from the men to Kemp, her hope of searching the secret corridor while Malcolm was occupied rapidly dwindling.

"Why don't you just help me into my dressing gown and then go off to bed," Julia suggested. If Kemp left then Julia could sneak away while the men worked.

"I won't leave you unattended! What would Mr. Barton say?"

She considered pointing out that Malcolm was not only her abductor, but he was alone with her all the time. But one look at Kemp's determined face told her that excuse wouldn't work.

And so she paced and waited.

It took over *two hours* for the men to repair the leak, which meant it was slightly before two in the morning when Julia finally managed to slip into the corridor.

As much as she wanted to rush to the window and spy, she took her time, making sure to examine every inch of floor as she went.

But by the time she reached Malcolm's study, she was beginning to despair. If the bracelet wasn't in this stretch of hallway, then she had no idea where it—

"Looking for this?" a deep voice asked.

Julia jumped and shrieked.

"Sorry, I didn't mean to startle you." Malcolm emerged from an alcove Julia had somehow never noticed before. Something glittered in his outstretched hand: the clasp on the pearl bracelet, which was set with small brilliants.

Julia took the bracelet without speaking.

He stepped into the middle of the corridor and gestured to the alcove. "Come inside."

Julia peered and saw it wasn't an alcove at all, but another panel doorway, this one into his study.

The room looked different now that she was inside it—bigger, the colors richer, the smell of books, leather, and the lingering scent of Malcolm's cologne combining to form a heady mix.

"I'm going to have a whiskey. Would you like one?"

Julia startled; nobody had ever offered her spirits before—even though she'd sneaked a sip or two when she was younger—because it wasn't the sort of thing a lady drank.

"Yes, please," she said, deciding she would probably need something stronger than ratafia to get her through the next few minutes.

Malcolm turned to pour two glasses, leaving Julia with her thoughts, which were zinging around the inside of her head like so many moths banging against light cover.

You'd better think of something to say, Julia.

What could she possibly say? He knew that she'd watched him, the only question was *what* exactly she'd seen.

You'd better have a believable lie ready.

Julia stared at his back as he poured their drinks, unable to look away from him even though she'd seen him dressed in the same clothing only hours earlier. What was it about him that she found so intriguing?

Was it merely the attraction of wealth and power?

Or perhaps just the sheer mystery surrounding him. What was he hiding behind his mask? Beneath his clothing? He never even showed himself to the women he did such wicked, intimate things with. Did anyone ever see him?

Norris, surely? A man could hardly remained fully covered in front of his valet. Could he?

Thinking of him taking off his clothing had her pulse racing.

Malcolm turned to her, and all her thoughts fled.

He handed her a glass, his expression grim as he stared down at her.

The pulse fluttered at the base of her throat and she was grateful for the high neck of the dressing gown she wore.

He sat down in the chair next to hers rather than behind his desk. "How long?"

She opened her mouth to ask him what he meant—to buy herself a little more time—but found herself saying, "I found out about the doorway four nights ago."

A muscle jumped just below his eye. "Did you enjoy watching?"

"Wh-what?"

"You came back a second, third, and fourth time so I suppose you must have." A small smile curved his lips and humor glinted in his eye.

He wasn't angry… he was *amused!*

"I thought you'd be furious," she said.

"Why?"

Julia sputtered. "Because—well, you're so private."

"In general, that is true. But I like the thought of you watching me fuck another woman."

The squeaking noise she made was mortifying.

He chuckled and sipped his drink.

"But… *why?*" she finally managed.

"Because it makes me hard."

Julia's jaw dropped open, thankfully without the noise this time.

His gaze lowered to her throat, and then back up to her lips, which she'd parted to get more air—air that was suddenly hot and crackling as his pupil flared.

He wants me.

The thought was like a spark to a powder keg. The emotion that roared through her was so rare that it took her a moment to identify it. It was power that his look ignited.

For once in her life, Julia felt powerful.

"Do you want to do those things to me, Malcolm?" she asked, her voice low but firm.

He answered without hesitation. "Yes."

Julia rejoiced inside at his admission, but she could see from his face that he wasn't finished.

"But I'm not going to do those—or any other things—to you."

Julia felt as though he'd slapped her.

"I apologize for what you saw and—"

"No." She pushed up out of her chair. "Don't apologize for something *I* did. *I'm* the one who came back again and again."

"Julia, this isn't—"

"Stop treating me like an ignorant child! You didn't shock me"—she stopped, pulled a face, and then said, "Well, truthfully, you *did* shock me," she admitted, "but you didn't disgust me or—or damage me." She made an exasperated noise. "Don't you understand? I came back time after time because I want you to do all those things to me, Malcolm."

Thankfully, Malcolm didn't laugh at Julia or mock her for her embarrassing confession.

Indeed, he didn't respond in any way other than to stare at her with his opaque gaze.

The uncomfortable silence stretched and stretched, until she was in agony.

And then the truth smacked her in the face like the backlash of a tree limb, stinging and painful. Julia had obviously misread his earlier expression; it wasn't desire she'd seen on his face, it was discomfort.

Malcolm was not rendered speechless by lust; he was trying to contrive a way to reject Julia without hurting her! After all, why in the world would he need *her* when he apparently had unlimited access to beautiful and skilled women?

Julia had been a fool.

"I'm sorry," she mumbled. "I need—I need to leave."

She took several steps toward the mirror but then realized she didn't know which of the wall sections led to the corridor. There was a proper door, of course, not that she knew where it led. But surely anywhere was better than where she stood right then.

She darted toward the door but his hand closed around her wrist and he jerked her back, roughly turning her to face him.

Julia flinched at the harsh expression on his face as he glared down at her. "You have *no* idea how much I want you," he said grimly.

She swallowed hard and his eye dropped to her throat to track the motion.

"More than any woman in years. Maybe more than I've ever wanted a woman in my entire life," he sounded as if he was speaking more to himself and the admission stunned him.

They stunned Julia, too.

Hadn't he said he loved his wife? Did he mean—but no, he'd said that *wanted* Julia, not that he *loved* her.

"What are you saying," she asked.

His eye moved slowly upward, until their gazes locked. "It doesn't matter what I want, Julia, because when this is all finished—what I'm doing to your father and your family—you will hate me so much that you'll never want to see me again. And even if you don't," he said when she opened her mouth to argue, "this"—he waved a hand between them—"whatever you think there is between us, it can *never* happen."

"Why? Tell me why it can't?" she begged, hating that she sounded like a whiny, sniveling child but unable to stop herself.

He gave a frustrated groan and shoved his fingers into his hair hard enough to make him wince. "You are making it *very hard* for me to do the decent, honorable thing, Julia."

"Then don't do it!"

He backed away from her, as if she were some sort of contagion, and yanked out his pocket watch, glaring at it. "I can't do this right now, Julia. I have to go somewhere—"

"*Now?* But it's two-thirty in the morning!"

He stalked over to the wall that held the window or mirror or whatever it was, and pushed on the upper panel, opening the door with a soft click. "Go back to your room, get some sleep, and pray that you wake up tomorrow having come to your senses."

Julia did some stalking of her own but stopped in front of Malcolm instead of the door. "I *am* in my senses. It is *you* who are behaving irrationally."

"Go," he growled.

"I won't change my mind, you know—you can't bully me into it."

His gaze was flat and shuttered. "What I *can* do is keep you from entering this corridor again. From now on, you will find it locked."

Julia glared up at him, struggling to hide her pain. "If you think that will stop me from seeing you then you are not as clever as you think." She stormed from the room, momentarily triumphant at getting the last word.

Unfortunately, that feeling didn't even last until Julia reached her room.

Chapter 25

The evening before had been so traumatic that Julia had forgotten today was Christmas, not that she had anything to celebrate or anyone to celebrate it with.

All she could think about was Malcolm and the cold look he'd given her right before he'd ordered her out of his study as if he never wanted to see her again.

His lie had been pitiful. Where in the world would he be going at two-thirty on Christmas morning?

Was he even going to come back? Or would he just leave his own house rather than face her again?

The door opened to her chambers and Kemp entered for the second time that day.

Julia forced a smile onto her face. "Happy Christmas, Kemp."

"Happy Christmas to you too, Miss Julia. Are you ready to go to breakfast yet?"

Kemp had come at her usual time and Julia had sent her away—that had been hours ago—because what was the point of getting out of bed? So she could eat a lonely breakfast? And then a lonely dinner?

Julia opened her mouth to send Kemp away but the maid disappeared into her dressing room. "Do you know what you'd like to wear today?" she called out cheerily.

Julia didn't care what she wore.

"Miss Julia?"

Her voice was so pleasant and hopeful that Julia grudgingly left her warm bed and slipped on her robe. "The dark green wool, please."

"Lovely choice," was Kemp's muffled reply.

"It's too late for breakfast. I won't bother with anything to eat."

Kemp emerged bearing the gown, her forehead puckered. "Er, but it is Christmas."

Julia opened her mouth to ask what that had to do with anything, but Kemp said, "And Cook has made something rather special. Norris, Mr. Butkins, and I thought we would join you."

"You will?" she asked in a high-pitched, too-emotional voice that made Kemp look vaguely uncomfortable.

"Of course we will, it is Christmas."

Julia threw her arms around the older woman and squeezed hard enough to make her grunt. "Oh, how did you know I needed that today, Kemp?" she choked back her sob at the last minute, but her chest still shook with it.

Kemp patted her shoulder. "There now, it's Christmas," she murmured, sounding flustered. "Don't cry, Miss Julia."

"No, I'm not," Julia lied, wiping away a few stray tears before releasing poor Kemp, whose normally pale face was flushed and very pretty. It suddenly occurred to Julia that the maid was not as old as she'd originally thought. The combination of stern clothing and her sober demeanor made her seem far older.

"Are you sure, Kemp? You must have a family you'd rather be with today. Perhaps somebody… special."

Kemp gave an uncharacteristically nervous laugh. "There is nobody special, Miss Julia. And I have no family nearby. You'll have to be my family today."

"I'd be honored."

Kemp's lips twitched into a brief smile before she banished it. "Come," said briskly. "Let's get you ready, shall we?"

***

"Happy Christmas!" Norris and John called out when Kemp and Julia joined them in the dining room a short time later.

Julia wanted to fling her arms around both men but wisely refrained. Instead, she said, "Happy Christmas! Thank you *so* much for joining me for breakfast."

The two men blushed and stammered.

"If I'd suspected you'd dine with me I wouldn't have been so very late—it's more of a nuncheon than a breakfast. I can't imagine which of you convinced the others to step outside convention," she teased.

John coughed, glanced at the other two, and then said, "Actually, it was Mr. Barton who suggested you might like company today."

Julia's smile faltered slightly. "Oh. It was kind of him to think of me before he left."

The three servants exchanged quick, meaningful, looks.

Before Julia could commence prying Norris said, "Ah, here is our Christmas feast."

Three footmen entered bearing loaded trays.

"You are right here, Miss Julia," John said, gesturing toward the head of the table, where several wrapped gifts sat next to the place setting.

"Oh, dear!" Julia said. "I forgot your gifts in my room. I'll just run and get them."

"Let James fetch them," Kemp said.

"We can open them later," Norris suggested.

"Do sit and eat first," John begged.

For once, Julia wouldn't be budged. "It won't take but a minute."

Julia hurried from the dining room and through the corridor, a silly smile on her face as she thought about their reactions. The paintings were small so it was no problem to pile them up in her arms.

As she hurried back, she studied the wrapping paper. She'd not wanted to ask for any from the store, so she'd painted her own, using newspapers, and was quite pleased with her result. They weren't pretty foil and—

"*Jule!*" a familiar voice shrieked when she entered the greenhouse.

Julia's head whipped up just in time to move the three slim packages to her side, barely preventing them from being crushed by the careening form of her brother Richard.

***

Malcolm watched the Harlow twins enjoy their joyous reunion from a place of concealment, smiling at the sound of Richard's laughter and Julia's girlish squealing.

He'd not known what to expect when he'd shown up at Brookfield bright and early that morning. It had been years and years since he'd gone out in public, but the errand was one he hadn't want to entrust to Joe. Not because he wasn't capable, but because this was *his* gift for Julia.

A young housemaid—rather than an upper domestic—had answered the door to the pretty little manor house. She had been startled to see a masked stranger, but it had seemed to Malcolm that she'd been less shocked by his face than the fact that there was a visitor on Christmas morning.

The servant's surprise had been nothing to Nanny Potter's.

"You want to take Richard to London?" the old woman had repeated, visibly befuddled.

"Er, yes, ma'am. And you, too, of course," he'd added hastily.

"And Miss Julia is staying with *you?*"

"Not *with* me alone. She has a chaperone for the duration of her stay."

Nanny Potter, who had to be eighty, if a day, had resembled a tiny, fluffed up bird as she'd perched on the horsehair settee, her neat puff of white hair as pure as freshly fallen snow, her faded blue eyes surprisingly sharp.

"Why is Miss Julia with you?" she'd asked.

Malcolm hadn't told her why and had no intention of doing so. Instead, he'd lied. "Her parents were called on a journey to the north quite suddenly and Mr. Harlow—an old friend of my family—asked if she might stay with me."

"And you want to bring Mr. Richard up to see her?"

"Yes, ma'am, as a Christmas surprise."

"In your private rail carriage," she added flatly.

"Yes, ma'am."

Her shrewd old eyes narrowed. "It occurs to me that you might be the Barton of Barton's Emporium."

"The very same, ma'am."

A huge smile broke out on her face at that information. "Barton's is reputed to be quite a miracle of modernity. A lady in our village— Mrs. Logan—visited your London store last summer and dined out on the fact for months."

Malcolm had chuckled. "Well, you will be able to do her one better ma'am because I will give you a private tour."

"On Christmas Day? But surely it is closed?"

"Ah, but I have the keys, Mrs. Potter."

That had made her laugh, but she'd sobered quickly. "Richard is a good boy—and so sweet and kind, but—" she'd frowned, her mouth tightening. "To speak plainly, sir, it surprises me that Mr. Harlow would allow Richard to visit his sister considering he has always refused to acknowledge the relationship. He is *very* insistent on keeping Richard out of sight. As he pays for everything, I wouldn't want to anger him by going against his word."

"Well, you needn't worry about all that, Mrs. Potter. I will take care of Thomas Harlow." In more ways than one.

She brightened at that. "That is such a relief. Richard will be tickled to go on a train. We've only been once before and he adored it, so this *will* be a treat. Except—" she cut him a pensive look.

"What is it, ma'am?"

"It's just that Richard doesn't like to be away from home very long. He gets… anxious—quite agitated, really—and could never stay anywhere overnight."

"Don't worry, ma'am, the journey is just under two hours and I will make sure he is in his own bed tonight."

The old lady had looked delighted. "Well then, that's settled! Let me get Mary to fetch Richard."

Malcolm had been eager to meet the man who Thomas Harlow refused to acknowledge and whom Julia had bartered her future to save.

As it turned out, the lad—or young man, for he was twenty, the same age as his twin—was just as charming and friendly as both Julia and the old lady had described him.

Just like his sister, he was fine boned, pale, and had enormous blue eyes. In shape and color, they were the same as Julia's, but unlike the fierce intelligence and burning curiosity in her eyes, Richard's gaze was sweet and placid.

Nanny introduced them and then explained—painstakingly—how Malcolm would take him to see Julia.

But Richard was clearly too fascinated by Malcolm's appearance to pay attention.

The instant Nanny Potter stopped talking he said, "What happened to your face? Why are you wearing that mask?"

Nanny made a despairing noise and cut Malcolm an apologetic look. "Oh, Richard—you know you shouldn't ask people personal questions until you are better acquainted."

Malcolm had smiled. "It's fine, Mrs. Potter." To Richard he'd said, "The left side of my face was badly burned and it scares people to look at it. So I keep it covered."

Richard had pondered that and then said, "My Papa said I scare people. He said I shouldn't go out and about at *all*. Didn't he Nanny?"

The old lady's face twisted painfully.

Malcolm had fiercely regretted that he'd not *softened up* Thomas Harlow a bit the night before. What sort of miserable fucking pillock could say that to his own son?

"You don't scare me," Malcolm had assured Richard.

"You don't scare *me*, either," Richard said right back, laughing.

Nanny Potter had given Malcolm a grateful look and patted the lad's shoulder. "Aren't you going to tell Mr. Barton *thank you* for taking you on the train to see Julia?"

"I'm not afraid of trains," he'd proclaimed proudly. "Nanny was, but I told her they were safe. And it was, wasn't it, Nanny? Didn't I tell you? It was safe."

"Yes, it was very safe, Richard."

"Nanny said you'd take me in a *private* rail carriage," he'd spoken as if Malcolm hadn't been sitting there when the woman had explained it all. "Who will be in it?" he'd demanded.

"Er, just me, you, and Mrs. Potter."

"The last time we went on the train we sat in third class and there was a little girl in the seat in front of us. She turned around and made faces at me the whole way." His huge blue eyes had narrowed with suspicion. "There won't be any staring little girls, will there?"

Malcolm had laughed. "I can promise that no little girls will be staring at you."

Richard had briefly looked relieved, but then his smooth brow had furrowed again. "I will need to be back by my bedtime. Won't I, Nanny?"

"Yes, luv. Mr. Barton will have you back by bedtime."

Richard's smile had been pure sunshine. "And I'll see Julia after riding on the train."

Malcolm had always appreciated his luxurious private rail carriage but never had it brought him as much joy as it did Richard Harlow.

Malcolm had smiled so much on the brief journey back to London that his face had hurt by the time he'd escorted the pair up to the rooftop greenhouse

He couldn't have planned their arrival more perfectly, as Julia had just stepped away from the dining room, leaving Malcolm free to pass the visitors into Butkins' capable hands and nip off before Julia returned.

Malcolm lingered just long enough to watch the brother and sister embracing and laughing and crying—on Julia's part—before he silently slipped out of the greenhouse and made his way to his study.

You did a lovely thing, Mal. Why won't you go and join them?

And a happy Christmas to you, too, my dear Sukey, he retorted as he sat down at his desk and flipped through the neat stack of documents that he'd instructed Butkins to prepare for today.

Right on top of the pile was the letter he'd told Tommy to send last night. He smiled, well pleased at the other man's obedience.

When he saw that everything was in order he toggled the lever that rang a bell in the servant quarters.

He'd kept the staff on for today but would give everyone except the upper servants a two-week holiday starting tomorrow. Butkins, Kemp, and Norris would take staggered, extended, holidays after New Year's Day.

James opened his study door a few minutes later. "Yes, Mr. Barton?"

"Tell Parker to have the carriage brought round immediately."

"Very good, sir. And, er, if I may be so bold—Happy Christmas, sir."

"The same to you, James."

"Thank you, sir."

Once the door shut behind the servant Malcolm unlocked his desk, removed two envelopes, and slid them, along with the stack of documents, into his satchel.

You deserve some happiness, Mal. Why don't you join the people who care about you?

Malcolm ignored the questions. He was still wearing his coat and hat from earlier, so he headed directly for the lift.

Christmas is a day for friends and family. Why do you insist on punishing yourself with solitude?

Malcolm thought about the contents of his satchel and smiled, albeit unpleasantly.

Oh, you are mistaken, my dear, I'm not punishing myself, at all.

Indeed, Malcolm was about to go and punish somebody else—two somebodies.

In fact, it was his Christmas gift to himself.

Chapter 26

You have to let me go, Jule. You'll make me miss my train,"
Richard said, squirming in Julia's embrace.

She didn't bother to remind him that the journey he'd be
taking was solely for *him* and would never leave without him.

Julia shuddered to think what Malcolm had paid to hire an
engineer to pull his private car back to St. Albans.

"*Jule*," Richard whined.

Julia released him and grinned at him. "I'm sorry. But I don't know
when I'll see you again so I had to get as much unbreaking as possible,
Rich."

Her brother gave a distracted smile at their old jest. When he'd
been little, he'd thought the word *embracing* was *unbreaking*.

"I need my unbreaking, too, Julia." Nanny Potter slid her frail arms
around Julia and hugged her with surprising strength.

When they finally stepped apart, Julia had to look down to meet
the older woman's eyes. It seemed like her beloved Nanny got smaller
each time she saw her.

"With all the excitement I never got a chance to tell you how
blooming you look, my dear."

Julia blushed; what sort of person *bloomed* while in captivity?
"Thank you, Nanny."

"I hope you will tell Mr. Barton all that is proper for me. I'm
mortified that he slipped away before we thanked him for his
generosity."

Julia smiled, even though she was furious at Malcolm for hiding
himself away. "He despises being thanked; that is probably why he
made himself scarce."

Either that or he was afraid Julia would fling herself at him. Again.

"*Nanny*, we're going to miss our train." Richard's voice was loud
and strident.

Nanny gave Julia a wry smile. "We'd better go."

John opened the lift door. "Ready to go?" he asked.

"I suppose I can do it once more," Nanny said, grimacing as she stepped into the metal box that would take them both away from Julia until who knew when.

"I'm ready!" Richard bounded into the lift—which he'd already ridden up and down at least four times—followed closely by James, who was laden with bags and boxes, most of which were gifts for Richard, who'd gone on a tour of Barton's with the specific instruction from John that he and Nanny should both choose whatever they wanted.

It had been all Nanny and Julia could do to keep her brother from taking half the store.

"Goodbye!" Julia waved to her dearest people in the world. She waited until the door slid shut before dashing away the two tears that had managed to escape.

She turned to Kemp, who'd waited silently a few steps behind her. "What a lovely day, Kemp. Thank you so much for sharing it with us."

"It was an honor, Miss Julia. Your brother is delightful and made the day quite festive."

Julia gave a watery chuckle. "Yes, Richard is a one-person celebration."

"He seems very happy," Kemp said, as the two of them walked back to Julia's part of the house.

"He loves Nanny and they have a peaceful and predictable life together, which is very important to my brother. I *do* worry what will happen when she dies." It had shocked Julia just how frail Nanny had looked since she'd last seen her—almost a year ago, thanks to her father's draconian refusal to allow Julia to visit her twin more than once a year.

As usual in Malcolm's labyrinthine house, Julia became disoriented and was surprised by how quickly she ended up at her room.

"Would you like an hour before I come and dress you for dinner, Miss Julia?" Kemp asked.

"Will Mr. Barton be coming to dinner tonight?"

Kemp's eyes slid away. "No, Miss Julia."

Julia's face heated with embarrassment but it was nothing to the pain in her belly. So, he was simply going to ignore her until he finally sent her back, was he?

If you let him.

"Will you please tell Mr. Barton I wish to see him?"

Kemp didn't look surprised; nor did she look especially happy. "Now?"

"After dinner will be soon enough." That would give her time to prepare and arm herself as best she could.

Because that is what tonight would be—a battle. And she knew exactly which weapon she needed to decimate and dominate her opponent.

"Kemp?"

The older woman paused, her hand on the doorknob. "Yes, Miss Julia?"

"I need something from the store."

"Of course. If you know what you want, just write it down and I'll have somebody fetch it for you."

Julia smiled. "Oh yes, I know exactly what I want."

***

You're worthless and weak, Malcolm told himself for the dozenth time since agreeing to see the girl.

Don't do that, Mal. Don't call her a girl, *as if she is a child who doesn't know what she wants. She's a young woman, not an infant.*

Malcolm squeezed his eye shut and let his head fall against the chair back. Just because he'd agreed to see Julia didn't mean he needed to lose control of himself.

You could do with losing control. How long has it been, Mal?

He ignored the taunting question. He could control himself; he'd been doing it for days and days.

If you really wanted to do right by Julia you could just send her home now, couldn't you? The voice wasn't Sukey's, but his own beleaguered conscience.

And it spoke the truth. Malcolm no longer needed to hold her hostage. Tommy Harlow would do everything Malcolm wanted, so would Nadine and Carl. He could let her go.

But if he let her go right now, she'd walk right into a bloodbath.

And who would she blame for that, I wonder?

Malcolm grimaced.

There was a light knock on the door.

"Come in."

Kemp stuck her head in first.

Not in the six years the woman had worked for him had she given him such a severe look.

Malcolm's face heated because he deserved the look. "Happy Christmas, Kemp."

"The same to you, sir. Miss Julia is here to see you, sir."

He heard the disapproval in her voice and saw it on her face.

He didn't care.

"Show her in."

Kemp frowned but opened the door wider and stepped back for Julia to enter.

Malcolm had seen the dress before—of course he had, it was his store and he knew every single item he sold—but he'd never imagined it would look like *this*.

One trip up and down her body was not nearly enough for his eye or brain, he needed a second, and then a third.

He'd seen a plate of the dress when he'd flipped through this season's clothing orders and had not been especially taken by it.

Now, after seeing it molded to Julia's body—the polished black cotton looking so much like leather—Malcolm decided that he would cancel all future orders for the gown because he didn't want any other woman wearing it.

The gown came with three possible bodices and Julia had chosen the most concealing—a high neck with long tight sleeves that made her look as if she were encased in black leather.

Large onyx buttons fastened at the side of the neck and cut across the bodice. The skirt was narrower than usual—an edgier design that the dressmaker, a young Englishman, had argued was the coming trend—and was smooth-fronted with a froth of black ruffles cascading down the back.

Malcolm swallowed down the moisture that had pooled in his mouth.

And then swallowed again.

At her throat were the black pearls he'd given her and her only other jewelry was her bracelet.

Like Malcolm, she wore black leather gloves covering her hands, making the two of them a matched set.

Well, except for his mask. And all the burns beneath it.

She cleared her throat, making Malcolm realize that he'd kept a lady standing just so he could ogle and drool.

He swallowed for the fourth or fifth time. "Please, have a seat." He gestured vaguely toward the seating area, unable to take his eye from her for even a second.

When she moved, he saw a brief flash of silver beneath her skirts and knew immediately which shoes she'd chosen from the store. They were black kid with an oversized silver buckle that was studded with brilliants. At four inches the heels on the shoe were ridiculously high, quite the tallest he'd seen. Wearing them brought her head almost to his shoulder.

Rather than sit, she stopped in front of him and held out her hands. "This is for you."

Malcolm was surprised to see a rectangular package; he'd been so busy staring at her person that he'd not even noticed she was holding anything.

"It is a Christmas present," she explained with a faint smirk when he looked at her like a dunce.

"Thank you," he said, and took it, a smile curving his lips at the wrapping paper. It was newspaper—which is what the few gifts he'd received at the orphanage had been wrapped in. Socks, always a pair of socks knitted throughout the year for each of her charges by Mrs. Thomas.

Malcolm laughed when he saw the story on the front of the package. He looked up and grinned at her. "I like it."

Her cheeks flushed and he could see that she was pleased, rather than horrified, by his crooked smile. "The actual gift is *inside* the wrapping, Malcolm."

"Ah, is that how it works?"

"But I am glad you like the paper. I'd planned to just paint the newspaper until I saw this story."

By *this* story she meant a photograph of Barton's Emporium and an article about a charitable program the store contributed to every year.

"It's very kind of you to give gifts to orphans, Malcolm."

Malcolm ignored her—and the uncomfortable heat in his face—and stared down at the package, turning it around and around in his hands.

"Aren't you going to open it?"

He looked up. "I didn't get you anything."

Her eyes widened and then she laughed.

The sound punched him in the chest, driving the air from his lungs. She was a marvel, every single thing about her was beautiful, even the sound of her laughter.

"What do you call this?" She gestured to the gown she wore.

He laughed, although the sound was more of a drowning man's breathless gasp. "That's another gift for me," he assured her gruffly, allowing his eye to wander her body yet again, since she'd invited him to do so.

"All you've done is give me gifts since the day I woke up here," she said. "Please, open my present."

As Malcolm tore into the paper, he tried to recall the last time he'd opened a gift on Christmas and couldn't.

Not since me, Mal, Sukey whispered, the sound faint and sad.

That was true. The last person to give him anything for Christmas had been his wife.

The paper fell away and fluttered to the floor and Malcolm stared, utterly entranced.

It was a painting—of him.

He was sitting in the greenhouse and he recognized the bench—there were six total, each one a little different—and knew it faced the bay leaf tree which was a favorite resting spot for the finches.

The painting showed him full face, which would have meant that the painter was up on a limb with the birds.

His pose was relaxed and he was looking directly ahead, wearing a faint smile and looking… content.

"The hands were easy."

He looked up at the soft words.

"Because they are gloved," she explained. "Remember? I told you—"

"That you couldn't paint hands."

She looked pleased that he'd remembered, as if he didn't remember every look and word.

"How did you paint this? I mean, did you see me there?" he asked, stammering over the words.

"I saw you talking to the gardener—Mr. Bobbit—one afternoon. And when he left, you sat for a moment."

"And where were you?"

"I hid because I didn't want to disturb you. You looked so peaceful."

Now that she'd mentioned Bobbit, Malcolm recalled the day. The fussy gardener had come to his office to nag him, insisting that Malcolm come and look at some plant rot or fungus. Exasperated, but amused, Malcolm had put aside his work and gone to look at the problem. And then he'd told the man what he'd already told him once: do what you think is best.

Once Bobbit had left, he'd sat for a moment, thinking about Julia and how Kemp said she spent a great deal of time in the hothouse. One thought had led to another and he'd wrestled with himself, yet again, about whether or not to spy on her.

Malcolm smiled, amused that she'd painted him while he'd been thinking about *her*.

"Why are you smiling?"

"Because I am pleased," he said. "Both that you'd think me worthy of painting and also that you'd give me such a thoughtful gift."

Her beautiful face became even more lovely, her shy, pleased smile making her look angelic, although Malcolm knew that she was no angel.

She was far, far more interesting than a mere angel.

"I'm happy you like it," she said, shifting on the settee, her magnificent shoes peeking from beneath her skirts.

Malcolm wanted to correct her; he didn't *like* it. He loved it. And the fact that he could appreciate a painting of himself—when he couldn't stand looking in the mirror—dumbfounded him. But somehow she'd managed to make him look interesting, rather than just broken; worthy of knowing rather than simply worn out.

Give her something in return, Mal. It couldn't have been easy to ask to see you. You owe her.

Malcolm thought he owed her the exact opposite—he should send her packing—but he was sick and tired of that struggle.

So, instead, he took his dead wife's advice for a change and smiled at Julia. "I'm glad you're here with me tonight."

***

Malcolm's words—so unexpected and intoxicating—made Julia weak with relief.

"Me too," she said quietly.

He turned away and propped the painting on the mantlepiece and then stood back to look at it.

Julia was delighted that he seemed to like it. She believed it was the best painting she'd ever done and couldn't help wondering if it was because of the subject.

"Would you like some champagne?" he suddenly asked.

"Yes, please—I adore champagne." Julia studied the room while he opened the bottle. She'd been too anxious and distracted to pay attention the last time she'd been in it. It was masculine, yet not oppressively so, the dark wood floors and rich brown leather furniture lightened by exquisite oriental rugs.

As much as she tried not to stare, her gaze pulled in Malcolm's direction.

He was looking at her, his hands moving competently on the bottle.

"Thank you for bringing Richard and Nanny to me. It was the best Christmas gift I've ever had."

He popped the cork and then deftly filled one glass.

Julia frowned. "You aren't having any?"

He hesitated, and then poured a second glass. "Your brother is charming and Nanny Potter is a delightful woman."

"I wish you would have joined us."

"I thought you would like to have some time together."

"You were missed," she said softly.

The uncovered side of his face was facing her and his expression seemed grim.

But when he turned to hand her the glass, Julia thought she must have been wrong because he wore a faint smile.

"Thank you," she said, watching the bubbles for a moment before looking up at him. "Are we celebrating something?"

"You tell me—are you staying?"

Julia's heart thudded painfully at his direct look and she had to scrape together every last bit of bravery to say, "I'm here, aren't I?"

His smile was disarming, boyish, and charming and it even reached his icy eye. He lifted his glass. "Then yes, we are celebrating. Here is to tonight, then."

Malcolm clinked his glass against hers and they drank. He gestured to the settee. "May I sit next to you?"

"Please do."

The entire piece of furniture shifted when he sat, even though he'd lowered himself carefully. He angled his body toward hers, his gaze hooded and introspective, as if he'd surprised himself, somehow.

"May I ask you some questions?" she asked, when it became clear he was content to just stare at her.

"You may."

"How many?"

"As many as I feel like answering."

Julia laughed. "I suppose I'd better ask the most important questions first, then. Have you watched me—through those mirrors?"

"The only time I watched you was when you arrived."

"Was I n-naked?"

"Yes. I watched Kemp undress you and put you to bed."

The effect of his words on her body was both immediate and electric and she set down her glass with trembling fingers.

"I wish I could apologize," he said, his low voice a rumble. "But I'm not sorry."

"Well, at least you are honest."

"Are you angry that I saw you?"

Julia knew she should lie, but she couldn't. "No."

A slow, wicked smile transformed his face, making him look almost satanic in his black mask. "Do you like thinking of me watching you?"

Rather than trust her voice, she nodded.

His expression was darkly amused, but he didn't speak.

"You watch other women, too—don't you?"

"Yes."

Jealousy sank its poisoned fangs into her. "Why do you do it?"

"Why did you come back to watch me over and over?"

Even though Julia's mouth had fallen open, she couldn't draw in enough air.

He chuckled. "My turn to ask some questions. Was the tutor the only one?"

She chewed her lip.

"Come—the truth and only the truth."

Julia knew she shouldn't, but the words came tumbling out, "No, there was my stepmother's footman, Matthew. He was before Solomon." She risked a look at him but couldn't read his expression. Was he angry? Disgusted? Disappointed? "Do you think that makes me a whore?"

"*What?*"

He looked so scandalized that it was actually amusing.

"It's what my father and Nadine called me—more than a few times."

His jaws flexed and his expression went flat. "Did they."

It wasn't a question and the sudden coldness in his eye made her shiver. Julia changed the subject. "You never told me how you found out about Solomon?"

"You haven't finished answering my question," he said coolly. "Who else other than Solomon and Matthew?"

Julia's temper, which was generally difficult to rouse, flared. "Why should I tell you?"

"Because you like it when I answer *your* questions."

She opened her mouth to argue, but then sighed; he was right, after all. "That was it, the two of them."

"To answer *your* question, I found out because I sent a private inquiry agent to discover why you were in town at this time of year, among other things."

"Things about my father."

"Yes. How many times did you make the beast with two backs with your lovers?"

Julia had just taken a sip and choked, spewing champagne all over his trousers.

Her eyes flew open. "I'm so sorry!"

He took out a handkerchief and daubed at the fine dark wool of his evening clothes before refolding it to a dry spot and returning it to his pocket. "I deserved a bit of spit and a great deal more for my crudeness. You can chalk that up to me being jealous."

"Jealous? Of *me*?"

"Jealous of Solomon and Matthew," he corrected, his pupil swallowing his iris. "You are exquisite, fresh, charming, lively, and clever."

Nobody had ever said such things to her. It thrilled her but left her feeling strangely frightened and vulnerable. What would he think if he saw how needy and scared she was?

"I can't imagine there is a man alive who wouldn't want to be your lover," he said.

She shivered at the word *lover*. It sounded so … grown up.

Julia turned her burning face to the floor.

But he wouldn't let her escape. He leaned close and took her chin, gently, but firmly, tilting her head until she was forced to look at him.

"You aren't just beautiful, Julia, you are also full of life. And kindness. You've brought joy and happiness into my house and my servants adore you."

What about you? she wanted to shout. *Do you adore me? Have I brought joy and happiness to you?*

Of course she didn't.

Instead, she mumbled, "Kemp, Norris, and John have been very kind to keep me company." She stared at his full, shapely mouth rather than his eye, which seemed to peel the skin from her bones.

"Have they?" Those sensual lips curved into a slow smile as he softly stroked her chin.

When Julia risked a glance up, she was caught by his penetrating stare, scooped up as easily as a fish in a net.

"Ah, Julia," he murmured, shaking his head, his expression a jumble of sadness, regret, and desire.

And then he leaned forward and kissed her.

Chapter 27

Malcolm saw himself doing it—kissing her—but couldn't make his body stop.

He hadn't kissed a lover since before the fire; who the hell would want to get that close to his face, even masked?

But Julia hadn't flinched or looked revolted when he'd held her chin and forced her to look at him. Instead, she'd leaned closer, her pupils swelling obscenely large as she parted her petal-soft lips.

The yearning look had been a sledgehammer to his self-control.

Malcolm groaned as he kissed her. Christ! She was sweet—like some mythical nectar of the gods—her mouth so soft and hot.

And she knew how to kiss, opening to him like a blooming flower, tilting her head to take his tongue deeper without any urging from him.

Malcolm shuddered when the tip of her tongue darted into his mouth. He closed his lips around the sleek organ, trapping it and gently sucking.

She gave a surprised, breathy laugh and then fucked into his mouth, delving into him with greedy, deep strokes—caressing his teeth, gums, and the ridged architecture of his palate.

Bloody hell!

Malcolm reluctantly released her, allowing her to come up for air. He stroked the sensual curve of her jaw as he trailed kisses over her whisper soft skin, wishing like hell that he could feel the satiny texture with his fingers.

"What are you thinking?" she asked.

Malcolm blinked, momentarily disarmed by the question—the sort only young and fearless lovers would ask.

When he didn't immediately answer, she filled the awkward silence. "It's just… well, I know so little about you while you know everything about me. And you obviously know so many other—"

"Other?" he prodded, caressing the fine down on her jaw with his lips, inhaling her intoxicating scent.

"Things."

"What sort of things?"

She growled, sounding like an angry kitten. "You want to make me say it out loud, don't you?"

Malcolm smiled. "Yes."

And then he kissed her scandalized frown.

Julia opened to him immediately, just like she'd done before. This time, Malcolm explored her, giving himself over to his hungry desire and penetrating her deeply and thoroughly, devouring her.

"Mmm," she hummed against him, but then abruptly pulled away, her silky eyebrows drawn down. "Stop distracting me and just tell me."

"Tell you what?" he asked, his wits no longer under his control.

"You've known a l-lot of women?"

He frowned at the odd question. "I don't think you really want to know about that."

"I wouldn't have asked if I didn't."

Malcolm sighed. "I'm forty-three years old, Julia—more than twice your age. I've lived two lives to your one, so of course I've known a lot of women." Not to mention quite a few men, but he kept that to himself.

She looked so goddamned stricken that he quickly added. "But none like you." It was the truth.

"You mean young and ignorant?"

He gave a bark of laughter. Partly, he meant that. He'd never been with a twenty-year-old when he'd *been* twenty, but it would be cruel to tell her that.

"No, I meant perfect," he said—again, it wasn't a lie.

Julia rolled her gorgeous eyes at him, but Malcolm saw something other than exasperated amusement; he saw worry. About him? About what they were about to do?

Malcolm dropped his hand and put some physical distance between them. "We can stop right here and now, Julia."

"You mean—"

"I mean I'm grateful for the kisses. You needn't do anything more to please me."

Her brows knitted and she blinked her stained-glass blue eyes rapidly, as if she were fending off tears.

Good Lord.

"I *want* you," he assured her, relieved when her anxious expression eased a little. "Christ knows I want you," he muttered more to himself. "But I've abducted you, forced you to stay in my house, exposed you to, er, lurid behavior, and now—"

"I'm young, but I'm not ignorant, Malcolm. Soon—too soon—I will be married to a man who despises me and doesn't even want to look at me." She took his hand. "Please, I w-want this, Malcolm."

Her begging went straight to his already eager cock. Malcolm gritted his teeth. "You want what, Julia? To throw yourself away on a scarred, debauched old man who abducted you?"

Julia bit her lower lip but couldn't hide her smile. "You're not *that* old."

Malcolm barked an appreciative laugh. "You little witch."

She moved her hand to his knee and every muscle in his body tightened, as if she'd grabbed his ballocks.

"I am a woman and I know what I want. I want to be with a man who wants *me*. And I want *you*."

Malcolm growled like the beast he was, grabbed her waist with both hands, and lifted her onto his lap.

She gave a surprised yelp but didn't resist. Indeed, once he'd settled her across his thighs she wiggled against him, like a small cat getting comfortable.

Malcolm ground his molars when her lush bottom rubbed against his hard shaft, visions of flipping up her skirts and plunging into her battering his self-control.

Patience.

Yes, well that was easier said than done.

She reclined against the arm that cradled her, her soft blue eyes flickering over his face, settling on his mask.

"I want to see you—Malcolm, all of you."

***

Julia felt his massive body stiffen beneath her. And not in a good way.

"No." His tone was cold and she could almost *hear* the slamming of doors as the warmth leaked from him gaze and his eye shuttered.

"That's not—"

"Fair?" he guessed.

"I was going to say that's not very flattering to me."

"I don't follow that logic."

"Do you think I would agree to—to be *with* you and then change my mind when I saw your scars?"

"That's not why I said *no*."

"Then, *why*?"

"Because it is not something anyone should have to see."

"I'm not just *anyone*."

His lips twitched into a faint smile. "No, you're not," he agreed, his warm look making *her* warm. "You're more important and therefore I don't want you to see me even more than most other people."

She scowled. "Do you believe I am so superficial?"

He paused, as if he actually needed to consider her question before answering.

Julia gasped. "I can't believe you need to *think* about that!"

"Some people—well, some people, no matter how nice or good they are, cannot stomach deformity of any sort."

"I am not that sort of person!"

"I'm sorry. I didn't mean to offend you. But I hardly know you, Julia—we've not even been acquainted a month."

His words stunned her. Not the least of which because they were true. What *did* they know about each other besides the strong physical attraction between them?

But then one didn't need to know—or even like—another person to have sexual intercourse, did one? She'd given her maidenhood to Matthew—a man who had the intelligence of a turnip, albeit a very, very handsome turnip—and hadn't even known his last name.

She'd practically forced poor Solomon into bed and she'd never had a conversation with him that hadn't sent her to sleep.

Soon she would be engaging in the sexual act—*for the rest of her life*—with Sebastian, who was not only a stranger, but who loathed her.

Julia looked up into Malcolm's patient gaze. "I might not know a great deal about you, but I like what I *do* know."

"I like what I know about you, too," he admitted. "I never meant to imply that I didn't."

"Then why do you think I shall cringe or wince or be disgusted?"

"Trust me, you couldn't *not* do those things."

"I'll have you know—"

"Actually, let me amend that. I don't care what your reaction would be. I won't undress or show you my face because *I* would not like it."

"Showing yourself to me?"

"To anyone."

She chewed her lip, and then blurted. "Do you ever show yourself to *her*?"

"Her?" he looked comically perplexed.

"The woman you've been with—the blond one," she clarified, when she recalled that he'd been with *two* women on one occasion.

His stern features relaxed. "Oh—you mean Maisie. No, of course not." He laughed, but there was no amusement in it. "And I assure you that she is *extremely* grateful for her blindfold."

A nasty serpent slithered around in her belly at the sound of the woman's name on his tongue. "Does she know you are here with me?"

"What?"

"Does she?"

"No—not that she'd care if she did."

"But—"

"I don't think you understand, Julia—I pay her to be with me."

Embarrassment flooded her as she took his meaning: the women were prostitutes. How could she be such a simpleton?

"Does that revolt you?" he asked.

Julia opened her mouth to confess the mortifying truth about her and Matthew, but then Malcolm stroked a hand down her throat in a way that was shockingly intimate.

She shivered with pleasure before she could stop herself, intensely aware of the huge body beneath and around her.

"Does it, Julia?" He stroked her again and she leaned into his hand and closed her eyes. He smelled so *good*, like leather and some expensive cologne that was clean and citrusy and positively *edible*.

"Bloody. Hell," he muttered, shifting beneath her.

Julia opened her eyes. "Am I too heavy?"

"No. Does it?"

"Does it what?" she repeated, pressing her neck against his motionless hand, needing more. Why had she never noticed how arousing it felt to be touched on the throat?

He flexed his hand, the fingers closing just enough to make breathing difficult.

"Mmmm." Julia squeezed her thighs together, magnifying the already pleasurable pulsing in her sex.

His delicious grip loosened. "Julia?"

"Hmm?"

"Does it disgust you that I pay whores to pleasure me?"

She sighed when she realized he was intent on pursuing the point rather than continuing his lovely stroking. "No, it doesn't disgust me." She didn't tell him that it made her burn with jealousy. That was the *last* thing she could say—not without sounding like a schoolroom chit with her first infatuation.

He cocked a skeptical eyebrow at her. "Really?"

Her face heated under his probing look. And also at what she had to confess. "I'd be a hypocrite if it disgusted me because I paid Matthew to, er, be with me."

He looked so stunned that she gave a nervous laugh. "What?" she taunted with more bravada than she felt, "Does that disgust *you*?"

"You paid your stepmother's footman to take your maidenhead," he repeated, his expression strangely flat.

Well, when put like that it did sound rather disgusting.

When Julia tried to turn away, he caught her chin and held it. "No, it doesn't disgust me at all," he said in a rough tone. His lips curved into a smile that was both sensual and cruel. "Tell me, Julia, did you like watching me these past few nights?"

"You know I did," she shot back, annoyed and aroused by his confidence in such matters. "Will she be back again?"

"Who?"

"Are you being purposely obtuse?" she snapped. "Maisie, that's who!"

"Maisie never left; she's here, now."

"*What?*"

"Well, not in this room, obviously, but—"

"Are you saying that she *lives* here?"

"Sometimes."

Julia shoved herself off his lap—or tried to, but he held her in place with irksome ease, and she didn't really want to leave, anyhow.

But she was so angry and jealous that she couldn't think straight. What kind of man *was* he to have her in his chambers while another woman waited for him somewhere else in his house?

"Is she waiting for you? In your bedchamber or that wicked room across the corridor?"

He chuckled.

"Don't laugh at me."

"I'm not. I'm laughing at the situation."

"Why?"

"I'm here with you. What does it matter where she is?'

"If I had not asked to see you tonight, would you have gone to her, for—for pleasure?"

"That is why I employ her," he stated it mildly, as if they were talking about a charwoman or parlor maid.

Julia felt as though she'd been kicked by a horse, the pain in her chest making it difficult to breathe. She pushed up to her feet and this time he didn't stop her. Julia marched toward the door.

"Come here, Julia."

Julia stopped but didn't turn. "Why should I?"

"Are you jealous of Maisie?"

She whipped around, only to discover that he was a step behind her. How did he move so fast!

She scowled up at him. "Don't be absurd. Of course I'm not jealous of a p-prostitute." Her lie sounded woefully unconvincing.

He went to his desk and did something to the odd, black lacquer box that sat on the corner.

"What are you doing?"

"Taking care of a problem."

"What problem? What is that—"

The door opened and Norris stood on the threshold.

"Yes, sir?" the tall, thin valet asked, carefully not looking at Julia.

Even so, Julia's face burned with embarrassment. She'd begun to think of Norris—and Kemp and John—as friends. Now she wouldn't be able to look them in the eyes. What must they think of her not only coming to see Malcolm but all but begging to do so?

Malcolm didn't even glance at his servant, keeping Julia pinned with his gaze. "Tell Maisie I don't need her. Pay her for the entire time and send her home in one of my carriages."

"Of course, sir."

"That is all."

The door shut behind him and Malcolm asked, "Better?"

Julia despised herself for the surge of relief that flooded her at the knowledge the other woman would soon be gone. "What about the second woman? Amanda?" she spat the name out like a fly she'd discovered in her tea.

His faint smirk was even worse than his grin. "She was only here for the night."

"But *Maisie* you keep here all the time and move about like a chess piece? She just comes and goes at your whim?"

"Yes." Something in his frosty gaze told Julia that she would soon be doing the same thing.

"She—she—" Julia chewed her lip. "I saw her that night—the night she was beneath your desk. Why was she under there?"

He looked perplexed by her question. "She was pleasuring me with her mouth."

Frustration and raw lust collided inside her at his matter-of-fact words. "I *know* what she was doing! I meant why under your desk, of all places?"

"Because I like to have my cock sucked while I work."

Julia clutched the back of the settee for support. "How can you just *say* such a thing?"

"Because it is the truth. Or would you rather I lie?" His gaze was both intent and detached. As if he were interested in her reaction but had no personal stake in it.

Julia couldn't get the memory of what she had seen that night out of her head, and God knew she had *tried.* "And that's why you k-keep her there? Just to—just to—"

"Just to suck my cock. Yes."

How utterly … *degrading.* Julia's sex clenched so hard at the thought it almost doubled her over. She was twice as swollen and wet as she'd been when she'd been sitting on his lap. She really *was* a whore.

"Often?" she asked, her voice high and breathy.

His lips twitched slightly. "Define often?"

Julia's head spun. What sort of deviant kept a prostitute kneeling under his desk, *servicing* him like some despot of old?

What sort of woman was not only aroused by such a barbaric, sexual, crude beast of a man, but envious of the prostitute he used and treated like a mindless vessel?

Because that is exactly what she craved: to *be* that woman.

Oh God. How could she want that so badly?

Judging by the way he was smiling, he knew it; he could read her face as easily as he read one of his business reports.

He held out a hand. "I don't want to waste our time together talking about a whore. Come," he said, the gleam in his single eye knowing and indulgent. "Let's go somewhere we can be more comfortable."

As Julia stared at his outstretched hand she wanted, in the worst of ways, to tell him she was leaving—that she never wanted to see him again. That he was a vile swine and could go back to his prostitute and be welcome to her.

Instead, she put her hand in his.

Chapter 28

The room Malcolm led Julia to was his favorite in any of his houses—and it was unique. Not because of the furniture or the shape of the room. No, the layout in all his apartments was the same. And they all contained valuable—some would say priceless—works of art.

But the art in this room was some of his most precious, and Malcolm didn't want to miss even an instant of watching Julia as she took in the various paintings and *objets d'art*.

She was so utterly spontaneous, as if she'd never been taught to hide her feelings—although life would teach her that soon enough, he feared—and every emotion she felt: surprise, curiosity, and—yes—arousal flickered over her beautiful features.

"William Blake is the artist," he said when she stopped and stared at the two paintings, which were side-by-side. "*The Great Red Dragon and the Beast from the Sea*, and *The Great Red Dragon*."

Her lips parted in awe. "They are grotesque, and yet it is difficult to look away from them."

Malcolm suspected she might describe him the same way.

He watched her investigate the other art, amused when she froze in front of the series of Shunga woodblock prints, one hand lifting to her mouth as she stared at the octopus fucking the woman.

"Japanese," he said, biting back a smile when she hastily moved past the woodcuts toward a single sheet of parchment protected by thick glass.

"An engraving from the *I Modi*." It wasn't an original—those had all, tragically, been destroyed—but it was still very old.

Her steps faltered as she approached the massive four-poster bed—a work of art in its own right. It had been carved by the English industrialist, Edward Fanshaw, who'd once been a woodworker and now made furniture as a hobby.

It took her a moment before she noticed the picture over the headboard. "Oh."

"That is by a contemporary artist—Gustav Courbet. It is titled *The Origin of the World*."

Malcolm had paid a foolish amount for the painting—a woman's torso, her sex exposed, but her identity erased—and didn't regret even a penny.

He laid a hand on the small of her back, just above her bustle. "Do you like my art?"

She nodded dumbly and turned slowly to him. "I have never met anyone like you."

"I could take that several ways," he teased.

Her full lips pulled into a wry smile. "I meant it as a compliment."

Malcolm inclined his head. "Thank you. Did you wear that gown with me in mind?"

Her hand immediately went to the large onyx buttons and she looked enchantingly flustered. "Oh, well, I thought—"

"That I might not be able to manage tiny buttons or hooks?"

She hesitated, and then nodded.

Malcolm took her hand and led her toward the fire. "It's true that I find buttons quite challenging," he said, not entirely truthfully. "So why don't you undress for me, Julia."

She blinked up at him and Malcolm couldn't recall seeing such a look of profound stupefaction on another human being's face.

He suspected it was a look that he would see often if they spent much time together.

He settled into one of the huge leather armchairs he had in every room, built for a man his height and size, and looked across at her, curious as to what she'd do next.

She swallowed convulsively, her fingers toying nervously with the button. "You want me to—"

"I want you naked; I want to see every inch of your body."

She flinched, as if he'd shouted, but then her chin tilted bravely. "Yet I am not allowed to see you?"

"You can see my cock."

Her chin, so brave only a few seconds before, sagged.

He smiled and set his hand over his tented placket, lightly stroking himself while enjoying her wild blushing. "See what you do to me, Julia?"

Her breathing was rapid and ragged, her eyes riveted to his crude fondling.

Would she leave now? Part of him—although not the part he was absently stroking—hoped she did. While she wasn't a virgin, she was close enough that he knew he'd feel guilty about debauching her for a long, long time.

But then he thought about why she'd been in London at this time of year. She had pursued sensual adventure doggedly and been punished for it. She deserved to know how much pleasure her body was capable of receiving—and giving.

Malcolm was hardly the knight in shining armor a woman like her deserved, but then he suspected that wasn't what Julia wanted. Indeed, he could see by the lust in her gaze that she needed something darker, something raw and visceral.

That was something Malcolm could give her.

She worried her lower lip, lowered her lashes, and then said, "Will you take it out so I can see it?"

Yet again, she surprised him and his balls clenched so hard he had to squeeze the sensitive crown hard to suppress his arousal. He barked a laugh. "Vixen."

"Please, Malcolm?"

"Undress," he ordered roughly, ignoring her request. If he took his prick out and stroked himself in front of her, he'd last all of ten seconds.

She tossed her head like a willful filly but obediently flicked open the button at her wrist that held the short gloves closed.

Malcolm was breathing heavily by the time she'd slowly tugged off all ten fingers and tossed the gloves onto the settee.

"Look at me, Julia," he said when she lifted her bare hand to the button at her throat.

Her fingers trembled, but she met his gaze.

"Are you wet and swollen—between your legs?"

Her hands froze and her lips parted.

"Are you?"

She gave a jerky nod.

"So am I."

Her gaze dropped to his lap.

Malcolm pulled the placket tight against his shaft, the crown pressing against a dark, spreading stain on the black wool.

When her pink tongue darted out to moisten her lower lip he stopped being amused by her innocent reactions and had to bite the inside of his cheek until he bled to keep from saying the things he wanted to say—ordering her to do the things he wanted her to do.

Patience.

Already he was moving too fast—making her disrobe for him like an experienced courtesan. But they had so very little time together.

Her fingers resumed their work on the few buttons of her bodice and once it was loosened, she gave a slight shrug to shift the garment off her shoulders before carefully pulling off the skintight sleeves and then laying the bodice over the back of the settee.

Her throat flexed as she swallowed and then swallowed again, but she held his gaze as she bent her elbows to reach the closures at the back of her waist.

Malcolm's fingers twitched to help her—to peel her from her clothing like a ripe, juicy fruit from its skin—but he made himself wait.

Patience.

Once she'd unfastened the skirt, she slid her hands around to the front and untied the tapes that held the petticoat, cage, and bustle, letting the heavy garments fall to the floor with an audible *whoosh* and leaving her standing in simple white undergarments.

As much as he adored the wicked black gown, Malcolm was ridiculously grateful that she'd not strayed from her original simple style when it came to her chemise, drawers and corset. She would look good in anything, but unadorned virginal white suited her beauty like a plain frame suited a masterpiece.

"Come here," he said. "I am dexterous enough to pull a few tapes and remove the rest."

Her blush, he saw now, spread from her cheeks to the tops of her lush, full breasts.

Malcolm's gloved hands looked enormous and obscene pulling the narrow white tape that held up her petticoat.

He let the garment slide to the floor. Leaving her only in her drawers, chemise, and corset. Malcolm stood, towering over her, her eyes wide but filled with anticipation and desire as she looked up at him.

He had to bend low to kiss her, caressing her mouth gently, teasing and playing with her lips and tongue before her hands landed softly, like butterflies, on his shoulders. Malcolm slanted his mouth and plunged into her, thrilled when she responded just as eagerly, her fingers tightening and pulling on his coat.

All too soon the thin skin on his left side began to burn from bending so low, so he straightened up, her lips clinging to his as he pulled away.

He closed his hands around her waist, easily spanning the front of her body before pushing lightly on the boned fabric, so the hooks and eyes separated.

The sensual sigh of relief she gave made him throb with need and his mouth watered as he looked at her plump, dark-tipped breasts thrusting against the thin chemise.

He tossed the corset aside without looking, earning a nervous giggle from Julia when the garment knocked against a brass statue of Priapus and set it wobbling.

"Oh goodness," she said, her gaze fixed on the big cock and balls with legs. "I didn't notice that before."

"Arms up, sweetheart."

She was caught off guard by his rough command and obeyed without hesitation.

Malcolm lifted the garment and then let it fall from his limp fingers, his body frozen in shock as he soaked in her beauty.

"Fuck."

Her hands came up to cover—or at least try to cover—her full, lush breasts, but they spilled out of her small hands.

He forced his gaze up to face.

"Shy?" he asked, hoping his smile was reassuring and not predatory—which is what he was feeling.

She gave a jerky nod. "Can I keep my—er, do I need to take off my drawers just yet?"

"You don't need to do anything you don't want to do." He reached up and caressed her jaw, obsessed with the smooth, sweet curve of her face.

"I *will* take them off," she shakily assured him. "But just not right now."

He smiled and nodded. "Unbutton my coat, Julia."

She swallowed and looked down to where she held her breasts, her brow furrowing as she realized her conundrum.

Malcolm watched with interest as she tried to figure out how to unbutton the coat without uncovering herself.

Finally, she sighed. Some of the tension leaked from her slender shoulders and she lowered her hands.

Malcolm feasted on her glorious breasts as she made short work of the few buttons. He wanted to touch her, but sensed she was walking a fine line, so he kept his hands to himself and turned so she could help him off with the closely fitted garment, observing her in the mirror, her dainty hands like small white stars on his black clothing.

She was staring up at him, unaware that she was being watched, and her expression was… hungry.

Christ. She really did want him.

She undressed for you, Mal—what did you think she wanted? Do you know how difficult that is for most women?

Go away, Sukey, you're not needed here.

Smug laughter echoed in his head.

Once his coat was off, he turned to her, his entire body pulsing with the need to claim her.

He swooped down and captured her mouth, kissing her until they were both breathless and her body had relaxed against his.

When Malcolm pulled away, he met her gaze and then slid a hand from her waist, which he'd been massaging, over her pelvis, not stopping until he cupped the heat of her mound.

"I want to put my mouth on you if you'll let me."

She nodded, looking eager rather than shocked, which told him the intrepid Lily, at least, had treated her to this particular pleasure.

Malcolm took a cushion from the bed and tossed it to the floor before lowering to his knees, joints popping. She was still wearing her high heels and hose and he slid his hands around her dainty ankles and gently pulled her feet apart, until she was at the perfect height.

Malcolm's hands shook as he parted the split in her drawers, exposing her blond bush to his greedy gaze.

"Gorgeous," he muttered, thrusting his nose into her damp curls like an ill-behaved dog.

She gave a half-yelp, half-laugh and grasped his shoulders to steady herself.

He inhaled deeply, filling his lungs with her essence. "Fuck, you smell good."

She gasped, either at his raw action or crude words, or both.

Malcolm stroked up her legs, which were surprisingly muscular—all that riding to hounds, he assumed—and wrenched his hungry gaze from her delicate cleft to meet her wide-eyed gaze, suddenly frustrated by the barriers between them, especially his damned gloves.

He wanted to plunge his bare fingers into her silky wet heat and feel *her*—not the inside of his blasted gloves.

Surely you're brave enough to show your hand when she's been brave enough to bare herself to you?

Malcolm ignored his dead wife's taunting.

Instead, he remembered that long-ago whore and how she'd almost vomited when she'd seen his hand. He'd forgotten her name, but her horrified expression was indelibly engraved into his mind's eye.

No, he'd keep himself covered. He could enjoy her plenty with his lips and tongue

He cupped her breast, caressing his thumb over her already taut nipple, making it harder.

She moaned and her eyelids fluttered.

"Watch me," he ordered, pinching and stroking and teasing until her back was arching toward him, begging for his touch.

And then he released her, smirking at her desperate, demanding whimpers.

"Shh," he chided, and then lowered his hands to part not only her drawers, but the swollen pink lips hiding beneath.

"My God, Julia," he whispered as he stroked open her delicate petals and revealed her pearl. "Perfect," he muttered, and then lowered his mouth over her engorged clitoris, intoxicated by her sweet, clean musk.

She groaned and steadied herself by laying her hands on his head, fingers tangling in hair on one side, and caressing smooth, unfeeling leather on the other.

Malcolm stroked her slick folds with his thumbs while ravaging her with his mouth, lips, and tongue, his eye never leaving her face.

She kept her heavy-lidded gaze on him as he sucked and teased her engorged peak, working her until she squirmed and begged, "Please… please… *please.*"

"Malcolm!" she suddenly cried out, pulling his hair until his eyes watered, her entire body going rigid before the floodgates broke open and she shuddered and bucked with passion.

He released her sensitive bud and thrust his tongue into her cunt as deeply as it would go, reveling in the way her tight passage squeezed and flexed, his balls aching as he imagined how she'd feel around his cock.

As her climax slowly ebbed from her body Malcolm lapped at her gently, careful not to touch her too-sensitive clitoris.

Although he felt strangely drained by the sheer ferocity of her orgasm, he was still as hard as iron.

And God, he wanted more.

***

Julia's head spun from too much sensation—too much pleasure—too much *everything*.

Malcolm had consumed her like she was a piece of fruit, devouring her. He'd thrust his tongue *inside* her, using it as if it were his sex organ, his gaze rapt and worshipful even while he stripped her bare.

Julia's thighs trembled from the force of her climax and she had to lean against him to steady herself.

He smiled up at her with slick, swollen lips. "Legless?"

She nodded.

He stood with a slight grunt and then took her by the waist and tossed her onto the bed.

She laughed. "Thank you… that was… well, I don't have words."

When Julia tried to pull her legs modestly together, he laid his hands on her thighs. "I'm just getting started." He smirked. "Unless you are too tired?"

Amazingly, her sex clenched at his wicked look, ready for more.

Julia let her legs fall open.

"Mmm. Can you spread wider?"

She complied without hesitation, so eager to please him that she opened herself until her hips ached.

His pupil flared as he drank her in, tracing a finger lightly over the sensitive crease between her sex and her thigh. "Good girl."

Julia's inner muscles spasmed at his gruff praise, the effect of the simple words on her already overstimulated sex both immediate and electrifying. For the second time in as many minutes her back arched off the bed as a sharp, sudden climax ambushed her.

Even before the pleasure had fully ebbed Julia's cheeks burned.

As much as she wanted to hide, she forced her eyes open.

"Bloody hell," Malcolm murmured, staring down at her as if she'd just done something miraculous. "Did you just—"

"Yes," she blurted, before he could utter anything else that might shock another orgasm from her and prove just what a wanton whore she really was.

He stared, unblinking.

Julia turned away from his probing gaze.

"Hey there." He slid a hand around her jaw and turned her to face him. "Why do you look so miserable?" he gave a breathless laugh. "You just had an orgasm without either of us even *touching* you."

Julia squirmed. "Is that—it's—"

"What, luv?" he murmured, his brow furrowed with concern.

"It's abnormal to be the way I am, isn't it? I'm some sort of—of deviant." Julia pulled her thighs closed and this time he didn't stop her.

Instead, he leaned down on the bed, bringing his face close enough that she could see the magnificent icy blue of his iris and the beginnings of his night beard.

"You're not a deviant, sweetheart."

Julia tried to turn away, but he wouldn't let her.

"No," he said, although she'd not spoken. "I won't let you shame yourself for this. Do you think I'm a deviant for what I do?"

She opened her mouth, hesitated, and then said, "Well… yes, a little."

Malcolm laughed, a deep belly laugh that was so warm and comforting that Julia had to smile with him.

"Let me rephrase that," he said. "Do you think my desire for sex is the mark of a deviant?"

"No, but then you're a man and it is different for men."

"Society—a large part of it—believes that," he conceded. "But do you really want to please the nameless, faceless mass of society?"

"Of course not, but—"

"Worry about what *you* want and need, Julia. And what your lover likes and needs." He cocked his head. "Do you regret what you did with Lily? Because society would surely point its finger and call you a deviant for that. But do you wish it hadn't happened?"

Julia thought about Lily and those two lovely years when they'd been both best friends, and, yes, the adult word lover applied, too.

She met Malcolm's gaze. "I wish I hadn't been caught," she admitted. "But I wouldn't change it if I could."

"Do you think you will regret what we are d—"

"No," she said firmly.

His smile, when it came, grew slowly and it made her already hot face scald. "May I continue?" he asked, caressing her jaw with the back of his knuckles.

She nodded, suddenly shy.

He gestured to her drawers. "Can we take these off you now?"

Julia fumbled with the drawstring and then lifted her bottom while he pulled off the damp linen and tossed it to the side, leaving her in nothing but her stockings.

"Much better," he said, lightly stroking her calves. "We'll leave these on, I think." He dropped his hands to her ankles. "Will you open for me as prettily as you did before?"

Julia's leg muscles jumped and twitched as she opened them.

Malcolm caressed the sensitive skin of her inner thighs, the feel of his hands and gaze on her feeding the banked fire inside her.

"Yes, that's perfect." His gaze dropped to where his fingers, clad in cool, impersonal leather, spread her lower lips gently, exposing her fully to his scorching hot gaze. "You have the most beautiful cunt I've ever seen."

She shuddered at his filthy talk.

"You like that, don't you?" he murmured, slicking his finger from her swollen bud to her opening. "Don't you, Julia? You like me to say crude, nasty things to you while I touch you." He pushed a finger into her, not stopping until his knuckles rested against her sensitive flesh. "Don't you?" he repeated.

"Yes," she said, although it was more of a gasp as he worked his finger in and out of her with slow, deep thrusts.

"You look delicious stretched around my finger," he rumbled. "I can't wait to see how you look taking my cock."

A mortifying noise slipped out of her but Julia couldn't bring herself to care.

"Christ, but you're tight!" he said, the words almost accusatory.

He buried his face in her sex again, but this time, he maddeningly avoided her throbbing peak. Instead, he thrust his tongue in beside his finger as he worked her, filling the room with the wet, pornographic sounds of grunting and sucking.

Julia basked in the utter depravity, but her clitoris—or *clit* as Lily had wickedly called it—begged to be touched. She slid a hand down over his hand—the one holding her open—and groaned when she circled the tight bundle of nerves.

"Yes," he urged, pulling back to watch while she fingered herself. "Don't stop." He gave her bud a hard suck that made her squeak.

Julia squirmed as a second finger breached her, whimpering at the uncomfortable stretch.

"You're tight, but you can take it," he said, easing the thick digit into her by careful degrees, until her passage was full. He groaned as if he were in pain. "So. Fucking. Tight."

She clenched at his crude words and the sensation that rippled out was delicious, making her want more, deeper, harder. Julia dug her heels into the bed and shoved against his hand.

"Yes," he hissed as she bucked and ground into him. "Fuck my hand."

He shoved her finger away and lowered his mouth over her core, his wicked tongue stroking while his powerful arm pumped harder and faster, meeting the thrusting of her hips.

Julia lost herself in pleasure and not caring how she appeared, squirming and begging.

This time, when she orgasmed, her inner muscles closed around his thick fingers rather than emptiness and it intensified the exquisite contractions over and over again, until she drifted on a cloud of bliss.

She was only vaguely aware that he was still moving between her thighs, the rhythmic stroking of his tongue sending her into a fugue state, and didn't immediately notice that his tongue was moving down, down, down—

Julia clumsily pushed up onto her elbows, trying to pull her legs shut. But his arms tightened like iron bands and he spread her even wider, pushing her knees tight against her chest.

"Malcolm? What are you—ah!" she gasped when his hot tongue licked her *there*.

How could he? It was so dirty! Perhaps it had been an accid—

"Malcolm!" Julia yelped when he did it again.

He just chuckled and closed his mouth over her tightly puckered hole and *sucked*.

Julia groaned. Good Lord! It was the most deliciously filthy thing she'd ever felt. She tried to squirm away, but it was only a token struggle, a sop to her conscience.

Sensual pleasure at the soft, hot pressure of his lips and tongue on such a taboo part of her body warred with mortification at what he must be tasting and seeing.

Whatever he found, it clearly excited him and he sucked her harder, nibbling and tonguing until she was shamelessly shoving herself at him, needing him deeper, wanting more.

When he suddenly pulled away, Julia whined like a needy, shameless animal.

His bruised lips curved into a faint smile as the thick tip of his finger lightly circled her hole. "You are so beautiful. I want to explore every single part of you."

The lust-filled rasp of his voice was as erotic as his actions and Julia whimpered, her hips twitching.

"You want more, don't you?"

She had to bite her tongue to keep from begging.

He chuckled, easily reading her desire. "You'd like me to fuck your tight little hole with my tongue, wouldn't you?" His eyelid, which was already low, drooped even lower. "Imagine how good it will feel—slick, hot, and thrusting. Is that what you want, Julia, to feel me sliding deep inside and worshipping even the dirtiest part of you?"

To her shame, she nodded.

He grinned evilly, lowered his mouth over her, and shoved his tongue into her.

Julia moaned, folding herself almost in half so that she could watch him at his filthy labors.

Even though she could barely breathe in such a position it was worth it to meet his dark gaze as he turned words to deed, fucking into her with deep, slippery thrusts, his hands keeping her spread wide as he feasted.

Julia shuddered when his finger began to circle her overworked clitoris. He was careful not to touch her directly at first, working her slowly up to her need, until Julia was once again groaning and bucking her hips—or trying to, but he kept her pinned and immobile.

He gave her pucker a last, hard suck and then smirked up at her. "Need to come?" he taunted, flicking her tender bud hard enough to sting. He laughed at her pained gasp and did it again. "Well?"

"Please." The word burst out of her even as shame flooded her as she imagined how she must look to him: knees high against her chest, thighs spread wide, every part of her exposed and swollen.

She couldn't regret her begging when he lowered his head and once again drove her toward bliss.

This time, he let go of her thighs when she came, easing the ache in her sore hips, as she shook and shuddered.

Julia forced her heavy lids up and met his blazing blue gaze. His expression was one of fierce, intense desire as he tended to her—licking her clean as if she were the most delicious, precious thing he'd ever tasted.

A different sort of warmth than that she'd just experienced—this one more cerebral—spread through her at the sight of this huge, powerful man *worshipping* her.

Julia shivered, almost afraid of the emotion.

"You're cold," he said, pulling away, concern furrowing the part of his brow she could see.

Before she could demur, he pushed up onto his hands and knees and came up beside her, pulling the counterpane and blankets over her.

"Shouldn't I get underneath?" she said, the last word distorted by a yawn.

"Later. Just rest for now."

"Don't you want some blanket?" she offered sleepily.

"I'm not cold." He pulled her body close to his and Julia snuggled against the impossible softness of his waistcoat and trousers, resting her head on his biceps.

"Mmm," she rubbed her knee against his, yawned, and then murmured, "I've never felt such soft wool."

"It's blended with cashmere," he said, his voice a low rumble.

"S'nice." Julia could barely keep her eyes open. "I don't know why I'm so tired."

He chuckled. "Half a dozen orgasms will take it out of a person."

Which was when Julia recalled that *he* had not enjoyed any release. "You didn't get to—"

"Shhh. Just rest."

She struggled to push herself up, but his arm tightened around her and he held her in place firmly, but gently. "It doesn't matter, Julia."

Julia didn't agree at *all*. Her memory of that afternoon with Solomon—and how unfulfilling it had been—was still fresh enough that she burned with embarrassment that she'd just done the same thing to Malcolm.

"But I want to," she said, and then ruined her claim by yawning.

He slid his fingers through into her hair and began plucking out the few pins that hadn't already fallen out.

"Later, sweetheart," he murmured, the endearment making her neck feel boneless. "For now, just rest."

She fought against another yawn but lost the battle. "P'rahaps just for a moment. You won't let me fall asleep?"

"No. I won't let you fall asleep."

Chapter 29

Julia blinked to clear the sleep from her eyes, momentarily confused as her gaze flickered around the unfamiliar room.

Then she saw the paintings above the fire—they were called dragon-something, although they didn't look like any dragon she'd ever imagined—and recalled where she was: Malcolm's bedroom.

One thought struck her like a slap. *He let me fall asleep!*

Julia pushed up and tugged the blankets up over her bare breasts and looked at the other side of the bed; she was alone.

She reached down between her thighs—as if to assure herself that he'd really had his face down there last night, for what must have been *hours*—and felt the slightly abraded skin where his night beard had chafed her.

Yes, it really *had* happened.

She squeezed her thighs together and smiled at the sensations that lingered in the area—as if he'd pleasured her so deeply that she was permanently branded.

Julia's smile slid away; why was she alone?

Like her suite of rooms this one was also windowless so it was impossible to tell what time it was. How was she supposed to get back to her rooms?

Julia glanced around and saw a servant pull, right beside the bed.

But if she rang for a servant they would know that she'd been with their employer.

Fool. You think they don't already know?

Julia grimaced. Yes, it was likely the whole house knew.

But what were her other choices? Cower in bed all day?

Julia was just leaning over to pull the servant cord when she spied a dressing gown across the bench at the foot of the bed.

She pushed back the blankets, padded over to it, and slipped it over her shoulders. On the floor were slippers that were clearly meant for her feet.

A quick glance around the room showed her no gown, petticoat, or any of Malcolm's clothing. In fact, there was nothing personal at all—no photographs, no books on the nightstand.

She wandered into the huge bathroom, very similar to the one in her own suite of rooms. It was pristine, as if it had never been used.

When she opened the door to the dressing room, she discovered it was empty.

This wasn't Malcolm's room, at all.

Julia frowned; he'd just brought her to another guest room, not even trusting her enough to bring her to his own chambers.

Suddenly, she needed to get out. Rather than head for the servant cord, she turned toward the door.

Half of her expected it to be locked, but it opened easily.

Julia hovered on the threshold, trying to recall what turns Malcolm had taken to get her there.

Honestly, she'd been far too agitated to pay attention. He might have brought her to the room by hot air balloon for all that she remembered.

Well, she had two options. Julia decided to go left.

The corridors were like those outside her chambers, so she wasn't wandering one of his *secret* hallways.

Julia listened at every door she passed and when she heard no sounds she peeked inside. Thus far she'd found two more bed chambers, a large, mostly empty room with several huge tables, shelves full of ledgers, and dozens of rolls of paper that turned out to be architectural plans, several linen closets, but not a living soul anywhere.

She was just dithering which way to go when she heard John's voice coming from the corridor on the left.

Julia smiled; John would take her back to her chambers.

But a different voice came to her ears just as she approached the open door and Julia skidded to a halt.

"—no, I already told them to have it finished on the eighth or they wouldn't get paid. They signed the contract—tell them to re-read it if they are confused as to the terms," Malcolm said, his voice not loud, but stern.

"Yes, sir," John answered.

"Next," Malcolm said, sounding oddly breathless.

"I've received a second letter from Jean-Louis in Normandy about the—"

"Tell him not to use the Barton's label on any of it. They've had terrible weather and the lavender will be sub-standard. Next."

Julia crept up to the doorway and peeked around it.

John was standing a few feet inside, his arms filled with papers he was shuffling. Beyond him was a room unlike anything she'd ever seen. There were racks of cast iron things, thick canvas pads on the floor, leather bags hanging from the ceiling on heavy chains, and strange padded benches.

Right now, Malcolm was hanging from a metal bar that was embedded in two of the exposed wooden beams.

The reason his voice was breathy was because he was lifting his entire body with only his arms, raising himself up and touching his chin on the bar, lowering himself slowly, and doing it again.

And again.

He wore loose white cotton trousers and a smock-type shirt with short sleeves.

His left side was to her. Although he still wore his mask, his arm was bare up to his bulging biceps.

The skin on his arm was shiny and red and whorled, as if it had been melted, stirred, and allowed to settle. His elbow and parts of his forearm were covered with odd patchwork sections of lighter skin.

His hands were curled around the bar and there were just two fingers and a thumb on his left hand, the last two fingers were stumps.

The burns were terrible and Julia shuddered to think of the pain he must have suffered, but nothing about him revolted her.

Indeed, looking at his bare arm had quite the opposite effect. His bulging muscles were massive—perhaps as big around as her waist—and exquisitely defined beneath the shiny pink skin.

"Did you have any responses to the latest batch of telegrams," John asked, shifting the armload of documents slightly as he stared up at his employer.

Malcolm pulled himself up, giving a low grunt. He paused at the top and said through clenched jaws, "No, that's all. You may go, Butkins."

John turned, saw Julia, and then yelped, flinging up the armload of documents.

Julia pulled her head away from the door and slapped a hand over her mouth to keep from laughing.

"Good God, Butkins! You scared the hell out of me," Malcolm growled. "What the hell are you yelping about?"

"Erm, sorry sir."

Julia heard the sound of papers being shuffled.

"What the devil is wrong with you?" Malcolm asked.

"I thought I saw a spider."

"A spider," Malcolm repeated in a flat, disbelieving tone.

Julia choked and snorted behind her hand, backing away from the door, not stopping until she was around the corner, where she could chortle and choke on her laughter.

John barreled around the corner a moment later. He gave her an accusatory glare and hissed, "What are you doing here?"

"Just looking," she whispered.

He took her arm and marched her down the hallway. "Mr. Barton wouldn't like to find you watching him in his gymnasium."

"Oh, I wondered if that's what that was. He is very strong, isn't he?"

"Let me escort you back to your room, Miss Harlow," he said, ignoring her question.

"Thank you, I'm afraid I was quite lost."

John didn't look at her as they walked. "How are you this morning?" he finally asked in a subdued voice.

"I'm fine. Why?"

"Oh, no reason." He was in profile to her, his cheek shockingly red.

Julia bit back a smile when she realized he was concerned for her—or for her virtue, at least. "Are you worried Mr. Barton shocked me last night, John?"

"Shhh," he hissed, his eyes darting about frantically, as if somebody might be listening.

Well, given that the house positively seethed with hidden corridors that was a distinct possibility.

John stopped in front of a door and opened it.

Julia gawked; it was her sitting room.

"Goodness! I didn't realize I was so close."

John ushered her inside but left the door open as he pulled the servant cord and turned to her. "You shouldn't wander around by yourself, Miss Harlow."

She frowned at his chiding tone. "I'm not a toddler, John."

"No, I know that. But, er, there are things you shouldn't see."

"What sort of things?" she asked, although she could guess.

He frowned. "I'd rather not—"

"I know about the women."

"W-women?" he blurted.

Julia gave an exasperated sigh. "The prostitutes—Maisie and the other one."

"Good Lord! But—but how?"

"What does it matter? Mr. Barton told me he sent her away." Julia narrowed her eyes. "Did he or was he lying to me?"

"No, no, he wasn't lying. She is gone." He grimaced when he realized what he'd said. "I shouldn't have told you that—and *you* shouldn't ask me such things because my first loyalty is to Mr. Barton."

Julia brushed aside his scold. "Does he go to that room—the gymnasium—often."

John gave her an exasperated look.

"What?"

"I just told you I can't answer questions about him—ah, hello Mrs. Kemp." His shoulders sagged with relief when the maid appeared in the open doorway. "I had better go, now."

"Must you? We were having such an interesting and *informative* talk," Julia teased.

He hurried out of the room as if he had vicious predators on his heels and Julia couldn't help laughing.

Kemp pursed her lips, but Julia knew the older woman was amused. "You shouldn't tease him, Miss Julia."

"I know, but I can't help it; he blushes easier than I do."

"Let's get you into the bath," Kemp replied.

If Kemp thought any differently about Julia for spending the night with her employer, she didn't show it.

"Which gown shall I set out for you today?" Kemp asked as Julia lounged in the enormous bathtub a short time later.

"The green velvet," Julia said. "And I'll need my painting smock."

"Shall I have James bring your paints and easel out to the greenhouse?"

Julia thought about the picture she wanted to paint and smiled. "No, I shall paint in my sitting room." This was a painting she would need to keep private—as the subject was a *very* private man.

Chapter 30

Malcolm told himself, yet again, that he was doing the right thing.

Somebody needed to end this madness and it needed to be *him*.

Nothing good could come of dallying with Julia, and he was losing control, something he never ever did.

It was better for both of them that he'd left Julia alone to sleep last night before he could do something foolish and irreparable.

Like fuck her.

If he'd stayed it would have been a goddamned catastrophe.

It would have been glorious.

Well, he couldn't disagree, even though the thought was less than helpful considering that he was trying to take the moral high ground rather than utterly debauch her.

And what you did to her last night was the high ground?

Malcolm gritted his teeth.

A little bit of tongue work is one thing—it never got anyone pregnant—sticking my cock into her, on the other hand, and—

"Sir?"

Malcolm looked up; Butkins was standing in the doorway and he'd not even heard him enter.

"What is it, Butkins?"

"I know you didn't wish to be disturbed, but—"

"But here you are disturbing me. What?"

"Miss Julia wishes to speak to you."

"Tell her I'm not here."

Butkins hovered.

"What?" he barked.

"She asked if you would be coming to dinner?"

"No."

"Very good, sir."

The door closed behind him and Malcolm slumped back into his chair. There, that was what he should have done all along. Dining with her, playing cards with her, sharing secrets with her as if they were school chums, taking her bloody skating, for fuck's sake! And, worst of all, allowing himself to touch her.

Allowing himself to want her and imagine they might be able to have—

Damnit! He was doing it again: fantasizing about the impossible.

Malcolm was not the sort of man who yearned for women he could not have. Indeed, he'd never suffered an unrequited affection— either before or after his marriage—and the experience befuddled and displeased him.

Not that Julia was rejecting him, precisely, but she was too young and inexperienced to understand that what she felt was mere infatuation; she was only fascinated by him because she'd never met anyone who'd been open about their sexuality, and a warped sexuality at that.

She would tire of the novelty of him soon enough. And when she did, she'd realize that all he had to offer was a scarred, broken body and a corrupt, debauched soul.

But for Malcolm? Well, it wouldn't be so easy for him to forget Miss Julia Harlow; he'd be the one who suffered.

Malcolm pushed back from his desk and paced the room, organizing his addled wits. Soon—very soon—this entire charade would be over.

He had Sheehan and his cunt of a sister and Tommy, all lined up like ducks in a row. Only one last duck evaded him, but Malcolm knew he'd not need to wait long for Brian Harlow to waddle into his snare.

Until then, he'd keep his mind, eye, and hands off Julia.

***

Malcolm's resolve lasted all of two days.

He'd spent a miserable and exceptionally unproductive forty-eight hours yelling at Butkins for minor—or entirely imagined—infractions.

Not only that, but he was constantly hard from remembering how Julia had looked that night, spread and needy and writhing beneath his mouth and fingers. He could recall the sweet flavor of her cunt without any effort—and it was ruining him for any other food or drink.

He'd considered summoning a whore—not Maisie, but somebody who'd evoke no memories of Julia, not that anyone could compare to her—but he was too infuriated to reward himself. He didn't deserve an orgasm—he was an idiot for allowing his obsession to grow to such proportions.

For forty-eight miserable hours he suffered with an erection: he didn't even jerk himself. It had been years since he'd gone without sexual pleasure whenever he wanted it.

Malcolm told himself he could do it; he could keep away from her. After all, in only a few days she would be gone forever.

He'd received word from Joe that Brian had arrived in London, finally, although he'd showed no signs of coming to see Malcolm. But he would. Oh yes, he would.

Malcolm could only imagine the scene between Brian, Tommy, and Nadine Harlow, all huddled together in Harlow's London home like spiders in a bowl, trying to find some way out of the trap that Malcolm had set for them.

It would only be a matter of days—a week at the most—before one of them acted.

Once that happened he could get Julia out of his house and himself way from temptation.

Although it wasn't pleasant, he could tolerate a few more days with a relentless erection.

He'd become spoiled by too many whores and too much cock sucking and it had softened his brain. He'd become—

A timid knock on the door interrupted his internal rant.

"Come in!" he barked, unsurprised when Butkins opened the door and then hovered on the threshold.

"Come or go. But do not hover, Butkins."

Butkins stepped inside and closed the door but did not advance into the room. "Miss Harlow is refusing dinner. Again."

"Goddammit!" Malcolm roared. "How many meals has she missed?" He knew the answer, of course, but needed to buy time to think.

"Er, seven, sir."

He let out a stream of curses that made Butkins's face pale.

"Tell her to get herself to the dining room and eat or I shall have her strapped to her bed and force-fed."

Butkins's jaw sagged.

"Oh, for Christ's sake, man! I'm not in earnest, but she won't know that."

Butkins nodded and swallowed. "And shall I tell her she'll be dining alone?"

"No." He barked. "Tell the manipulative little vixen that I shall join her."

***

Kemp, normally the most placid of creatures, flapped around Julia like an agitated hen while Julia sat at the dressing table, fussing with her already perfect hair.

Kemp looked at the watch pinned to her bodice. Again. "Oh, Miss Julia, you're already fifteen minutes late."

"My stepmother says that it is wise to keep a man waiting."

"Not Mr. Barton, Miss Julia. He is the *last* man you wish to make wait. He is—"

The door to Julia's chambers swung open hard enough to smash against the wall. The man under discussion filled the doorway with his massive frame.

"Out," he ordered in a low, menacing growl.

Kemp fled.

He shut the door ungently, his single eye raking her coldly. He snorted, his lips twisting into a sneer. "You don't look like a woman fainting from hunger. Somebody has been feeding you."

Julia shrugged with an insouciance she was far from feeling.

He took a step toward her and it took all her strength to hold her ground.

"You've manipulated me, haven't you?"

She lifted her eyebrows. "Perhaps."

He gave a chuckle that made the hairs on the back of her neck stand up. When he reached for her cheek, she flinched.

"Shhh," he soothed, cupping her gently. "You wanted my attention, now you have it, Julia. What can I do for you?"

She lifted her chin defiantly—and perhaps she rubbed her cheek against his palm. Maybe just a little—and said, "Have you called her back?"

"Called who?"

Julia scowled. "Maisie!"

His eye widened briefly and he gave a bark of laughter.

"What is so amusing about that?"

"No, Maisie won't be coming back."

"But you'll have some other woman?" she demanded before she could stop herself. Julia wanted to slap her own face. What was wrong with her? Why couldn't she shut her mouth?

250

Malcolm's pale blue eye turned icy and cruel. "Will I fuck another whore? Is that what you are asking me? That is a safe wager, Julia. Utterly safe."

Molten jealousy bubbled in her belly and rose up in her throat, choking her. She *hated* him in that moment.

His gaze stripped her bare, exposing her humiliating yearning. He stroked her lower lip with his thumb. "Are you offering to please me, Julia? Hmm? Is that what you want—to be my whore?"

Shock exploded inside her like a pyrotechnic display and Julia opened her mouth to tell him to go to the devil.

But before she could speak, he pushed his thumb between her lips. "Suck."

Her jaw dropped open in shock and he took advantage of her reaction to shove the thick leather clad digit all the way to the joint, his lips curving into an unspeakably decadent smile.

"Go on. Show me you deserve my cock."

Humiliation, disbelief, and anger collided inside her at his crude order, but those emotions were swamped by a lust so visceral it made her head spin.

"No?" He cocked his eyebrow and began to withdraw his thumb.

Julia clamped down hard enough to make him wince. "*Tsk, tsk*, no teeth, sweetheart."

Her face scalded at his mocking smile and her own shameful behavior; she should just release him now and tell him to get out.

But if she did that, he would leave and never come back. This was it; this was her last chance to get what she wanted: him.

And so she sucked.

***

Be kind to her, Mal. She just wants to please you.

Well, look who has come back. Thank you for sharing what is patently obvious, Sukey.

It would be clear even to a dead man that Julia was all but exploding to give herself to him. Her desire to please him was insanely flattering and arousing and made him feel a hundred feet tall.

Too bad it was nothing but infatuation.

If he took her—made her his—and then continued with his plans for her family? Well, it would be his undoing. Because she would hate him with the heat of a thousand suns after he destroyed her life.

Her eyes, which had been huge and startled when he'd stormed into the room, now sparkled with anticipation.

She was like a kitten—playful, trusting, and without guile, showing every emotion on her expressive, surpassingly lovely face.

And Malcolm was a pig who wanted to put his big club of a prick between those plush lips and fuck her face as roughly as he would a back-alley whore.

Her pale, delicate hands landed on his leather-clad fist, bringing to mind dainty, wholesome butterflies alighting on something blackened and stunted. Her eyes met his as her lips tightened around his thumb. Even through the barrier of the leather he felt her tongue cradle his finger and blood surged to his cock.

"You drive me mad; do you know that?" He snorted. "Of course, you do," he said before she could answer. "I think of you day and night. What little sleep I *do* get, you have ruined for me, because all I see when I close my eyes is *you*."

Her magnificent eyes glittered with feminine satisfaction at his accusation.

Malcolm laughed harshly. "My own personal siren luring me to the rocks."

When she would have pulled away to speak, he shook his head. "No talking—keep sucking until I tell you otherwise."

Her eyes hazed with lust at his vulgar command and her instant submission made his balls so bloody hard they felt like stone.

Decades of iron will and self-control reasserted themselves. He was accustomed to deferring his pleasure with whores, now he could exercise that restraint with the real thing—a woman he wanted, and one who was rapidly taking him apart, piece by piece, without even trying.

"Good," he praised in a voice roughened by unholy lust. "But that's just a thumb." Her eyes scrunched up and a notch imposed itself between her elegant brows, her full lips going slack around his digit.

Malcolm took advantage of her momentary inattention to reach around her and grab the cushion from a chair. He tossed that down to the floor. "Kneel."

Her eyelashes fluttered and more color stained her already pinkened cheeks.

Malcolm waited patiently. *If you know what's good for you, sweetheart, you'll send me packing.*

Instead, she shakily lowered herself to her knees and swallowed noisily when she stared at his grotesquely tented trousers.

Malcolm spread his feet enough to lower his prick to the level of her mouth. "Open my trousers and take me out."

She looked like she might faint—which would be the best thing for her—but, again, she surprised him, her elegant fingers fumbling with the buttons.

"I shouldn't take you in this room like this," he muttered, dropping a hand to her hair and carding his fingers into the thick locks, wrenching her head back.

She stared up at him with startled, wide eyes, her lips parting. "Why not?"

"Hush," he ordered, tightening his grip until she winced. Rather than knock any sense into her, Malcolm watched as the pain sent a fresh wave of lust rolling through her body.

"I should put you under my desk—use you like a whore for my pleasure."

She groaned, the sound so low and needy he almost came. Yes, his little Julia didn't just like pain, she craved humiliation. In that moment, she reminded him so much of Brian Harlow that his vision briefly hazed.

He was a sick, perverted bastard to find the comparison arousing.

But then he already knew that.

"That's enough," he ordered gruffly when she'd undone all but two of the buttons. "Reach in and take me out."

"But… may I not take them off?"

"No," he barked.

She cut him a mulish, rebellious look that drove him wild: his Julia might be submissive with a taste for pain, but she was no doormat.

Malcolm caught her wrist, surprising a gasp from her, squeezing the fragile bones hard enough to hurt her and get her attention. "Tell me to leave."

Her lips parted and hurt flooded her eyes.

Part of him cheered her on. *Say it to me—leave! Leave now. There is nothing good for you here. I'm as hollow and empty as an abandoned building that will collapse on top of you, taking you down with me.*

But her delicate jaw hardened and a fierce light glinted in her eyes. She tugged her hand away and pulled open the two sides of his trouser placket, making an adorable squeaking sound when his eager prick thrust its way through the opening.

All her bravery disappeared when faced—literally—with his cock. Her mouth opened in awe—an expression that sent indecent ideas frolicking through his filthy mind—and her eyes widened comically.

She swallowed and then looked up at him. "It seems larger than I remember."

Malcolm laughed, genuinely amused. "That's your effect on me."

"Really?" And then she blushed at whatever she saw on his face. "You are teasing me."

"Perhaps a little."

She swallowed, the delicate cords of her throat flexing enticingly, begging to be filled and fucked. "What should I do, Malcolm?"

"What do you want to do?"

She nibbled her lip, her gaze wary as it slid over his shaft. "I'd like to touch you."

"Then do so."

She smiled as if he'd just given her a diamond tiara, her small hand making him look obscenely huge as it wrapped around him. "It's so smooth and hot."

"Haven't you touched one before?"

Charmingly, she blushed and shook her head. "I wanted to, but with Matthew everything happened too quickly, and Solomon wouldn't let me. He said it was… profane."

Fucking fools.

"Stroke me," he ordered.

She gave him a caress so soft that he shouldn't have been able to feel it, but it rocked him to his core and Malcolm hissed.

She looked up, her hand freezing. "Did that hurt?"

"Do it harder."

Her delicate hands were torture as she slid across his hot, wanting skin. "Like this?"

"Yes," he grated. "Just like that." He watched her raptly, storing away every expression like a squirrel hoarding nuts for the cold, lonely years ahead, when she was some other man's wife.

She became bolder, her grip tighter as she slid his foreskin down. "How interesting," she murmured, eye to eye with his leaking slit. "It is to protect you, isn't it?" she asked, her eager, innocent curiosity so bloody enchanting it hurt.

Malcolm wished like hell that he had two eyes to watch her. Consume her. "Yes. It is where I am most sensitive—right below the crown."

"It is similar to me, in a way."

He nodded, saliva pooling in his mouth as he thought about her clitoris tucked beneath its sweet little hood. He was briefly tempted to toss her onto the nearby settee and examine her as closely as she was doing him and then suck her to orgasm a time or five.

But then she smiled mischievously and slid his foreskin all the way back, tilting him so she could see the underside.

Malcolm gritted his teeth against the feel of her hot breath against the fragile, sensitive skin.

Then the wicked little enchantress looked up at him with those huge blue eyes and said, "Here?" And licked him.

She could have licked the bottom of his shoe with that expression it would have made his balls, already snug to his body and full, clench painfully hard.

"Fuck." He had to force the word through jaws that felt welded shut.

She looked startled, her cheeks coloring, but then she smiled, and it spread across her face like a sunrise.

"You like that." She looked justifiably proud of herself and then glanced down. "Oh," she said leaning closer. "You're becoming wet," she swallowed hard, her eyelids suddenly drooping.

"Is teasing me making your sweet pussy all swollen and slippery, Julia?"

Her lips parted and a soft grunt escaped, the wealth of need in the faint sound making him drunk with desire.

"That was a wicked thing to say," she whispered.

He lifted an eyebrow. "Pussy?" he taunted.

Rather than become flustered, as he'd thought, she lowered her mouth and tongued his slit in erotic retaliation.

Malcolm squeezed his eye shut and drew in a shaky breath, the image of her tongue on his cock branded onto his brain—probably for the rest of his life.

When he opened his eye, she was staring, rapt.

"You see the power you wield, Julia?"

She nodded, the corners of her mouth curling up slightly.

"You like that, do you?"

Again, she nodded. "I want to please you—tell me how."

Christ and hell and damnation.

***

This was, Julia decided, even better than having Malcolm's mouth between her thighs. This was the power she'd felt before, but instead of a meandering river, this was a tidal wave crashing through her, spreading through her veins to every part of her body.

It was the sort of feeling that could become addictive.

She already wanted more.

"I want to please you—tell me how."

His nostrils flared and his hot blue gaze turned black.

Julia made him do that—with only words. What could she do with her mouth?

"Take the knob into your mouth and suck," he said roughly, his raw need thrilling her. "Mind your teeth and don't try to take too much or you will choke yourself—which could be bad for both of us."

"But Maisie took all of you."

He snorted. "You are a competitive little thing, aren't you?"

"Tell me how she did it," she persisted.

"Practice," he said dryly. "*Lots* of practice. You will see once you have me in your mouth that I feel larger than I look—that is the nature of cocks."

"You sound… knowledgeable."

"I am."

Have you—" she couldn't bring herself to complete the sentence.

"Have I sucked cock?"

The words and image they evoked robbed Julia of speech and it was all she could do to nod.

"Yes, I have." His unabashed smirk and blunt confession sent delicious ripples of naughty pleasure shimmering through her body.

"That thought arouses you." It was a statement, not a question— he didn't need to ask because he knew; he saw into her darkest and most depraved thoughts as if she were made of glass.

A sensual smile curved his lips and he slid his huge hand around the base of his equally huge shaft. He closed his fist and pumped himself, the sight of black leather against his ruddy skin intoxicating. His fingers moved to the part he called the crown and squeezed, making more fluid leak from the slit.

When she looked up, she saw he was watching her. "It's making you wet to imagine me on my knees with my lips wrapped around a thick, hard jack, isn't it?"

Julia was beyond wet; the thought was rendering her nearly blind with desire.

What was wrong with her?

That is a question you need to quit asking, she told herself. *Accept that you are a depraved wanton and let that be an end to the tiresome subject.*

A certain amount of tension drained out of her at the decision and she looked up at him.

Malcolm gave a slight nod at whatever he saw on her face and aimed the head of his cock toward her mouth. "Suck it."

Julia immediately complied, inhaling the earthy scent of him mingled with some trace of soap or cologne—perhaps bergamot or lavender. She opened her mouth, thinking it would be wide enough, but it wasn't close. She had to all but unhinge her jaws to take him in and not drag her teeth on him.

Respect for Maisie mingled with jealousy.

This was going to be a challenge.

The fat end filled her mouth and she laid her hands on Malcolm's hips to steady herself.

"Wrap one hand around the root so you can control how much you take in."

Julia's fingers didn't meet when they wrapped around his girth; small wonder that he did not fit easily in her mouth!

"Hold me tighter," he ordered gruffly. "Yesss, like that." He lowered his hand to her hair and stroked gently. "Teeth, luv."

Her jaw had drifted closed while she'd been concentrating on what her hand was doing. She opened wider, recalling what he'd said about the underside of the crown. With a bit of adjustment, she had him angled so she could use her tongue to cradle and stroke the spot.

He all but purred. "Good girl," he murmured, his eye glinting with smug humor when she stiffened at the strangely potent praise.

Once she'd found the spot that made him shiver, she moved her hand, mimicking the stroking he'd done earlier.

He shuddered, his jaw taut. "God, yes, stroke me while you suck."

It was not as easy as it sounded, but she soon established a slow, even rhythm. Keeping her teeth in mind, she gradually took him deeper, stopping when she felt as though he might choke her.

Julia moaned with frustrated despair when she saw she'd barely taken half of him.

"Forget about throating me, sweetheart. Suckle my slit and feast on my desire for you."

Oh, the things he said to her…

She withdrew until only the bulbous end filled her mouth. It was thicker than the shaft and reminded her of a large hot plum, not that she'd ever attempted to stuff an entire plum in her mouth.

She found the slit with her tongue and earned a low, rumbling growl of approval.

Every reaction from him caused her own body to respond, her muscles to flex and tighten, her breasts to become heavier, and her sex to become slicker, needier.

"That feels wonderful, Julia."

She preened at his praise and the dark undertone in his low, rough voice, wanting more words, more moaning and shivering. She stretched her jaws wider, careful not to chafe him, her tongue sliding down the pulsing underside of his shaft as she inexorably lowered over him.

"Mmmmm."

His groans of pleasure were an aphrodisiac unlike anything she could imagine and she wanted more, taking the fat crown deeper and deeper and—

Julia gagged, her eyes watering and her throat convulsing. Big hands lightly but firmly cupped her jaws and he carefully withdrew.

She doubled over, hacking and coughing and staring up at him through tearing eyes.

"I can do better," she rasped when she saw that he was tucking himself away. "Let me try aga—"

"Hush. Come here." He gently lifted her off her knees.

Julia swayed, face burning as she stared up at him. "You didn't like it?" It shamed her how childish and foolish and gauche she must appear to him.

His eye flickered over her face and he pushed a loose lock of hair behind her ear. "I liked it very much. However—unlike you—I have not had servants sneaking me food so I am hungry."

She gave a watery chortle. "That was clever of me, wasn't it?"

"Very. Come, let us eat the fine meal the chef has been holding for us."

She nodded and then glanced at the mirror, stunned when she saw her full, slick lips and flushed cheeks.

"You look even more beautiful than usual," he assured her, turning toward the door.

Julia clutched his arm, halting him. "Are we—is everything—" she broke off and bit her lip. "I don't want you to ignore me again, Malcolm. I want—"

He laid a finger across her lips. "I'm tired of resisting my desire for you, Julia."

Her heart leapt. "We will spend every evening together?"

"Every evening for the rest of your stay," he corrected.

"How long is that?"

"Not long. Two—maybe three more nights at most."

"No! You said before that it would be longer."

"I was wrong," he said, his gaze once again shuttered.

Julia wanted to stomp her foot and shake him until the warmth came back into his eye. But she knew that would only make him retreat faster and farther. Instead, she worked on the desire he had just admitted to. "What if you can't bear to send me back, Malcolm? What if you want to keep me forever?"

His expression chilled her. "Make no mistake, Julia. Nothing that happens will change my mind. I *will* send you away when everything is over." He hesitated and added, "And once you find out what I've done, you will never want to see me again."

"What could you do that is so terrible?"

He ignored her question as if she'd never spoken. "Come, let us go to dinner."

Julia followed him without arguing, but her mind was churning.

Two, even three, nights with him would never be enough.

Malcolm might refuse to keep her.

But then Julia could always refuse to go, couldn't she?

Chapter 31

Malcolm was staring sightlessly at the same report he'd been staring at for an hour, recalling last night—both before dinner, when Julia had *practiced*, and after dinner, when Malcolm had done some *practicing* of his own.

He'd been grateful when she'd not wanted cards and chatter after their meal. Instead, they had retired to his favorite guest room where he'd spent most of the night reacquainting his mouth with her body.

It had taken some effort to distract her from her stated goal of intercourse—she was nothing if not dogged—but Malcolm had discovered that his Julia became just as malleable as anyone else when subjected to repeated and protracted orgasms.

He'd had his tongue and fingers in and on every part of her, so why he was resisting engaging in the *ultimate* deed with her, he did not know. Did he believe she'd find some consolation—after she'd learned the depth of destruction he'd visited upon her family—if they'd never actually fucked?

Malcolm snorted at the foolish thought.

He'd resisted her considerable efforts last night and had—yet again—left her exhausted and sleeping, compounding his cowardice by eating his breakfast just after dawn to ensure he didn't encounter her accusing gaze over coddled eggs and kippers.

Something told him that she'd be less amenable to sensual manipulation—no matter how fulfilling—tonight.

The door to his office opened and Butkins entered.

"I told you I didn't want to be disturbed." Allegedly because of all the work he had to do, but really because he'd wanted to fantasize about last night… and what might happen tonight.

"Er, Mr. Smith is here, sir."

Malcolm glanced at the clock and frowned; it was just after three. A visit from his friend in the middle of the day was unusual. Smith must have something important to say.

"Send him right in."

"It will take me a moment to go fetch him."

"Fetch him from where?"

"He is waiting in the greenhouse, sir."

Malcolm snorted. "With Miss Harlow?"

"Yes, sir. She was painting when he arrived."

"How long has he been here, Butkins?"

His secretary's pale skin flamed. "Er, perhaps a quarter of an hour."

"And nobody thought to tell me until now?"

"Well, sir, it seems he… er, sneaked in."

Malcolm sighed.

"I'm terribly sorry, sir."

"It's not your fault. If Smith wants to get in somewhere, he'll get in. Go and fetch him."

Malcolm allowed himself a laugh when Butkins shut the door; Smith and his bloody meddling. The man was a force of nature once he sank his teeth into something and Malcolm knew from his last visit—when he'd barged into Malcolm's library so he could meet Julia—that his controlling friend had decided it was time for Malcolm to marry.

"She is perfect for you and you for her," Smith had insisted.

"Julia would be perfect for any man, Smith. While I—I am a debauched, damaged pervert twice her age."

"More than twice, actually."

That had made Malcolm laugh.

He could only assume the other man was back for more of the same today. Why Smith was so damned determined to see him wed was anyone's guess.

Malcolm shuffled his papers into a neat pile and was just tucking them away when the door opened.

"Ah, what a pleasant surprise, Smith—three times in one month."

Smith grinned as he sauntered into his study looking perfect and elegant dressed in his day attire—clothing Malcolm rarely saw him wearing. "Thank you for seeing me, my friend."

"Oh, I had a choice?"

Smith laughed. "No, not really. You need to get new locks, my friend. Especially in the employee stairwell."

"Thank you. I shall pass that along to store security," he said dryly.

"You are welcome," Smith said without irony.

"Drink?" Malcolm lifted the decanter with Smith's spirit of choice.

"Why not? It is still the festive season for a few more days, after all." He settled into a chair while Malcolm poured them both a glass.

"How did you celebrate Christmas?" Malcolm asked as he delivered the drink and took the chair across from his friend.

"Doing this and that, here and there."

"As forthcoming as ever," Malcolm murmured.

Smith chose to ignore his sarcasm. "I just had the most delightful conversation with Miss Harlow."

"So I heard. I hope you know that all of your creeping about will make poor Butkins gray before his time."

"I need to keep in practice."

"Yes, but do you need to practice your housebreaking skills on *my* house?" Malcolm asked plaintively.

"What are friends for?"

Malcolm sighed. "I give in. What did you and Julia talk about?"

"You, of course."

All the good humor he'd been feeling drained away. "I hope you've not been filling her head with foolish dreams?"

"No, only fertilizing the ones she already planted herself."

"Goddammit, Smith!" Malcolm slammed down his glass, no longer amused. "You, of all people should understand what I'm about to unleash on her."

"That is true," he admitted, unperturbed.

"And you don't think that might have some impact on whatever dreams she's, er, *planted* about me?"

"Some, but not as much as you think."

Malcolm gave a disbelieving huff.

"What? You think she feels any love or affection for Carl Sheehan, Nadine Harlow, or even Thomas and Brian? After what they've all done to her?"

"She doesn't know what they've done to her and I plan to keep it that way," he shot back. "The last thing I want to do is trample the few good memories she might have of them after they are gone."

"She's an adult and deserves to know."

"That isn't your choice to make," he snarled.

Smith merely sipped his drink, utterly uncaring of the menace and anger swirling between them.

"Stay out of this, Smith. It's none of your concern."

"I beg to differ."

"And what gives you the right to interfere in my bloody life—or hers, for that matter?"

The change in the other man's demeanor was subtle—a slight flaring of his nostrils, a thinning of his full, sensual mouth, and a chill in his usually warm gaze. "While you were unconscious and in mortal peril, I spent the last hours of Sukey's life with her."

"I know that," Malcolm growled. It was one of the great regrets of his life that he'd not been the last one to see his wife alive.

"You have always been jealous of that," Smith said, easily reading his thoughts, as usual. "But you *should* be grateful, Malcolm." He made a dismissive wave with one elegant hand when Malcolm opened his mouth to argue. "That isn't what I want to talk about now. What I want to talk about is her last words to me."

Malcolm's hand tightened hard enough to crack the crystal tumbler and he thrust it aside. "You said she was unconscious."

"I lied."

Malcolm was out of his chair and clutching Smith's lapels in his fists before the impulse had even registered. "How *dare* you keep that from me?"

Smith didn't struggle or resist in any way. "Go ahead and hit me, I deserve it. But before you do, know that I did it because she made me promise not to tell you. She didn't want you to know how she suffered for three entire days."

"*Three days*! I was told she died only hours after we were pulled from the fire. I was awake the second day in the hospital and might have spoken to her. You *cheated* me out of that time with her." The anguish was so suffocating he could barely breathe.

Smith stared up at him, unafraid and unapologetic. "It was *her* wish."

Malcolm flung him away and stepped back, glaring while Smith calmly straightened his clothing.

"You want all of it?" Smith asked.

"I wanted all of it fifteen years ago, goddammit!"

Smith shrugged. "A deathbed promise surpassed my duty to you. Until now."

"Why are you telling me *now*?"

"Because I might actually be able to fulfill the second promise Sukey demanded of me." Smith held out his glass. "A bit more, if you will."

Malcolm scowled but snatched the glass and stalked over to the decanter. When he returned, Smith had settled into his chair and looked as cool as ever.

"Thank you," he said, when Malcolm rudely shoved the glass into his hand.

"Go on," he said, his voice harsh. "Tell me the rest."

"She made me promise that I'd see to it that you'd not blame yourself, that you'd marry, have children, and live a long, happy, fulfilling life. For fifteen years I've watched and waited for a chance to fulfill my promise to her, Malcolm," Smith went on, relentless. "Sometimes I thought you might be happy going on the way you were. I even hoped you might find a prostitute you could love—a woman who would know about your proclivities and perhaps share them." He shrugged at whatever he saw on Malcolm's face. "I'm sorry if you find that insulting, but whores are people with wants and needs—my friend Nora Fanshawe taught me that—and they can make the best mates in the world for men like us."

"I'm not insulted," Malcolm growled. "I'm amused—bitterly—that you're so bloody stubborn and refuse to accept how women—whores included—react to me, which is with revulsion at worst and toleration at best."

"Did Julia react like that?"

Malcolm hesitated only a fraction of a second before opening his mouth to answer, but it was long enough for Smith to shove his foot into the doorway he'd opened.

"No, I didn't think so," Smith said.

"She hasn't *seen* me."

"That's not true."

Malcolm thought his head might explode. "What the hell are you talking about?"

"Why don't you ask Julia?"

"Because I'm asking *you*, damnit!"

Smith picked a piece of lint from his sleeve before looking up. "She saw you in your gymnasium, so she's seen your arm and neck. She knows what is beneath your clothing."

"When? How—? Never mind!" he snapped before the other man could speak. "My arm is a far cry from my face and you know it."

Smith heaved a put-upon sigh that made Malcolm want to strangle him.

"And why are you talking about such things with a woman you've only met once—well, twice. Or have you been sneaking into my house daily?" Malcolm wouldn't put it past the man.

Smith grinned at that. "I'd like to say that women just trust and confide in me"—Malcolm snorted—"but the truth is that I am the only source of information Julia has about you and she's smart enough to use me."

"And you're devious enough to encourage her."

Smith ignored the accusation. "Let Julia hear the truth and allow *her* to make her own decision, Malcolm. I think you will be surprised by how she views matters."

Malcolm stared down at his clenched fists, fighting the hope that his friend kept throwing at him.

"I know revenge will not bring her—*them*—back, Smith. But I cannot allow those bastards to go about their lives without punishment, even if it means I destroy what Julia might feel for me." He looked up. "They have been *ruthless* in their pursuit of what they want. Not only the fire that did this to me, but another in New York that killed *five* people." He squeezed his eye shut at the horror of what that family had suffered.

"I know about that, Malcolm," Smith said softly. "And I also know more."

He opened his eye and gave a soft, disbelieving laugh. "And you think telling me that makes me want to pull back from what I am about to unleash?"

"I don't want you to pull back."

"I don't understand? You just said—"

"There is one more thing you should know, Malcolm. One thing that will tip the scales irrevocably."

"What?" Malcolm asked, afraid to hear his answer.

Smith opened his mouth, but a loud rap on the door stopped him before he could speak.

"What the hell do you want, Butkins?" Malcolm raged when his secretary entered.

"I'm terribly sorry, sir, but it's Mr. Harlow—he is downstairs in the store. He refuses to leave. The guards have taken him into the stockroom, but he is causing quite a commotion, demanding to see you."

"It's not like Tommy to make a scene," Smith said.

Butkins cleared his throat. "I'm sorry, sir. I should have said it was *Brian* Harlow, not Thomas Harlow."

Malcolm opened his mouth to tell Butkins to summon the police to deal with the man—and that he would see Brian when he bloody well wanted to see him.

But Smith spoke first. "Show Mr. Harlow up."

Both Malcom and Butkins gawked at him.

Smith met Malcolm's disbelieving gaze and shrugged. "Once I tell you what I came to say you will relish what you have to do, rather than feel guilty. I promise you."

Malcolm hesitated a long moment and then turned to Butkins. "Bring him up—make sure nobody sees him."

When the door closed behind his secretary Malcolm turned to Smith and said, "Now, tell me this piece of information that you think will make me easy about destroying a young woman's life."

Chapter 32

At almost fifty years of age, Brian Harlow still managed to look golden and angelic—at least at first glance.

But as the other man came closer Malcolm wasn't surprised to see that his blond curls had become brittle, the gold color too bright for nature. His rounded face, so like Julia's, had hollowed, and his body, once pleasingly slender, was now spare and gaunt.

Well, time had touched them all, hadn't it?

Brian glanced around Malcolm's study; his lips parted in wonder. "You've got quite a house, Mal—and filled with so many treasures."

"I've had fifteen years and not much else to do but acquire them."

Brian's wondrous expression dissipated, replaced by one that screamed guilt—the same expression he'd worn that morning fifteen years ago, when he'd come to say *goodbye* to Malcolm in his sickbed.

Why had it taken Malcolm so long to recognize the expression for what it was? Not just revulsion—although there was plenty of that, too—but raw guilt.

"Can I get you a drink?" Malcolm asked as his erstwhile lover chewed his lower lip—yet another mannerism he shared with Julia.

So, Brian was nervous. As well he should be.

"Er, whatever you're having."

Malcolm poured two glasses of brandy, a drink he knew Brian hated, and approached the other man's chair, not stopping until his knee touched the arm, forcing Brian to tilt his head at an uncomfortable angle. He smiled down at him and handed him the glass.

"A toast," he said, raising his glass, "to long delayed reunions."

Brian gave him a tentative smile and then raised the glass to his mouth, taking a sip so small it barely wet his lips.

Malcolm swallowed the contents of his glass, hissing in a breath at the burn. It had been years since he threw back a drink like that—fifteen years, not since that night.

He went to his desk and purposely turned up the gas lighting so Brian would be forced to look at him.

"So," he said, leaning back in his chair. "My secretary says you were quite vocal about seeing me today."

Brian set down his glass, the crystal chattering against the wood as his hand shook. He swallowed several times. "I'm sorry about that, Mal. But I—I, well, I can't bear to drag this out any longer. The situation at Tommy's house is—"

"Dire?" Malcolm suggested with a laugh.

"Yes, that sums it up nicely."

"Tommy and his wife are at each other's throats, are they?"

Brian's gaze slid away. "Er, Nadine isn't there. She left."

"Oh? To where?"

"I don't know—neither does Tommy."

All the lying he'd done and yet Brian was still terrible at it.

"Do you think your brother will forgive her?" Malcolm asked.

Brian snorted. "Forgive her for foisting off bastards on him? And her *brother's* bastards, at that? Not bloody likely."

"Perhaps they really are Tommy's? Twins run in your family, after all."

"No, she admitted it—after Tommy forced her to."

Malcolm clucked his tongue. "Tommy beating his wife? An ironic turn of events for that pair, isn't it?"

Brian blinked at him, his brain clearly scrabbling for a suitable answer. When he couldn't come up with one, he shrugged. "No court in the land would blame him for beating her."

"No," Malcolm agreed. "But her lover might blame him. Or has Tommy already taken care of Sheehan?"

"Sheehan wasn't at the address you gave Tommy."

"He wasn't?" Malcolm said, his eye widening with mock surprise. "Why, he must have escaped. I shall have to discipline my men for that. I would imagine Tommy might want to watch his back if Carl is on the loose."

Brian swallowed, and whatever he forced down looked both unappetizing and painful.

"Tommy will take care of it," he finally assured Malcolm. "But he would be able to focus on the problem better if he could have his daughter back."

"*His* daughter?"

Brian flinched but nodded. "You should let the girl go, Malcolm."

"You came all the way to London to tell me that, did you?"

"You don't need to keep her; Tommy will do what you want, but it will just take time. You can trust me on this. The poor girl must be frightened out of her wits being held hostage—it would be a kindness to just let her go."

"Why are you so concerned about her? She told me that you haven't seen her in fifteen years—it sounds as if you've been a stranger to her."

"She told you that?"

"Among other things."

Brian didn't know how to take that, so he left it alone and reverted to the reason for this visit today. "The marriage—her and Basingstoke—it's more important than you think, Malcolm."

"How so?"

Brian's eyes crawled slowly over the leather that covered Malcolm's left side. He swallowed yet again, as if he couldn't assemble the right words.

"You mean the marriage is important because Tommy has made some rather poor investments and needs the military contract the Duke of Angleton is dangling in front of him?"

Brian gaped.

Malcolm laughed softly. "I can't imagine that his grace will take kindly to a cit's daughter jilting his son. What a disaster it would be for Tommy to alienate such a man, wouldn't it?"

Brian briefly closed his eyes. When he opened them, they pulsed with raw fear. "I know you think destroying Tommy is exactly what he deserves, but…" He stopped, as if he'd hoped Malcolm would interrupt him.

"No, please—do go on," he urged. "I am utterly *fascinated* to hear why I shouldn't destroy the person who murdered my wife and unborn child. Well, *one* of the people."

Brian looked terrified, but not startled by that information. "I swear to God that I only found out about what Carl and Nadine did a few days ago. I was… shocked and devastated."

Malcolm ignored the egregious lie; he would come back to it later. "But you knew that Sukey was pregnant back then—she told you, didn't she?"

"No! Tommy just told—"

"Lie to me again and I will kill you right now—and I will take my time doing it."

Brian's throat worked convulsively. "I didn't know for certain—I swear, Mal! Neither did Sukey. You know how long she'd wanted to have a baby and it always ended in heartache. She wanted to wait to tell you until she was certain. Besides, you'd been working so hard on the deal that she didn't want you to worry."

"Why didn't you tell me about it when you came to see me in the hospital—before you left?"

"I—I thought it would only make things worse if you thought she'd been pregnant." He hung his head. "God, I'm so sorry that I left you like that, Mal."

Malcolm's jaw tightened at the sound of his pet name on this traitor's tongue.

"That's quite all right—I told you to leave, didn't I?"

He'd told Smith that, too. But Smith had refused.

"You did," Brian said, assuming a martyrish expression. "Even so, I shouldn't have left you while you were… like that

He laughed and Brian flinched at the harsh sound. "Don't fret yourself, I didn't blame you. Much. We were lovers, but we were never really close, were we, Brian? It was Sukey who brought us together and held us together. And without her … well, we were like the pages of a book without the binding." Malcolm was enjoying watching the other man's Adams apple bob up and down, up and down. He liked to think of all the things Brian was swallowing and wonder which words he'd finally set free.

"I cared for you," Brian said, after the silence had stretched out too long. He cleared his throat. "I still care."

Malcolm grinned, amused—but not surprised—when the other man winced at his crooked smile. "Why, that warms the cockles of my heart, Bri."

"I'm so sorry about Sukey. *So*—"

"Shut up." He didn't raise his voice, but Brian's jaws snapped shut immediately.

"You are still a beautiful man, Brian. Angelic is the word Sukey used for you." His mouth twitched into a genuine smile. "She loved you, Brian—even knowing your weaknesses. *Brian has the face of an angel, the vanity of a schoolgirl, and the heart of a hen*, she once said to me." Malcolm chuckled, genuinely amused by the other man's furious flush.

Brian's eyes narrowed to slits. "If I remember correctly, you were more than a little vain yourself once, Malcolm."

"Oh, I was." He nodded vigorously. "I was a handsome bastard back then, wasn't I, Bri?"

"You're still very handsome." Brian had to force the words out and his face turned beet red when he heard how false he sounded.

"That's kind of you. But you needn't pretend with me. I know you. You never could bear broken or ugly things, could you Bri? I remember that dog I found half-dead near our rubbish bin. One eye, three legs, scarred all to hell from some rat or cock pit. Sugar, I named her—a sweet little bitch she was, but you couldn't even bear to look at her. *The dog is an abomination*, you said, *it would be a kindness to put her down*. I think you were glad when the poor thing got run over by a carter, her spine crushed. Even then she dragged herself to me and licked my hand. But that's a dog for you, isn't? Loyal through and through. No other creature quite like it. The best I could do to repay that loyalty was to put Sugar out of her misery quickly. Poor Sukey cried and cried—even I bawled like a babe. But you? You were dry-eyed."

Brian couldn't seem to find his words.

"Don't look so stricken," Malcolm said, reaching for the ties that held on his mask, amused by the other man's widening eyes. "I reckon you thought the same about me—that it would be a mercy to put me down?"

"No! Of course I didn't—"

"One-eyed, scarred even worse than poor Sugar." Malcolm pulled the second tie and then tossed the mask to the desk with a clatter. "Hell, even *I* thought it would be a mercy to put me down."

Brian's lips parted in horror, his eyes flickering across Malcolm's ruined face, revulsion coloring his still-beautiful features.

"So, no," Malcolm said, smiling at the other man. "I wasn't angry when I saw the way you looked at me when I was lying in that hospital bed, nothing but a raw, open wound. It's a bit like the way you're looking at me now, Bri."

Those words must have reminded Brian that he'd come to Malcolm on a mission and that he'd better master his expression sooner rather than later.

Brian forced a shaky smile. "Surely you still remember the good times we had, too, Mal?"

"Oh, yes. I can remember those, Bri."

"Perhaps…"

"Perhaps?" Malcolm repeated, genuinely intrigued.

"Perhaps you could see your way to relenting? Just a little," he added hastily.

"Relent how?"

"Let the girl go."

Malcolm shrugged. "What is the hurry? The wedding isn't for several weeks."

"Basingstoke and his family are in town and they've been asking about her. It is… awkward."

"Hmmph. Awkward," he said, as if pondering.

"Yes, very."

"What about the other items on that list I gave Tommy? You want me to *relent* on all that, too?"

Brian's expression went from hopeful to wary. "No, no, not all of it."

"Carl and Nadine for example—they can still get what they deserve for killing Sukey, hmm?"

The other man was quick to nod. "Yes—yes, of course. They're the ones who came up with—"

"And the lad—Richard, his name is?"

Brian frowned. "Er, yes… about him. It was quite unusual that you mentioned that matter, Mal. As a matter of fact, Tommy—"

"So, should Richard get to keep that house?" Malcolm asked, amused by the flicker of irritation on Brian's face at the interruption. "No, wait! I'm sorry"—Malcolm snapped his fingers. "I forgot that Tommy already signed Brookfield over to those hungry creditors. He's just waiting until the girl falls in line and marries to toss the boy out." He shrugged. "Well, it's not as if Richard Harlow *cares* where he lives, is it? An asylum will be fine for the likes of him."

"Er, I'm told he is too slow-witted to notice his surroundings," Brian said, encouraged by Malcolm's tone. "Actually, it would be a mercy to put him with his own kind."

"You've been told? You mean you've not seen him?"

Brian frowned. "No, why would I?"

"Indeed, why," Malcolm agreed.

Brian's cheeks darkened and he swallowed again, his gaze flickering to Malcolm's ruined face and then darting away, only to slide back again. "You agree then? About the girl and the house?"

"It's always been hard to say no to you," Malcolm said, his words deliberately noncommittal.

Brian smiled, clearly delighted. "Shall we seal our bargain?"

"Hmm? Whatever you wish, Bri."

Elation vied with relief on Brian's face as he stood and approached Malcolm with an outstretched hand.

Malcolm remained seated, his own hands on the arms of his chair. "I thought we might seal it in a more personal way."

"P-personal way?"

Malcolm grinned and suggestively palmed his groin, grimly pleased when the other man flinched.

"Oh," Brian said.

"Unless you'd rather not touch——"

"No, no! That is an excellent idea," Brian hastened to say, his face a sickly gray as Malcolm spread his thighs.

"You needn't go under the desk." Malcolm barked a laugh. "We're too old for such games." He pointed to the floor. "Right here will be good."

Brian sank clumsily, landing with a thump.

"Ah, you on your knees. Now *that* brings back those good memories you were talking about, Bri."

Brian's eyes darted nervously from the left side of Malcolm's face to the erection that tented his trousers. He swallowed yet again and managed another smile, although it was more of a rictus. "You used to love it when I knelt beneath your desk. I did, too——it was one of the most erotic things I ever did, Mal."

Malcolm only smiled, willing to let Brian script this part of the play.

Brian inched forward on his knees and Malcolm spread wider to accommodate him.

"I've thought about you often, Mal——about this——" Brian said, warming up to his unexpected role. He reached for Malcolm's placket. "To be honest, there have been many, many times I've wanted to come back to you, but——but I was afraid." He gave a breathy laugh while his shaking fingers worked on the buttons. "Sukey was right about me—— I'm hen hearted." He reached the last button but Malcolm set a gloved hand over his fingers before he could open the placket.

Brian jerked his hand away and then hastily shoved it back, trying to cover his actions with a smile. "What is it, Mal?"

"You mean you'd consider coming back to me, Bri?" he asked softly, rubbing Brian's hand with his thumb.

Disgust flared in Brian's lovely blue eyes. "It has actually been my dearest wish for years, Mal," he spoke softly, managing to put a lover's adoring look on his face

Malcolm assumed a pensive stare as he held the other man's jittery gaze. Finally, after he'd made Brian wait so long that he looked in danger of bursting into tears, he released his hand. "I'd like that very much, Bri."

Again, Brian's Adam's apple danced, his lips curving into the same tremulous smile as he reached for Malcolm's cock.

"No, take my trousers down, Bri."

The other man's jaws flexed, but he nodded and Malcolm lifted his hips while Brian awkwardly tugged down his trousers, exposing the burned skin of his left leg along with his erect prick.

Brian cut him what was probably meant to be a sensual smirk but looked more like a death mask. "You always were hard for me even before I touched you." He allowed himself a smug smile at this proof of his desirability.

"Mmm hmm," Malcolm admitted. "I was hard for you even before you walked in the door, Bri."

"Were you imagining this? Hoping for it?" Brian teased, becoming more comfortable now and extending his freakishly long tongue to lick the pearl of liquid from Malcolm's slit as he stroked his smooth, cool hand down Malcolm's shaft.

Malcolm's groan grew into a throaty chuckle. "There's no denying I've missed your mouth on my cock, Bri."

Brian grinned. "And I've missed *this*," he said, giving Malcolm's shaft a squeeze.

"A handsome man like you—I'm sure you've not been lonely."

"No, I've never been lonely," Brian admitted.

His fist ceased its practiced stroking when he realized what he'd said.

"Of course, I've never seen another prick as beautiful as yours, Mal." He wisely quit talking about his lack of loneliness and lowered his plush lips over Malcolm's crown.

Malcolm watched the other man service him from beneath lowered lashes. He was impressed by Brian's display of enthusiasm. It only faltered when he forgot and looked at Malcolm's face or glanced at his left leg.

He decided to help him with that problem and threaded his fingers into Brian's thick golden curls and forced his head down and down, holding him immobile while jamming his dick as far as it could go.

And keeping it there.

Brian shuddered and then squirmed, but Malcolm didn't let up.

"I remember how you like it," Malcolm gritted, holding Brian full of cock until he could feel his slim body begin to slip into a full-blown panic, jerking and twitching beneath his unbreakable grasp.

But as terrified as Brian might be, Malcolm knew he'd be as hard as iron from the rough treatment.

Still, he didn't want to actually *kill* him—yet—so he let him up.

Brian gasped and choked, but he wasn't as bad off as Malcolm had thought. Indeed, he'd forgotten how long the other man could hold his breath.

"I hope I didn't hurt you," Malcolm lied.

"No, no, I'm fine," Brian hoarsely assured him

"No coming for you until I allow it," Malcolm chided when he saw Brian's arm move toward his own placket. "Not until you've earned it."

"Of cou—"

Malcolm rammed his prick deep and commenced to fuck his face in earnest, plunging all the way to his root with each brutal thrust.

"So good," he muttered.

Soon tears ran down Brian's cheeks, his swollen pupils telling Malcolm that his enthusiasm wasn't *all* for show; the man genuinely loved to be force-fed a cock.

He was tempted to use Brian's mouth for hours—the way he used to—but the tight leash he'd kept on his rage was slipping. If he didn't finish everything soon, he'd probably give in to his urges and kill the man.

So, he gripped Brian's head with both hands and pumped into him with savage, punishing thrusts, his balls heavy and tight as he made Brian choke and gasp, over and over.

"Such a good little bitch—taking me just like I remember," he hissed, his hips bucking off the chair with each thrust. "I want your throat," he ordered, even as the head of his cock battered the back of Brian's throat, riding his face so hard he'd probably not be able to speak right for a week. "That's right, whore, you know the way I like it. Swallow," he snarled.

Brian's throat flexed so tight that Malcolm almost forgot what this was all about.

That couldn't happen, ever.

It was time to end this.

He was so close, it didn't take much, just a few more driving thrusts and he was there.

"I'm coming," he grunted, hilting himself until Brian's nose was buried in his pubic hair. "Take it all, cunt," he ground out, his shaft thickening as he pumped jet after jet of spunk down the other man's unresisting throat, his vision going black with the vicious pleasure of his release.

Distantly, he realized Brian was gagging and squirming and gave a breathless laugh.

"You want to breathe, do you?" he asked, pulling out.

Brian gasped and sputtered for breath.

Malcolm slapped his face, hard. "Clean me up."

Brian startled at the brutal blow but eagerly complied, milking the last drops from Malcolm's balls and licking his shaft and sac clean.

When Malcolm shoved him away Brian laid his head on his thigh—the unburned one—breathing in harsh gasps. "God, that was so good," he wheezed, giving Malcolm a genuinely worshipful look.

Malcolm smirked when the other man's gaze drifted to the left side of his face and then quickly darted away again. "Wasn't it, Mal? Good I mean?"

Malcolm reached over and took the mask off the desk, quickly tying it back on before pushing Brian's head away and pulling up his trousers.

"Yes, it was good." That was the truth; the man knew his way around a cock.

Brian's swollen lips curved smugly at the praise and he looked relieved to find Malcolm once again safely covered by the mask and trousers.

"Can I come now?" he asked, reaching for his tented placket.

"No."

Brian blinked at his abrupt denial. "But—"

Malcolm grabbed Brian's chin, forcing the other man to meet his gaze. "You're still one of the best cocksuckers I've ever known, Brian," he grinned, allowing all the loathing he felt to show on his hideous face, gripping Brian's chin painfully hard when he tried to pull away. "But you're nowhere near as good as your daughter."

Chapter 33

Julia blinked, shaken from the strange, dreamlike state that had swallowed her while she'd watched her lover use her uncle like one of his whores.

Julia hadn't known that her Uncle Brian was married or that he had any children.

And how did Malcolm know Brian's daughter?

Just what was going on?

Julia staggered back from the small mirror and bumped into the cool window behind her—the window that looked into the wicked room where she'd watched Malcolm with the two women a few evenings ago.

Had it really been only a few nights ago? Because it felt like a hundred years.

She shook her head, as if that could clear the confusion that fogged her thoughts. Why would Mr. Smith—who'd seemed so kind and helpful—unlock the panel-door to Malcolm's secret hallway for her and then all but order her to spy on him in his study?

Stay until the end, Miss Harlow, no matter how shocked you might be by what you see. Malcolm has his reasons. The best reasons in the world, Smith had assured her when she'd asked him why.

The things Julia had seen and heard about Nadine and Carl and the twins, her father's duplicitous plans for Richard—and Malcolm's seeming agreement with that plan—and the wildly erotic but viscerally disturbing scene she'd just witnessed between her uncle and Malcolm—had left Julia's senses feeling abraded and raw.

Why had Malcolm done *that* to her uncle? And how could Julia find such sexual violence erotic? It didn't matter that she'd not seen Brian Harlow for fifteen years, he was her *uncle!* Truly, she was beyond redemption if she—

"—not true!"

The sound of her uncle's shouting yanked Julia from her bewildered state and she eased back to the window.

Malcolm was reclining in his chair, his posture that of a lazy, sated predator, while her uncle stared across the room at him, his face a mask of outrage.

What had he said? What had Julia missed?

"I would have known it even without the proof, Bri," Malcolm said, his derision as sharp as a razor. "Richard is the spitting image of you when you were young."

"Proof? What proof?" her uncle demanded.

Malcolm yanked open the top drawer of his desk and threw a letter across the room, smirking when the other man scrabbled to catch it. He watched her uncle read with a cruel, hate-filled expression twisting his face, which was once again masked.

When he had removed his mask earlier it had astounded Julia almost as much as hearing about her father's plans for Brookfield. It hadn't shocked her because Malcolm was so hideous, but because he chose to show himself to a man who so obviously did not want to see him. A man he clearly loathed in return.

Jealousy had eaten at her that he would share himself with her uncle but not with her.

Indeed, it was almost laughable how jealous she *still* felt—especially given all the other revelations she'd just heard.

Brian Harlow whimpered and looked up from the letter that trembled in his hands. "Christ, Malcolm—please tell me you aren't going to show this to—"

"To Tommy? Why, yes, as a matter of fact. The moment I decided to let you in today I sent a messenger with a copy of that letter to your brother. I would imagine he's in quite a… state after reading it."

Brian slumped into a chair, the crumpled letter falling to the floor. "He'll kill me."

"He very well might," Malcolm agreed, looking cheerful. "Ah, you and sweet Jenny McQueen, eh? I was more than a little surprised, Bri."

Julia startled at the sound of her mother's maiden name. *What?*

"She was a beautiful lass," Malcolm went on. "But really, fucking your brother's wife, Bri? *Tsk, tsk, tsk.*"

Julia gasped, waiting for her uncle to deny it.

But Brian Harlow looked like a drowning man. "It wasn't my idea, Mal—Jenny was, well, I'm sure you heard stories about her. She was always on me—whining that Tommy was cold and didn't want her. She knew what I did with Sukey and she—she wanted—Ugh." He shoved a hand through his curly blond hair. "Christ, Mal! She all but forced me to fuck her! Even after the brats were born and she should have known better, she was still after me."

"Tommy never guessed the twins were yours, Bri?"

The words echoed in Julia's head so loudly that she almost missed her uncle's response.

"—blond, blue eyed—looked enough like Tommy not to cause trouble." He gave a hysterical laugh. "Hell, he might actually be glad to learn they *aren't* his. He was bloody stricken when that old nurse told him the boy was no better than an imbecile."

The horrified confusion that Julia had been feeling turned to white hot rage at his cruel words about her brother. Julia clenched her fists and pressed them against the glass, ready to smash it and storm into the room.

Yet again, Mr. Smith's warning came back to her. *Stay and listen to all of it, no matter how badly you want to walk away.*

Brian Harlow's whining voice—Julia refused to think of him as her father—sliced through her fury.

"She should have been grateful to get away with it once and kept her legs together, but then the silly bitch got pregnant *again*." His laugh was bitter and disbelieving.

"She didn't get pregnant without help, Bri," Malcolm said, his gaze cold.

Brian looked momentarily disconcerted, but he recovered quickly, a sneer distorting his features. "The woman wouldn't leave me alone— what else could I do?" He laughed. "Anyhow, she'd not been with Tommy in years when she got pregnant the second time, so she couldn't pass off another bastard; he would *know* it wasn't his. There was only one way to take care of the problem, but she wouldn't listen."

"Ah, did she threaten you, Bri? Is that why you did it?"

"Did what?" Brian demanded, his voice high and sharp.

"Is that why you killed her?"

Blood roared in Julia's ears.

"What in the name of God are you talking about?" Brian's voice sounded far away to Julia, even though he was shouting. "I refuse to stand here and listen to—"

"Was it Nadine or her brother who first put the idea into your head, Bri? Probably Nadine. I suspect she's always been the brains in your little cadre."

Brian sputtered, but Malcolm wasn't finished.

"I didn't recognize Nadine until she came here in person. She's changed a great deal since her days at that old birch house where she used to work—under a different name, I might add. Now what was that place called?" Malcolm stroked his chin. "Something improbable like *Madame Tessa's* even though Tessie Gordan was no more French than I am."

"I don't know what place you mean," Brian croaked.

Malcolm laughed. "I know you went there, Sukey told me about it. That's one of the few things you and Tommy share, isn't it? A craving for pain with a healthy dose of shame on the side?"

Brian just stared.

"I'll wager Nadine was damned good at her job—whipping men until they beg is probably as natural as breathing to her. But she would have been too smart and too ambitious to be happy in such a place for long. If I had to put money on it—"

"It was all Nadine's idea!" Brian blurted. "She wanted Tommy, but I didn't understand what she was up to until after. I swear! I didn't want to do it, Mal—I just wanted to give the stupid bitch something that would make her lose the child before she told Tommy and ruined my life. Nadine said the tincture—or whatever it was—came from a midwife. I never thought it would bloody *kill* Jenny!"

Julia stared, open mouthed, as the vile words poured out of his mouth, the truth echoing in her head: he had *killed* her mother.

She staggered back from the mirror, as if she could back away from the truth.

She had to get out—away—

Stay until you hear all of it, Miss Harlow. No matter how painful.

More? There was more?

Julia's entire body shook and she felt like she was breaking into a thousand pieces.

He'd killed her mother.

She could hear the distant sounds of voices—shouting and begging—but there was a buzzing in her head and it was getting louder and louder.

No more. She couldn't take any more…

***

"It was a mistake!" Brian shrieked even though Malcolm hadn't argued with him.

"A mistake," Malcolm repeated. "Just like Sukey was a mistake?"

Brian's eyes widened. "God no! You can't think I had anything to do with that! I only learned of that a few days ago! I never—"

"Your brother already told me that you knew. So did the other two. Quit lying, Brian. Your job that night was to get me good and drunk—drunker than I ever recall being in my life—and then unlock the door for Carl, wasn't it?"

"No! I didn't—"

"But why did you leave Sukey there, Brian? Why didn't you—"

"They told me it would just be a small fire—enough to damage that ship Leeland wanted so badly, but not enough to hurt anyone," Brian wailed, tears running down his cheeks. "Surely you can't believe that I'd—"

"Why did you agree to help them, Brian?" he could barely force the words out.

"I didn't agree! They forced me!"

"They?"

"It was that bastard Carl! He threatened to tell Tommy everything about Jenny if I didn't help."

"So, it had nothing to do with the twenty percent of the company that Tommy promised if you joined their little plan?"

Brian's eyes threatened to roll out of his head. "Bloody hell! Who told you—"

"Quit lying!" Malcolm shouted. His blood thundered so loudly that it took him a moment to realize the noise he'd been hearing wasn't inside his head—it was the rattling of the panel door, as if somebody were flinging—

The door suddenly banged open and a blue whirlwind swept into the room.

Malcolm blinked at what had to be a hallucination: Julia.

"Julia?" Brian gasped, convincing Malcolm that he wasn't imagining things.

"You *murdering swine*!" Julia yelled as she launched herself at Brian Harlow.

Malcolm leapt from his chair and charged across the room.

Julia was clamped onto Brian's back, her legs wrapped around him, hands clawing and pummeling his face and head while he writhed and howled beneath her fury.

"*You killed her! You killed her!*" The words were so thick with rage he could barely understand them.

Malcolm slid his hands beneath her arms and tried to pull her away, but it was like trying to pry a limpet off a rock.

Brian suddenly shrieked, the sound blood-curdling.

Malcolm slid his whole arm around Julia's slender waist and pulled.

"My *head*!" Brian screamed, stumbling after them as Malcolm hauled Julia away, her teeth still clamped to his ear.

Malcolm shifted her until he could see her face. "Julia—darling! Let him go."

Her eyes were wide and crazed, her teeth still buried in the torn cartilage, blood streaming down her chin.

"*Now*, Julia!" He had to shout to be heard over Brian's squealing, but it caught her attention and she let go so suddenly that Malcolm stumbled back a few steps while Brian fell onto his arse, screaming and writhing.

Malcolm swung her into his arms and kicked at the other man. "Get up and get out of here!"

"But—my *ear*!" Brian sobbed, clutching his head.

"I don't give a damn. Get out or I'll let her go. And this time I'll hold you for her." Malcolm turned to Julia, who'd begun to shake badly.

"Julia, darling?" he murmured, only vaguely aware of a door opening and rapidly receding footsteps.

"He killed her," Julia whispered.

"I know, love. I know."

She broke then, her body shuddering with sobs.

Malcolm lowered them both onto the settee, holding her close. "Go ahead and cry, sweetheart. Let it out."

And then he closed his eye and grieved with her.

Chapter 34

Are you going to kill them?"

Malcolm startled, jolted from his fugue by Julia's question. According to the clock on the mantlepiece, they'd been on the settee for a little over an hour.

"I thought you'd fallen asleep," he said, shifting her in his arms so that he could see her tear-stained, but still unbearably lovely, face.

She was staring at something over his shoulder, not meeting his gaze. "Are you?" she repeated. "Is that why you thought I'd hate you? Because you're going to kill them?

"No, I won't kill them." He paused and admitted, "At least not personally. But I have engineered matters so that they will do it for me." He cleared his throat. "I suspect they've already begun. Sheehan has gone missing and Nadine is no longer at your father's house."

"He's not my father," she said, the words lacking heat—or any emotion at all.

Her blue eyes finally slid to his. For the very first time, Malcolm could not tell what she was thinking.

"How much did you hear?" Malcolm grimaced. "And see?"

"All of it."

He sighed. "Let me guess: Smith."

She roused herself and Malcolm admitted that he liked the anger that flared in her gaze better than her dead, lifeless stare—even if that anger seemed directed at him. "Why didn't you tell me about all this? Why was it Smith who told me?"

"Because Smith is an interfering, manipulative—"

She snorted. "Manipulative? This from the man who engineered a situation where four people will exact revenge *for* him?"

"That's right, Julia. And I won't stop what I've started—no matter how much you beg me to do so."

"You think I want to *stop* what you've started, Malcolm? They deserve to die—all of them." The pure menace in her soft voice made the hairs on the back of his neck stand up.

"You might think that now, Julia, but Brian is your father and Thomas Harlow stood as father to you, he raised you—"

"Brian Harlow *killed* my mother! The only person who might have loved me and Richard!" Her chest heaved with plenty of emotion now, her eyes pure blue fire. "Do you think I could ever forgive that?"

Before he could speak, she went on, the poison pouring out of her. "As for *Thomas*. Don't you know what sort of *father* he was? He exiled my brother and then lied to me and plotted to put Richard in an asylum while forcing me into a marriage with a man I hate." Her eyes narrowed. "And on that subject—"

"I was lying to Brian," Malcolm assured her. "I've got the deed to the house in my drawer—with your name on it. I bought it from the man your—er, Tommy—signed it over to."

Her expression, so hard and wild a few seconds before, softened. "You did that?"

"Bloody hell, Julia! You didn't think I'd let Richard be tossed out of his house?"

She threw her arms around his neck. "You did that for me, didn't you?"

"Of course I did."

Her body tensed and she made a muffled noise that sounded suspiciously like a gulp.

Malcolm prayed that she wasn't going to cry again.

But when she released him a moment later, her eyes were blessedly dry.

"All my life I tried to make Thomas Harlow love me—or even *like* me. Instead, he belittled me and ignored Richard. He beat me so badly I couldn't leave his house for *weeks*—and not only once, Malcolm. Those years away at school weren't only a revelation when it came to sensual matters, I also saw that my life with Nadine and my—and with Thomas—was neither healthy nor normal. Their cruelty manifested itself in a hundred small ways and culminated with what he would have done to Richard even *after* I bartered my future away."

She held his gaze captive, magnificent in her fury. "How could you think I would hate you for punishing people such as them?"

He hesitated, and then said, "I'll admit I didn't know about what Brian did to your mother until today—thanks to Smith—which certainly changed a great deal."

"Mr. Smith told you?"

"Yes, right after he was telling *you* things, apparently."

She shook her head, marveling. "Does Mr. Smith know *everything*?"

Malcolm shuddered. "*Please* never say such a thing in his hearing."

Julia gave a startled laugh but sobered immediately. "I will *never* blame you for anything you do to Brian and Thomas. As for Carl and Nadine," she gave an ugly laugh. "I will hunt them down myself if whatever you've planned does not work."

"And your younger brothers?" Malcolm demanded. "Do you think *they* will thank me when their mother and father are dead?"

"They never knew Carl."

"They know their mother and they know Thomas."

"Nadine—in her relentless quest to ape the aristocracy—ensured that her sons would be hard-pressed to pick her out in a crowded room. It is their grandmother who has given them the only parental love they've ever known. As for Thomas Harlow," she snorted bitterly. "Do you think he will be kind to them now that he knows the truth?"

"No," he admitted. "That is unlikely."

"Impossible, is more like. Trust me when I tell you Dorian and Dominic will be better off without scheming killers for parents."

Malcolm somehow doubted the boys would accept their loss that easily, but then he did not have Julia's experience or history with any of the people involved. Nor was he prepared to do anything to stop what he'd set in motion.

"Do you care for me at all, Malcolm?"

He gaped at her unexpected question. "Of cou—"

"Did you really believe I'd hate you for seeking justice from four people who *murdered* your wife and unborn child and caused you unspeakable physical and emotional pain?"

"It's not that—"

"Oh, Malcolm." Her shoulders sagged and she gave a sad half-laugh, half-sob. "What am I going to do with you?"

"Nothing, Julia."

She blinked. "What did you say?"

"You'll do nothing with me. Instead, you're going to leave this house as you should have after overhearing everything. My carriage will take you to Brookfield, where you will stay until the Season begins. I have it on good authority that the Countess of Bankton will be in London and will, I daresay, be pleased to chaperone you."

She shook her head, her expression wondrous. "You didn't hear a word I just said, did you?"

"Just because you did not react as I expected regarding your—" Malcolm struggled to find the least offensive words.

"Murderous relatives?" she suggested coolly.

Malcolm sighed. "Just because you don't hate me doesn't mean there is a future for us, Julia. Your family wasn't the only thing that stood in our way."

She stared up at him with the strangest look on her face. "You can't stop, can you?"

"Stop what?"

"Inventing reasons why you don't deserve to be happy." He opened his mouth, but she wasn't finished. "I didn't really understand until Mr. Smith"—Malcolm growled at the sound of the meddling man's name but she just raised her voice and spoke over him—"told me how you blamed yourself for not rescuing your wife."

"He had no *right* to share that."

"Somebody had to, Malcolm, because you are intent on not just punishing those who actually set the fire, but yourself for not stopping it, for not—"

"I *failed* her! I was supposed to protect her and I—"

"Almost died in the process," she snapped. "And you have not stopped blaming yourself for being alive. So now you think to punish yourself yet again by throwing away what we have. By mapping out a life for me that doesn't include *you*. Treating me like a chess piece to move around in your own private game against yourself. But you have forgotten one thing—do you know what that is?"

Malcolm didn't think that was the sort of question it would do him any favors to answer. Instead, he waited for what she had to say.

"You have forgotten that it is *my* happiness that you will be throwing away if you punish yourself." Her lips curved into a smile that shot right to his balls. "Shall I tell you what I'm going to do?"

He swallowed, his necktie suddenly uncomfortably tight. "Er—"

"First, I'm going to take off this mask." She lifted her hands to his face.

Malcolm's hands caught her wrists and he held her arms immobile. "No, you're not."

"Yes, I am. It's only fair."

He snorted. "What have I told you about fairness, Julia?"

"I know what you told me—but that was before, and now is different."

"And why is that?"

"Before I was your captive but now—well, I'm your betrothed."

A startled sputter burst out of him.

"That's not very flattering to me, Malcolm."

"I'm sorry, but you're *already* betrothed—to another man."

She cocked her head and cut him a flat look.

"Fine, that engagement is effectively over," he agreed, his heart flooding with relief. "But that doesn't mean I recall asking you to—."

"Will you marry me?"

"Julia—"

"It's a yes or no question, darling."

"No."

Pain flashed across her beautiful face but was gone quickly. "Then I'll just have to live with you in sin, as your mistress and—"

"*No.*"

She shifted on his lap, until she was straddling him.

"Julia, what are you doing?"

She placed her hands on his shoulders and rose up until she was staring him in the eye. "I love you."

Malcolm knew his mouth was open but could not close it.

"I love you," she said again, the words shaking him from his stupor.

"You can't do this, Julia?"

"Do what? Love you? Too late, I already do."

"You can't throw your life away on me," he said quietly.

"Did you want to be on the stage when you were young?"

"*What?*"

"I only ask because you are *so* dramatic, Malcolm."

He gave an affronted laugh.

"I love you and want to spend my life with you. And it is *my* life to throw away if I want to." She leaned in and pressed a butterfly kiss to his slack lips.

When she sat back, the humor that had been sparkling in her eyes had turned serious. "Let me see you."

"No."

"I saw when you took off your mask earlier."

"That was different—you were far away, not inches from me."

"What are you so afraid of? That I'll run screaming in horror, or that I *won't* run?" Her eyes widened. "That's it, isn't it? You don't *want* me to love you and stay with you. You're afraid, aren't you?"

She's got you there, Mal.

Malcolm ground his molars so hard it made his jaw ache. *Now is not the time, Sukey.*

"Malcolm?"

His eye snapped back to the woman who was actually alive and in the room with him. "I'll never be able to give you the life you want, Julia."

"What life is that?"

He sighed.

"No, I want to know what life you think I want?"

"A Season, for one—I've heard you say it."

"Malcolm, that was something I wanted because I hoped I'd find my prince—that I'd find love." She smiled ruefully. "I've already found both—what in the world would I do with a Season *now*?"

"You're only twenty, Julia—"

"I'll be twenty-one in three months."

"Fine, you're almost twenty-one. I'll be forty-four on my next birthday."

"Nadine is eighteen years younger than my father."

He laughed bitterly. "And just look how well that marriage turned out."

Julia gave an exasperated sigh. "My point is that our age difference isn't that unusual. Lily's husband is forty-six and they are deliriously happy." She frowned. "Is that your only reason for resisting me—my age?" She began to lower her arms. "Or is it because you don't love me and—"

"No." Malcolm seized her arms to keep them around him. "No, that's not it."

Her smile was luminous. "You *do* love me?"

Oh, just say it! Say it and set me free, Mal. Say it and forgive yourself.

Julia slid her hand around his neck and pulled him toward her. Her kisses were different than before, more insistent and needy.

His tattered control snapped and he wrapped his arms around her, crushing her mouth with his.

Don't throw this away. Forgive yourself, Mal. Sukey's voice was softer, fainter, and Malcolm suddenly knew—with a stab of sadness—that was the last he'd hear from her, no matter what decision he made today. From now on, he'd be able to blame nobody but himself.

Malcolm crushed Julia to his chest so tightly it was difficult for him to breathe—no doubt even worse for her—and did something he'd not done in decades: he prayed.

Please make this the right decision.

Malcolm pulled away and the two of them filled their starving lungs with air.

"I love you, Julia."

Her darkened eyes widened. "You do?"

"I do, with all my heart. You don't need to look at my ravaged face to prove anything," he told her. "I'm accustomed to wearing this mask and can—"

"I love you. All of you."

This time when Julia reached up to remove his mask Malcolm didn't stop her.

***

Malcolm was right that the damage appeared far more severe up close.

Julia's eyes burned with tears and she grieved for the pain that he must have suffered.

"May I touch you?"

Only when he exhaled did she realize he'd been holding his breath. He nodded.

The skin was so soft she feared damaging it. "Does this hurt?" she asked, feathering her fingers over his cheek.

"I feel some sensation in a few areas and none in others."

His eye was gone, as was all but a vestigial part of his ear.

Julia laid a hand over the patches of skin on his neck. "Why do these look different?"

"Those are called grafted skin, which was taken from another part of my body."

"I've never heard of such a thing."

"It was an experimental procedure fifteen years ago—only now does the medical establishment even begin to accept that grafting can work. A French physician pioneered the process. I took a great deal of risk to try it, but to *not* try it—well, that would have been worse."

He wasn't entirely without hair on the left side of his scalp, but he kept it shaved close to his head.

Julia turned his face until his eye met hers and her heart ached for the dread she saw in his beautiful blue gaze.

She lowered her lips over his and kissed him. For a long moment he was motionless beneath her and Julia explored him at her leisure, her sadness slowly sloughing away as she nipped and nibbled and probed the wet heat of his delicious mouth.

He'd still not responded when she finally pulled away, her pulse pounding with arousal.

She smiled. "You've not driven me away or scared me off and I still love you."

His expression was one of disbelief.

Julia groaned. "What can I do to make you belie—"

"No, I believe you."

"Then what is it? Why are you looking at me as if I'm mad?"

"No, not mad, just… utterly unexpected."

"You've known me for weeks and yet you still believe I would reject you because of your scars?"

"The first woman who saw me—and only my hand, mind—almost fainted, Julia."

"Did she love you?"

He frowned. "What?"

"Did she love you?"

"No! She was a whore."

Julia tried to ignore the jealousy she felt in the pit of her stomach—it was in the past. She took his right hand. "May I?"

He gave an abrupt nod.

She struggled to peel back the snug leather. "Do you really like it so tight?"

Malcolm's lips twitched into an unexpected smile. "The tighter, the better."

Julia narrowed her eyes at him, her face heating as she understood his crude innuendo. "You are naughty."

His smile grew wider and he nodded. "Yes."

Julia did a terrible job of hiding her answering grin and turned back to her labors. The leather was exceedingly thin.

"Do these tear easily?"

"They do not usually last more than two or three days."

Her head whipped up. "You replace them every two or three days?"

He shrugged. "They are the only gloves that yield adequate sensation." He sounded defensive.

Julia wanted to suggest that he *not* wear them but decided to leave that struggle for later. They would have the rest of their lives, after all.

She tugged off the last finger and held his hand in both of hers, her finger tracing the tissue-thin skin on the top before turning it over to find the underside mostly undamaged.

She set down his hand and picked up the left.

"That one is worse."

Julia ignored him and went through the same painstaking process. The hand beneath was, indeed, worse, burned on both top and bottom, the last two fingers nothing but stumps.

She lifted both his hands and placed them on her face, cupping her jaws the way he so often did. "Can you feel my skin?"

"A very little with the left but"—his lips curved into a painfully sweet smile—"but I can feel you with the right."

"And how do I feel?" She rubbed her cheek against his palm.

"As lovely as you look."

His words warmed her and she leaned forward to kiss him. But he pulled back.

"What is it?" she asked.

"I can't live a normal life, Julia."

"You mean you can't m-marry," she stumbled over that word, blushing scarlet, "or have children?" she asked, feeling bolder the more she spoke, the angrier she became at him for denying himself and trying to deny *her*.

"Obviously I can do those things, but I cannot socialize normally. I won't go to parties or dinners or the theat—"

"I don't *care* about those things."

"You say that now, but once the novelty has worn off—"

"Will you come with me to visit Richard and Nanny?"

He opened his mouth, hesitated, and then said, "I would prefer that they came here, but yes, I would go there."

"Will you agree to meet Lily and her husband? Perhaps invite them over for dinner?"

Again, he hesitated, but then said, "Well, if you like Lily and Smith likes Bankton, then I suppose I could be convinced to socialize with them, too."

"Do you have a home in the country?"

He looked as if she'd asked him if he ran through the streets naked. "No—I've rarely even *been* in the country."

"Would you be willing to try staying in the country during hunting season?"

This question gave him the longest pause of all. "Would you be hurt if I went to the country but didn't go hunting with you?"

"Not at all." She waited and then asked, "Well?"

He nodded slowly. "We might be able to negotiate some sort of agreement on that subject."

She didn't bother to hide her smile of triumph. "You, my small family, my few friends, horses and hunting, painting—*those* are the sorts of things that are important to me, Malcolm. I'm not sure why you ever thought I wanted balls and parties." She rubbed her bottom over his thighs, purposely stroking over his erection and hiding her smile in his lapel when he hissed.

He did nothing but sit for a long moment, and then, slowly, his arms circled her body and she felt him sigh. "Once you are mine, Julia, I will never give you up."

Julia closed her eyes and smiled; finally. "Now, will you please take me to bed?"

Chapter 35

It was the first time Malcolm had walked through his own house not wearing his mask.

What was even more stunning was that he'd not recalled that he'd left it lying on the desk until he was almost to his bedroom.

A complex stew of pain, fear, shame—and yes, even hope—had churned in his belly when Julia had uncovered his face.

And then had come the most shocking part: she hadn't run or flinched or paled.

She had stayed.

Actually, she'd done more than just stay. She had touched him and told him she loved him.

Malcolm had watched her more closely than he'd ever watched anyone in his life, searching for signs of quickly concealed disgust or revulsion.

But all he'd seen on Julia's face was sadness, sympathy, and something he was beginning to believe really was love and not just infatuation.

Malcolm had used his private corridors to lead Julia to his room. After all, he might allow her to see him, but that didn't mean he would ever feel comfortable baring his face to others, even those servants who'd served him longest and best.

He stopped beside the panel that led to his chambers, but when he reached out to open it, he felt a hand stay his arm. "What is it?" he asked.

"That's my room!"

He looked down to see her staring at the mirror into her own chambers.

"Yes, it is," he agreed. The panel beneath his hand clicked and swung open.

"You mean—"

"My room is right across from yours."

"Is it *really* your bedchamber this time?"

He couldn't help laughing. "Yes, it really is."

"And you've been sleeping so close to me all this time?"

"It has been… torture to be so close and yet not look at you or touch you." Malcolm gestured her inside. "After you."

He crossed his arms and leaned against the panel she'd just shut, watching her inspect his private domain. Malcolm was unsurprised when she stopped in front of the portrait that hung opposite what he thought of as his reading chair.

She stood in front of the painting and studied his dead wife. Her throat flexed as she swallowed once and then again, before turning to him.

"Your wife?"

"Yes." And because that seemed too abrupt, he closed the distance between them and said, "It was painted shortly before her death when we were in Antwerp on business. We met a painter there, a man named Alma-Tadema at some function or other and he asked if she would sit for him." He snorted. "Well, I suppose lie for him would be more accurate."

They both turned to look at the nude. It wasn't large—perhaps ten by twelve inches or so—but it was magnificently potent.

"It's called *Caldarium*, which is an old Roman bath, apparently."

Sukey had never looked more attractive—lush and ripe and alive, posed on a marble dais covered with an animal hide and overflowing with pillows in luxurious silks and velvets, holding an ancient grooming tool called a strigil. Whatever the hell that was supposed to mean.

"The artist hadn't yet delivered it, which is why it didn't burn up with everything else in the fire." The photographs of them together, the letters they'd exchanged when he'd had to travel on business. Everything else was gone.

"Does it bother you to have it hanging in here?" he asked her.

***

Oddly, Julia found that she didn't mind the thought of a naked painting of his dead wife. The woman in the portrait looked like somebody she would have liked to know, her eyes wicked and laughing.

"No, it doesn't bother me. I like it." She turned to him. "Does it make you feel guilty to be with me?"

He looked startled by her question. "You mean would she be angry to know I've moved on?"

"Have you moved on, Malcolm?"

He lightly traced her cheek and Julia pressed her face into his palm, thrilled that there was no barrier between them.

"I'll always love her, Julia. But I no longer yearn for her. I yearn for you."

She turned her lips to his palm and kissed it, her tongue darting out to taste salt and the faint smell of leather.

He growled, his eyelid drooping.

Julia pushed him back lightly. "Sit," she ordered.

His eyebrow lifted in surprise, but he lowered onto the settee.

Once again, she straddled him.

"What are you doing?" he asked when she reached for his placket. "I thought you wanted the bed?"

"I want you, Malcolm. Every single time we come into a bedroom you make me delirious with pleasure and then leave while I am sleeping." She unbuttoned the entire placket and then pulled the flaps apart, hissing with pleasure when his thick member thrust up through the open trousers, the mushroom head wet and almost purple he was so hard and engorged.

She stared at it, her mouth flooding with anticipatory moisture as she recalled the taste and feel of him.

"Julia?"

"Up," she ordered.

He snorted but obeyed.

She tugged his trousers down to his knees.

"Just leave them there," he said as she clambered down off the settee.

Julia ignored him; she wanted to see all of him.

Once the sinfully soft cashmere was down to his ankle boots, she unbuttoned the right boot first, slipped it off, and then pulled off the trouser leg.

He groaned. "Is this really necessary?"

Julia smirked at how petulant he sounded and peeled off his stocking.

He had nice feet: large, but well formed with elegant arches and long toes. She smiled to herself and dragged a finger across his sole.

"Julia!" he shouted, almost levitating off the couch.

She chuckled. "Ticklish."

"You witch," he hissed.

She turned to his left leg, removing the boot and stocking with more care.

His ankle and knee had more of the paler skin, the grafts he'd called them, and the smallest toe was missing.

Julia sat back on her heels and looked up at him as she lifted his foot, her eyes locked with Malcolm's as she pressed a gentle kiss on the damaged skin on his ankle.

His eye flared with heat and he lunged forward with remarkable speed, grabbing her by the upper arms and lifting her up so quickly she squeaked.

When she was straddling him again, he held her by the shoulders, his eye roving over her as he shifted his hips beneath her. "Hold up your damned skirts," he ordered.

Julia laughed but complied. "I thought I was in charge of this seduc—" she moaned when his hot, hard length thrust through the split in her drawers and nudged at her entrance.

"You were saying?" he mocked.

"Nothing," she muttered, every particle of her being focused on the blunt crown pressing against her.

His hand slid between her thighs and they both groaned when his bare finger glided through her wet sex.

"My God you feel divine," he said, stroking her lips and teasing her throbbing bud.

Julia took a deep breath and began to push herself down.

"Not yet."

Julia whined. "Why not?"

"I want your bodice off—"

Julia opened her mouth to complain.

"One word of complaint and I'll put my trousers and mask back on."

"That's *blackmail*."

"Was that a complaint, Julia?"

"*No!*"

"Good, now help me get this off," he said, his fingers already moving to the hooks on her blue velvet.

Julia pushed his hands aside. "I can do it faster."

Indeed, she'd never undressed so fast in her life.

Not until he pulled her chemise over her head and tossed it aside did she consider how she looked: clad from the waist down and naked from the waist up.

"Mmm, this is better," he said, gently squeezing and spanning her waist with warm, strong hands. "So soft," he murmured, his hot gaze scorching her breasts.

Julia arched her back and groaned as his thumbs caressed her aching nipples, her eyelids fluttering when his hot mouth lowered over her breast.

But then a cold button grazed her hot skin and she hissed, her eyes flying open.

"Coat off, too," she said, her voice breathy but firm.

For once, he didn't argue, keeping his gaze fastened to her chest while she unbuttoned his coat. The garment hadn't even hit the floor before he ducked his head again and latched onto her breast, holding her firmly with both hands.

Julia let her head fall back, luxuriating in his hot, soft mouth. She was floating on a wave of bliss when he nipped her.

"Shhh," he muttered when she yelped, laving and kissing and sucking the nipple to soothe away the pain. "Sit up higher," he said, trailing kisses down her breast when she did so, his fingers pushing between her lower lips.

"Fuck," he muttered, the crude word making her jolt, as always. "Your cunt is so damned soft." He sucked in a mouthful of thin skin on the underside of her breast while breaching her with his middle finger, commencing to stroke her with deep, languid thrusts.

Just when the sucking crossed the border between sharp pleasure and pain, he released the tingling skin and lifted her heavy breast to investigate. "Mmm. You mark up so prettily." He gently licked the abraded flesh, the wet sounds of his rhythmic pumping between her thighs both arousing and embarrassing.

He sat back and chuckled at whatever he saw on her face, his hand still moving. "What is making you blush so prettily, Julia? Is it the sound of your greedy, soaking wet cunt?"

She glared at him through a haze of lust, her hips pulsing to take him deeper.

He grunted, his expression shifting from amused to feral in the blink of an eye. "I want to bury my cock in you so damn bad." He circled the engorged bundle of nerves while forcing a second finger into her.

"Does it hurt?" he asked when she whimpered, his fingers stilling.

"No," she assured him, rocking her hips, willing him to continue.

He made a frustrated noise and withdrew from her body.

"What are you doing?" she demanded.

"This bloody skirt is in my way." He shoved his hands beneath the waistband of the expensive blue velvet and a loud *riiiip* filled the room.

"Malcolm—you've ruined it!"

He ignored her protests and shredded the cage and petticoats, as well, until she wore nothing but stockings and her drawers.

He paused and surveyed her a moment before muttering, "These must go, too," and tore her drawers in half, pushing the tattered remnants down her thighs. "There," he said, a satisfied smile curving his lips as he stared at her mostly naked body.

Julia laughed. "You might have just taken them off me."

He grunted dismissively and then lifted her by the waist and laid her out on the settee as if he were arranging a doll.

Julia was still adjusting to the sudden change in position when he shoved her legs wide and lowered his mouth to the apex of her thighs. She moaned and tilted her pelvis, opening herself wider to him.

Malcolm slid his arms beneath her thighs and pulled her tight to his marauding mouth, obliterating what little remained of her wits.

***

Some remote part of Malcolm's brain pointed out that he might be suffering from a type of insanity.

It was as if a decade and a half of sensory deprivation was being satisfied all in one moment. Why had he ever believed that his fingers were too damaged to appreciate and feel the silken heat of her cunt? The satiny smoothness of her breasts and the intriguingly rough nubs of her nipples?

Malcolm stroked her thighs as he buried his tongue as deeply as it would go.

He was vaguely aware when she came, and then again, but not until the third time—when he heard begging—did he realize how deranged he must appear.

"Malcolm—I *can't*," she whined. Her hand—which had been pressing his head to her sweet little pussy only moments before—pulled at his hair.

He reluctantly released her and sat up.

"Did I hurt you?" he asked when she heaved a sigh and slumped back.

She regarded him through lust-slitted eyes. "You almost killed me with pleasure." Her gaze dropped to where his cock jutted between his thighs. He'd leaked so much that it looked as if he'd already ejaculated.

Julia reached down to run a finger over his wet crown and then raised it to her lips and sucked, her dark blue gaze riveted to his face.

"Fuck, Julia!" Malcolm twisted around on the settee—wincing when sweaty skin caught on leather—turning his body until he was kneeling between her sprawled legs. "If I make four strokes before I come it will be a miracle," he muttered.

Her smirk was pure sin, and when her hand dropped to her sex and spread her swollen folds for him, he lost what little control remained and launched himself at her, entering her slick body with one long thrust.

Julia cried out and arched off the settee.

He paused, buried hilt deep. "Did I hurt you?"

She bit her lip and thrashed her head from side to side. "No," she said in a strained voice. "But… need a moment."

Malcolm covered her face with kisses. "Sorry, love," he whispered, relieved when her tight muscles began to soften beneath him.

It seemed like two hours later but was probably less than a minute when her legs wrapped around his buttocks, pushing him that last impossible bit deeper. "I'm ready."

It *might* have taken six strokes before Malcolm exploded inside her, his entire body spasming with what felt like the most prolonged, intense orgasm of his life.

He kept his weight braced on his elbows while his cock jerked inside her, her tight passage milking his balls until they ached.

"Sorry," he slurred groggily when his arms suddenly gave out and he slumped down on top of her.

Two small hands snaked around his back and kept him from pushing back up.

"I'll crush you," he protested.

"No. I like it," she wheezed.

He'd get up in a minute. Just a minute.

***

Sometime later…

"I'm *sure* that nothing is permanently damaged," Julia laughed. "Stop asking me that."

Malcolm grimaced. "Fine. But don't let me do it again tonight. You'll be too sore."

She rolled her eyes at him.

He yanked her tightly against his chest. "Look who is a cheeky little monkey."

"Did you just call me a monkey?"

"Mmm-hmm." He kissed her thoroughly and when he pulled away, she'd forgotten all about the monkey comment.

Malcolm sighed in pure bliss and rolled onto his back, wincing slightly at the pull of skin on his side.

"What is it?"

He looked up and saw that she was pushed up on her elbow, looking at him.

"Nothing."

"No. It was something. You grimaced."

"Julia—"

"I will pester you until you tell me. That's something you might not have realized about me—my ability to single mindedly pester."

He sighed. "The skin on my side is a bit dried out. I'll have Norris take care of it later."

They'd moved from Malcolm's sitting room to his bedchamber after he'd fucked her with all the finesse of a seventeen-year-old and then fallen asleep and crushed her beneath him.

As a debut performance it had been lacking on his part.

"What does Norris do to help you?" Julia asked.

"There is a salve he applies."

"Let me put some on now."

"Julia—"

"Where is it?" She rolled away from him and pushed off the bed, looking around his bedchamber, as if the tin of salve might be on the mantelpiece right below his favorite Shunga print, which was—roughly translated—*Client Lubricating a Prostitute.*

It seemed to snag Julia's attention, momentarily diverting her from the fact that she was naked.

Malcolm smirked and pushed himself up so he could watch her. He had an impressive collection of erotica, although nothing like Smith's—he'd been the one to lure Malcolm into the expensive hobby—and he kept some of the best in his chambers.

Julia moved on to a smaller Shunga print, this one depicting a whore about to suck a man's improbably huge cock.

"Do you like them?" he asked, stroking his own cock, which was rousing as he watched her peruse his erotica.

"Yes," she said, her voice scratchy, her back muscles tensing when she stopped in front of a slightly larger canvas.

"That is by a man named Tassaert," Malcolm said.

It hadn't been expensive when compared to most of the items in his collection, but it was among his favorites. Although Tassaert was still alive, he had stopped painting years ago and his work was quite rare.

This particular painting was one he'd done several versions of. It depicted a woman being ravished by three androgynous lovers, one of whom was actively engaged in cunnilingus.

Julia stepped closer to the painting. "Are these three men or women, I cannot tell?"

"Does it matter?"

She turned at that, her expression startled but thoughtful. "No, I suppose it doesn't." Her gaze dropped to his slowly stroking fist. "Hmm. What do you have there?"

"Come here and see."

"Not until I put some of the salve you mentioned on whatever is sore."

Malcolm growled. "Later."

Julia set her hands on her hips and growled right back.

He released his eager cock, defeated by her utter adorability. "It is in a silver tin in my bathing chamber—near my shaving things."

She smirked triumphantly and padded into the other room, her generous rump bouncing enchantingly.

"Where is the spot that needs it?" she asked when she returned with the tin.

He lifted his left arm and pointed to his side.

She winced. "Oooh, it's bleeding."

"Just a little."

"What happened?"

"Sometimes I twist or turn the wrong way."

"Is it alright to put this directly onto it?"

"Yes, rub it in well."

She scooped up a bit of salve and dabbed it on.

"You can rub harder than that, Julia. It doesn't hurt." In fact, it felt damned good. Far better than Norris's hand.

"That's plenty," he said after a moment.

"Anywhere else?" she asked, her expression charmingly hopeful.

"A bit here." He pointed to his forearm.

She squinted. "It's not bleeding."

"No, but it's sore," he lied.

Once she'd finished, he pointed to a spot just above his knee. And then near his hip.

"Anywhere else?" she asked yet again, so eager to help that Malcolm shouldn't be such an arse, but he couldn't help it.

"Right here." He pointed to his cock. "On the end."

She gawked, frowned, and then slapped his shoulder.

"What?" he protested, fisting the base of his erection and struggling to keep a straight face. "It really does… ache"

She snorted and turned, as if to take the tin back to the bathroom, but Malcolm caught her arm.

"Come up on the bed," he said, taking the tin and tossing it aside while she complied. "Straddle me," he ordered after she'd clambered up beside him.

Once she was settled, he put his hands on her waist and stared up at her. "Thank you," he said, serious. "That felt good."

She gave him an unusually shy smile.

"What is it?" he asked, tracing a finger across her soft belly.

She shrugged.

"Tell me, Julia. I can be quite a determined nag," he warned, his words a teasing echo of hers from earlier.

"I didn't use the word *nag*."

"No, but I am. Now, what is it?"

"I don't have much to offer, so it would make me feel useful if you would allow me to do things. To help."

Malcolm frowned. "What do you mean you don't have much to offer?"

"You don't need money," she snorted, "not that I have any. I'm pretty enough, but there are thousands of pretty women in the city. I'm not talented or especially clever or—"

"Stop."

His harsh bark made her startle.

"It's the truth, Malcolm."

"You make me want to get up in the morning. You make me believe I can have things I'd given up on: love, a wife, children, a family. Do you think that is *useless*? I was initially attracted to your beauty, but it did not take me long to realize that is the least impressive part of you, Julia. Don't ever say you have nothing to offer; you are *everything* to me."

A tear slid down her cheek and he wiped it away with his thumb and then pulled her down on top of him, wrapping his arms around her and holding her tightly while she snuggled into him, as if she could burrow right into his chest.

"You make me so happy, Malcolm. I just worry I won't be enough for you."

He stroked her silky hair. "I worry about the same thing, too, sweetheart." He pressed kisses against her head, inhaling the intoxicating scent of woman. "You make my life worth living, Julia. I love you so much it hurts."

She cuddled harder and gave a suspiciously damp sniff. "I've waited so long to hear that."

"I'll tell you every day, darling."

"I love you too, Malcolm." The last word was strangely distorted.

"Is that—did you just *yawn* Julia? While I am declaring my undying love for you?" he teased.

"I'm so sorry. I don't know what is wrong with—" Another yawn drifted up. "Why do I always get so tired when I'm with you? No, wait," she said, "I know—*five orgasms will do that to a person.*"

Malcolm laughed. "Just rest, love."

"You'll be here when I wake up?" she asked sleepily. "You won't just go without saying anything?"

Malcolm tightened his hold on her. "I'll be here when you wake up tomorrow, and every morning after, darling."

Epilogue

Three months later

H appy birthday, darling," Malcolm said, giving his wife a large velvet box.

Julia opened the box, her blue eyes going wide. "Oh, Malcolm, how lovely," she said, lightly tracing her fingers over a diamond necklace that had cost more than all the other jewelry he'd bought added together.

He cocked his head and put a finger beneath her chin, tilting her face up. "Why do you look less than pleased."

"Oh, no! I love it! I do. It is exquisite and beautiful and—"

"—and it was not what you were hoping for," he finished.

"Well, I must admit I'd thought—" she broke off and flushed, biting her lower lip.

After three months of marriage her blushes were rarer, but they still appeared when he forced her to articulate some of her thoughts—especially the wicked ones.

Like whatever she had in her head just then.

"Yes?" he prodded.

"You are terrible. You know what I wanted."

"I do."

"I am ready for it," she said. "I know you think I'm not, but I've—"

Malcolm laid a finger across her lips. "Shh." He took the necklace from its silk nest and clasped it around her long, slim neck. "Lovely," he said when he stood back.

Julia glanced in the mirror and smiled. "It is very beautiful, thank you."

"*You* are very beautiful." He corrected, and then held out a hand. "Come, your birthday guests await."

***

Julia smiled as she glanced around the dining room, the sight of all her friends and family gathered together causing a warm feeling in her belly.

Beside the fire were Richard and Nanny, who were chatting and laughing with Lily, her husband Robert, and his recently widowed sister, Mary.

Julia had never met Mary before, but she'd recently moved in with Lily and the earl, so her friend had asked if she could come tonight.

"Mary is so sad-eyed and quiet it's hard to remember she's even in the room," Lily had assured her.

Dorian and Dominic, who were home for the Easter break, were working on an intricate puzzle that was set out on a large table in the other corner, their ginger heads close together.

Her little brothers had taken Thomas Harlow's death harder than Julia had expected, certainly harder than the news of their mother's demise in the same freak carriage accident that had plunged both to their deaths.

Interestingly, it was Malcolm's company that cheered the twins the most. They'd taken to him quickly, haunting his steps whenever they came to visit, and pestering him with endless questions about the emporium and all its interesting innovations.

Julia knew they mourned their parents, but it really was true what she'd told Malcolm: neither Nadine nor Thomas had ever spent any time with them. They would have grown up with ample money and luxuries but no love to speak of.

They had been delighted to discover they had an older brother and were touchingly careful in the way they treated Richard, behaving less boisterously so as not to agitate her gentle twin.

In another corner of the room was Mr. Smith—or Smith as she now called him—who was talking to Edward and Nora Fanshawe.

Julia was still a bit intimidated by the big, brusque industrialist, but it enchanted her how much Edward loved his wife and she was pleased that Malcolm had another friend.

Although Nora was older than Julia, the two of them had immediately taken to each other and Julia absolutely adored her. Already Nora felt more like a sister than a friend.

Thanks to Nora's patient mentoring Julia was also becoming a better painter, although she would never be even half as good as the other woman. Still, Malcolm appeared to love her paintings and that was good enough for Julia.

Thinking of her husband made her look for him. He was standing with John, the two of them actually *talking* for a change, rather than Malcolm just barking orders at his gentle secretary.

She suspected that John Butkins would never be entirely easy about socializing with his employer, but he, too, had become a good friend to Julia and she considered him part of her new family.

He was kind, considerate, and clever and he also knew her husband better than almost anyone. She was grateful that he lived in their house and was thrilled that he would be coming with them at the end of the summer when they removed to the country house Malcolm had leased not far from Lily and Robert.

John's presence would be a normalizing influence on Malcolm, whom she knew was nervous about not only leaving the comfort of his lair, but also living in the country for the first time in his life.

As Julia looked around at the people in the room, she couldn't believe how much her life had changed in only a few months, and how happy she was.

She knew that Malcolm had worried when Brian's body had been discovered in a seamy part of Paris, dead by the hand of an unknown assailant.

"You aren't a little bit sad?" he'd asked that night, after making almost careful love to her.

"Will you think me unnatural if I say that I'm glad?" she'd asked.

"I'll think you perfect, just as I always do."

"And what about Carl?" she had dared to ask.

"He will not be found."

Julia had left the matter at that.

Was she cold not to have mourned the passing of the only father she knew, as well as the death of one she never would know?

Perhaps. But Julia had decided that that was something she could live with.

And a Second, More Wicked, Epilogue

Later that same night…

Malcolm was buried in Maisie's hot, skilled throat when he heard the knock he'd been expecting.

"Come in!"

The door opened and Julia squinted into the gloom before her eyes settled on Malcolm and Maisie.

He made sure she got a good look at what Maisie was doing before he tapped the kneeling woman's jaw, her signal to sit up.

"Happy birthday, darling. Come in and shut the door."

Julia was like a beautiful, exquisitely colored bird that was poised for flight. And for one long moment, Malcolm thought she would fly away—that this gift had been too much, too soon, even though she had hinted, in her not very subtle way, that such a thing was one of her deepest, darkest fantasies.

But sometimes fantasies were best kept to the imagination, so Malcolm hadn't been quite sure this was the gift she wanted. He still wasn't…

So, he watched and waited.

His diamonds still glittered at her lovely throat and the gown she wore—*not* the one she'd worn to her birthday celebration earlier, but one that she would have discovered upon going to her bedroom afterward—was the shade he liked best on her, the pale pink of a virgin's blush, all the more striking because the gown was cut for a courtesan, the bodice low enough that her nipples rose over the tight silk.

She straightened her spine and deliberately shut the door without making a sound.

Malcolm smiled and he knew it was an insufferable, smug expression. He gestured with his chin toward the mirror.

She had to visibly wrench her gaze away from him.

Her lips parted at what waited for her on the other side of the glass.

His gaze never left her, but he knew what she was seeing: Two identically beautiful, black-haired, blue-eyed, intensely masculine angels, naked and erect, their muscular bodies glistening with oil.

The only thing they wore were matching black leather straps around their cocks and balls, keeping them erect for his wife's birthday pleasure.

When Julia turned back to him, there was a faint smile on her angel mouth. "For me?"

"All for you."

She caught her lower lip in a gesture that made his cock, already throbbing and wet, leak like a firehose.

"They have their instructions," he said, when he saw a glimmer of uncertainty. "All you need to do is go in and enjoy yourself."

She swallowed again, her glance flitting to Maisie, a small frown marring her brow. "Are you going to—" she looked from Malcolm's cock to Maisie's mouth.

"Come in her?" he suggested.

She squeezed her eyes shut briefly but then opened them and nodded.

Oh, her face was so easy to read that it really wasn't fair. Malcolm knew she'd be both aroused and displeased at the thought, the warring emotions confusing her.

"She is here to keep me hard for you, Julia. I will save my orgasm for you."

Malcolm snapped his fingers and Maisie lowered her mouth and went to work.

Julia's smile was sudden and brilliant and wicked.

And then she turned and pushed the panel open.

***

As Julia closed the door between Malcolm's study and the room with two gorgeous strangers, she realized her body had never before held so much conflicting emotion.

When she'd entered that room and saw Malcolm with that woman—the one who looked so disturbingly like Julia herself—she'd been blasted with jealousy, fury, and lust.

Her thighs had become embarrassingly wet as she'd struggled to master her emotions.

Be careful what you ask for, or you will surely get it...

Malcolm had given her exactly what she'd asked for and the sight of it had almost overwhelmed her. It had also been… delicious, especially when he'd snapped his fingers, bringing the other woman—so beautiful and skilled—to heel like an obedient hound.

Julia shivered—ashamed and aroused by her unworthy reaction. Both emotions were smothered by the eagerness she felt for the room beyond. The men—the second part of her birthday gift—were waiting for her.

Julia pushed open the door.

"I'm Phillip," the one on the right said, coming toward her and shutting the door behind her.

"And I'm Peter," the other said, his god-like body stretched out across the bed like an offering, his hand languidly stroking his hard shaft.

"How will I tell you apart?"

They both laughed, the fascinating musculature in their bodies flexing. "You won't," they answered together.

"Shall I undress you?" Phillip asked, jarring her rapt gaze from his brother's ruddy erection.

She nodded.

He moved behind her, his hands light and deft. "What are those straps you wear," she asked.

"These?" Peter's elegant, long-fingered hand slid to where the leather bound his shaft and sac. "They are to keep us hard for you."

"They will make sure we do not come until—and if—you decide we may," Phillip added, his breath hot on her neck.

"You mean you will not orgasm unless I tell you?"

"Yes," they both answered at once.

"We're here for your pleasure," Peter said, his hot blue gaze burning over her as his brother lowered her gown from her shoulders.

Beneath it, all she wore was an almost torturously tight corset that ran all the way down to mid hip. It was the exact same shade of pink as the gown.

She had blushed when Kemp laced her into the corset, still embarrassed by her lack of drawers—something she'd not worn in months, not since her wedding day, in fact.

"No more drawers," Malcolm had declared at dinner that night. "They just get in my way and I want you accessible at all times." He'd then slid his hand beneath her gown, pushed aside her drawers, and made her orgasm right there at the dinner table.

"Beautiful," the two men murmured as Julia stepped out of her skirts and cage.

She gave a slightly nervous giggle. "Do you always think the same things?"

"We are right now," Peter replied, the muscles in his forearm flexing as he squeezed his shaft.

Phillip's hands moved to the corset.

"No. Leave it on."

She jolted at the sound of Malcolm's voice, amazed that she'd forgotten for a moment that her husband was watching.

"In fact, pull it tighter. And turn her toward me as you do it." Phillip immediately complied.

Julia was already laced so tight it was difficult to breathe.

"Those are my instructions," Kemp had answered when she'd asked her. And yet the thought of being bound tighter—suffering for Malcolm's pleasure—sent at trickle of desire sliding down her already wet thighs.

She watched her reflection as Phillip retied the laces, imagining her husband's hard cock and aching desire.

"Naughty girl," Malcolm chided with a chuckle, reading her thoughts as easily as ever. "Kneel, Peter," he ordered sharply.

She watched in the mirror as the twin slid from the bed and move toward her, his phallus slim and elegant like the rest of his body—nowhere near the size of Malcolm's.

It occurred to her, suddenly, that he'd purposely chosen these beautiful men. They were muscular—astoundingly so—but they were not large or tall. Their bones were aristocratic and elegant and they were only five or six inches taller than her.

Objectively, they were far more attractive than her brawny husband. But her sex pulsed hardest at the thought of him sitting in the other room, a woman servicing his huge cock—which Julia considered hers—while Malcolm thought only of *her*.

He'd be lusting at what he saw, wanting her, but—perversely— giving her to these two perfect men.

She suddenly knew that he would suffer as deliciously as she had at seeing him with Maisie.

***

Jealousy tore at Malcolm like savage, snarling dogs.

The men in that room represented everything he could never give her: beauty, youth, and perfection.

310

And it ate at him like acid.

It also made him harder than he'd ever been in his life.

He set a staying hand on Maisie's head; he would come too soon if she continued.

Instead, he wrapped his hand around his shaft, squeezing the base like the straps the men in the other room wore.

Peter knelt at Julia's feet while his brother stood behind her, caressing her hard nipples and kissing her neck.

"Go ahead, Peter," he ordered.

He grunted when the man's slender fingers exposed Julia's wet pink perfection. "Lovely, he said, his voice rough. "Now take her bud between your lips and suck."

Julia jolted at his words, her eyes burning into him even through the glass. Her lips parted and a soft whimper escaped her as the man between her thighs covered her tiny nub with what Malcolm had been assured was an unparalleled mouth when it came to pleasuring both men and women.

Julia's lids had drooped and she was breathing through her mouth, her tightly corseted body trembling. She was so bloody responsive he knew she was already cresting toward her first orgasm.

"Enough, Peter," he said, enjoying a cruel, private smile at the look of disbelief on her face. Malcolm had never denied his lovely wife an orgasm before. And Julia did not like it.

"Bind her the way we discussed earlier," he ordered, resting his hand absently in Maisie's hair and twisting a lock of it around his finger, tugging her down onto his cock, pulling hard enough that she whimpered, a shudder running through her body.

Maisie liked her pain almost as much as Julia did, blindfolded, she could imagine that Malcolm was anyone, so everyone was happy.

"You may touch yourself, Maisie," he said, loudly enough to be heard beyond the glass, smirking at the disgruntled frown that shifted Julia's lovely features.

The two men were skilled at their jobs and he'd paid handsomely for their presence here tonight. He'd hardly imagined it was possible to find one such exquisite specimen, let alone two.

It had been Smith, of course, who'd discovered them.

What Julia had once said was true: the other man really *did* seem to know everything.

The twins stepped aside when they'd finished binding Julia's arms and legs.

Christ. She was a bloody masterpiece: stretched and bound and pulling restlessly against the leather cuffs on her wrists and ankles. She was perfect—almost.

"Draw her arms up tighter and spread her feet another six inches, that should stop her willful thrashing."

He chuckled at Julia's startled, mulish expression and then glanced at Maisie. She was rapidly approaching her climax and her lips and tongue had become clumsy on his cock.

"You may come, Maisie," he said, drinking in Julia's outraged face as he allowed the other woman something he was depriving her.

Malcolm snickered quietly; he could practically hear his wife's teeth grinding.

Once the men were finished, he gorged himself on the sight of her, bound so tightly she couldn't move—her breathing constricted so that her breasts swelled high with each breath.

"Good. Now gag her."

A yelp slipped out of Julia and she squirmed—or at least tried to, but she couldn't move an inch.

Peter held up the gag, a rather devious contraption fashioned on an actual scold's bridle but made especially to fit Julia, the metal and leather parts lined with velvet so it wouldn't chafe or hurt her.

"Malcolm," she whined, her cheeks flushed, her breathing ragged.

"Yes, my dear?"

"Do you really need to do this?"

"Of course not," he said, agreeably. "Peter, return the—"

"No!" she said, although it was more a of gasp. "It's—please, I want it."

He knew she did. But now he would make her beg for it.

"Oh, well … I'm not sure it is such a good idea," he said. "Perhaps another—"

"Please, Malcolm."

"Please, what, darling?"

Her eyelids fluttered but did not shut. "Please have Peter put it on me."

"It?"

She heaved a sigh, the action doing fascinating things to her breasts. "The gag. I want to be gagged."

Malcolm grinned at her anguished tone; he would go straight to Hell for being such a sadistic bastard, and by God, would he enjoy the journey.

"Give her the scarf," he ordered.

Peter put a small red scarf in Julia's left hand.

"If you want to stop—for any reason or no reason—just drop the scarf. Understand?"

"Yes, Malcolm."

"Good. Drop it now."

The scarf fluttered to the floor.

"You do that and everything stops." He spoke seriously, not wanting her to hurt herself in an effort to please him.

"Yes, Malcolm."

Peter returned the scarf.

"Ready, luv?"

"Yes, Malcolm."

"Gag her, Peter. Make sure it is nice and snug."

Malcolm stilled Maisie's bobbing head; all his attention riveted on the scene on the other side of the glass.

"In olden times some men used scold bridles to discipline willful wives," he said as Peter carefully fit the thick but soft leather bit between her lips, adjusting the metal rings that sat on either side of her face.

Julia's eyes were wide as the myriad straps tightened and secured the bit, spreading her lips wider.

"All right?" he asked once the device was secure.

She nodded jerkily.

Peter next slid a wide posture collar around her neck. It ran from just below her chin to the bottom of her neck. It was stiff boiled leather, reinforced, and lined with fur.

"This keeps you upright and also will stop the strap from chafing your lovely throat," he explained.

Not to mention that she looked fucking gorgeous wearing it.

Malcolm stared in worshipful silence; he simply could not get enough of her.

His angel was almost ready.

***

Julia could not stop staring at her reflection. She looked like one of the wicked drawings she'd seen in Malcolm's impressive and arousing erotica collection.

The black strappy device that kept her jaws wide and the other thing—the collar—that kept her chin high… well, they were the most erotic things she'd ever seen.

"You look very beautiful, Julia," Malcolm said, the lust in his voice sending a bolt of pleasure to her core that would have doubled her over if she'd not been bound so cruelly.

"The plug, now."

One of the men, she'd lost track of who was who, disappeared and returned a moment later, holding an anal plug.

"I know you recognize this, darling."

Julia's body clenched at the sight of the plug, which was slightly bigger than the one he'd inserted in her a few days ago.

Malcolm had started using them on her a month ago—a different one every week, each a little larger than the last.

He had called it *training*, but had refused to tell Julia what, exactly, the training was for.

The twin slicked it with oil and then lowered it against her hole.

"You remember what to do? When he presses it to your anus, you bear down—as if you are on the commode."

It had been mortifying with only her and Malcolm. Having a veritable audience—Malcolm *and* the three prostitutes—rendered her face so red that she doubted she could have blushed harder.

He chuckled softly at whatever he saw on her face.

Something cool and slick pressed against her back hole.

"Don't forget to use the silk cloth if you need it, darling."

Her hand clenched tighter around the scarf, as if she might accidentally drop it. She tried to shake her head to make sure he knew she didn't want to stop, but of course she couldn't.

"That's a good girl," he soothed.

Julia bore down as the object pushed into her, stretching and stretching until it hurt, and then abruptly narrowing, her body drawing it inside, the flat stem snug against her spread cheeks.

"That wasn't so bad, was it?" Malcolm asked.

It actually embarrassed her how much she liked the sensation of fullness; how naughty it made her feel to go about her day with nobody but her and Malcolm aware of what was beneath her skirts.

She clenched at the thought and then whimpered at the pleasure that rippled through her.

His low laugh warmed her. "I knew you would enjoy it, darling. Now Peter is going to use the marble phallus on you while his brother performs cunnilingus."

Just when Julia thought she couldn't become more aroused, he used *that* word. The only person she'd ever heard use it was Lily. She'd believed it sounded wicked coming out of her friend's mouth.

Malcolm made it sound positively filthy.

Julia could see the men in the mirror.

Peter had a marble cock—a dildo, she knew they were called—and was oiling it while Phillip spread her lips and commenced to pleasure her.

Julia was already so aroused that her orgasm crashed down on her within only seconds, pleasure rippling from both her sex and her anus, which was clenching around the hard plug.

"Now, Peter."

She was shuddering and whimpering when something big, cool, and hard pushed into her sheath. Her rippling inner muscles gripped the hard stone and she'd never experienced such intense fullness.

"Slowly but deeply, Peter."

Time blurred as over and over the stone phallus and hot, sucking mouth drove Julia toward almost unbearable bliss.

They were torturing her with pleasure.

Just when she couldn't take a moment more, a low, raspy voice ordered, "That's enough. Release her and carry her to the bed."

Warm, gentle hands unbound her, soothed her skin with caresses, and then carried her to a mattress as soft as a cloud.

Julia knew she must have fallen asleep and it took her a moment to realize what woke her. She was on her side and there were two mouths, both between her thighs, licking and sucking the entrances to her body.

Her eyelids fluttered open and the first thing she saw was Malcolm, sitting in a chair beside the bed, still completely clothed from head to toe, fingertips to mask.

It didn't bother her to see him like this now—she got to see every part of him every night—and understood his desire to protect himself with strangers.

"Hello darling," he said, giving her the sweet smile he saved just for her.

Julia smiled, her body already tensing with yet another impending crisis. "No Maisie?" she teased in a breathy voice.

"I wanted to enjoy this without distraction."

"This?" she repeated groggily.

His smile was slight, but mysterious.

"On your back, Peter. Phillip, lift her up."

Julia found herself being gently lifted and manipulated by soft, strong hands, until she was kneeling over Peter, straddling his hips.

"Take him inside you, Julia—slowly."

She shivered at Malcolm's erotic command and held her lover's gaze as she sank down all the way, taking another man's shaft deep inside her body as Malcolm watched.

"So lovely," Malcolm praised, stroking himself faster. "Are you sure you want this?" he asked.

"Yes, but I want it with *you*."

"That would hurt you."

Julia knew he was right—he was easily half again as thick and far longer than the slender twins. But she still ached for him.

"Shhh," he said, seeing the mutiny in her gaze. "Be a good girl and do as I say."

A shudder wracked her body at the familiar, but still potent, words. "Yes, Malcolm."

His nostrils flared at her submissive tone and he turned to Phillip and nodded.

The plug came out easier than it had gone in, with only a moment of resistance. Julia had, in fact, become so comfortable with it that she'd forgotten it was inside her.

Malcolm released his shaft but didn't close his trousers as he came and sat on the bed beside her.

"Give me a kiss, sweetheart."

Julia grabbed his coat and yanked him closer, earning a startled look before her mouth crashed over his.

She didn't realize that she was grunting and nipping and whimpering like an animal until his big hand smoothed down her back, caressing her and petting her while he gentled her with his kisses.

"All you alright, darling?" he murmured when he pulled away.

"I am now that you're beside me."

"Are you sure you want to do this?" he asked again.

"I'm sure."

He nodded. "Lie down on Peter and I will help Phillip prepare you."

Julia didn't want to let him go, but she also wanted to take two men inside her, just like the postcard she'd fantasized about for months and months.

She gave him one last, lingering kiss and then lowered her body over Peter, tucking her face into his neck. One of his hands landed on her back and he caressed her, his heart beating fast and strong while Malcolm's large hands spread her open.

***

Malcolm could not recall a more arousing evening and there seemed no better way to end it.

He couldn't have his cock inside her for double penetration—at least not her first time—but that didn't mean he couldn't help prepare her for the experience.

He lowered his lips over her slightly reddened pucker and Julia moaned and shivered as he soothed and sucked and probed her tight hole with his tongue, fucking her gently and deeply, slicking and stretching her until she'd gone as limp as a rag beneath him.

He glanced at Phillip and the other man slid a slender finger past Malcolm's caressing lips and tongue, breaching her easily she was so relaxed.

But a second finger made her stiffened, so Phillip paused while Malcolm again worked her until she was writhing and whimpering, pushing back for more when a second finger eased in beside the first.

The younger man knew what to do and Malcolm gave himself up to pure voyeuristic enjoyment while Phillip skillfully stretched her with his fingers, until she was ready for his cock.

Malcolm held her cheeks spread while Phillip positioned himself and slowly eased his length inside her body.

God! She looked so damned beautiful being stretched and filled, her taut skin sheening with sweat as she took a second cock inside her.

"Does it hurt, darling?"

"No …s'good," she slurred, her hips gently pulsing, pulling Phillip's prick deeper.

Malcolm nodded at Phillip and he slid all the way inside, sheathing himself to the hilt in Julia's delectable body.

Julia shuddered and moaned. "So full."

Malcolm kissed her side and murmured. "More?"

"Mmm-hmmm."

"Fuck her," Malcolm ordered. "Slowly, but deeply."

The men knew how to make it good for her, timing their thrusting so that one of them was inside her at all times, keeping her full of hard cock but not overwhelmed.

Malcolm stroked his prick and watched the three perfect bodies writhing and bucking, a beautiful ballet that he no longer had to observe alone in a darkened room, but which he could now share with his lover.

***

Julia was dozing, her body floating as she chased a delicious but elusive pleasure.

A low chuckle vibrated from her sex up her body and she opened her eyes slowly, blinking as she looked around her, trying to remember what had happened and where she was.

Oh, yes—the twins, Peter and Phillip.

"Ah!" she cried out, her thoughts momentarily scattering as a skilled mouth closed over her clitoris and suckled.

Julia lowered her hands to a familiar handful of hair on one side and warm, soft skin on the other.

"Malcolm," she murmured. Spreading her thighs wide and tilting her pelvis to aid his erotic labors.

He grunted his approval and his finger pushed into her body, the opening sore from the earlier activity but not painfully so.

Julia floated on a warm cloud of bliss as he worked her through first one orgasm and then another.

She stopped him when he would have embarked upon a third.

"No. Come up here." She tugged on his hair lightly.

He gave her one last long lick with the flat of his tongue before he came up to lie beside her, his huge body naked and hot alongside hers.

"Everyone is gone?" she asked, although she already knew that— he'd never bare himself for anyone except her.

"Just me and thee," he murmured, kissing her with lips that tasted like her.

Julia slung a leg over his hip and straddled him, taking his thick, hot length slowly inside her sore body as she lowered herself down.

"Mmm," he moaned, flexing his cock inside her. "Fuck me, Julia," he begged. "Need to come."

Julia rode him hard, the way she knew he liked it, not surprised when his climax came quickly.

"I'm an embarrassment to men everywhere," he sighed a moment later. "Shooting my load in thirty seconds like a green boy."

"I believe it was closer to ten seconds," she teased.

Malcolm laughed. "You are right."

Julia smoothed back his hair. "My poor darling—you've suffered all night long waiting."

"Mmm," he kissed her. "You're worth waiting for."

"You mean *we're* worth waiting for," she corrected.

He frowned, clearly running the words through his mind.

"What?"

She raised her eyebrows, waiting for it to hit him.

He pushed up abruptly, lifting her off the bed in the process and making her giggle.

"Julia!" He grabbed her face in both hands, his eye blazing with love and something else: hope. "Are you saying—"

"Yes. At least that is what Kemp believes. We both suspected as much but thought to wait another month to make sure." She gave him a mocking look. "You are not very observant—didn't you notice I had no courses?"

His mouth hung open.

Julia laughed. "Well, *say* something."

"You're pregnant," he said, as if he needed to hear the words spoken aloud.

She nodded. "Are you happy?"

He seized her in a rib-cracking embrace. "There should be a new word for what I am, darling."

"Need… breathe," Julia gasped a moment later.

He released her immediately, his expression frantic. "Did I hurt you?"

"Don't be silly."

He sighed, visibly relieved. "When is the date?"

"Probably in late November or December."

He set his hands on her stomach and caressed her softly. "We'll need to be careful with you."

"But not *too* careful, I hope. I loved tonight, Malcolm. Thank you."

He smiled. "It was lovely."

"I wish you had been there instead of the two of them."

"I would have hurt you, luv."

"But Smith said—"

Malcolm squawked, "*What?*"

Julia collapsed in a fit of laughter. "You should have seen your face; I *do* love teasing you. And no, Smith is for once not guilty of subversion."

She grabbed Malcolm and held him close. "You gave me a wonderful birthday present, so let's finish off the day alone together. I love you," she murmured as she closed her eyes.

"I love you, too, darling."

And together they drifted off to sleep.

Who are Minerva Spencer & S.M. LaViolette?
Minerva is S.M.'s pen name (that's short for Shantal Marie) S.M. has been a criminal prosecutor, college history teacher, B&B operator, dock worker, ice cream manufacturer, reader for the blind, motel maid, and bounty hunter. Okay, so the part about being a bounty hunter is a lie. S.M. does, however, know how to hypnotize a Dungeness crab, sew her own Regency Era clothing, knit a frog hat, juggle, rebuild a 1959 American Rambler, and gain control of Asia (and hold on to it) in the game of RISK.

Read more about S.M. at: www.MinervaSpencer.com

OUTCASTS SERIES:
DANGEROUS
BARBAROUS
SCANDALOUS

THE REBELS OF THE *TON*:
NOTORIOUS
OUTRAGEOUS
INFAMOUS

THE SEDUCERS:
MELISSA AND THE VICAR

S.M. LaViolette

<u>JOSS AND THE COUNTESS</u>
<u>HUGO AND THE MAIDEN</u>

VICTORIAN DECADENCE: (HISTORICAL EROTIC ROMANCE—SUPER STEAMY!)
<u>HIS HARLOT</u>
<u>HIS VALET</u>
<u>HIS COUNTESS</u>
<u>HER BEAST</u>
<u>THEIR MASTER</u>

THE ACADEMY OF LOVE:
<u>THE MUSIC OF LOVE</u>
<u>A FIGURE OF LOVE</u>
<u>A PORTRAIT OF LOVE</u>
<u>THE LANGUAGE OF LOVE</u>
<u>DANCING WITH LOVE</u>

THE MASQUERADERS:
<u>THE FOOTMAN</u>
<u>THE POSTILION</u>
<u>THE BASTARD</u>

THE BACHELORS OF BOND STREET:
<u>A SECOND CHANCE FOR LOVE (A NOVELLA)</u>
<u>THE ARRANGEMENT (A NOVELLA)</u>

Keep an eye out for two BRAND NEW series coming in 2022:

<u>THE BELLAMY SISTERS</u>
PHOEBE
HYACINTH*

<u>THE WILD WOMEN OF WHITECHAPEL</u>
THE BOXING BARONESS*
THE DUELING DUCHESS*
THE CUTTHROAT COUNTESS*

ALSO BY AMY KNUPP

<u>Henry Brothers Series</u>

Untold (prequel)

Unraveled

Unsung

Undone

<u>North Brothers Series</u>

True North

True Colors

True Blue

True Harmony

True Hero

North Brothers Box Sets:

North Brothers Books 1-3

North Brothers Books 4-5

North Brothers: The Complete Series

<u>Hale Street Series</u>:

Sweet Spot

Sweet Dreams

Soft Spot

One and Only

Last First Kiss

Heartstrings

<u>Hale Street Box Sets:</u>

Meet Me at Clayborne's

Clayborne's After Hours

It Happened on Hale Street (all 6 of Amy's stories)

<u>Island Fire Series</u>:

Playing with Fire

Heat of the Night

Fully Involved

Firestorm

Afterburn

Up in Flames

Flash Point

Fire Within

Impulse

Slow Burn

Island Fire Box Sets:

Sparked (books 1-3)

Ignited (books 4-6)

Enflamed (books 7-10)

OR

Island Fire: The Complete Series

Themed Box Sets:

Friends to Forever (Friends to Lovers Romance)

Working It (Workplace Romance)

ABOUT THE AUTHOR

Amy Knupp is a *USA Today* Best-Selling Author of contemporary romance and a freelance copy editor. She loves words and grammar and meaty, engrossing stories with complex characters.

Amy lives in Wisconsin with her husband and has two sons, four cats, and a box turtle. She graduated from the University of Kansas with degrees in French and journalism. In her spare time, she enjoys traveling, breaking up cat fights, watching college hoops, and annoying her family by correcting their grammar.

For more information:
www.amyknuppbooks.com